Life Sentences

MARTIN MULL

HARD CIDER PRESS

Copyright © 2025 by the Estate of Martin Mull
All rights reserved under International
and Pan-American Copyright Conventions
Published in the United States by Hard Cider Press,
a division of County Highway LLC, First Edition 2025
Printed in Hudson, New Hampshire, by Kase Printing

Design by François-Xavier Delarue
Cover Art by Martin Mull
Typography by Ksenya Samarskaya & Céline Hurka
ISBN: 979-8-9991467-1-7
@hardciderpress / @countyhwy

Manufactured in the United States of America

MARTIN MULL. A MEMORY.

It was all the fault of Steve Martin, really. It was he who first put me in a guest bedroom with one wall covered by a large photorealistic painting of a bathtub with a rubber ducky.

What the hell is that? I thought.

But I knew Steve, and I knew he would know all about the artist, and soon he showed me more of Martin's work, and of course he knew him by his first name, and then he shared with me the pleasure of his company.

I was elated to discover not only that Martin Mull was a very funny man but that he was the only person I knew who played the same jazz chords as I did on the guitar. We thankfully fell into friendship, strumming away at standards and ballads of the thirties and forties.

Steve took me to his gallery openings and soon I bought my very own Mull. My collection grew from several to many. But never too many. And never too much time in his joyous company. Holidays in Montecito, tea in his garden in Brentwood, dinner at our house up on Mulholland, where he would come and stare critically at his pictures on our walls. Everywhere we went we loved playing guitar together.

The last time I saw him, the lovely, funny, kindly Bob Saget was making a documentary about him at our house, and we played guitars happily as they filmed, and then I'm sure I spouted bullshit eloquently for the camera, for I speak it fluently. Tragically, both Bob and the documentary came to an abrupt end soon after, with Bob's unexpected and miserably early death on the floor of a bathroom in Florida. *Don't go to Florida* I had texted Bob, as it was in the midst of Covid, but little did I know he would never return.

I must call Martin, I thought. We must play together again, and I kept meaning to call, only to make the horrible discovery one day that I'd left it too late.

This book in part makes up for it, as Martin writes wonderfully about aging and the approach of the inevitable, revealing stories that are often thinly disguised episodes of real life, as all the best writing is.

So I missed calling him, but, as age crept over him, he didn't miss recording in his fine and funny prose what he was thinking and feeling at that time—his ironic observations on the body's inevitable decay, always effortlessly expressed in his playful way with carefully chosen words. For, of course, like everything else he did, he wrote wonderfully. And honestly. No longer about painting but about suddenly realizing your time has passed. About feeling an outcast in another time. And about how that's not so bad.

When people talk about the complete Renaissance Man, I always remind them that was Machiavelli. Martin had none of that Italian in him, he simply could *do* everything: paint, write, act, draw, and play guitar, all wonderfully well. I miss him. But I'm grateful to have these stories to remind me what a clever bastard he was.

And of course I have his pictures.

What a man.

— Eric Idle

Table of Contents

State of the Artist: 1
Life Drawing: 11
Additional Information: 63
Real Estate: 79
Second Team: 99
Miller's Island: 147
Concession: 269
The Encore: 283
The Last Two Months of Ed Furst: 311
Warren Pace: 353

Life Sentences

STATE OF THE ARTIST

How many hours before I can unashamedly go back to bed? Not to read. Not to watch TV. And I certainly don't go to bed to *think* (though I seem helpless not to). All I really want to do is sleep—to take a microdose of the ultimate lights-out that looms on my diminishing calendar. I take my drugs, count my breaths (in lieu of sheep) to seventy-seven, remembering each as a year of past events, hoping that before I hit eighty, the sandman will show up. And then, as has been well said, "perchance to dream."

Dream while you can, I say. Because I'm certain that once one's eyes close for good, there will be none of it. When you're gone, you're as gone as yesterday; as gone as when under anesthesia; time is removed from the equation. With sleep there is the sense of time passed, the clock continues to tick. With anesthesia, sodium pentothal et al., the clock stops; hours that never had the chance to exist are removed from time itself: under at 10:30 and awake at 10:31, even though the clock says 5 p.m. That interim, I think, must be what the big sleep is like (except there is no 5 p.m. on the other side).

Now, about dreams, and why I find them so meaningful. It's not the improbable scenarios, the impossible architecture, the inexplicable nudism in public gatherings, the tractionless running, the disembodied voices. Nor is it the suspension of natural laws, of gravity, of time itself. It's not even the surreal ability for recollection (peoples and places from the past emerging clearly defined in the present). It is who *I* am in the dream. In dreams, I am always (whether coping, panicking, or merely observing) a younger man, my body functioning without gimp or rusted joints. I am young again.

But would I really want to be twenty again? Thirty, forty? I think not. Oh, I wouldn't mind having a liver or lungs that were uncompromised by years of self-administered poison. And I wouldn't mind if both my hips were bone instead of one of them being titanium. But, for the most part, I'd rather be the age I am. In many ways it's a simple case of "been there, done that." It's also a matter of finding the energy.

I think the energy for earlier adventures came from the fact that they were just that: adventures. Projects and endeavors undertaken with no knowledge of the outcome; experiments, shots-in-the-dark, unhampered by the cynicism that would stop such foolishness today. (I say foolishness because there was little thought of failure, of repercussion.) Every sunrise promising a chance to dive headlong into work, into art, into romance, into anything that presented itself as a challenge. That each day would be followed by another, equally promising, was unquestioned. There was plenty of time.

And now there isn't plenty of time. So, if life was reasonable, it would seem that I'd be trying like crazy to load up my days with last-ditch efforts, to paint the last paintings, write the last paragraphs, see the last sights. I should be playing my days like a football team down a touchdown and faced with the two-minute warning. But that's not the case. Instead, it seems that I'm scratching around for something, anything, to fill the time.

Think of it as a two-ring circus. In ring number one: a sequined showgirl doing an arabesque on a galloping horse. In ring number two: A disheveled clown loses his baggy pants while bouncing on a trampoline. It's impossible to concentrate on one without being distracted by the other; and you can't even say for certain which is the main attraction. If, as I often fear, the COVID-19 pandemic is just an idealist's flag being waved before a stampede of regulations and restrictions, then I suspect I'll just be trampled on the road to good intentions like everyone else. But, if it's allowed to be just the flu, then I've got some serious decisions to make.

I rise creakily from the chaise where I've been reading, pausing a moment to ensure that my knees will hold, and realize that I can see eighty with my naked eye. Jesus, how can this be? In my dream last night, I was thirty. But it's too easy to sit and ruminate on questions of mortality, to play the victim of time's arrow. Addressing the time remaining with a to-do list is a lot healthier. So, I'm back to needing a plan.

For the last fifteen years, I have been painting as much by habit as anything else and edging toward a feeling of remove, looking at the work of the previous sixty-five years as a critic might—as if it were done by someone else—and trying to see a sense of direction, an endgame, as it were. Because, at seventy-seven, I think whatever I might set down on paper or canvas needs to be a culmination, a distillation, an after-the-fact manifesto. Where would I find the energy for that? It's too easy to laze the day away, crawl under the covers by eight, and summon the antic distractions of dreamland.

But all of this folderol about motivation is really beating around the bush. It's not a question of where or when or how to jump into the water. It's a question of whether the water is even still there.

The reason why my seventies feel so different from the "driven" years preceding them is simple. I have reached a point of self-definition—the sense that I am what I was destined to be, and that, like any old stone building, I am beyond remodeling.

My attitudes toward everything social, artistic, political, and religious are immutable. (And these clothes fit comfortably, even if I am down to one outfit.) You could say that this rigor mortis befits an old man, and you'd be right. Unfortunately, I find myself living in a world that is perpetually teenaged—rampantly adolescent in its reckless, authority-shunning, destructive ideations and, saddest of all, completely disrespectful of anything that has gone before. In short, I find myself standing still while a world I know nothing of is barreling past me. Embittered old fart? You bet.

It would be one thing if I was simply irrelevant; a harmless, wasted vestige of the 20th century. But, as an old, white, male heterosexual, I am seen by many as the enemy.

I've never considered myself to be much of an ideologue, or even of having a particularly biased view of things. I have my likes and dislikes, my tastes, my preferences, but not to the point of a vocal condemnation of opposing views. Hence, my paintings are not journalistic in nature—chronicles maybe, but more intimate than expressions of a worldview, more like diary entries. That said, they do all tend to reflect a certain segment of American life. Specifically, the American life I've led. (I use the past tense because I see little to no hope for its continuance.)

I would like to think that my pictures of what would, no doubt, currently be labeled "my people" are rendered fairly—the depiction of silly pleasures, romance, and moments of self-reflection alongside disasters both real and imagined. I would hope that they are all painted with a nonjudgmental brush, created emotionally as they are physically: a product of disparate bits and pieces: a collage. True, my paintings are sequestered in the past, in a time with a much different flavor than the present. Nostalgia, however, seems to be a hard emotion to conjure in a world so bent on change. There are many headless statues of Robert E. Lee that can attest to this.

Now, with so much of the art world focused on social equity, my paintings are being seen as either a left-leaning condemnation of the soft white underbelly of America, a pulling back of the curtain to reveal a shallow and deeply prejudiced, Ozzie-and-Harriet-loving horde. Or they are seen as a self-agrandizing, insensitive anthem to a previous status quo—an adoration of a conservatism that has worn out its welcome—and I, as their author, a narrow-minded Norman Rockwell wannabe, who can't get with the times. They are neither. They are paintings, and they are only "about" themselves.

I subscribe to all the art magazines, and, as flagships, the contents are telling. Even though art is, by definition, not "about" anything, the works that fill the pages of these periodicals are *only* "about" something. Inept and crude, the works are rescued from the bin only by their loudly proclaimed moral stances. Sadly, museums have followed suit. Masterworks have been removed from the walls in favor of a more "diverse" presentation, regardless of quality. The powers that be have not only bought the emperor's new clothes, they are wearing them.

Alexander Woollcott was once asked to review a play entitled *For Our Time Only*. His review was a terse: "Not timeless enough." I rest my case.

I'm ranting, I know. But my outrage isn't sponsored by a desire to save the world of art. I am much more self-centered than that. What angers and frustrates me is that this social shift has diminished (if not extinguished) my desire to paint.

I haven't painted for nearly a year.

And that's what this is all about. The dreams, the pangs of aging, the old Caucasian's conservative outrage—none of it the real issue at hand. The issue is that I'm not painting. I had painted, almost daily, for over sixty years and had always assumed that it was selfsame with living. Not just what I *did* but what I *am*. I always felt that the urge to make paintings would still be there in full flower on the day I drew my last breath. That it would be my heartbeat that went first. Instead, it's the other way around, and I am muscling through my days with the sense of vacuum one must feel when they lose a spouse.

The paints, pencils, and paper are still there. My studio is still where I spend my time. But the pilot light has gone out.

The purist in me would like to think that having an audience is unimportant; that the making of the art is the end in itself. That I should keep on making my pictures whether anyone ever sees them or not. But having an audience feeds those other two, less noble addictions: fame and fortune. And the nature of these beasts is "enough is never enough." I'd hate to think that it's the absence of something as transparent and fleeting as praise, both vocal and fiscal, that has doused the pilot. But that could be.

I could force the issue, I guess. Stretch a canvas and attempt something that would be an uninspired self-cannibalization of work that went before, but I see no point.

Is painting without an audience like the sound of the falling tree in the forest? It depends on the painter and, perhaps, the extent of his or her madness—the extent to which one allows oneself to relinquish all else that ties you to the real world. For me, the process of making art is already insular enough; to make it and then just shelve it would underscore the insularity to the point where it would have to be considered a form of madness. Seen from afar, this madness could be perceived as "poetic"; seen from within, it has to be devastating. I'm not ready to give up the other pleasures I derive from sanity. I'm not ready to go there.

So maybe being a painter has run its course.

And if the painter has left the building, he's

not the first. Last night, as I fought my insomnia, I conjured the image of myself as a hotel. A hotel where many different people have stayed and then departed. There was an alcoholic songwriter who spent quite a while there, an actor, a screenwriter, a skirt-chasing roué, a twice-failed husband, and several young boys—all of them now checked out and never to return. But their luggage has been left in their rooms, and in my dreams I rummage through it.

So it's back to dreams I go, hoping to be informed as to who the current resident of the hotel might be. And hoping that, somehow, against all odds, he's still a painter.

Good night.

LIFE DRAWING

Teaching art was not his dream job. No child grows up with the dream of *teaching* art. Would his childhood friends, who had visions of being firemen or baseball players, ever be satisfied with anything less than actually rescuing a baby from a blazing inferno or hitting a homer in the bottom of the ninth? Well, of course not.

Woodley was no different. He wanted to <u>*be*</u> an artist. Actually <u>*do*</u> it. He wanted to make beautiful paintings and drawings, works of art that would find their place on the hallowed and sanctified walls of museums—nationwide, worldwide. (He envisioned high-quality reproductions available in the museum bookstore, coffee-table books with lavish foldout sections, postcards, gummed stickers for the young and impressionable.) He wanted to make work that was coveted and collected by the well-heeled people who not only had the wherewithal to afford his work but, more importantly, had the education to appreciate it. He knew he could do it. He had the talent. His mother told him so.

Life Drawing

Everyone who saw his drawings told him so. "Looks just like me!" friends would exclaim when he drew their portraits. Because he had a knack for wielding a pencil, a pen, a crayon, anything that could leave a mark on a page. He could draw with uncanny certitude and astounding accuracy. He had read somewhere that drawing was the essential backbone of making great visual art. At least it was the fundamental skill behind what *he* considered to be great art. (He had no interest in so-called "modern" art; saw it as a cheap bailout for people who *couldn't* draw and, as such, nothing more than a splash, drip, and smear campaign against the old masters he revered.) He envisioned himself as the man who would put *real* art back into the museums, the galleries, the glossy art magazines that disappointed him on a monthly basis. No other career possibility engendered even a wisp of consideration. So Woodley Frye went to art school.

Early on in his four-year stint at the Waterbrook Institute of Fine Arts, he discovered that the "modern" art that he so adamantly dismissed was the soup of the day. No one gave two shits that he could draw like the giants of the fifteenth century. While other (in his estimation, less talented) students were garnering praise for "pushing the envelope," he was considered a Luddite, yesterday's papers. But he stuck to his guns. He did all of his assignments in a timely and workmanlike way, never missed a class, vocally defended his work in critiques despite the catcalls and snickers of his fellow students. His pursuit of skills no longer needed or wanted was not a flunkable offense (if anything, they wanted to keep him around as a source of mocking amusement), so, after four friendless years, he was awarded his diploma.

Did having a BFA make him an artist? No, of course not. That would require a lifetime of effort. An effort that he would never cease. But now, out from under the umbrella of academia, he was faced with the issue of putting a roof over his head. He had read enough artists' biographies to know that even the great ones had spent a good chunk of their salad days driving taxis, hauling carcasses in slaughterhouses, bricklaying for the WPA. He realized that he would have to find something to put food on the table that still gave him enough free time to push the paint around.

So, two days after he received his BFA, he pounced on an opportunity to be a drawing instructor at the Orton School of Art—an undersized institution situated a few miles south and west of Springfield, Illinois. (The buildings, in their previous incarnation, had been a food-processing plant—there was still a slight scent of chicken in the hallways, an occasional waft of brussels sprouts in the teacher's lounge.) Orton catered to students whose portfolios had not been impressive enough to grant them entrance into a more prestigious venue. Students who, though generally bereft of talent, still had the means to pay the hefty tuition. As a rule, most colleges, universities, and respected art schools required that their faculty hold masters degrees, but Orton was far enough down the academic food chain that they were glad to have Woodley.

And Woodley was glad to have Orton. Though teaching was not the most artistically satisfying choice, it was, at least timewise, a very workable one: three days a week, six hours a day. Springfield was far from the Paris he had contemplated as a student, but he made the best of it. He found affordable housing—a small, two-bedroom cottage with a detached, one-car garage, which he immediately converted into a painting studio. His concession to his new career as a teacher was limited to the purchase of a corduroy sports coat with leather elbow patches, which he thought looked professorial. He'd only be a teacher until his paintings caught on, he reasoned, so he bit the bullet. It was a bullet he would chew for the next eleven years.

. . . .

The class had finished early (half of the students were no-shows, a phenomena that Woodley learned to expect) and Woodley was anxious to get back to his studio. The drive from the campus to his home usually took him about thirty-five minutes. But today it seemed like he was hitting every red light. He had little patience behind the wheel, every second on the road was a second that could have been spent painting. He hated to stop for red lights and hated, most of all, the light at the intersection of the secret, uncongested backstreet he had discovered and the unavoidable multilane Werner Boulevard. If you hit the Werner Boulevard light on red, you might as well bring a lunch. It took forever.

Today, he hit the Werner Boulevard light as red as a setting sun. Three cars waited ahead of him as well. Having hit that light a few times over his years of commuting, he knew the timeline well: It would stay red for about a month, go green for a nanosecond, then a flicker of amber, and back to red for another month.

So he sat there, drinking in the landscape. Well, *landscape* was a fairly forgiving word for it. What he saw was the homeless encampment that had blossomed in the culvert that ran under Werner Boulevard. While the drivers of the cars ahead of him were hastily rolling up their windows and locking their doors, Woodley felt no such angst. He watched the haggard residents with an artist's eye; taken in by their colorful, mismatched clothing, the strong, weathered features of their faces, the sculpture-like, akimbo stances they took while displaying their handmade signs—signs abloom with inventive spelling and magical calligraphy. He felt no fear of them, only compassion. His social excommunication at the Waterbrook School had made him an underdog sympathizer. And these people, struggling through their hand-to-mouth existences, were certainly underdogs. Even their dogs were underdogs. No, he wasn't fearful at all.

Only one car had made it through the green, and as Woodley inched his Volvo forward he was approached by a slim, raggedy man with a plastic bucket of water and a roll of paper towels. Wordlessly and unbidden, the man began to wash Woodley's windshield. Not just a slapdash, lick-and-a-promise job, but a thorough, even-under-the-wiper-blades, even-in-the-corners, cleaning. Woodley was impressed.

"You're an artist," Woodley said with a sweeping gesture toward his now spotless windshield. The man looked up from where he was carefully folding his used towels—a soldier furling a flag at a funeral no more deliberate.

"What?" said the man.

"Oh, I mean, you did a good job. Very clean. Never been cleaner. Thank you," said Woodley as he struggled to get at his wallet, a difficult task given the constraints of his seat belt.

"It was pretty dirty," said the window cleaner, obviously waiting for something more negotiable than verbal praise.

"Anything worth doing is worth doing well," said Woodley, as he contorted himself in an effort to free the wallet from his pants pocket. He had a habit of reverting to the pedantic when he was flustered. The man tucked the towels under his arm and turned to go.

"Look, if it's too hard, I'll catch you next time," he said.

"No, no, no... hang on... I just.." said Woodley, continuing to struggle. And, at that point, the car in front of him slipped through the window of green. Woodley would be next. If he was going to tip this guy, he would have to hurry.

Finally, with a grunt, Woodley freed the wallet from his pocket. He quickly fished inside it and discovered that he had only three bills: two singles and a fifty. A fifty-dollar tip was, of course, out of the question, but a two-dollar tip seemed insulting, considering the man's impeccable workmanship. (Woodley had been thinking more in the five-dollar range.) Could the man give him change for the fifty? An absurd idea. The man was wearing rags. Woodley fluttered and flailed, flummoxed.

"Like I said, next time is fine," said the man, stepping back.

"Wait!" Woodley shouted. "Can you take a check?"

The man shuffled back to the driver's side window as Woodley pulled his checkbook from his jacket's more accessible inside pocket.

"I guess," said the man, holding out his hand.

Woodley hastily wrote out a check for twenty dollars. (How he arrived at that amount he had no idea. Likewise, he had no inkling as to where the idea to write the guy a check had come from. A *check?* It would have to be useless to a man who was homeless, shoeless. (Was he shoeless? Woodley wasn't sure. For all his artist's ability to take visual inventory, he hadn't bothered to look at the man's feet.) Well, shoeless or not, he was beyond any doubt: *bankless.* Probably wanting for ID. A *check?* The man could never cash it. What was he thinking?

But the light was going to change any minute.

"What's your name?" Woodley asked hastily, his pen poised over the pay-to line.

"Raphael," said the man, "R-A-P-H..."

"A-E-L, Raphael... got it," said Woodley hurriedly. "What's your last name?"

"I just go by Raphael."

Woodley filled in the check, handed it to the man, and in this brief moment of eye contact, was suddenly struck by the man's extraordinary face. He was about to tell Raphael that there was a great Renaissance painter with the same name and that he looked exactly like someone from that period, the same chiseled profile, the same noble manner, the same... but the light had turned to green.

Scooting through the intersection, he saw Raphael in his rearview mirror, folding the check as carefully as he had folded his towels, and putting it into his pocket.

Woodley finally arrived home, checked his messages (none), and changed into his paint-encrusted jeans and denim work shirt. He grabbed two Pepsis and a bag of pretzels from the kitchen and headed for the studio. Time to paint.

He approached his craft with a monkish diligence. Even on those days when his presence was required at Orton, he would spend at least four or five hours in his garage-studio—on his off days, he could easily spend ten to twelve, often forgetting to eat. Once his consciousness entered the rectangle of whatever canvas he had before him, the rest of the world disappeared. Though he considered his job as a teacher to be just that, a *job*, he didn't see the hours he put into his painting as work. (And neither would anyone who watched him in his studio. He would spend most of the time just sitting in his sagging, threadbare, overstuffed chair, staring at a canvas that hung on the opposite wall, now and then adding a tiny stroke or dab of paint, then wiping it out, then repeating the process. Work? In terms of calories spent, he might as well have been curled up on the couch watching *Wheel of Fortune*.)

But he was helpless to spend his time otherwise. He had no friends, knew no one in Springfield save for his fellow faculty members with whom he made no attempt to socialize. He wasn't stupid (actually, quite bright), wasn't humorless (actually, could see irony and absurdity with the best of them), and wasn't physically grotesque (no missing body parts or other abnormalities that could be off-putting), so he *could* have made friends. But whatever muscle it took to socialize had been atrophied by the ridicule he had endured at the Waterbrook Academy. Those snot-nosed, rich-kid, talentless bullies who had thought themselves to be so "creative" had only succeeded in creating Woodley's misanthropy. Though they had been unable to take away his passion, they *had* dented it. He found that he no longer had any desire to paint people.

So now, at the age of thirty-two, he was painting landscapes. Not the industrial-hazed, colorless landscape of Springfield, but digging deep to extract landscapes pieced together from memory and imagination. Though nowhere near as satisfying as his figurative work or his portraiture, it was not without its challenges and rewards. He was determined to make magic where he could. Rarely, but often enough that it would enfold him like an addictive drug, he would see something in his painting that seemed beyond his doing. Where did *that* come from? Did *I* do that? These "happy accidents" were enough to keep him going.

The painting he was currently coaxing into being was similar to many he had done over recent years: a sprawling, woodsy panorama, rendered in anal-retentive detail—every leaf and twig crisp and defined, every pebble given the attention and respect of Gibraltar. No people.

After three hours of painting (he had added a red wheelbarrow in the lower right corner and then wiped it out), the light in his one-window garage was beginning to fade. He could turn on the overhead incandescents, but preferred natural light. So he rolled up his garage door to grab the last rays of daylight.

That's when he saw Raphael, standing statue-still in his driveway, Woodley's check in his hand.

Backlit by the setting sun, Raphael had an imposing presence. Woodley startled at the unexpected sight.

"Can I help you?" Woodley managed.

"Mr. Frye?" said Raphael, reading the name off the check. (Woodley instantly realized that his name *and* his address were on the check. He had all but invited the man to his home.)

"How can I help you?" Woodley asked again, trying to hide his annoyance at having his work interrupted.

"I can't cash this. So I'm returning it," said Raphael.

"You're *what?* Jesus Christ... you're *returning...?* How did you...?"

"I walked," said Raphael as if it were obvious.

"Of course you did," Woodley exhaled. Woodley shook his head in disbelief, then took his wallet from his back pocket. He offered the two singles.

"Sorry, but this is the best I can do right now."

"*Two* dollars?" said Raphael, unhappily. "I walked all the way over here."

"I'm sorry. That's all I have right now," said Woodley, turning toward the garage.

"I saw a fifty in there," said Raphael.

The remark erased any cordiality that Woodley had tried to assume.

"And it's going to *stay* in there. Look, you washed my windshield. I never asked you to. And I certainly wouldn't have asked you to if I thought it was gonna cost me fifty bucks! Now, if you'll excuse me." And, again, he turned away.

Raphael didn't budge.

"I understand that, Mr. Frye. I'd be more than happy to work for the balance." A small smile crossed Raphael's face, as if he knew he had the upper hand.

Woodley didn't know what to say. For the next few pregnant moments he just stared at the man. The *man*? He was more like a boy. Probably early twenties. He was suntanned, long-haired, on the tall side—six-foot, at least. Woodley's trained eye could see that there were some serious muscles under the ratty cotton pullover, but he saw no threat of physical confrontation. Instead, he saw what had occurred to him when he had watched the man clean his windshield—that he was from another age, that his bone structure and bearing would have put him right at home in Florence in the heyday of the Medici. He wasn't quite Michelangelo's David, but he was damned close.

Woodley removed his glasses and rubbed his eyes. "Look, I'm sorry," he said, now feeling sympathetic. "I understand that you need money, and I appreciate that you're willing to work for it. I really do. But, to tell you the truth, I'm not that much higher up the food chain than you are." Woodley could see that his attempt at light humor had fallen on deaf ears, so he changed his tack.

"OK, you seem like a decent guy, but... Jesus... Raphael... I don't have *any* work for you. If I did, well, I'm sure you would be a terrific worker... I mean... my windshield has never been cleaner... but, I..."

Raphael held up his palm like a kindergarten teacher calling for quiet.

"There's a lot I could do," said Raphael. "Your lawn needs mowing, your gutters are full of leaves, your mailbox is loose on its post, the 6 on your house numbers has come undone and is hanging like a 9, and your garage door needs grease. When you opened it, it sounded like someone stepping on a cat." Then he flashed a big, toothy smile. It was genuine, it was earnest.

Who *is* this guy? wondered Woodley. He obviously wasn't stupid, and he certainly was observant—the little bungalow had indeed been sorely neglected. It could use some TLC.

"Well?" asked Raphael.

By now the sun had nearly set and Woodley's thin, denim shirt offered little protection against the crisp, late-October air. He was in no mood to stand in his driveway, educating this uninvited interloper about the nature of economics. But the man showed no sign that he was leaving any time soon. Woodley shivered, then he caved.

"Come on in the studio, we'll talk about this," he said.

Raphael followed Woodley into his studio. When Woodley closed the garage door after them, he had to admit that it *did* sound like someone stepping on a cat.

In a perfect world it would have been a job interview, a convivial business meeting, one side with something to sell, one with something to buy. But in a perfect world you wouldn't have both parties as societally disassociated as Woodley and Raphael: Raphael, the hobo dropout, Woodley the head-in-the-clouds "artiste." So it took some doing for an actual conversation to begin. Woodley broke the ice. "You want some pretzels?" he asked, offering the half-eaten bag.

And this act of kindness was all it took to open Raphael. After finishing the whole bag, he began his autobiography, his clear, black eyes never leaving Woodley's.

He was twenty-three and a survivor of the foster home system. His mother had been fourteen when she had had him, and had died of a heroin overdose eight days shy of her twentieth birthday. His father could have been any of six different men, none forthcoming, and none traceable. Woodley could hear that this was going to be a long story. He tried to conjure the tolerance and interest one gives a drunken stranger in a bar, the ear one lends to a verbose seatmate on a coast-to-coast flight.

At the age of five Raphael became a ward of the state, bouncing from one dysfunctional family to another. He had no brothers or sisters, no aunts, uncles, or cousins. No grandparents. Because he was never in one place for very long—thirteen different homes in eleven years—he had made no friends. He became a loner who would lose himself in books.

"Books?" said Woodley hopefully. "Comic books," said Raphael, forging ahead. He had hated school and dropped out at the age of sixteen. He ran away, living for a while at the Springfield YMCA, getting room and board in exchange for janitorial duties at the facility. His love affair with smoking pot began at the Y and, shortly thereafter, evolved into his becoming a low-level dealer. He thought he was street-smart. Thought he could smell a cop a mile away. He was wrong. He got nailed trying to sell a half pound to an undercover narco who looked just like Jerry Garcia. His public defender was useless. He was sentenced to four years at a minimum-security prison. That was where he got the tattoo that encircled his bicep. The tattoo originally had read: S A T A N, but, after realizing that good behavior and claiming to have found Jesus could lessen his sentence, he had it altered to read: SAinT ANthony.

Life Drawing

That did the trick. After serving less than half his sentence, he was deemed rehabilitated and released. He left prison with nothing but the clothes on his back. Having no job, and hence no money for dope, proved a blessing in disguise—he weaned himself from the weed and was clean. Clean, but homeless.

He learned of the encampment under Werner Boulevard from a fellow panhandler and soon became a fixture there. For the last two years, his sole source of income has been the dirty windshields of kindly passersby. His goal in life? To own an Arby's franchise.

Woodley had been listening more with his eyes than his ears, studying the man's near-perfect, near-David face as he spun his white man's Uncle Remus tale. "Arby's": Woodley heard the word just as his gaze landed on the embroidered medallion on Raphael's baseball cap: "Arby's," it said. The confluence of sight and sound brought Woodley back to the moment.

"Could you take off your cap?" asked Woodley, like a dentist asking someone to rinse.

"My cap? Why?" said Raphael.

"Because I have an idea how you can earn the fifty."

"No problem," said Raphael, removing his cap and shaking out his hair.

"My God," gasped Woodley. "You look just like his portrait of Bindo Altoviti!"

"Bindo *who?*"

"I'm sorry. Of course you wouldn't know this," said Woodley, apologetically. Woodley then took a deep breath and went into teacher-mode. "There was a painter named Raphael, same name as you. Anyway, he painted a picture of a guy named Bindo Altoviti in 1515. You look just like the guy."

"No kidding," said Raphael, uninterested.

"Raphael, I'm an artist." Woodley gestured toward the landscapes that were hanging on the walls, stacked in the corners. "These are mine."

"No shit? I thought they were posters."

"No, I painted them. Listen, I'd like you to model for me."

Raphael stiffened defensively. "Oh, no, no, no. You mean take my clothes off? Ain't gonna happen! I went through enough of that shit at the Y, don't even ask about prison." He jumped to his feet, replaced his cap on his head. "I'm outta here!"

"Hold on!!" Woodley barked. "No clothes off. Nothing like that. I just want to draw your face."

"My *face?*"

"That's all. Your face."

Raphael considered the offer for a moment, then, cooler now, said, "I don't know. I may look like an idiot to you, but I'm not. I look around at these pictures and I don't see any people in them. I don't see any *faces*. Something doesn't smell right."

And now it was Woodley's turn to tell *his* story. He told Raphael about how he had been made an outcast in art school for his old-fashioned ways, how he had come to feel distant from his fellow man, how that isolation had removed his beloved drawing of people from his repertoire, and how their chance meeting had given him inspiration he hadn't felt in over a decade. Raphael's face did not betray any understanding of what was being said, so Woodley cut to the chase.

"I'll pay you ten dollars an hour just to sit here with your clothes on," he said.

"Just to *sit* here," echoed Raphael.

"That's right," said Woodley.

Raphael sat back down, removed his cap, and started to laugh. "How 'bout a hundred an hour and I'll take my clothes *off?*"

"Not a chance. Just your face," said Woodley, and both men laughed. The deal was done.

Raphael proved a worthy model, sitting stone-still while Woodley scratched away with his charcoal. All of Woodley's skill and command as a portraitist came bounding back. After all, portraiture was what he did best, where his true talent resided. He could see that now. Drawing this face that could have easily been Bindo's made him feel like a new man. He drew like a man possessed, finished one rough sketch and was about to start another when he realized that Raphael had fallen asleep. Time had flown. It was one-thirty in the morning. Woodley would never make the man walk back to the encampment at this hour.

He nudged his muse awake and led him to the spare bedroom.

. . . .

The next morning, Raphael was still asleep when Woodley rose and dressed himself for work. Woodley wasn't surprised. For a moment, he thought that the young man might be exhausted from the long walk to his house, but then realized it was more likely the ecstasy of sleeping in an actual bed. Woodley wouldn't deny the kid a couple more hours of dreamtime. He bolted down his instant coffee and, before leaving, taped a note to the inside of the front door instructing Raphael to make sure it was locked before leaving. Still buoyant from the previous evening's drawing session, he went into his studio to have a quick look at what he'd done. The cold light of day did nothing to diminish his excitement—the drawings were better than he'd remembered. He even felt reinvigorated as a teacher, now certain that he had something to impart. He pulled the Volvo out of the driveway and headed for Orton. Maybe it was something mystical, or maybe it was just the clean windshield, but the world looked somehow brighter and sharper.

As was his usual pattern, he arrived at the school twenty minutes before his life-drawing class was to begin. Normally, he would use this time to visit the teacher's lounge, have a second cup of coffee, wolf down whatever form of sugary pastry survived the morning rush, and put on his teacher's face. Today, he went straight to the classroom—a smallish room with high frosted windows (it still, after all the years, smelled of beets and pickles)— and set to work rearranging the dozen benches and easels so the students would be virtually on top of Magda, the seventy-eight-year-old Russian model. (Magda presented a motherlode of drawing possibilities. With nearly three-hundred pounds of her, cascading like lava down her five-foot-three-inch frame, the ripples, folds, and bulges offered a challenging visual geography. And once she had her Harlequin novel wedged comfortably on the ledge of her stomach, she sat as still as a corpse.)

Magda was already there when Woodley arrived. Already out of her oversized chenille bathrobe, sipping a cup of tea and scrutinizing the arriving students with her Eastern European eyes as they straggled in. The students seemed confused by the new seating arrangement, but settled in nonetheless.

"Good morning!" Woodley piped. He was unusually cheerful. "You're probably wondering why I moved your benches so much closer to Magda."

"She smells like Bengay," grumbled Roger, a black-clad, goth sophomore, known for his bad attitude. Woodley ignored the remark and forged ahead.

"Today, we're going to do something different," he said.

"It's hard to breathe, man," Roger said. This time his aside engendered a smattering of giggles.

"Roger, please. A little respect," said Woodley impatiently.

Woodley began to pace the way he'd seen other professors do.

"Now listen up, gang, I want you all to forget that Magda has anything going on below her neck. Today, I want you to draw her portrait. Just the face. In fact, Magda, you could put your robe back on if you want to."

"Nyet. Too hot," said Magda.

"Up to you," said Woodley. He collected himself with a deep breath, then tapped one of the students' sketchpads. "*This* is where you're going to make your magic. You're going to be surprised. Now I don't want you to think that you're just drawing a *head!* No. You're drawing a *person!* Find that spark. Find that intangible... find that..."

"Smell?" whispered Roger.

Woodley shot him a look that said, "That's enough," and turned his attention back to the other students.

"Okay, you've got two hours. Let's see if there's *any* talent in this frigging room."

Alice, a mousy-looking, pigtailed girl in bib-overalls, took this last remark like a bullet. Woodley instantly regretted his tone. "I'm sorry, that was cruel," he said. "It's just that last night... I... well... it's a long story..." He toyed with the idea of telling his students of his breakthrough and realized it would fall on deaf ears. Instead, he just said, "Get to work," and walked out of the room.

An hour later he was back, looking over the students' shoulders to see how their work was progressing, offering comments and suggestions to those who seemed most at sea. The drawings were dreadful, not even an interesting struggle, just mindless, cartoonish scribbling.

One student had elected to use red chalk. When Woodley asked him why, he said, "Because she's a communist." The next hour seemed interminable.

Once the class had been dismissed, Woodley looked at their work, which was now pinned to the bulletin board. There was only one of their hamfisted efforts that even resembled a human being, and it looked like a clumsy police artist's sketch of a perp. Hopeless. But rather than beating himself up for his ineptitude as a teacher, he thought about his *own* work. That was really all that mattered to him. He needed to find Raphael again.

He took the long route home, not caring about hitting Werner Boulevard's endless red light, in fact, hoping for it, wanting those extra minutes to reconnoiter the encampment for his muse. He sat through two red lights, scanning the grounds. He looked everywhere. Raphael wasn't there. Woodley headed for home, his disappointment shrouding him like inclement weather.

Ordinarily, he would jump on the gas after he crossed Werner Boulevard and hot-foot it home to his studio, eager to have that peculiar peace of mind that only comes from burying oneself in one's life's work. Not today. Last night's session with Raphael had spoiled him. He now felt little desire to get back to his landscapes. The sprawling, rural scenes were decent enough, showed him to be a capable painter (a real estate lady had borrowed one for staging a house she was selling; a retired couple had paid him $50.00 for the one they hung in their fishing cabin), but his heart just wasn't in it. Not after the unbridled glee he had felt drawing the Medici Man. And then he thought to himself, "Why should *I* be allowed to only do what my heart desires? What about mailmen? What about meter-readers? What about snow-tire salesmen? Do dentists have their heart in everyone's mouth? Come on, Woodley, life could be worse. Make the best of it." And these were the thoughts that ping-ponged and caromed until he pulled into his cul-de-sac. That's when he heard what he thought were gunshots.

It wasn't gunshots he heard. It was the sound of a sixteen-pound sledgehammer banging into a metal post. Woodley pulled into the driveway and saw Raphael—capless, shirtless, and sweat-drenched, the hammer swinging from his hands like a John Henry manqué. Raphael waved at Woodley and pointed to the mailbox, now hanging perfectly straight on the iron post. "Ta da!!" he said, proudly.

Before Woodley could respond, Raphael was by his side, grasping his arm, and directing his attention to the side of the house.

"Look, Mr. Frye! Your house numbers! Your number 6!" he shouted. "It's not a 9 anymore!"

And it was then and there that Woodley knew that his muse had come home to roost.

. . . .

Woodley and Raphael hashed out the details of their new arrangement. When it was all settled, they both felt like they had won. It was fairly simple: Raphael would continue to model for Woodley on a nightly basis in exchange for room and board. Any other tasks around the house that Raphael decided to take on would be paid for on a per-job basis. (Fixing the mailbox and house numbers, for instance, netted him an additional twenty dollars.)

Thus began a seismic shift in Woodley's life. It was almost like he had a son. While Woodley was off at school, Raphael would spend his days searching for and fixing problems around the aging cottage. He kept the tiny lawn as meticulously as a country club greenskeeper. He vacuumed, did the laundry for both of them, and was always available to model. Woodley felt like he had grabbed the brass ring and reciprocated with fatherly attention. He bought him clothes, a cell phone, helped him open a bank account. For the first time in his young life, Raphael was making honest money, and, though Woodley was far from well-off (he barely broke even at the end of the month), he nonetheless dug deep into his savings and bought Raphael a used VW Bug. Two months ago, Woodley would never have imagined it, but here he was, sitting in a DMV parking lot, grinning like a proud papa, as his "son" emerged, waving his first driver's license.

Yes, Woodley's life had changed. So it should have come as no surprise to him that his work would change as well. That they were all pictures of Raphael did not change, but the new portraits were looser, freer, often done in a flurry of activity, and much less concerned with the microscopic detail that had once been his signature. There were drips and smudges, bleed-throughs, and swatches of brilliant color, slathered on with apparent abandon. He wasn't putting both eyes on one side of the head like Picasso, but the work definitely had taken on a more modern look. Woodley was astonished. Astonished, mostly, because he felt good about it. He compared his new work with his older drawings and paintings and the older ones seemed as stale and unemotional as medical illustrations. Why, he wondered, had he, for so many years, fought the intrusion of anything modern into his thinking?

The reason hit him like a runaway bus. Fear. That's all it was. Fear of the unknown. Fear that straying too far from the norms that were established centuries ago would send him on a slippery slope to oblivion. Now he was determined to push the envelope as far as possible. If the release and joy he was feeling night after night in his little garage studio was oblivion, then bring it on!

The combination of disenchantment and limited studio space (but mostly disenchantment) had kept Woodley's work modestly sized. His landscapes were never larger than those that graced a wall calendar. Now, as his ideas burgeoned—the act of painting had almost become an athletic event—he needed a bigger arena to express them. He ordered fresh canvasses that barely fit through the garage door. (On his commute to and from Orton, he would often see an unused billboard and lapse into fantasies about a masterpiece.) Bigger was better. Compared to life pre-Raphael, *everything* was better. He painted like a dervish.

And, in that firestorm of activity, he soon discovered that along with overcoming his fear of the contemporary, he had overcome other fears as well. Most notably, the fear of showing his work. He saw two truths simultaneously. First, that it had been the negative reception his work had received at art school that had made him loath to show his paintings, had made him gun-shy about ever opening himself up to further ridicule. But, second, he realized that it was the praise and acknowledgment that his drawings had garnered when he was a boy that had fueled his desire to be an artist in the first place. The gushing of parents, the astonished, raised eyebrows of his elementary school teachers. It was the praise that pushed him, gave him his *raison d'être*, that validated his being. It was the *praise*, not some rare genetic stamping that made him unable to stop drawing. Praise, hosannahs, accolades. He needed these things. And, realizing this—that his so-called drive could be nothing more than a social/neurotic need—didn't dampen his newfound enthusiasm. Why should it?

Art was a form of communication, wasn't it? And communication demanded a speaker and a listener. An audience. But, currently, his audience was limited to Raphael, who, of course, would give him a thumbs-up—his lack of any sophistication, let alone any knowledge of art, prohibited anything more than this digital blessing, and he certainly wasn't going to bite the hand that fed him. No, Raphael didn't really count.

And then, because everything was currently falling into place like toppling dominoes, an opportunity presented itself.

It was an Orton tradition that there be an annual faculty exhibition. It was the highlight of the school year. Teachers from the various departments—painting, drawing, ceramics, photography, and sculpture—were invited to show their work in the school's makeshift gallery. (It was the only opportunity to do so for most of the faculty, their work being lackluster at best.) Exhibiting was not mandatory, and Woodley had always declined the offer. His excuse was always the same: My work is a *work in progress*. But it was progress that had recently been made, so, to the surprise of the faculty (and to himself, truth be told) he accepted the invitation. He suffered under no delusion that the audience at Orton would be erudite or able to comprehend what he was up to (he knew these people too well), but it *would* be an act of putting his paintings in front of warm bodies. Baby steps.

Woodley chose two of his largest, most ambitious, semi-abstract portraits of Raphael for the exhibit. In for a penny, in for a pound, he reasoned.

The exhibit space (ordinarily the cafeteria) was high-ceilinged, long, and narrow—almost the proportions of a bowling alley. (It had housed a conveyor belt in its previous incarnation as part of the food-processing plant, and still held the faint aroma of broccoli and bacon.)

The exhibit was a catchall, more akin to garage sale than gallery. Vernon Cox, the sculpture teacher, had created some contraption that seemed to be made of coat hangers, saucepan handles, and duct tape. He entitled it *Rapture*. Cokie Stier, the ceramist, displayed a selection of lopsided bowls that had the signs of the Zodiac glazed into their lids. Jojobo Chia's photographs took up most of one wall: a misty, black-and-white panorama of plastic bags, beer cans, cigarette butts, used condoms, shredded lottery scratchers, sneakers flung over telephone wires, and other detritus that defined the gloom and depression of inner-city Springfield. Janis Jans, the other painting and drawing teacher, hung her series of limpid watercolors depicting women in various stages of lesbian romance. Under the No Smoking sign, the diminutive jewelry instructor, Chin Lu, had nailed up a pair of rhinestone-encrusted handcuffs. Otto Orton, the namesake and current president of the college, though admittedly a businessman with no artistic talent whatsoever, put up a few of the paint-by-numbers that had occupied him after hip surgery. Woodley, with one wall virtually to himself, would clearly be the star of the show.

Woodley worked his way through the small crowd—mostly students, faculty, custodians in their Sunday best, and Springfield locals who were lured in more by the open bar than a need for culture. He had toyed with the idea of inviting Raphael to the opening of the Orton Faculty Show but decided against it for two reasons: He didn't want to reveal the "secret sauce" behind the work; and, there being an open bar, he didn't want to put temptation on the table for Raphael, who had, after all, spent two years in prison because of drugs. Wasn't alcohol a drug? He would go it alone.

He sauntered to where his paintings hung, making himself available for any questions or comments. He didn't have to wait long. He was instantly awash in compliments, in praise, in admiration. It was just what the doctor ordered. Roger, the black-clad, smart-mouthed Goth, fist-bumped him. "Your stuff is *hot*, man!" The shy, pigtailed, bib-overalled Alice gave him a quick peck on the cheek and retreated, crimson-faced. Magda (he, at first, didn't recognize her fully dressed) air-kissed him on both cheeks as if he were the Tsar himself, returning from a successful military campaign. The burly sculpture teacher, Vernon Cox, gave Woodley a bear hug that could have qualified as a Heimlich. Even Lars Phleck, the art history teacher, a stern and dyspeptic man who seldom spoke to anyone without his notes, waxed rhapsodic, pointing out merits in the paintings that Woodley had not imagined were there. Woodley felt like he had won an Oscar.

The last time he had been this much the center of attention was his eleventh birthday party, when he had drawn caricatures of his fawning aunts, uncles, and cousins. He shook more hands than a gubernatorial candidate. And, while it seemed that everyone wanted a piece of him, wanted to get as close to him as possible, there was one man who lingered on the periphery.

He was older—probably late sixties—not a faculty member, not a parent, and, judging by his attire (an expensive looking blazer and black turtleneck), he was not from Springfield. He was just staring, unblinking, at Woodley's paintings. Woodley couldn't help but notice. Emboldened by his newfound notoriety, Woodley approached the man.

"Welcome," said Woodley, extending a hand, which the man seemed to examine before shaking. An odd duck, thought Woodley.

"Are you the artist?" he said, pointing at Woodley's paintings.

"I am indeed."

"Name?"

"Woodley Frye."

"Fry...? With an 'e'?"

"That's me," said Woodley.

"Hmmmm..." said the man, returning his silent gaze to the paintings for a full thirty seconds. Woodley thought the man might be crazy.

"Never heard of you," he said, finally, as much to himself as to Woodley.

"I teach here," Woodley said, as if that would explain his anonymity. The man didn't seem to hear him, and continued to stare at the paintings. After another awkward silence, the man finally turned to Woodley.

"Who do you show with?" the man asked.

"*Show* with? You mean, like a gallery? Oh... I don't... I mean, I've never... I just."

"I find that hard to believe," said the man, extending his hand for a second handshake.

"I'm Howard La Salle," he said formally. "The La Salle Gallery in Chicago. That's me. I'm sure you've heard of it, unless you've been living under a rock." Howard smiled for the first time, then began his pitch.

"This work is extraordinary, Mr. Frye. You should be showing regularly. Are you aware of that?"

Woodley could only manage a weak, "Really?"

"Genius doesn't serve anyone if its products stay locked in a closet," said Howard. Woodley had the feeling that this was a sentence Howard had practiced.

"I don't want to keep you from all of your fans who want to talk to you, so let's just cut to the chase. I imagine you have more work like this. If you do, the La Salle Gallery would be delighted to give you an exhibition."

"You're kidding," said Woodley, pleasantly blindsided.

"I'm as serious as cancer," said Howard with a little laugh. "You *do* have more work like this, don't you?"

"Yeah, lots," said Woodley, still wondering if this was all a dream.

"Well, I want to see it. Can I visit your studio?"

"Sure," said Woodley. Was this really happening? "When?"

"Well, how about right after this flea market closes?"

"You mean tonight?"

"The iron is hot, Mr. Frye."

Howard liked the work in the studio as much,

if not more, than the work in the faculty exhibit. They talked long into the night, Howard listening intently to Woodley's ramblings about his early training, his initial loathing of anything "modern," and his unexpected metamorphosis into the artist he was today. Woodley pulled out his drawings, showing Howard the ones that he felt were his "breakthroughs," and expounding at length about where it all might be leading. His breathless speech about "figure/ground," "negative space," "deconstruction," and "surface tension" only ceased when Howard suddenly brought up money.

"I think the big paintings can go for ten to twelve thousand; the drawings for three to five," he said, confidently.

"Oh my God!" said Woodley, not believing his ears. He had never thought of his work in terms of financial gain—certainly not financial gain of this magnitude. He instantly had visions of quitting his teaching job, a larger studio, an assistant, maybe. "Oh my God," he said again.

"You just keep making these things and I'll take care of everything else," said Howard.

With the ball now in his court, Howard laid out the details. It so happened that the gallery had an open date in two weeks—the artist originally scheduled had suddenly decided to go into filmmaking and had abandoned painting completely. The timing couldn't be better, and Woodley had more than enough work to fill the space. Howard handpicked fourteen paintings and drawings for the show and instructed Woodley on how to wrap and ship them to Chicago. It was a done deal.

. . . .

It was nearly two o'clock in the morning when Woodley walked Howard to his car. While they were exchanging their final handshake, Raphael's VW pulled in beside them. Woodley had been so consumed by the evening's events he had not noticed that Raphael wasn't home. He was *always* at home. Where the hell had he been?

Raphael, acting like nothing was amiss, walked to where the two men were standing. Howard stuck out his hand.

"*You* must be the model!!" he exclaimed. "I can see why Woodley was so inspired. How *very* nice to meet you!"

Raphael shook Howard's hand quickly and, after apologizing for being "very, very tired," headed for the house.

Howard watched him go. "Boy, those kids love their weed, don't they?" he said, chuckling knowingly to himself.

"What are you talking about?" said Woodley.

"Weed, pot, marijuana. You can smell it a mile away," said Howard. "It's probably on my hand from when he shook it." Howard laughed and held up his hand to Woodley's face.

"Want a hit?" he said, teasingly.

Woodley inhaled, obligingly.

"I don't smell anything," he said.

"Hey, maybe I'm wrong. No biggie," said Howard with a shrug. He moved to his car and slid behind the wheel. "Tonight, we made art history, my friend. See you in two weeks!"

And as he watched the Mercedes disappear under the streetlights, Woodley sniffed his hand again.

It had been quite a night; quite a tornado of unexpected events, and it wasn't over. Woodley had to prepare himself for a possible confrontation with Raphael.

Though he had complained of being very tired, Raphael was not in his bedroom. He was in the kitchen, sitting at the little Formica table, methodically spreading peanut butter on a stack of Ritz crackers. He was so engrossed in his culinary art that he didn't notice Woodley staring at him—not just staring, but examining, looking for the telltale sign of glassy eyes. Woodley knew Raphael's face better than he knew his own. If there was something off, he'd see it. No glassy eyes, nothing untoward, but still there was the mystery of where Raphael had been.

"Where were you tonight?" Woodley asked as calmly as he could.

"Huh?" Raphael said, a little startled. "Me? Oh, I was with some friends." Woodley stiffened:

a lie, right off the bat. Woodley was fairly certain that Raphael had no friends.

"Friends, huh, anyone I know?"

"No," said Raphael, returning his attention to his snacks. Woodley decided to go right for the jugular.

"Have you been smoking pot? My friend said he smelled it on you."

"Jesus, Woodley. Can I just eat my crackers and go to bed?" Raphael said in a huff. This amped Woodley's suspicions—Raphael *never* called him by his first name, always Mr. Frye. Something was up.

"You *have*, haven't you! Well, I must say, I'm very disappointed," said Woodley, pulling up the other kitchen chair and sitting, hoping for an intimacy that would make him more counselor than accuser. "Given your history, Raphael, you know what a bad idea that is. You don't want to go back to..." Raphael cut him off sharply.

"*Stop!*" he said. "You have *your* thing. I have *mine!!*" Woodley was dumbstruck. He had never heard this tone from Raphael. "What are you talking about?" Woodley asked.

Raphael forced a triple-decker peanut-butter-and-Ritz combo into his mouth and stared coldly at Woodley while he chewed. Once his mouth was clear again, he let it all out.

"You had your big show tonight. Your fancy-schmancy Orton Faculty show. Your big-ass party. Your dog and pony, look-at-me-ain't-I-somethin'… your… your stupid show-and-tell. But you know something? You would have had *none* of it if I hadn't sat there like a zombie, hour after hour, while you scratched away with your stupid drawings and… and… Damn it, Woodley, open your eyes. The pictures are all of *ME! ME!!* Don't you see it? It would have been *my* big night, too! It *should* have been my big night! *My* fifteen fucking minutes of fame! But was I *invited?* No! No, of course not. Don't even *think* about taking the little homeless guy to the big fancy-schmancy party because… I don't know why. Embarrassed? Was that it? Or maybe you just hoped I'd stick around your pathetic little house and fix things. Do your fucking laundry or something. I don't know. You're a hard man to figure, Woodley. Well, I didn't stick around the house. I went out in my piece of shit VW that you made such a big fucking deal about buying me, and I went back to the culvert to see some people that treat me like a *person* and not just something to draw, not like a goddamn bowl of fruit in a goddamn painting. And, yes, I got high! I got high and laughed like I haven't laughed in a long time. So you had *your* big party, and I had *mine!* And, by the way, I hope someone told you that the paintings are messy, sloppy, and too fucking big. So, yes indeedy, I got high. I still am. You want a cracker?"

Woodley rose to his feet and pointed at the door. "Get out!"

Life Drawing

"I had no choice," Woodley said to the mirror the following morning. "I heard what I heard and had to kick him out." But it wasn't something he was happy about. He liked Raphael. Beyond "liked," he felt he had become some kind of surrogate relation (not a father, he was only a dozen or so years older; not a brother, they were too different in too many ways; not a roommate, there was clearly a hierarchy in the home; it was something unnameable). He would miss him, even though he knew that keeping him around, especially after the blistering harangue Raphael had unleashed, would be counterproductive. Healing a wound that deep would have required countless heart-to-hearts and confessionals that would have taken time that Woodley, selfish or not, simply didn't have right now. He had his first gallery show to put together. He had paintings to finish, to wrap, crates to build, shippers to contact. The old Raphael would have been a great help with all of it, of course, but not the one revealed at the kitchen table. The mirror looked back at him and told him the truth: "The last thing you need right now is a spoiled brat pothead keeping you from your date with destiny." Woodley walked out of the bathroom and felt a pang of remorse as he passed the empty guest bedroom. He steeled himself to go to work. He opened the now silent garage door, forgetting for a moment that it was Raphael who had greased the wheels.

Woodley had never worked harder. Fueled in equal parts by panic and excitement, he added the last bits to the paintings Howard had selected, then carefully wrapped and crated them. He finished the job only moments before the truck arrived to take them away. The truck was enormous. Seeing this, Woodley decided to add his portfolio of earlier, photorealistic drawings to the shipment. Once again, in for a penny...

He signed the bill of lading, shook the driver's hand, and watched as the truck groaned its way out of the driveway. He returned to his studio. The walls were empty—he had long ago trashed the labored landscapes that preceded his "Raphael period"—and, if it weren't for the paint stains on the floor, the garage would have been just that: an ordinary garage. He stood for a moment in the middle of the studio, a wave of longing enveloping him. It could have been the unadorned white walls, could have been the melancholy of exhaustion, or it could have been that the only evidence that Raphael had ever been a part of his life was in the back of a truck. He had to admit it: He missed the guy.

Raphael had fallen off the planet since the night of his eviction. There was a part of Woodley that wanted to try and find him—he was, no doubt, back at the encampment, licking his wounds. If he wanted to, Woodley could show up with an Arby's take-out lunch for the boy and try to smooth things over. Why didn't he? Because, in an odd way, Woodley felt that *he* was the one who had been abandoned, not Raphael. "That's crazy," he told himself, "I'm overthinking this whole thing. Just let it be one of life's little hiccups. I did a good deed, helped a guy out, paid him a few bucks, maybe even taught him a few things that'll help him down the road. Let it go. He's young. He'll be fine."

Woodley packed his bags for Chicago.

. . . .

Woodley was stopped in his tracks when he rounded the corner and saw the gallery. Huge black letters formed an imposing rubric on the window under the La Salle Gallery sign: WOODLEY FRYE—VISIONS OF RAPHAEL. It took his breath away. When he entered the gallery his breath was stolen again. Howard had done a beautiful job hanging the work. It looked like a museum.

The large paintings that adorned two of the walls were lit in a warm glow by the gallery lights; the drawings had been framed exquisitely and were clustered along a third wall. The portfolio of early, photorealistic drawings (Woodley's last-minute addition) sat on a table in Howard's office. (Woodley assumed this was so Howard could show his collectors how the paintings had evolved.)

Howard had thought of everything. As Woodley walked past the aproned man, busily setting up the table for the canapés and fine wines that would be served to the high rollers, he felt that he had arrived. He even said it aloud, "This is the real deal."

La Salle greeted Woodley with a broad smile and a fraternal hug, then ushered him into his office, a spotless den of high-end black leather and chrome. He handed Woodley the price list. Woodley's hand actually shook as he read it. La Salle had priced the work even higher than he had originally suggested. The paintings ranged from fifteen to twenty thousand, the drawings were at least four thousand. Even the sale of a couple of pieces would give Woodley a wherewithal he'd never dreamt of.

"Seem okay with you?" asked Howard. He grinned slyly—as if he were "the brains" behind some intricate bank heist.

"I have no idea," said Woodley.

Howard laughed. "Of *course* you have no idea. You're the *artist!* Artists don't know shit about business. That's why you have *me*. Trust me, Woodley, I know my clientele and I know what they want. They're gonna eat your stuff up!"

"I don't know how to thank you," said Woodley, meekly.

Again Howard laughed. "Oh, I think my fifty percent commission will be plenty of thanks."

He slapped Woodley on the back. "Now let's go get a hamburger. You're gonna be on your feet for three hours tonight, yakking to people you don't know. *I* know these people, and believe me, you don't want to deal with them on an empty stomach."

It was the best hamburger Woodley had ever had. Howard grabbed the check before it ever hit the table. "Your money's no good in *my town*," he said. Howard further suggested that Woodley should go back to his hotel and grab a little nap before facing the daunting circus of an opening. Woodley felt the circus had already begun, and that Howard was the ringmaster, so he did as he was told. He flopped on the bed but, of course, couldn't sleep. He tried to watch TV but found it inane. He read and reread the price list La Salle had given him. He had the angst of a teenager on the night of the prom. He was already showered and dressed when Howard called him and told him to come a little early—there was already a line at the door.

La Salle's openings were a magnet for the upwardly mobile of Chicago. When Woodley arrived, there was already a small sea of Armani suits and designer dresses swirling around the refreshments table. In this ocean of shiny, black gabardine, Woodley (in his corduroy sports coat with the leather elbow patches) stood out like a horse in church: He was obviously the artist. He lingered near his wall of paintings, girding himself for any questions the gallery-goers might have. No one approached him. Oddly, there were very few who even seemed remotely interested in the paintings. Maybe that's the drill, he thought: get your drinks, chat a bit with your cronies about your new Tesla or your timeshare in the Bahamas, and then, saving the best for last, look at the art. But, as the evening wore on, he could see that a different pattern was emerging. After taking what seemed like a polite lap around the exhibition, giving little attention to the large paintings or framed drawings, the attendees were drawn to Howard's office. Woodley looked through the large glass wall that separated Howard's office from the gallery. He could see Howard passing around the unframed drawings—the pre-breakthrough, photorealistic studies of Raphael that Woodley had only shipped as an afterthought. People were grabbing them out of Howard's hands, out of each other's hands. They were like kids in a candy store.

"What the hell?" Woodley said aloud. He knocked on the window, hoping to get Howard's attention. Howard turned, held up a "one minute" finger, and, after a handshake with one of the Armanis, came out of the office.

"What a business!!" Howard all but shouted.

"What's going on?" asked Woodley, truly confused. "No one is looking at my paintings!"

"I know," said Howard. "It's the strangest thing. I thought they'd love them, but they don't. What they *love* is your model! They think he's beautiful! They want to see *him*!! Is he coming?"

"No," said Woodley flatly.

"Well, that's a shame." Howard shook his head.

"I tell you, I've never seen anything like this. I've had portrait shows before. Lots of them. But this is a first. Everyone coming up to me with the same question: 'Who *is* this guy?.' Women and men alike, asking, 'Is he single?' I had an indy filmmaker wanting to cast him as Sir Lancelot; a lady who runs a modeling agency claimed he was the perfect fit for the Ralph Lauren catalog and demanded his phone number. They want *photos* of him! *Photos!!* Not paintings!!"

"Jesus Christ," was all that Woodley could say.

"Well, we don't have any *photos*, do we. So I offered them the next best thing. I showed them your studies. They're almost like photos. Some of the clients thought they *were* photos. I lied a little bit—told them that this was your *new* work, that we hadn't even had time to frame it. Well, long story short, I've already sold two of them. I wish we had more."

"But..." Woodley barely uttered.

"I've got to get back in there," said Howard, "these people are crazy."

Woodley's ego was determined to get *something* out of the evening. "Do any of them want to meet the artist?" he asked in a pathetically hopeful voice.

"Don't take it personally, but I don't think they give a shit," said Howard, spreading his hands in a "beats me" gesture and reentering the free-for-all.

Woodley stared through the window at the clients pawing through his drawings as if they were baseball cards in a thrift shop, like half-price socks and underwear at a department-store fire sale. How different this was from the Orton reception. Apples and oranges, he tried to think. Apples and oranges.

Though the opening was scheduled to go from 6 p.m. to 9 p.m., it was over by 7:30. The last guests made their exit, leaving just the bartender fishing his tips out of a jar, an exhausted Howard, and a shell-shocked Woodley.

"It's still early. You gonna drive back tonight?" asked Howard softly.

"Huh...? Oh, no. I'm pretty tired. I'm gonna go back to the hotel," said Woodley, robotically.

Howard placed his hands on Woodley's shoulders. "How 'bout a smile, huh? We sold three drawings. Two more on hold. That's *something*. I've had shows where *nothing* sold. You should feel pretty good about it."

Woodley nodded silently in response, turned, and walked out of the gallery. As he plodded the seven blocks to his hotel, the ubiquitous Chicago wind picked up. As if it were a message from on high, a gust grabbed the price list he held in his hand and blew it into the lake.

. . . .

He fell on the hotel bed like a toppled statue. "I don't get it," he said to the ceiling. Yes, I showed nothing but portraits of Raphael, and yes, it was probably stupid to title them *Raphael I*, *Raphael II*, *Raphael III*, all the way to *Raphael XIV*, as if it were all about *him*. But, come on, when people look at the *Mona Lisa*, they think of Da Vinci. They have no idea her name was Lisa Gherardini. Couldn't care less. She stopped being a human being when she became a painting. Same thing for Van Gogh's mailman. Does anybody say, "Hey, there's Joseph Roulin? I wonder what he's up to. Is he still delivering mail?" Never. They say "I love Van Gogh." Same thing with Whistler's mother. No one clamored for photos of Anna McNeill Whistler, or even bothered to learn that was her name. Maybe I should have just titled the paintings *A Study in Red*, *A Study in Yellow*, *A Study in Green*. Pulled the same trick Gainsborough pulled when he called his painting *The Blue Boy*. That kid was every bit as easy on the eyes as Raphael, but no one asked for *his* phone number, or even his name. Because he was a *fucking painting!!* Sure, I'll bet those morons I saw tonight have paintings on their ultra-modern condo walls, and I'll bet they're all those mindless red squares or doodled splashes or "expressionist" slatherings of paint that dry up as lifeless and inert as used toothpaste. And as for portraits? Oh, I'm sure their high-priced decorator put family portraits around their spotless, cream-and-beige living rooms: all photos.

Here's one of Tiffany when she got her degree from Tufts (gender studies). Here's one of Dylan on a pony when he was six. This is one from when we got married. "Oh, my God! Look how long my hair was!" Sure, they have portraits, but would never think that one could be *painted*. So what did he expect? That these people would recognize *art* when they saw it? It had been a fool's errand. All of it. From the get-go. From the day he decided to be an artist, putting all his eggs in one basket, spending every waking moment pursuing the elusive magic of the painted image. He had seen in Raphael a glimpse of the past—the noble forehead and aquiline nose, the piercing onyx eyes of the fifteenth-century nobleman—and had hitched his wagon. Because he loved the past. The past was when *real* art was made. Well, he'd better love the past, because that's where he was now. Back to square one.

Woodley wasn't sure he had ever really fallen asleep, but he must have, because he was unsure where he was when the phone rang the following morning.

"Woodley? It's Howard. I wanted to try and catch you before you left. I've got the numbers from last night, thought I'd run them by you." Woodley hoisted himself to a sitting position and tried to clear his head.

"Numbers?"

"The postmortem. You want to get a pencil and write this down, or can I just tell you? It's pretty simple."

"I don't have a pencil. I'm still in bed."

"Well, like I said, it's pretty simple. We sold four of the old drawings. After the discount I always give my inner circle, the grand total was eight thousand four hundred dollars. Now, as we discussed, my cut is fifty percent, so that leaves four thousand two hundred for you."

"Four-two, for me," said Woodley, slowly waking.

"Right. But here's the thing. You remember how we talked about framing and shipping costs being *your* responsibility? Well..."

"No, I don't remember that," said Woodley, now fully awake and certain that the subject had never come up.

"Well, we *did*. Anyway, those costs come to four thousand two hundred and twelve dollars."

"So, you're saying that *I* owe *you?*"

"Nonsense. You owe me nothing," said Howard quickly and officially. "I'm not going to end what I see as a promising relationship over twelve fucking dollars. We'll call it even."

"Even," said Woodley, flatly.

"Even, Steven," said Howard. "Safe trip back." And he hung up.

. . . .

The trip back from Chicago seemed twice as long as the trip to. It took forever to push the Volvo out of the wet, grey womb of Chicago's inner city—another lifetime to guide it through the smoky stop-and-go of the industrialized suburbs, then the featureless sprawl of tract housing. Finally, with these tired attempts at civilization behind him, he was in the endless pastureland of central Illinois: acre after acre of cornstalk stubble, thrust like rows of broken cutlery through the dusting of snow. The land looked like the classifieds section of a newspaper—the perfect canvas for his emotions. Had he been in a healthy frame of mind, he would have used this lack of distraction to focus, accurately and chronologically, on the events in his life since Raphael and Howard had entered it.

Woodley was not in a healthy frame of mind. He felt burned, betrayed, the fall guy in some Ponzi scheme perpetrated by Life itself. In short, he was sulking. Sulking like a six-year-old told to go to his room. "Why me?" and "Life's not fair" alternated as his mantra as he entered the Springfield city limits. And there it was: the Orton School. The cinder-block walls, the rusted tin roofs—it looked like a Stalag in his current mindset. He saw it now as it had originally been intended: a food-processing plant. A place that produced products that would ultimately turn to shit. Wasn't "food processing" a polite-company way of describing the digestive process? "Everything I've done has turned to shit," he thought. It was a thought that, for a split second, made him want to drive into a tree.

Life Drawing

And then, after hitting this nadir, the strangest thing happened. He had a positive thought: "Hey, I *did* sell four drawings. And Howard had said that he'd had shows where *nothing* sold." And, slowly, like a runner catching his breath after a marathon, he began to rebuild his confidence. He saw where he had gone wrong. He had simply tried to be something he wasn't. He had tried to be contemporary, cutting-edge, modern. All things he wasn't. He had let the excitement of painting people again throw him off course—had gotten over-eager, hasty, and sloppy, and had defended the new work as the conquest of some obscure debilitating fear. What bullshit. On top of that, he had let the praise that the "new" work had garnered at the Orton show go to his head. Well, the "new" work hadn't gotten a second glance at the La Salle Gallery. It was the drawings he had done *before* he went on this fool's errand that had sold. "Those drawings are who I *am*. And, art world be damned, they *had* an audience. Howard had said he could have sold more if he'd had them. Well, he's *going* to have more. I'm not done drawing Raphael!" Woodley's thinking had done a full three-sixty—he was actually excited about the future when he pulled into his driveway.

And there it was, spray-painted on his garage door in letters two feet high: ASSHOLE!!

He knew who had written it, and, in his new resolve, couldn't let it be the last word. He had to find Raphael. He couldn't lose him now. He backed out of the driveway and headed for the Mercer Boulevard encampment, knowing that's where Raphael would be. He rehearsed his *mea culpa* as he drove. Raphael would surely understand that he had kicked him out for his own good. He would accept an apology, maybe even make one of his own. He would, of course, invite Raphael to all of his openings from now on. He'd give him his share of the pie. He'd...

As he neared the Mercer Boulevard intersection, he could see a burgeoning cloud of dust over what was once the homeless encampment—the bulldozer, like a prehistoric beast, eating giant mouthfuls of cans, bottles, abandoned clothing, remnants of tents, the rusted, dirty detritus of meager means. Food processing.

And, as he sat there, the roiling dust congealing on his windshield, Woodley waited and waited for the light to turn green.

ADDITIONAL INFORMATION

The thought began as the end of a dream and dovetailed into wakefulness. It was an odd thought to have in a dream—coming at me not as one of the surreal and fractured impulses that usually bombard me during my REM cycle, but more as a complete vocalized sentence.

It was more like a remembered song lyric. "*You need to get a physical*," was the thought. Not a very dreamlike message or a terribly catchy or poetic phrase for a song lyric (is there even a rhyme for "physical?"), but the words grabbed my attention, as if they had been scribbled on a Post-it with "TO DO!" written importantly across the top. I tried to put it out of my head and go about my morning business (shit, shave, shower, coffee) but it nagged me.

It had been years since I'd had a physical. Many people would find that irresponsible. I like to think

Additional Information

of myself as a take-care-of-business kind of guy, so that kind of nagged me as well. Maybe it was time for me to bite the bullet, drop my pants, and cough.

I had hoped it would be simple—surrender an hour of my life in exchange for many more healthy years to come. I pictured the doctor, bopping my knees with his little red rubber hammer. I knew he'd press the stethoscope to my heart and listen for the lub-dub as intently as one would listen to strange sounds coming from one's attic. I assumed he would look deeply into each ear as if he could actually see through my head. I expected the wooden stick, like the remnants of a popsicle, to be scraped around inside my mouth. I knew I'd have to take deep breaths and hold them. I was pretty sure of all of this. What I didn't anticipate was the paperwork.

Before I retired (eighteen years ago), I worked behind the counter at the windowless Avis Rent-a-Car kiosk in Logan Airport. Those of you old enough to remember will recall that Avis's motto was "We Try Harder." In my twenty-two years there, I came to realize that "We Try Harder" simply meant that we have more paperwork. At times, it felt like I was asking for a last will and testament before loaning a Ford Pinto for the weekend. Long-term leases engendered forms that rivaled the US Constitution. After nearly a quarter-of-a-century of this, you can imagine how I felt about paperwork. I hated it.

So, when the pudgy little nurse behind the glass partition handed me the clipboard and a ballpoint pen, I came very close to throwing it back at her and storming out. That would have created a scene, however, and I had no desire to offer a sideshow for the other patients who were in the waiting room. The "good citizen" prevailed. I lowered myself into the frayed Naugahyde club chair and began to fill in the blanks.

The first few lines were easy to answer. Name, address, occupation, next of kin, insurance. The usual. Then I got to the top of page two:

Which of the following best describes your present physical condition?

Very good _____*Average* _____*Poor*_____

Now, if there is one thing my years at Avis taught me, it's this: Don't lie. It will only come back to bite you. I've seen people's lives all but destroyed over a misrepresentation of mileage, near-bankruptcy born from a simple fib about gasoline purchased. Tempting as it was to just breeze past this line of questioning, I knew I had to answer honestly. I'm eighty-three years old. There is no way on God's green earth that anyone is going to believe that I'm *Very good*. And, since I could no longer do things that were relatively easy just three years ago, I doubted that I'd even get away with *Average*. I had no recourse other than to check *Poor*. It was the next line that threw me.

Additional Information

If you answered Poor, please list any and all contributing factors:

Oh, boy. Where does one start? I certainly didn't want to be called in again because my answers were incomplete, so I decided to throw the whole book at it. Be completely honest, from top to bottom, stem to stern: the whole one hundred seventy-one pounds of meat and gristle, the various and sundry fluids, the hairs and their follicles. I started at the bottom. The parts that touched the earth.

My Toes: With the exception of my toenails (inaccessible to clippers because of general flexibility issues, they have come to resemble the tusks of small desert animals), my toes are fine. Just dandy. I've got the ones that went to market, the ones that stayed home, the ones that had roast beef, the ones that had none, and the ones that went whee-whee-whee all the way home. All ten, just dandy.

My Feet: The bottoms of my feet, dry as summer sidewalk, are no longer arched. If anything, it feels as if they are arching in the other direction, giving me the sensation of walking on irregular cobblestones, on small logs. I have tried to use arch-increasing insoles but it feels like I have my wallet in my shoes. Because of this unfit-for-military-service flatness of my feet, I have no balance problems per se. If anything, I have the opposite problem: my balance is so sure and anchored that it often rivets me in place and generates anxiety about moving. The skin on the top of my feet is thin, as translucent as theatrical scrim, little blue veins scrambling around like an inner-city road map. (I should add that these feet of mine often go to sleep. This feeling, that my feet are twice their size, and filled with a numbing ginger ale, makes me tentative when they finally "awaken." The first steps can be a tricky business. Three times I have fallen. I have learned, like a swimmer waiting an hour after eating, to wait until full feeling returns before leaving my recliner.) What else? Oh, I've been told, more than once, that I walk like a duck. I have a friend with diabetes who lost both of his feet, so I'm not complaining—I'm just saying.

My Shins: I can't say when the hair on my legs started to disappear. It had to be quite a while ago, because I can't even remember them ever being hairy. If they were, not a strand is left. I imagine this is the result of eight decades of sock wearing, the constant abrasion of argyle on skin. Now the skin is so smooth and shiny that my socks have little to grab and are constantly slipping down my leg—annoying, but not painful, so it's probably not worth mentioning. I have barked my shins so often over the years that they feel like a washboard when I run my thumb up and down them. The shin as artifact: a physical record of countless collisions with inanimate objects, something that could end up in a natural history museum years from now, an example of the clumsiness of twentieth- and twenty-first century man. My activity level these days is such that all my shins really do is connect my feet to my knees. So, I guess, they're not a problem.

My Knees: There is an old joke that goes: "Doctor, I have pain in the joints," and the doctor says, "Well, stay out of them." Unfortunately, I can't stay out of my knees. There are days when they work like the proverbial well-oiled machine. And there are days when the simple act of crossing my legs feels like unanaesthetized amputation. I look in the mirror and I see a bag of walnuts, the left one more than the right, and I know that parts of them have slipped into the wrong place, are headed down my leg, one day to be part of my feet. When I undertake something as daunting as a flight of stairs, I become aware that the tendons and sinews are no longer like strong leather belts, but more like a fat man's suspenders. I have the feeling that flexing a knee is a lot like bending a piece of wire, sooner or later it snaps. I have heard that they now have very good knee replacements but the thought of being in a rehab clinic with young athletes who have blown out their ACLs, hearing them chattering away in sport-speak, and seeing them regard me as some form of ancient dust, takes that option off the table. The answer is to remain seated as often as possible. When I have to leave my chair, I take a moment to test my knees, like one would test the ropes holding up a tent before entering, and, satisfied that they will hold, plot my few steps to wherever I'm headed like a mariner crossing choppy seas.

My Thighs: Are human thighs considered "dark meat," like a chicken's? I don't know. I can say for certain that mine are not dark. Just the opposite. They are as white as an actor's teeth.

As a young man, a teenager, more honestly, I had rock-hard thighs. Today, they are barely larger than my calves and soft to the squeeze. (What had once felt like stone now feels more like rope—more accurately, the soft ropiness of a coiled bathrobe sash.) Their primary purpose in what has become my life is to serve as a lap: a place to rest a book, a tray with a sandwich on it, a television remote. They, too, are hairless as a newborn, marked here and there by small discolorations and bumps. No quarter-sized, maybe-malignant spots or moles—just not very pretty. I can see no reason why the doctor would even want to look at them.

My Privates: My privates are private. All I'll say is that, unlike the hairs in my ears, they're not enjoying a late-life growth spurt.

My Ass: My ass? Who am I kidding? I don't have an ass—just two, unfleshy extensions of my thighs. Two bony flaps, like an open book lying on a table. It's the kind of ass you would expect to see under a tennis skirt on a seventy-five-year-old socialite. There is nothing rosy or round about my ass. The only contour it has is achieved by putting my billfold in my right rear pocket and stuffing the left rear pocket with Kleenex. I am unpadded in that area, wooden chairs are a torture. As for the hole in the middle, that's nobody's business. It's my business's business. A few inches north of that hole (I think I have the right location), is my prostate. I am fully aware that men of my age can have prostates that are the size of a kielbasa or the winning summer squash at the county fair. I may have one that is trending in that direction, if my peeing is an indication. The stream is strong enough at times to put my mind to rest, but occasionally it's nothing more than a leaking garden hose. The traditional shaking of the member after voiding one's bladder does little to rectify the situation. A few drops always emerge unsolicited. I know that the doctor can check this. And I know *how* he checks this. Well, he can forget about it. I don't want anyone going two-knuckles deep into my inner recesses. I know that there are some who would pay three hundred euros to a hooker in Amsterdam for the same favor, but I am not one of them.

My Back: I find it very strange that I have been on this planet for eighty-three years and have never seen my back. I've seen portions of it, reversed in a mirror, but never the whole slab at once in true right-left. I know that I have a constellation of moles, like a child's follow-the-dots puzzle, and a scar or two, but that's it. I also can attest to the fact that it feels fused, the vertebrae between my alleged ass and the middle of my back welded as a steel bar, stiff as the trunk of an oak. I have never been able to touch my toes and am currently barely able to touch my knees.

On the positive side, I have no hair on my back. I have seen men at the beach whose backs look like woolen throw rugs, who must have to shampoo their whole body, and I have wondered where they fall on Darwin's charts.

My Stomach: I must wear my belt too tightly because all of my fat gets stopped at the border, not frisked and released, but incarcerated. I've heard the expression "muffin top." How dainty. Mine is not a muffin top, it's a whole bowl of bread dough, the size, shape, and consistency of an inflatable beach toy. I look down in the shower and see nothing beyond it, like a sailor seeing the curvature of the earth. I don't need an airbag in my car, I have one under my shirt. And the noises it makes! I lie in my bed at night and I might as well be at the zoo, listening to the animal's grunts, grumbles, and gurgles—the whines and groans of my refinery, my processing plant, turning hamburgers into poop. (I've been told that we have twenty-five feet of small intestine. That's a long way for a fart to travel. I give them credit for being so intrepid.) My belly button is an "innie." As a child, I was told by my father that it was the perfect place to keep salt when you're on your back eating celery. What he had hoped to give me was his wisdom. I wish he had given me his stomach instead. He had what is called a six-pack. My beer gut doesn't come in a six-pack, it comes in a barrel.

My Tits: Is there anyone, anywhere, who can explain to me why I have nipples?

My Arms: They're not what they used to be. The muscles haven't turned to fat, they have turned to some other mysterious substance. The shrunken, puckered skin that encases what was once toned sinew now seems more than ever a victim of gravity, falling heavily, draped like a wet towel on a rod. Do I still have the strength to do what I need to do? Yes, but only because I need to do so much less. My forearms (once a point of pride) are now like parts of an uncooked turkey. I take off my watch and the dent it has made remains unfilled. Hemingway said it best: a farewell to arms.

My Hands: In the unstoppable, ineluctable parade of aging, the hands are the drum major. Way out front. I have come to think that the hands are always at least five years ahead of the rest of the body. Maybe ten. I see mine now—thin crackled leather, dappled with liver spots and inexplicable bruising—and am reminded of piercingly detailed "art" photographs of old men with their hands lying motionless in their laps. Pictures taken with the hopes of giving us the appreciation (or maybe just the fear) of growing old. I try for the appreciation part and inevitably land on the fear. My fingers remind me of asparagus, the bulging knuckles like tiny piles of unfolded laundry. It's too easy to see my mitts folded across my chest in a coffin. If my theory that the hands are ten years older than the rest of me is true, then at least a part of me made it to ninety-three. That's pretty damned good, I guess.

I didn't anticipate the length of my "additional comments," and, though I had tried to write in the smallest possible print, I soon found that I had filled in all of the space on page two, front and back. Asking for blank paper from the little round nurse seemed a bad idea. I didn't want to have to explain myself. What to do? I hadn't even gotten to my *head* yet. My head: the corporate offices of my body, the lookout station for this bag of bones.

Fortunately, not an arm's length away, there was a stack of Xeroxed flyers for discount hearing aids, a bit of info on side one lauding the power and affordability of the little devices, stating, unabashedly, that they would "change your life!" and nothing on side two. I waited until the nurse left her station to burrow, her butt up, in the files and grabbed a handful, shoving them in the clipboard. Plenty of space for my head and neck.

My Neck: If I turn my neck slowly from one side to the other, it sounds like an intruder walking over broken glass. If I turn it rapidly, it's a firing squad. I know that this short stump that holds my head erect is made of bone and muscle, but it sounds like it's a box full of broken plastic spoons. (And it can hurt: The cliché "pain in the neck," like all clichés, is born from reality. Ice *is* cold. Pigs *are*

Additional Information

fat.) I have more skin there than I need. It looks like a hastily wrapped gift, the corrugated bumps and strings of whatever is inside clearly apparent, the Adam's apple hanging like an egg in a sock. If I were a woman, I would have nothing but turtlenecks in my wardrobe.

(I've said very little about coloration. Conventional wisdom and the US Census would tell you that I am White—and there are a few parts of me that really are, the tops of my feet [as I've said], the circle that lies hidden under my watch, and the half-inch square under my growing earlobes. The rest of me is more piebald—not the extreme contrast of a zebra or a pinto horse, more a selection of whites and off-whites, pale yellows, pinks, beiges, eggshell, ecru. Essentially a handful of wall-color choices. I could stand naked in your living room and disappear. I don't tan. I burn and peel, like the dashboards on old cars.)

My Head: the home office. Like my back, I've never seen the dark side of this moon, but I know the front better than any other part. That is to say, I know it currently. However, I look at photographs taken at the age of ten, twenty, thirty, even, and I'm hard-pressed to see any resemblance to the man I now see in the mirror. Not just the wrinkles, which one comes to expect, but structural changes. The bags under the eyes, like miniature pieces of carry-on luggage. The nostrils, twice the diameter of my youth. The mouth, turned downward, in direct opposition to the cute upward cant I see in my baby pictures. My eyebrows are a street-riot. And the eyes, the so-called windows to the soul: If they are indeed windows, then they need washing—washing with some miracle cleanser that can eradicate the wet, amber gloss of eight decades; erase the paint splat of red that surrounds the glazed and perplexed pupil. The damage of time is so apparent that I'm not even sure what color they are anymore. Without my glasses, the "E" in the first line of the eye chart looks like a swastika. My forehead looks like lined notebook paper, like a freshly plowed field. The hair that once grew on top of my head has decided to grow in my nose. I do my best to avoid mirrors.

My Heart: In my haste to get to my head, I forgot to mention my heart. Like all of my internal organs, I have no idea what it looks like. My innards could be spread out on a table next to someone else's and I couldn't begin to tell you which were mine. (I simply assume that the needed parts are all there, the kidneys, bladder, liver, et al., all the potential cancer havens, wet and pink and doing their jobs.) The only organ I can feel is my heart; the comforting, perpetual pulse of its beating. Still beating, even though it has been badly broken in the past. Broken when Millie decided she'd had enough and drove off with her muscle-bound trainer. Broken when, after I moved to Norwalk to be closer to my daughter, she decided to take her family to San Diego. Broken when my father called me an asshole on his deathbed. Broken by Nixon when he resigned. Broken by the Red Sox in game seven. Broken but operative—three words that pretty much sum up my current condition.

My Brain: My brain is me. Without it, I would be just so many chemicals and water. I find it difficult to describe my brain, since it would have to be my brain that is doing the describing. It would be like the accused rendering the verdict in a trial. My brain would have to step aside to assess itself and that can't happen. I've seen pictures of the brain and it doesn't look like much—a cauliflower gone bad, what I imagine a turtle looks like without its shell. And yet, all of the info is stored there, some of it retrievable, some of it not.

Actually, the memories are not so much stored as hoarded—bundles of information that I no longer need. Names and dates filed away regardless of importance; handy when doing a crossword puzzle, but useless for getting from A to B in real life. That's just the storage part. There is also the imagining part. Sadly, it's the imagining part that seems to have lost a bit of its muscle tone. Not that I was ever able to see the future, but, as a younger man, I had a sense that I could at least have a hand in designing it. I harbored the notion that one is somehow in control of one's destiny. (When you're working behind the counter at the Avis Rent-a-Car bodega at Logan Airport, you *have* to think that you can change your lot in life.) And yet, as I sit here, I can't imagine what lies ahead. When I try to envision what I have in store, the images are unpleasant, dark, breathless. So I try not to think about the future. Oddly enough, one *can* decide not to think about something; there is a power we possess that can even suppress the brain. I have no idea where that comes from. Maybe it's what people call "will." Maybe it's a part of the brain we don't know much about. All I know is that something compelled me to write this all down and it wasn't my plan to do so.

I reread what I'd written and, satisfied I'd been as truthful as I was capable of being, signed and dated it.

"I'm done," I told the nurse as I poked the clipboard through the opening in her glass cubicle. She arched an eyebrow in surprise as she looked at the number of pages.

"What's all this?" she said.

"Due diligence," I answered.

She removed all of the pages but the first one from the clipboard and handed them back to me.

"We don't need these," she said, "just your name and your insurance. That's all that's important."

I carefully folded the pages I'd written and put them in my jacket pocket. I wordlessly headed for the exit.

"Wait a minute, where are you going?" the nurse said. "Don't you want your physical examination?"

Additional Information

I tapped my breast pocket where the pages were nestled.

"I just had one," I said, and walked out.

As I was waiting for the elevator, a part of my brain remembered the dream/song that had urged me to get a checkup. Then another part of my brain informed me that "quizzical" rhymes with "physical."

Nope, I haven't lost my mind.

REAL ESTATE

The realtor could easily have been my granddaughter—just a little pixie of a thing—what my mother would have called "cute as a bug." Her huge, brown eyes sat on her forehead like pumpkin pies displayed in a bakery window; her dandelion-blonde hair was hacked and spiked in a cut that seemed self-inflicted in a moment of rage. Maybe it was chic. I couldn't say. My knowledge of chic, as well as my concern for it, vanished over half a century ago.

I stuck my head tentatively in the door of her cubicle and she flicked a few fingers at me in a wave of sorts, indicating that I should take the little molded plastic chair opposite her desk. At first, I thought she was talking to herself, then gathered from what she was saying that she was on the phone (though I couldn't see anything resembling a phone in her hands or on the grade-school sized desk in front of her).

"Of course it's a *laminate*, Henry... I never said hardwood... well, that's BS... no... I might have said that there *could* be hardwood flooring *under*

Real Estate

the laminate, but I never said... well, that's why there's such a thing as escrow, isn't it... what...? are you dealing with him or *her...?* I gotcha... right... right... no, she's the right age for menopause that's for sure... right... look, I've got someone here... yes... tell her I'll call her tonight... what...? well, tell her again. Bye." She pulled the little peanut buds out of her ears.

"What a business!" she said, offering her tiny hand to shake. "I'm Candy Cotton." She tapped the little engraved, plastic *Happy Homes* nametag on the breast of her navy-blue blazer, as if it confirmed her identity.

"I'm Mitchell Street," I said.

"Mitchell Street?" she repeated, and broke into a wide grin.

"There's a Mitchell Street turnoff on the parkway. I've sold properties on Mitchell Street! You don't, by any chance, live on Mitchell Street, do you, Mitchell Street?" she giggled.

"No," I said flatly. She stopped laughing.

My brain works in ways I don't always understand. When she made her little joke about my name, all I could think was, "Look who's talking!" Candy Cotton! She should know better. How many times in her life had she had to give last name first, first name last: homeroom roll calls, IRS forms, summer camp sign-ups, application forms? "Cotton, Candy." "*Cotton Candy!!*" Her classmates must have had a field day. I can picture her running to the cloakroom and burying her face in her coat in unbearable embarrassment; the teacher lecturing the class about how "sticks and stones can break my bones..." Her mother coming to fetch her with everyone watching and sniggering. Nights alone in bed, sobbing, inventing other names for herself, names that didn't conjure visions of sticky spun sugar on a paper stick. Names like Marisca Malone, Tiffany Pinter, Darla Fine. And she's making fun of *my* name?

I said none of this, of course. The thoughts themselves took only a second or so. Maybe less than a second. And while I was having them I did nothing to betray their presence. I have, over the years, developed a form of internal ventriloquism, an ability to have one thought and appear to have another. In layman's terms, I suspect it is nothing more than finally learning, after seventy-nine years, to keep my thoughts to myself. I just smiled at her in a bemused way that I have mastered since becoming old. It's a smile that I've found suggests an age-worn vulnerability, all threat removed by the passage of time. It puts most people at ease.

Candy folded her hands in front of her and returned my smile with one that seemed more practiced than genuine, the official *Happy Homes* smile.

"What sort of place are you looking for, Mr. Street?"

"I guess I'm looking for a place to die," I said.

Because sometimes my mental ventriloquism

doesn't work and I'll say exactly what I'm thinking. Sometimes the truth just has a way of coming out.

Candy's smile flatlined. The air in the tiny cubicle mustered itself like threatening weather. The poor girl was trying desperately to recover something from her *Happy Homes* internship that could cover a request such as mine. She'd been well-tutored in handling the usual: first-time buyers, divorcees, widows and widowers, developers, trust-fund babies, even lottery winners. All of these were people looking for a place to *live*, not die. She stared at me with those pie eyes for a long second, then picked up her pencil and silently placed the eraser end to her lips—an ex-smoker, I assumed. It was a gesture that would have seemed petulant if she were not so genuinely perplexed. I felt for her. She was totally at sea.

"I'm sorry," I said, "I didn't mean to be so… well, morbid. I guess what I'm saying is that I don't want to have to move again."

She let out a long breath.

"Oh," she said, relieved by this more acceptable wording. "I know, I know. Moving can be a very stressful time for lots of people, so I *completely* understand why you…"

"I'm pretty sure you *don't* understand in my case," I said.

I tried to keep any nastiness out of this last response, tried to make it more a statement made by a kindly Santa Claus—a twinkly-eyed reminder that I had many, many years on her, and that it would be simply chronologically impossible for her to understand my situation.

She blushed a bit and nodded her head in a sheepish acknowledgment of her inexperience.

"But let's assume that you *do* understand," I said, still Santa Claus, letting her off the hook.

"Yes, let's," she said gratefully as she, all business now, opened the leatherette binder of "availables" on her little desk. She thumbed through a couple of pages, then looked up with a thought.

"Is there a Mrs. Street?" she asked.

"No," I answered.

"OK," she said. I could see her wrestling with the urge to ask if I was divorced or widowed, knowing full well that either answer could precipitate a long, possibly uncomfortable, and ultimately fruitless explanation. You could almost hear her reminding herself to "be professional." I decided to rescue her.

"Currently, Ms. Cotton, you are the only woman in my life."

"Oh my!" she laughed. "I would think that a handsome man like you would have a little black book full of ladies," she said, condescendingly. Now *she* was playing Santa Claus.

"You're the one with the little black book," I said, pointing at her leatherette binder.

"Of course," she said, her realtor's demeanor instantly returning. "Can you tell me a little more about the kind of place you're looking for?"

I drew in a long breath, not really a sigh, but it probably seemed like one.

"I'm looking for somewhere that used to be," I said.

"Used to be," she repeated, in a tone generally reserved for psychiatrists.

"Someplace where your newspaper is delivered by a boy on a bicycle, where cars have fins on the back fenders, where gasoline is fifty-five cents a gallon, where ladies wear dresses, and men wear the pants in the family."

Once again, I'd caught her unprepared. She closed her leatherette binder.

"Mr. Street, I appreciate your candor and what I assume to be your sense of humor. But I'm going to need something a little more concrete to go on if I'm going to find you what you need. Let's get down to nuts and bolts if we can. How many bedrooms?"

How many bedrooms? How many beds? This is not a question you ask an old man who is currently spending most of his time reviewing his life. Cataloging it, arranging it, boxing it up into eras the way one boxes books or dishes before moving, placing the fits and starts into phases like art-world changes, hemlines, like presidential terms, trying to find benchmarks to separate the stages: childhood, the teens, the more difficult and worldly separations of adult life, and the unexpected onset of senescence. Each incremental change identifiable by a different bed—a bed that would soothe the exhaustion of whatever I had currently done and offer the chance to dream of what I would do next. The beds. Remembering so many of them, from crib to King, each a mile marker. Following them like a dotted line, wondering if it all had really happened, and more than aware that one of them will be where I last lay my head. And she asks, like it's a simple question: How many beds?

"Just one," I said.

"One bedroom," she said, reopening her binder. "Gee... we don't have many... I'm not sure we even... A one-bedroom...? Huh... Have you considered an apartment?"

"No. No apartment. It has to be a house," I said firmly.

"I see," she nodded, then held the binder in both hands and pressed it to her chest as if it were a Bible.

"I've got close to three hundred listings in here, Mr. Street, but I'm sorry to say, none of them are... You did say *one* bedroom, right?"

"With a yard."

"With a yard," she repeated, as if I'd asked for the moon.

"Mr. Street, I would love to find a home for you, but I'm not sure that what you're looking for even exists. I have a couple of very nice two-bedrooms, and lots of three-bedrooms, some of which have lovely yards. Maybe you could go the two-bedroom route and use the second bedroom for an office or storage. Does that sound like something that might work for you?"

"No, it doesn't. I don't need an office and I have nothing to store. I'm done."

"Well, I might be able to find you a little guest house. How about that?"

"*A guest house!!*" I said in audible italics. "No, no, no!! Out of the question! I'd have to share the yard with the main house people. I'd have to hear their music blaring, their dog barking, their moronic conversations escalating into fights that last long into the night. That's not going to work at all. I need a house to myself. Jesus Christ, I thought I made that clear."

I instantly regretted snapping at Candy. It was, after all, a perfectly reasonable suggestion.

She had no way of knowing that I had a personal history with guest houses. I could have told her the whole story instead of just offering the clichés of barking dogs and loud music, but I was in no mood to lay myself bare in front of a twenty-something pixie.

Here is the story I was in no mood to tell her. I'll try to keep it short.

. . . .

Many years ago, decades, actually, I was what is commonly considered a success. I say "commonly considered" because I was rich, and that is how most people measure success. I was financially well-off, but socially I was a pauper. I had no friends, not even acquaintances. I assumed this loner's lifestyle was partly the fault of my profession. I was an inventor—or at least fancied myself one. My days and nights would be spent in my garage, hunkered over my little workbench, bending wires, carving bits of wood and plastic, mixing chemicals, doodling drawings for potential projects. Picture Thomas Edison in his attic. At one point (I think it was in '81 or '82, I don't remember exactly), I was attempting to create a device that would fit on an electric toothbrush and signal the user when the full minute of recommended brushing was complete. After two years of trial and error, I thought I'd perfected it and sent the plans and prototype to an old friend at the patent office. He returned my plans to me with a note suggesting that, though it was probably unmarketable as such, it would be of great interest to the manufacturers of microwave ovens. Long story short, I sold it to Sears. Yes, I am the man behind the ticking sound and the little "time's up" bell you hear if you own a Kenmore.

The sale made me quite wealthy. So I plunged, head first, into the Great American Dream. I bought an imposing brick home with a tennis court, swimming pool, and nearly an acre of carefully manicured lawns and gardens. (Having no skills outside of my inventor's handiwork, I hired a young, athletic, horticulture student to look after the grounds and do any maintenance that might be needed. His name was Kit, and I let him stay in the apartment over the garage in exchange for his services.) I hired a decorator who quickly filled the house with high-end furnishings.

There was only one thing wrong with the place—I was the only one in it. I would walk around the rooms and hallways at night, the sound of my footsteps competing with the sound of my breathing. For the first time in my life, I thought that, despite my undeniably insular personality, I might be lonely. Maybe I *did* need people, human contact, conversation.

Throwing a party was, of course, out of the question, since I had no friends to invite. There had to be a way to get strangers into my home. I hit on the idea of an "estate sale" (though I had no intention whatsoever of selling anything in my home). Still, I knew that nothing enticed people more than the promise of finding a great deal on something that they probably didn't really need.

The following Saturday, I put up a large sign proclaiming the sale and the hours. I bought balloons to line the walkway to the house, hired a caterer, and waited. It didn't take long. By 7 a.m. the house was bustling with eager lookie-loos. One by one they would approach me and ask what I wanted for a specific item and, one by one, I would tell them that it was not for sale. Before they could walk away, I would introduce myself and direct their attention to the caterer's table, hoping that I could create a party atmosphere. My plan was an abject failure. Of the two hundred people who came through my house that Saturday, only three bothered to have a civil conversation. The others felt they had been the victims of a ruse and stormed out rather angrily. Their disappointment was only exceeded by my own. 4 p.m. and my home was empty again. Dejectedly, I went into my kitchen to rewarm my coffee (hoping that the sound of my ticking Kenmore might cheer me up), and that's where I saw her.

The light from the kitchen window bathed her in a glow, her hair a diffused aura like the spun-glass snow on a Christmas tree, her eyes two blue diamonds. Her posture couldn't have been better if she had a book balanced on her head.

"Oh, hello," she said, a little startled. She had a cut-glass creamer in her hand. "I was wondering how much you want for this?"

I was dumbstruck, nothing would come out of my mouth. I had never seen a more beautiful woman in my life.

"Am I too late?" she asked, peering down the hall at the empty house.

"I lose track of time when I'm around beautiful things, and I think this is really beautiful," she said, holding up the creamer. "It's a little cow, isn't it!"

"It was my mother's," I managed, still stunned by her beauty.

"Oh. Well then, I'm sure you want to keep it," she said, carefully placing it back on the shelf.

"No. It's yours," I said, automatically. "Free."

"Really!!!" she said, her dazzling blue eyes opening even wider. "I don't know what to say! Thank you, Mr...?"

And I introduced myself, as did she. Her name was Margrit. (I promised to keep this short, so I'll just say that we started talking and couldn't stop. Neither of us. It felt like kismet. She was an ex-model turned fashion photographer with a booming business, five years younger than me, recently divorced, smart as a whip and funny, and, on top of everything, she owned a Kenmore!) Before either of us was aware of it, the sun had begun to set. While she carefully wrapped the little cow creamer in tissue and placed it in her bag, I selected a very good wine from my cellar and suggested we sit poolside and celebrate the cow's new home.

Well, as the saying goes, one thing led to another. We sat together on the little wicker loveseat looking at the sunset reflected in the pool. It was magical. Feeling a boldness I'd never felt before, I placed my hand on hers. (I should tell you that, despite my ability to handle small gears and gadgets as deftly as a magician, I am fairly bumbling when it comes to human contact. A more seasoned suitor would have had Margrit in his arms by now, but I was too concerned I'd do it all wrong, grab the wrong appendage, scrape her porcelain skin with my stubbly beard.) I certainly had the urge and desire, what I lacked was the courage. I decided that the courage could be found in a second bottle of wine and excused myself to go fetch it.

I was reading the label on the bottle as I walked back toward the pool, so I didn't see him right away. When I did, I almost dropped the bottle on the flagstones. There, barely two feet from Margrit, stood Kit. He was in his bathing suit, a towel casually thrown over his shoulder. And it wasn't just a regular bathing suit. He was wearing one of those Speedos that leave nothing to the imagination. It looked like he had a long-necked summer squash tucked in his pouch. He could have at least held the towel in front of him, but he didn't. He was showing off. He saw me approaching.

"Hey!" he said, like nothing was amiss. "I didn't know you had company. I'll take my dip later." Then he turned to Margrit. "So nice to meet you," he said, shaking her hand. Seconds later he was gone.

"What a nice man," Margrit said.

"He's a *boy*," I corrected her.

"Yes, you're right," she said and proceeded to yawn in what I considered an overly dramatic way.

"I really should be going," she said, "I've got an early shoot tomorrow. Sorry to be a party pooper, Mitchell, but I need my beauty sleep."

"But you *couldn't* be more beautiful," I said, as she rose from the loveseat and gathered her purse and the bag with the cow creamer.

"That's very sweet," she said, but I could see the evening was ending.

I walked her to her car and before she slid into her seat she gave me a small kiss on the cheek. I made a move to up the ante, but she was already in and seat-belted. I watched as she pulled away, my fingers tracing the spot on my cheek where her lips had been.

I walked around the now deserted rooms of my fancy home. My heart was filled with Margrit, my brain with anger toward Kit. Everything had been going so well and then *he* had to show up. The more I stewed, the angrier I got. I decided to fire him. Not tomorrow, right then and there. I didn't care that it was two in the morning. I charged up the back stairs of the garage that led to his rooms. I didn't even bother to knock, just threw open the door, and there they were. Kit and Margrit, naked as newborns, doing their horizontal jitterbug on Kit's disheveled futon.

And *that* is why I have a thing about guest houses.

. . . .

"And what happened to the big, brick house," said Candy, her voice seeming to come from far away.

"What!? How did you...?" I said, focusing.

"You were mumbling in your sleep."

"Sleep? I fell *asleep?*" I was stunned.

"Just for a few minutes. You seemed to be in deep thought for a moment and then, bingo, you went out," she said, no hint of judgement in her voice.

"And I was mumbling?"

"A little. Something about a brick house, a gardener, someone named Margaret."

"Margrit," I corrected her.

"Well, as I said, you were mumbling, so I didn't get all of it." She turned her attention to her leatherette binder, leafing silently through the pages. Time stood still for a moment.

"I lost the big, brick house, Candy. I lost everything," I said, coming clean with a sigh. If she was capable of entering my dreams, then there was no reason to have secrets. Candy frowned with compassion.

"Oooh, I bet *that's* a long story," she said.

"No. It's a short one," I said. "Two words: Bernie Madoff."

"Oh, dear!" said Candy, and went back to her binder.

The air in the cubicle turned from that of an office to that of a closet. We both sat quietly for a moment. Candy closed her leatherette binder and gave me a look of concern.

"So, how are you…?" she said, pausing for the right word.

"Social Security," I said.

"Gee," she actually said, "that kinda limits what we can…"

"Look," I said. "Don't worry about my means. What's the expression? A means to an end? Well, I've got enough means to make it to the end."

She didn't seem convinced.

"Mr. Mitchell, after all you've told me, I'm thinking your best bet might be a retirement community. I heard you when you said you wanted a place that 'used to be.' I think you'd find a lot of people who feel the same way in a senior living facility."

"Please don't use the word 'facility,'" I said.

"I know it sounds cold, but it doesn't have to be. My grandfather had the same misgivings and ended up loving it."

"How old is your grandfather?" I asked.

"He's dead," Candy said softly. "You kind of remind me of him. He was a little shorter and a little fatter, but he had the same eyebrows. And, don't take this the wrong way, he was kind of grouchy the way you are. It bothered some people but I thought it was adorable."

I didn't know how to respond to that. It was an awkward moment that was mercifully broken by Candy reaching for her little earbuds.

"I'm sorry, I've got to take this," she said.

"Of course you do," I smiled.

"What are you talking about, Larry," she all but screamed into the air, "No… oh, please, there *can't* be mold… no, no, no, we did an inspection… she's just trying to get out of…"

And while she set Larry straight in no uncertain terms, Candy, the multitasker, opened the drawer of her mini-desk, retrieved a small booklet, and offered it to me. It was a full-color pamphlet extolling the virtues of "Silver Threads," a retirement community that appeared to be nestled in the Sahara. The cover alone was enough to put me off: people who looked old enough to be on Mt. Rushmore, playing shuffleboard and checkers, wheel-chairing up and down ramps that dominated the architectural landscape. A Disneyland for the dying.

I tried to keep my ventriloquist's smile, to seem like I was listening to her conversation with Larry, but my brain was racing elsewhere. What upset me most, as I thumbed through the brochure, was that, in all the pictures, people were depicted in groups. Socializing. Pretending to have an interest in each other. I had, years ago, disabused myself of any leaning toward group activity. I was a loner. Some people are just better off alone, and I was one of them. My one pathetic attempt to join the human race (the ill-fated estate sale) had erased all doubt on the matter.

That I had chosen a career that isolated me in a small garage workshop was no matter of chance. No fluke. I could never work in an office, never be part of a team. As a boy, I'd never played baseball or other sports—if I *had* to choose a sport, it would probably be fishing. I shuddered at the thought of spending my last days listening to ninety-year-olds trying to collate the memories of meaningless lives and being forced to look at countless photos of gangling grandchildren, of hearing stories that had no beginnings or endings, the disjointed ramblings of the memory-challenged, recollections of accomplishments that were so miniscule in the grand scheme of things. All of it would be unbearable. I hadn't even made it through half of the booklet before I started to sweat. I had a vision of myself baking on a sun-blazed patio, surrounded by wheelchairs and dying white-hairs in their pajamas, my ears assaulted by a cacophony of war stories while some enormous Haitian in a nurse's dress offered me lukewarm lemonade. I was about to scream when I felt Candy's hand gently tapping me on the top of my head.

"Mr. Mitchell?" she was saying. I opened my eyes.

"You fell asleep again," she said, kindly.

"I did?" I said.

"You did. Just for a minute or so," she said.

And then I must have fallen asleep again because the last thing I remember was Candy saying, "Mr. Mitchell, are you sure you're alright? You look white as a sheet!"

. . . .

When I didn't wake up right away, Candy called 911. Off I went to Mercy General. After three excruciating days of invasive diagnostics, it was discovered that I had a fairly rare form of arrhythmia. My heart would stop for a few beats, the blood would cease its travel to my brain, and I would black out. My little "naps" were, in fact, little strokes. The frequency, length, and depth of these blackouts were both uncontrollable and unpredictable. MRIs and CAT scans revealed an "inoperable valve fault." The inventor in me was convinced that, given the time and materials, I could come up with a gizmo that would fix it. But, according to my Pakistani cardiologist (who looked about nine years old), it was an age-appropriate breakdown that would remain broken for the long run. Unfixable. He also hinted (in that way that doctors have of saying something without really saying it) that the long run probably wouldn't be that long. In other words, don't get involved in a soap opera or start reading a five-hundred-page novel. That's how I ended up here.

My room is in a wing of Mercy General that they refer to as "custodial." (This is because political correctness doesn't allow them to use words like "hospice" or phrases like "pull the plug.") Yes, I finally got my one-bedroom, and I wish I could say that I have it to myself. But I don't. On the other side of the drawn curtain is a guy named Roy Something—a Polish last name that I could never pronounce, much less spell. Because of the curtain, I've never seen him, but I can hear him—his breathing sounds like a car driving down a gravel road. My guess is that he doesn't have long.

Real Estate

. . . .

My guess was right, Roy cashed his check last night. So now I *do* have my one-bedroom. I even have a window and it looks out on a lawn of sorts. Of course, none of this was what I had wanted. What had I wanted? I suppose, like most men, I had simply wanted to live forever, without pain. But que será, será.

My attitude toward socializing has shifted a bit since being here. I'm still a loner at heart, but I've started to see the value in human contact. Oh, I still play my little ventriloquist game with the nurses—having one thought and showing another, feigning interest in their little dramas—but I also chat amiably with them from time to time. And, of course, there's Candy.

Candy comes by every Sunday night, usually sneaking in something to eat that's not allowed. At first we talked about the weather, about real estate, about my health, but we soon found ourselves having little to say that would make for a real conversation. Then, one night, out of the blue, she asked me to tell her how it used to be. She asked if it was really true that newspapers were once delivered by boys on bicycles. She's a very good listener.

SECOND TEAM

If you start a sentence with the words "I am a writer," you can kiss off any hope of getting a look of admiration by ending it with the words "for television." Sorry, that's just how it is. Oh, it's *writing*, in a way—there's spelling involved, indenting, typing, punctuation—but compared to being a novelist, say, or an essayist plumbing the depths of some obscure and arcane existential dilemma, you might as well be hula dancing or stoking the blast furnaces of Bethlehem Steel.

The writing I did for television couldn't be further from the prose that manhandled my consciousness so many years ago when I was a flaxen-haired sophomore wandering the quad at Brown University. The crannies and crevices of my bursting brain were kindled with Kafka, joyous with Joyce, beckoned by Beckett. See? That last sentence? That's how I thought I would write back when I saw myself as a Booker Prize manqué. A far cry from:

BURT
Hi, honey, I'm home!

(Then, after countless writers' room conferences and decoding producer and network notes:)

BURT
(HE HAS BITS OF BIRTHDAY CAKE
 STILL IN HIS BEARD)
Hi, honey, I'm home!

So why would an aspiring novelist cling, white-knuckled, to the lowest rung on the literary ladder? For the money. The money is ridiculous.

After graduation, I was aimlessly wandering down the sidewalk of life when I accidentally stepped into show business. (The profundity of this metaphoric sidle into dog shit was lost on me at the time. Too pie-eyed was I.)

Henry Pollock and I had been roommates for our last two years at Brown. When he called me with the suggestion that we rekindle that situation in his two-bedroom flat in North Hollywood, I was staring out the window of my basement apartment at an unpromising, steel-gray winter's day in Providence. Hollywood?! It was a no-brainer in every sense of the word—literally no brain involved, just a mind's eye view of swaying palm trees and a young man's hormonal drive for adventure. The minute he hung up, I called the airline.

I took very little with me, my luggage more knapsack than suitcase. That was a wise decision because Henry's flat was small—more "holding cell" than living space. But it served our purpose. Neither of us would be hosting galas. It was simply an address to give the pizza-delivery man. For me, the lack of furniture or other domestic amenities only underscored my new self-definition as "tortured artiste," and I would wallow in that thankless morass, cross-legged on my single-size mattress on the floor, and attempt to grind out a page or two of what I had no doubt at the time would be a remarkable and highly praised first novel. I even had a title: *Faust's Regret*. Awful. I know. Fortunately, for the literary world, my time to work on this travesty was limited. I was broke. I had to get a job.

Henry had a job as a waiter at a nearby Olive Garden. Why? Because he was an actor, or at least he wanted to be, and waiters in NOHO (North Hollywood to the uninitiated) are all either actors, actresses, or screenwriters. (Clichés become clichés because they're true, OK?) He was well liked at the Olive Garden and was quick to use his charm and rugged good looks on any customer he suspected might be "connected." He was also quick to suggest to the Olive Garden management that I would be a good busboy. Within two weeks of my arrival, we were both employees of Olive Garden.

A word or two about Henry. He was laser-focused in his determination to become a star. He kept his body fit and rippled with muscle, kept his face tanned, his nails clean and buffed, his teeth regularly whitened. He looked the part. He just hadn't been offered the part. Any part. So, during the day, while I was scratching away at some mindless paragraph of *Faust's Regret*, Henry was traipsing through agent's offices up and down the strip and leaving his eight-by-tens with secretaries and assistants, with receptionists, with doormen. With anyone who might be looking for someone who looked like him. (The truth be known, if they were going after a certain look, then there would be thousands of Henrys to choose from. His looks were middle-American, high-school-quarterback clean, male-model sexy, and precisely the looks that every aspiring actor instructed his publicity photographer to shoot for and, if necessary, airbrush into reality.) He had no takers.

But Henry's vocabulary didn't include the word daunted. He continued to practice his "craft," watching as much television as his waiter's schedule allowed and mimicking the actors he saw, reciting the lines after they delivered them like a religious call and response. His optimism was almost annoying, especially when viewed from the bog of *Faust's Regret*. But, ultimately, I had to hand it to him. If opportunity ever did knock, he'd be ready.

. . . .

Opportunity knocked. Well, not so much knocked as ordered: fettuccine alfredo, side salad, and an iced tea, no ice. The guest, dining solo at the Olive Garden, was a late-middle-aged woman, well-coiffed, well-dressed, nothing really amiss, yet there was a sense, an aura really, of someone trying to fight the inevitable encroachment of aging and not getting too many points in the contest. Henry, as always, turned on his aw-shucksy warmth for his customer, and she seemed intrigued. Henry knew the effect he had on women of a certain age and was not surprised by her willingness to chat it up. What did surprise him ("surprise" is not a strong enough word), what hit him like a piano falling off a ten-story building, was the name on the credit card she had handed him at meal's end. KIKI KRUPP!!? My God!! He was at once thrilled and a bit embarrassed—he should have recognized her face from pictures in the trade magazines. Kiki Krupp, wife of Norm Krupp, the biggest sitcom producer in L.A.!!—maybe in the world, maybe in history!! Norm Krupp, the recipient of a roomful of Emmys and the creator of back-to-back-to-back blockbuster hits. (Currently, he had seven productions on the air, three of them in the Nielsen top ten.) There *is* a God! Henry thought.

Deep breathing to regain his cool, he hurried back to the table, feeling that the goose that laid the golden egg was in labor and sitting on his lap. He turned the charm up to ten, to fifteen. He praised her hair, her nail color, her "sparkling" blue eyes, even her handwriting on the credit card receipt. And, interwoven with all of this adoration, he managed to sneak in *his* whole story—his love of the theater, his classes, his frustrations with finding auditions. He blatantly snuck in a flirtatious admission that he would do *anything* to work with someone as worthy of worship (he actually used the word "worship") as her husband. She'd been around the block a time or two and construed his use of the word "anything" as a hint at a possible May-December tryst. (This was Hollywood, this was show biz, it wasn't out of the question.) She handed him back his pen and let her hand rest on his for a few seconds longer than what would be deemed appropriate. "I'll see what I can do," she smiled. Henry was barely able to say "Thank you" before his supervisor called his name from the kitchen. "Henry? Table twenty-six says their meatballs are cold!"

Henry hastily scribbled his name and phone number on the receipt. "If there's *anything* you could... I mean, My God... this is... oh, I don't know *how* I would ever be able to thank you," he blustered. She rose to her feet and, as she headed toward the door, looked back at him, flashing a smoky smile. "Oh, I think there's probably a way," she said.

Thursdays were for errands. Henry had arranged it so we both had Thursday off. Typically, we would do our laundry, sweep and vacuum the little apartment, and grocery shop (well, let's be honest, "groceries" meant alcohol and snacks).

These mundane and unimaginative endeavors, if taken alone, could eat up a whole day, so we made it a point to pool our efforts.

That's why I remember that particular Thursday. We both slept in, as was our day-off wont, but, instead of grumpily shoving his dirty socks and shorts into the gunny sack for the laundromat, Henry jumped in the shower like it was a regular workday. When he finally emerged in the kitchen he was dressed to the nines—well, not in a *suit* or anything, but way too snappy for our usual Thursday.

"What's up?" I asked him.

He seemed to be measuring his words when he said, "I've got a meeting."

"Oh, okay," I said, "work or play?" (I couldn't imagine it was *play* because neither of us had a lady in our lives at the time, and if it was *work*, it would have been a big deal and something he certainly would have mentioned.) "Neither, really," was his response. "I probably won't be back for a few hours." Faced with the fact that I would be doing the domestic chores all by myself, I probably said something grumpy. I don't remember, exactly. I just remember that he seemed like a man with a mission when he strode out the door.

It was nearly five o'clock when Henry returned. He seemed distracted and looked uncharacteristically disheveled. (Now I know that what I'm going to say next lacks any originality, is corny, in fact, but I'm not trying to be creative, I'm just reporting.) He had lipstick on his collar. Quite a lot of it. Enough that I had to mention it.

"Looks like someone I know got lucky," I giggled.

Henry saw no humor in the moment. "I don't know yet," he said flatly, "we'll see."

And with that, he disappeared to take his second shower of the day, an especially long one.

Our apartment was on the second floor, so when the doorbell rang, I would usually go to the window and look down to see who it was before letting them in. We didn't live in the safest neighborhood and one couldn't be too careful. So that's just what I did when the doorbell rang that evening. What I saw looked like the world's skinniest Hell's Angel, floral tattoos covering his arms and chest, his wild-haired head popping up from the tats like a gnome peeking out of a botanical garden. No way, I thought. But Henry flew out the door and down the stairs. I watched as the young greaser handed Henry a manila envelope.

I'd never seen Henry this excited. The envelope was opened, the contents in his hands before he even got back to the apartment. Henry quickly read what looked like a cover letter, scanned the other page, and let out a yell. "YES!!!"

He collapsed on the couch in a self-satisfied plop and read the pages again. "Andy!» he exclaimed. (I forgot to tell you, my name is Andy, Andy Parker, but this isn't my story, not yet.)

"Andy, I got an audition!!"

"Are you kidding me?"

"With Norm Krupp!!" he said, thrusting the papers at me. I read them quickly. He was right. He did indeed have an audition.

"How did this happen?" I asked, truly perplexed. A look came over his face that I had never seen before, and then, as if there are mysteries we mortals are not meant to understand, he said, "I have no idea."

I had no idea either. (It wasn't until much later that I was able to put two and two together, but by then it was small potatoes.)

The cover letter was not from Norm Krupp personally but from the casting director for his current hit, *Out in the Alley*, a sitcom about a professional bowler. The other page was from the show's current script. (These are called "sides," I would come to learn.) Henry was to learn and perform these lines. From what I could see, it was the smallest part in television history. Two short lines. They could have been delivered by an answering machine. I kept this observation to myself, of course, not wanting to do anything to dampen Henry's excitement.

As best as we could deduce from the page provided, here was the part: Josie, the bowler's daughter (played seductively by young Jenny Kerns) had been delving into online dating and would have her first in-person meeting with her potential suitor in the bowling-alley bar. Henry would play that suitor. According to the script, they exchange barely a greeting before Josie sends him packing. Not interested. Here are the actual lines:

> JOSIE
> So, like, what do you do? I mean for a living?
>
> KENNY
> I'm into chemistry.
>
> JOSIE
> Well, I'll be honest. I'm not feeling any.
>
> KENNY
> Hmmm. You know, I should tell you. I used my father's picture for the website. You said you liked older men.
>
> JOSIE
> And you said you were charming. So we both lied.
>
> (KENNY EXITS)

That was it. Not exactly *Hamlet*. But Henry immediately set to work, practicing in front of the mirror, trying every imaginable vocal inflection, every imaginable facial expression. He was determined to "be" Kenny.

I felt for him. I rehearsed with him, tirelessly trying to give him a "Josie" he could play off. We both knew the truth, it was a walk-on and, sadly, a walk-off. I suggested ways to up the ante of his character, to humanize Kenny. Maybe he stutters? Maybe he has a tic? Maybe he's shortlisted for a liver transplant and this is his last hurrah at ever finding romance? Absurd as it was, it was the liver transplant idea that perked Henry's interest. Not specifically, but the idea of giving this guy a backstory.

That's when I went to work. There was nothing in *Faust's Regret* that I could borrow, so I started from scratch. I worked all night, deciding to focus on the reference Kenny makes to his father's photograph and writing what could have been a eulogy to his father—a heartfelt, impassioned, character-revealing monologue that I thought Henry could use as an internalized motivation, something that could add weight to the few words he was given. I have to admit it was probably the best thing I'd ever written. I couldn't wait to show it to Henry.

Henry loved it. And I must say, even his cold first reading brought me close to tears. I had heard him, walking around the house, reciting speeches for his classes—Ibsen, Shakespeare, Albee—and never heard as much commitment as he managed with the page I'd supplied. I would, even now, hesitate to say that he has a gift, that he was a born actor, or that he was doing anything other than spinning his wheels in his pursuit of a thespian career, but you could have fooled me with the reading he gave to my monologue. Majestic. Henry knew it, too. He practiced the lines they supplied him with diligently, but he always prefaced them with what I'd written. Taken together, it was probably a three-minute speech, the last ten seconds of which were his actual lines. On the day itself, he would take a moment to silently recall this new preamble, and then, when the time came to actually speak aloud, the lines they had given him would be pure gold. That was the plan at least.

. . . .

Henry was a wreck. I don't think he slept a wink the night before his audition. I could still hear him reciting his lines, over and over, when I finally turned my light out about 2 a.m. The next morning, he was showered, shaved, and pacing when I stumbled into the kitchenette for my wake-up coffee. I could see a look of abject terror in his eyes, and was not surprised in the least that he asked me to accompany him to the reading.

"I gotta be at the Olive Garden by three," I told him.

"I called us both in sick," he said matter-of-factly. Of course he'd done that. He never had any intention of going alone. I should have known that.

And so, we set off for Krupp Castle: Norm Krupp's ten-story monolith on Sunset Boulevard. (Krupp owned the whole building, the ones on either side of it, and the nightclub across the street—the overriding impression, one that was, in terms of the TV industry, not inaccurate, was that he owned the whole town.)

We showed our IDs to the guard, and he led us to the elevator. (Henry had phoned ahead to clear me, stating that I was his agent.) Krupp's office was on the top floor, his waiting room only slightly smaller than a basketball court—lush furniture, gorgeous receptionist, and posters everywhere proclaiming his successes. A number of offices fanned out from the reception area, but there was no doubt which office was Norm's. His door, at the end of a hallway that seemed to rise like a stairway to heaven, was twice the size of the others and emblazoned with what looked like twenty-four-karat gold lettering stating simply: N.K. From our comfy, art deco chairs we watched that door as intently as one watches a car chase on the evening news. Then it opened. Out came Kiki Krupp.

You'd have to be blind not to see what I saw. An instant of recognition between Henry and Kiki that was tell-tale not because of how long it lasted but because of how quickly each looked away. She was quickly in the elevator and gone. I turned to look at Henry. Now, he may be an actor, but he wasn't actor enough to hide the look on his face—the cat that got the canary, the hand in the cookie jar, or, more up-to-date, the "Oh, oh!! They got my DNA" look. So two and two made four. My embarrassment for Henry wasn't because of what he'd done, it was because it was such a tired Hollywood maneuver. I didn't say a word. I didn't need to. He knew that I knew. We both reached for a magazine to cover our unease and, at that very moment, one of the office doors flew open and a slight, balding man stuck his head out. "Henry Pollock?" he more demanded than asked.

I could probably spend a lot of time telling you about the room, the décor, the "hot seat" where the auditioner sits facing the casting director, the producers, the tiny camera on the tripod, but more important than any of this geography was the presence of Norm Krupp himself. He greeted us warmly, shaking our hands, and stated, "I don't usually sit in on these things, but my morning is pretty light, so what the hell." He indicated for me to take a seat to the side of the producers and casting director and for Henry to take the "hot seat."

"Okay, you're reading for KENNY, right?" said the slight, balding man who had ushered us in.

Henry nodded "yes." (He had yet to utter an actual word.)

"Fine," said baldy, "I'll be reading JOSIE."

Now I have seen Henry in lots of different moods, but I've never seen what appeared before me when the casting director read his cue line. Henry seemed to inflate, to actually increase in size. His eyes darted to everyone in the room, landing lastly on Krupp's, and in a baritone I had never heard before, he began. Not with the scripted line that should have followed his cue, but with the soliloquy I had written for him. And he didn't just recite it, he *delivered* it. The room fell silent. Henry realized the mistake he had made and you could actually see the air rush out of him. "I'm so sorry," he said softly.

"Sorry?!!" Krupp almost shouted. "Are you *kidding* me? That was *amazing!*" The other toadies in the room concurred. "Where the hell did *that* come from?" Krupp asked.

Now I don't know if Henry was trying to shift the blame off himself or if he really was doing the noble, honest thing, but in response to Krupp's question he pointed at *me*. Krupp rose to his feet, crossed to where I was sitting and clapped a large, fatherly hand on my shoulder. "*You* wrote that? Amazing! Just amazing!" he said with a big shit-eating grin. "You have a beautiful future ahead of you, young man!"

And that, my friends, is how I came to be in the employ of Norm Krupp.

That all happened on the Friday following Henry's "visit" with Kiki. By the following Monday, Henry had a dressing room with the word KENNY on the door, and I had a small office with a desk at Krupp Castle.

. . . .

Second Team

I moved up the ladder pretty quick. Within weeks, I went from a low-level, staff-writer's assistant to a handsomely salaried writer/producer. The other writers, who were more than aware of my curiously meteoric ascent through the ranks, suspected some kind of ass-kissing on my part, vis-à-vis Norm Krupp. I swear that wasn't the case. The reason was simpler. I just played to my strengths. Here's what I mean. The medium is called "situation comedy." That means you not only need jokes, you need situations. You need stories. Well, I'm not a particularly funny guy. I don't tell jokes—certainly not as well or as readily as my co-writers (many of whom actually moonlight as stand-up comics, armed with an arsenal of one-liners about everything from mothers-in-law to body parts)—but I know stories. And when a sitcom is in year five (as was the case with *Out in the Alley*), new stories are hard to come by. But not for me. Inventing stories was my strong suit, and that's what fueled my ascent. (And, as you probably surmised, fueled the resentment felt by some other writers who had not risen in the ranks since their initial hiring.)

I could see how they might have thought I was kissing Norm's ass. He *did* spend an inordinate amount of time with me. Seldom did a day go by when I was not summoned to his office, where he'd offer me an espresso from his high-end machine, and then just chat. About anything and everything. After several of these tête-à-têtes, I started to get a sense of what was up. He saw me as a younger version of himself. That, and his genuinely avuncular manner, combined to create a mentor/disciple relationship. At least that's how *he* saw it. Frankly, it made me a little uncomfortable.

It wasn't anything he *did* that made me uncomfortable, it was what he *was*: rich and powerful. My unshakeable distrust of the rich and powerful had been set in stone during my years at Brown, where the better half of my classmates were trust-fund babies, lording it over us peons of lesser means, and generally being the kind of asshole who eventually becomes a governor. So it was a while before I could completely relax in Norm's presence. But I did. He sensed it, too. Whereas most of our chats had previously been about the show or my career ambitions, he suddenly began to talk about himself, and when he did, the façade of mogul dropped away, revealing a man who was, surprisingly, not terribly proud of his accomplishments. He felt he had sold himself short.

This fact was obviously one that haunted his days and filled his nights with insomnia. In truth, Norm Krupp was not a happy man. While the espresso machine hummed, he spilled out his guts like an Orange County housewife with her New Age shrink.

When he was roughly my age, and just starting in the business, it was fun. It was a chance to be silly for a living, to provide entertainment for people returning home after a lousy day on the job. He wasn't hurting anyone, and he was paying his rent. But he had considered it as a temporary "day job." It wasn't his dream. His dream, like mine, was to one day write the Great American Novel. (Why is my world so filled with cliché?) As he continued his tale of woe, I could see why he felt a camaraderie. I was transparent enough in my own longings that he knew he would have a sympathetic ear.

He decided to share a new problem that had reared its head. In the beginning, as he explained it, the stories and characters of his shows were bland, middle class, and purposefully inane. So he could do his work with essentially no real thought. Now he was being urged by the powers that be (lobbyists for every imaginable form of identity politics) to make his shows relevant. To make them more like real life. To invest them with all the Sturm and Drang that he would have put in his novel had he stuck to his guns back in the day.

This was a problem that split him down the middle. On the one side, he longed for the good old days when the plot was "Harry loses his hat" and the big laugh came from a spit take. On the other side, he wanted to address all the issues and challenges that had been set before him; to be a real, respectable writer; to show everyone that he could evolve with the times. He knew that the traditional sitcom was not the form for this, that it would take some real thinking outside of the box, and, sadly, at seventy-one, he no longer had the energy to do so. That's where his vision of me as the young Norm Krupp came into play.

It was April. We had finished the current season of *Out in the Alley* and wouldn't be back to the table until mid-July. My assignment: use the intervening time to write something that had never been done—a dramedy—something as deep as *The Iceman Cometh*, about a half hour long, with laughs. It was the look on his face that told me he wasn't joking. And it was the compensation he offered that made me say, "Can do."

. . . .

The hiatus was filled with lifestyle changes. Henry and I each found better places to live. My new apartment was a two-bedroom high-ender, in a glass and steel building that was, not surprisingly, owned by Norm Krupp. (You had to look long and hard to find any pie that didn't have Norm Krupp's fingers in it.) Henry bought a condo in Beverly Hills and was sharing it with Jenny Kerns, his costar and current paramour. My salary from *Out in the Alley*, along with the seed money for the pilot, would have granted me a fairly lavish lifestyle if I'd had the time to enjoy it. I didn't. I was virtually nailed to my desktop, every waking moment devoted to finding something, *anything*, that I could mold into a suitable solution to Norm's challenge.

Second Team

Over the two and a half months of endless rethinks and rewrites, I would have regular phone conversations with Norm, each time assuring him that the project was "coming along"—but the truth was that I had nothing. Then, one night, after killing half a bottle of tequila, I had a brainstorm. (Now, I say a brainstorm, that's not really true. It was something weirder. It felt like a little door opened on the top of my head and the idea just fell in.) Was it *War and Peace?* No. Was it *Macbeth?* Not even close. Was it, to use a hackneyed phrase, "good enough for television?" I decided it had to be. I wrote nonstop, well into the next day. When I finally typed the words FADE TO BLACK, I was completely spent. I slept for ten hours. A large part of me didn't want to get out of bed and reread what I'd written in the wee small hours, knowing that, as is quite often the case, it would be garbage in the light of day.

Well, to make a long story short (or, in this case, a short story even shorter), it was as good as I had thought it was. I had done it. All that remained was finding a title, and, in my newfound burst of ego, I stole from myself: *Faust's Regret.*

. . . .

I'll never forget the morning I walked into Krupp's office with *Faust's Regret* under my arm. My heart was racing, I was drenched in "flop sweat," and, at the same time, I was fully prepared to receive torrents of praise. Why wouldn't he praise me? I had done exactly what he had asked me to do. I wordlessly handed him the script, milking the moment. He nodded at me knowingly, cleared a space on his desk so he could give it his undivided attention, put on his glasses and began to read. For the next twenty minutes or so, I tried to be the proverbial fly on the wall. I didn't make a sound. Unfortunately, neither did Norm. Not a laugh, not a titter, not even a knowing or sympathetic "Hmmmmm." He turned the last page, and with no more emotion than a man going through his monthly bills, he placed my script on top of a stack of others on his desk. His look said it all.

"What do you think?" I ventured warily. Norm managed a semblance of a smile. "It's a start," he said. A *start?!* The word hit me like a bullet. I was speechless.

"I don't hear the funny," he continued. "Where's the funny?"

Now, two things: First, I thought he wanted me to tangle with the real troubles of the world, and to expect something that deep to be hilarious was asking the impossible. Second, I personally found the characters amusing—not fall-down, wet-your-pants, side-splitting funny, but lively and witty in a Noël Coward way.

"I'm sorry," was all I could muster.

"Don't be," he said, like a kindly scoutmaster.

"Like I said, it's a start. We'll give it to the guys in the writers' room and I'm sure they can funny it up."

"Right," I said, completely deflated.

There ensued a longish silence, which Norm broke. "*Faust's Regret*?" he laughed. "Where the hell did *that* come from? Kind of a downer title, Andy."

"Well, it was just a… I sort of… I… yeah. Nothing's set in stone, sir."

"No, nothing ever is," he said with a smile, putting a button on the meeting.

And, as if it were just a first draft of one of a thousand scripts, it was sent to the writers' room for dissection.

. . . .

Before I go any further, I should give you a brief synopsis of my script. Given my marching orders—that it should reflect all of the social ills and crises that dominate the evening news—I decided to set the story in an urban office shared by a dozen disparate social workers, each with their own agenda and area of concern. Every form of identity politics was represented. The pilot story revolved around a conflict over government funds—infighting over the monies—each of the workers contending that his or hers was the more needy issue. The humor—seen apparently only by me—came from the pompous, holier-than-thou postures of a few of the workers, and from revealing the inept bureaucracy of the government's aid programs. That was the idea that dropped into my head that fateful night.

Well, once the script reached the writers' room it was fair game. The first to go was the title. I expected as much. The new title was *Unofficial Business*. Next, it was decided that my unrelated characters should be related. First, it was suggested that a few of the workers could be married couples, then that was adjusted to make them all one large extended family. Then it was deemed too difficult to have an extended family of that size, so a dozen protagonists were reduced to four. Once that premise was in place, the notion of including children was put forth. And so it went, until, after only two days of discussion, the show was now about a laughably dysfunctional family with two impish and precocious children, and the family's heads now worked from home instead of the office. Also, instead of having jobs where they extend themselves, offering financial assistance to others, they are themselves on the dole—facing the challenges of daily life with good humor and lots of love. In short, it was a sitcom like hundreds of others that had been the fodder of TV-viewers for generations. Safe as milk.

I was astounded by what they had done, but much more astounded to learn that Norm loved it. At the time, it made no sense at all. With the perspective that age now allows me, I think I understand it a little better. I think Norm felt a sense of relief, and I think it was a sad kind of relief.

Second Team

(Now I'm thinking of myself as the young Norm, but turnabout is fair play.) I think he came to the realization that being an actual artist, a true visionary of the written word, was not to be. In an odd trick of fate, his dreams had been beaten by his successes—squashed by fame and fortune. And, though he probably could have rescued a vestige of his nobler intents from the mire of his wealth and pedestrian respect, he chose not to. He chose to make one more garden-variety, half hour of pablum. It was easier and he was too embedded in the genre to venture into the unknown. Maybe that's cruel. Maybe he was just too old. Maybe too tired. But, yes, Norm loved it.

I was devastated. Was this a joke? These guys in the writers' room were all gagmasters; maybe this was just one big one and I was the punchline. I honestly didn't know what was going on. I should have known my place, but I decided I had to confront Norm. I didn't even knock, I just barged into his office.

"Norm!! What the hell is going on?!" I demanded, nearly shouted.

Norm seemed unsurprised by the interruption, cool even, and gestured for me to take my usual seat. "Andy," he said, "I like you." And what followed that little blessing was an interminable silence in which he seemed to be gathering what he needed to say. Then he began, his voice that of a pedant, an elected official.

"Andy, I'm not going to affect some pretense of higher sensibility with you. I think you've supplied all the pretense this situation can handle. *FAUST?* You thought you could actually cite *Goethe* and ring a bell with the American TV audience? You thought you could *teach?* TV doesn't teach, Andy, it entertains. It entertains with as little information as possible. And our job as writers is to keep that information to a minimum. Our job is to homogenize. To find the least common denominator, to lower the playing field. To dumb-down. We're not in the *ideas* business, we're in *show* business. We make shows. If it's on TV, it's a *show*. Everything. Did you ever stop and wonder why, regardless of what happened in the world on any given day, the news still has time for weather? For sports? Because it's a *show*, Andy. A TV show. And are these shows the bricks that we use to build our lives? No! They're not the bricks, they're the mortar. The bricks are the *commercials*, the *ads*.

"Watch a little TV, Andy, and tell me, which has the greater production value. The tired multi-cams? The predictable single-cams? No!! It's the *ads!* These ads aren't just some stooge standing in front of a pie chart talking about recommended daily allowances. They're like mini-movies! They put our shows to shame. And they're everywhere, pouncing on every nanosecond of unprogrammed time. They're the locusts of the air waves. Full minute, thirty-second, fifteen, ten, five. The World

Series goes to seven games and a thousand more ads have a home. The Oscars run over by fifteen minutes and the sponsors pop champagne. *That's* our job, Andy. To make something so innocuous that the commercials can grab our imaginations.

"*Faust*, Andy? We're *all* Faust. We've sold our souls to the devil and he's let us drive Bentleys and eat at Spago's. Face the music, Andy. Your name is still on that script and that means a shitload of money in your pocket. You're not even thirty. By the time you're forty, you could be shearing sheep on your thousand-acre ranch in Montana, or whatever the fuck you want to do. Right now, you have the opportunity to take the money and run. I suggest you do it. Anything else I can help you with?"

I had been wrong about Norm's "inner fire" being doused by crass commercialism. He didn't have an inner fire; he was a businessman. So much for my being the young Norm or his being the younger me. I'm not sure I even said "Goodbye." I know I didn't say "Thank you." I just remember leaving his office and heading straight to the elevator and heading home. I poured myself a tall one, even though it was still morning, and turned on the TV. I watched it with Norm's eye. He was right. The shows were unbearably boring and the commercials were wall-to-wall with *Godfather* production values. I took a long nap and dreamt about shearing sheep.

If the decision to flee Providence and join Henry in Hollywood was a rash one, the decision I now faced had to be a calculated one. The average man does not easily look a gift horse in the mouth, and, in the end, I proved to be an average man. I bit the bullet. Norm had not intended his remarks to be cruel; he was just trying to open my eyes. Well, they were open, and what they saw was a pile of cash. I would do whatever it took to make *Unofficial Business* a hit. (My decision embarrasses me now; it should have embarrassed me then.)

As I said, the suits at the network loved the script, but they did have one note. They wanted one of the principal actors to be an older man. A grandfather was their suggestion. Why? Simple. If a good portion of your sponsoring comes from companies that sell vitamin-supplements, retirement plans, erectile-deficiency cures, and automated stairway lifts, it's a good idea to have someone with whom potential buyers can identify. Also, and probably more importantly, they had someone in mind for the role.

This last fact reminds me of a joke. I don't tell them well, but it's too on the money not to try and share it:

A jazz musician dies and goes to heaven. He discovers that there is a band that performs there and asks St. Peter about it. "It's great," St. Peter says. "We have Beethoven on piano, Bach on the harpsichord, Gabriel on trumpet, Benny Goodman, Gene Krupa..." The jazz musician is duly impressed. "Wow!" he says. "Who is the singer?" And St. Peter smiles and says, "Well, God has this girl he's been seeing."

The actor they had in mind was Monty Marshall. Monty was an actor's actor. For years and years he had been a fixture on Broadway, a devotee of the legitimate stage. He had won fourteen Tonys and countless other awards for his work. He did everything from Albee and Beckett to Lerner and Loewe.

What he had *not* done was work in television. In his interviews, he spared no disdain for the medium. Asking him to do television would be like asking Shakespeare to create greeting cards. But time can humble a man. Now in his eighties, Monty found himself in unfamiliar straits: He was broke. So, when the studio head (a lifelong fan of Monty's) offered the role of HUGO to Monty, he pounced on it. His heart was still on the legitimate stage, but his stomach needed to be filled.

. . . .

Armed with my new "team-player/take-the-money-and-run" mindset, I sat in on the casting sessions. It was an endless parade of humanity. Women whose lips and breasts had been reengineered to absurdity; men whose toupees fooled no one; and children, terrified of strangers, being coached and coaxed by parents/agents to the point of abuse. Each one looking to grab hold of the brass ring.

After three days of this shameless human vendue, we finally had our cast. (I was able to borrow Henry from *Out in the Alley* for a cameo in the pilot—he had become a hot property once his on-again, off-again dalliance with Jenny Kerns had become a steamy item in the gossip magazines.) Most of the cast were veterans of other sitcoms and all of them were in awe of Monty Marshall, who quickly became the mouthpiece for any of the cast members' questions and concerns.

I should mention that casting an actor in a sitcom is not like hiring a busboy at the Olive Garden. Busboys don't have agents. For the next two weeks, the office resembled Mission Control in Houston on liftoff day. Negotiations went on day and night—not just salary demands but contention over billing position: Who's on top? Who's before the credits? Who gets the special credit "And Starring"? (Henry was given "Special Guest Star.") There was a small war over who got which dressing room—Monty, the oldest and least mobile, got the one closest to the stage—and a brief stalemate with the leading actress, Susan Roth, when she was denied her own personal hair and makeup man. (The studio caved and she got him.) Finally, with everyone's egos and peccadillos assuaged, we had our cast.

Here was the cast: AL CORKER, the father, would be played by Jimmy Bondo. Jimmy was a veteran of many of Norm's sitcoms, and well loved in America. JUNE CORKER, the mother, was given to Susan Roth, a squeaky-voiced character actress best known for a floor wax commercial where she immortalized the line, "Not on *my* floor you don't!" BUD CORKER, the son, was an unknown who looked like a young Paul McCartney, and SUSAN CORKER, the daughter, was an androgynous teen who also vaguely resembled the young Paul McCartney. Henry's cameo would be as NICHOLAS BENDER, the oh-so-understanding social worker. And last, but hardly least, HUGO, the affable grandfather, would be brought to life by the incomparable Monty Marshall. That was our cast.

It was ten o'clock on a Monday morning when we all assembled for the table read. When I say *all*, I mean *all*. Everyone who could possibly be crammed into that windowless conference room was there. There was so much buzz about the new show (Monty Marshall's television debut, Norm Krupp's imprimatur) that every studio and network suit clamored for a seat.

It was the hottest ticket in town. The writers were all there, the secretaries, friends and relations of the actors, executives from rival networks, sponsor reps, actors from other shows. It was Times Square on New Year's Eve.

The actors took their seats at the long table facing their audience, busily marking their scripts with yellow highlighters. The executives greeted and congratulated each other and sidled into their seats. All was set. But where was Monty?

Now it may have been a brownout (LA electricity can be a bit iffy at times), or it may have been one of Monty's assistants following his instructions and flicking the light switch at just the right moment, but the lights dimmed noticeably, silencing everyone for a second. And when they came back up, there stood Monty, milking his entrance as if he were headed to center stage on Broadway. There was applause. Monty bowed humbly, as if receiving an award, and took his seat at the center of the table. He held the script up for all to see and, in his unique stentorian voice stated the title: "*Unofficial Business*!!" he declared. And so began the reading.

I must say, if there was still a part of me that lived outside the surreality of show business, that felt actual earth under my feet, it was swept away by the reading of the script. The actors rose to the occasion, piping life into lines I had thought were dead on arrival. There were volumes of laughter, appropriate sighs and gasps, and, after Monty's encapsulating coda, tumultuous applause. High-fiving, glad-handing, embracing, even. I've never shaken so many hands nor received so many kudos in my life. For a brief, exhilarating moment, I felt what it was like to be Norm, and it was intoxicating. (If someone sane had taken me aside and kindly pointed out that the entire event was moronic,

I would have coldcocked him.) The verdict was in, and it was unanimous. We had a hit on our hands.

. . . .

Rehearsals began immediately following the table read. The cast, the director, his assistants, and a handful of Krupp writers made their way to the airplane-hangar-sized stage 10 on the Majestic Studios lot. First order of business was a relaxed and chatty howdy-do from the director.

The director was an older gentleman by the name of Dodie Philbrick. Dodie was hired at Monty's behest. (They had pooled their talents on countless occasions, both on and off Broadway, and, though Dobie lacked any credentials whatsoever as a multi-cam sitcom director, Monty insisted that no one else would do. For Monty, it was a dealbreaker. In consideration of Monty's experienced judgement and, mostly, fearing a legal battle over his services if they went against him, the studio and network agreed to his demand. Dobie would be the director.)

Here's how the rehearsals worked. The actors, reading from handheld scripts, would "put the scene on its feet." Problems would be addressed, positions altered, entrances and exits designed, and, occasionally, spoken lines would be changed to suit the physical geography of the blocking. Dobie would generally let the actors find their own comfort zones, offering nominal suggestions. Given the years of collective experience the actors possessed it was hardly a case of reinventing the wheel.

Enter the "Second Team."

While all this is going on, the Second Team, the stand-ins, would be watching intently and taking notes. They would be the ones who would actually walk the scenes so the camera and sound crews could find their angles and pans, their two-shots, their close-ups, the look and sound of the final product. The actors would show the scene perhaps once, maybe twice—the lion's share of the work was done by the stand-ins.

So who were these stand-ins? They were all actors—at least that's what they'd say if asked—but, for a variety of reasons, the chance of ever being on the "First Team" had eluded them. Each had a glass ceiling imposed on his or her career by different circumstances. Mario, who stood in for Jimmy Bondo, was an ex-con who had taken acting classes in prison. He was handsome, if you like that swarthy Italian look, but he had the problem of being tattooed to a sideshow extent. Even his face, which always held a smile, looked like a detailed road map of Ohio. Mrs. Godinez was squeaky-voiced Susan Roth's stand-in. Mrs. Godinez (she eschewed the use of her first name; in fact, no one even knew it) was large—four hundred and fifty pounds large. With English being her second language, she had a tendency to mumble, and, more than her roundness, it was the mumbling which put her on the back burner for stardom. The two stand-ins for the children were, in fact, not children. They were "little people," both of them coincidently grandchildren of original "Wizard of Oz" dancers. (At this point, only exploitative reality shows had embraced the "vertically challenged.") And Monty's stand-in was his older brother: eighty-six, haltingly mobile, and unblessed with any of the talent that had found Monty. Collectively, they lent a carnivalesque atmosphere to the rehearsals. But, that said, no one worked harder or was more grateful for the opportunity.

Norm asked me to be his eyes and ears on the set. They had a canvas-backed chair made up for me—my name stenciled on the back indicating some importance. (I was trying to divine that importance when I noticed that everyone had the same personalized seating.) I really didn't know what I was doing there. The script was no longer even a facsimile of what I'd written; I didn't know any of the actors (Henry, being a two-line cameo, probably wouldn't show up until tape day), and I didn't know stage protocol. When can I speak? Who can I speak to? I truly felt like a fish out of water, and, as I looked around the enormous warehouse of the stage, I found my gaze landing on the stand-ins. In a way, it grounded me. They seemed somehow realer. I felt an odd kinship—not that they, too, were fish out of water, they were more like fish who had gotten stranded in a tide pool with no current, forever to swim in a small circle, never to enjoy the high seas.

I'd look at Mario, the tattooed ex-con, and wonder what he'd done to earn his stay in the big house. Was it robbery? Rape? Murder? Had he gotten all that out of his system? His story was already more interesting than the script. I forced myself to look away. My eyes landed on Mrs. Godinez, mumbling something to one of the middle-aged "children" and I wished I could hear what she was saying. And so it went. I rolled the script in my hands. I crossed and uncrossed my legs. I might as well have been on Mars.

. . . .

The schedule called for five days of rehearsal, the weekend off, then two more rehearsal days, with the taping on Wednesday. Monday through Thursday went by with little to no incident. Each day of rehearsal ended with a run-through of the show, followed by a confab of the writers and producers, who had taken copious notes throughout the performance. Lines would be tweaked, jokes eliminated or polished, exposition added where needed, etc.

The actors were not part of this "creative" confab. Instead, after the run-through, they would huddle in Monty's dressing room for their own assessment of the show's problems and merits.

This was unusual. (When I had visited the set of *Out in the Alley*, for instance, it seemed like the actors couldn't get away fast enough after a run-through, anxious as they were to get to their gym, their masseuse, their meds, or whatever they did besides act.) Not here. The "Monty Meet," as they called it, would sometimes last an hour or more. Norm (whose deep involvement with the project caused him to be present for all of the rehearsals and confabs) should have sensed that something was up.

Following the Friday run-through, the entire cast, with Monty in the lead, filed like soldiers into the sacrosanct writer-producer confab. "We need a meeting," said Monty. Given the orator's power and crystalline diction, his request had the weight of a dictator's fiat.

Monty instantly had everyone's attention. When his gaze settled on Norm, he began:

"Norm, we've both been around this business long enough that we don't have to mince our words. The show is shit. Ordinary, everyday shit. To say that it is beneath the capabilities of your actors would be a gross understatement. This is not even a point for argument. I know it, you know it, and, if this ever airs, America will know it. I come to you today—with the full support of the cast, I might add—with a solution to our, and by *our* I mean *your* problem. We make a silk purse out of a sow's ear. How? We air *live!* No tape. No film. *LIVE!!* What this show lacks is *risk!* A sense of the *daring!* The danger is the very meat that we, as actors, need for survival! Going live will put that meat on the table. We of the cast have talked long and hard about this and have concluded that it is the only way to instill excitement into a project so desperately devoid of it. Now, it would be very ecumenical of me to suggest that you think about it, but I'm afraid the situation is beyond pondering. The die has been cast. We, your talented and underchallenged cast, are all prepared to walk away and face whatever legal shenanigans that action may create if you refuse to let us ply our craft in the noble tradition of the theater. We either go *live*, or the show is *dead*. Norm, what say you?"

It was pin-drop time. The writer and producers were spooked, sitting stock-still like prairie dogs in terrified response to distant thunder. The only sound was Monty's measured, raspy breathing. It was Norm's turn to talk.

But he appeared frozen, like a man who has just learned that he has a terminal illness. Slowly his eyes went from Monty's to those of the other cast members. He saw nothing to betray any chink in their solidarity. He looked to the director, who nodded admiringly toward Monty, indicating his alliance. As I watched this drama unfold, tense as a showdown outside a western saloon, I swear that what went through my head was the old song: "There's No Business Like Show Business."

Second Team

Now a soundstage is a windowless, soundproof structure, so when it is silent, it is unnaturally so. It was this deep, outer-space, black-hole silence that surrounded the staredown between Monty and Norm. So silent, in fact, that we all almost jumped when it was finally broken by the sudden, repetitive, OCD clicking of a ballpoint pen. The pen was in the hands of Armand Lisher, second-in-command at the network. Armand was the highest-ranking minion under Allen Flesh, network president. When he was certain that he had everyone's attention, Armand rose to his feet, drawing himself to his full five feet six inches and straightened his Armani blazer. "We'd have to get publicity on it immediately," he said as a matter of fact.

Norm's jaw dropped. "Are you insane!!?" he bellowed.

Armand, who seemed calmly detached from the theatrics of the moment, smiled condescendingly at Norm. "I hope not," he said, then went on. "Not only do I think it's feasible, I think it might just be the shot in the arm the network is looking for."

"Well, my young friend," Norm said dismissively, "I think your boss might feel otherwise."

Again, Armand flashed his smarmy smile. "Not according to his text," he said, holding his phone up for all to see.

There was the briefest and subtlest smile exchanged between Armand and Monty and it spoke volumes. At least it spoke volumes to me. I instantly realized that it was all a setup. The pieces all fell in place. It was the *network* that had, from day one, insisted on hiring Monty. Allen Flesh wanted that feather in his cap. He was determined to get the legend on television and had assuaged Monty's small-screen trepidation by offering this carrot. From the get-go Monty had been assured that he would retain his reputation as a legitimate stage actor. Monty had been promised that his performance would be selfsame with any of the thousands of live performances he had given on Broadway. And Monty, financially strapped, had bent his high ideals and agreed to the deal. Yep, no business like show business.

Norm barely spoke in the three-hour meeting that ensued. He felt backstabbed. (But wasn't backstabbing an integral part of the business? Hadn't I been backstabbed when they completely rewrote my pilot? Come on, man, sauce for the goose...) And while Norm fumed, Armand made frantic calls to all the responsible departments. All factions of production were mobilized in a way usually reserved for the coverage of natural disasters, of new Popes, new presidents. By the end of a very long day, the ducks were lining up in a row.

It was late August. Typically, new shows wouldn't premiere on any of the networks until late September or mid-October, so *Unofficial Business* could stand alone, garnering all the industry buzz, all of the press, all of the watercooler gossip.

Second Team

Overnight, the "entertainment" segments of every newscast were devoted to our show; billboards went up; print ads, talk shows were clamoring for cast members as guests; the entire media apparatus went nuts.

Rehearsals resumed with a new energy. Dodie, the director, finally in his milieu, blossomed. Even Norm, a sucker for fame, succumbed to the excitement in the press, his name back in the forefront as it had been years ago. As I watched the rehearsals from my little canvas chair, I had to admit that, even though the writing was sophomoric at best and as predictable as a sunrise, the performances were getting more polished. The actors were all off-book, every line not just memorized but internalized, each word carefully parsed for maximum effect. I likened it all to a brilliant architect plying his skills to design a one-car garage.

I haven't mentioned Henry in a while. That's because, once he had gotten rich and famous, we had drifted apart. But now, with all the hoopla surrounding *Unofficial Business*, he made an effort to rekindle our friendship. (He wrongly assumed, since my name was still listed as the script's writer, that I had some sway, and he wanted his part beefed up from cameo to principal.) After telling him that I couldn't help him in the matter, we made a stab at a normal conversation. It felt forced and awkward. (I've often said that Hollywood is like high school with money, and fickle friendships are a big part of both.) We didn't speak again until after the broadcast.

. . . .

The day of the show arrived and, despite what I held as ambivalence, a one-foot-out-the-door distancing, more observer than participant, I had to admit, I felt the excitement. It was there when I set foot on the soundstage, like a form of weather—a Christmas morning, 16th birthday, first-pitch-of-the-World-Series tingle in the air. You could be deaf, dumb, and blind and still feel it. Crew members, usually attired in garb more suitable for camping or yard work, were in suits and ties. Makeup and hair stylists, also dressed to the nines, were gaily setting up their age-defying lotions and powders. Music was playing from unseen loud speakers—up-tempo rhythm-and-blues oldies—and stagehands were singing along as they gave the set a last look-see. It was magical.

Being an evening show, everyone had a late call—3 p.m. instead of the usual 10 a.m. The order of business was the following. 3:00 to 3:30: a run-through with the first team; 3:30-4:30: run-throughs (at least two of them) with the second team; 5:00-6:00: dinner; 7:45: cast introductions; 8:00: showtime. The run-throughs went off without a hitch.

Dinner would be served in a somewhat "upstairs, downstairs" manner. The crew and the second team would be served by the catering truck parked just outside the stage, as per usual. The first team, Norm, and the network and studio mucky-mucks would be treated to a special meal. World-famous Thai chef Bongkoch Songvisava had been flown in for the occasion, and the soundstage adjacent to ours had been transformed by the set decorators into a lavish Bangkok banquet. While those who actually worked the hardest would be dining on chicken fingers, macaroni and cheese, and coleslaw from the truck, the elite would be savoring som tum goong and pad krapow moo saap (Songvisava's prize-winning stir-fried basil and pork). Such is the Hollywood hierarchy.

Now I'd like to paint myself as a champion of societal equity, a defender of the little guy, a working man's pal, but the reason I chose to eat with the crew was simply a longstanding dislike for Thai food. (And a fondness I had developed for the catering truck's mac and cheese.)

Nothing more noble than that.

It was a life-changing decision.

Because there's no business like show business.

After the meal break, the cast returned to their respective dressing rooms to relax; Norm, and the studio and network brass, retired to the Green Room, a comfy couch-filled suite with huge viewing screens and an open bar that was tucked in a corner of the soundstage. Meanwhile, the studio audience had been admitted and was being roused to a fever pitch by the warmup man—a master at getting people to lose all sense of decorum (and, thus, gain the proper mindset for viewing a sitcom). It was barely controlled bedlam at 7:40, when the production assistants went to fetch the cast for introductions.

The assistant's scream could be heard over the cacophony of the audience. Something was terribly wrong. "Sick!! Sick!!" he exclaimed, running on stage and grabbing me like a man about to be thrown overboard. "All of them!!"

And indeed they were. Food poisoning. The first to fall ill were the little people, then Monty, then the rest of the cast. All of them now slumped over toilets. Within minutes another assistant ran onstage from the Green Room with the news that it, too, had turned into a vomitorium. Everyone sick as dogs. It was five minutes to showtime.

I have to hand it to the crew. Veterans all (they had probably seen their share of shit hitting the fan), they showed no sign of panic. I think I gained my strength from their composure. I was the only non-cast or crew member still standing, and, if a decision had to be made, it fell to me by default. I approached the second team who were huddled in a corner of the soundstage, dazed and confused. "You ready?" I asked.

And, at eight o'clock sharp, television viewers all across America were treated to the following: Mario, the tattoo-covered ex-con, comes through the front door of the set, walks to where Mrs. Godinez and the two midgets are seated at a card table, plants a kiss on top of her head, and says, "Hi, honey, I'm home."

. . . .

Because it all comes down to ratings. And for *Unofficial Business*, the ratings were strange indeed. The show had been much anticipated (press and promotion had done their jobs) so the initial viewership was high—off the charts, in fact. Within five minutes, however, the ratings plummeted—it seemed, for the moment, that America was not ready for amateur night in Dixie. Then (and I can only attribute it to the media sounding a siren of sorts that something worth watching, even for its oddity, was on television), the ratings started to creep back up. Yes, the show was a disaster, but nothing can grab an American television viewer like a good disaster. By the time the final credits rolled, our ratings were exceptional.

And the press!! The press!!! The press, whose swift sword can behead the best of efforts with a headline, sheathed their swords, commending and extolling Norm and the network for their egalitarianism—for not just being willing but making an aggressive effort to shatter the stereotypes of Hollywood. They waxed orgiastic over the cast. "Finally, *real* people!!" said *Variety*. "A video oasis for the everyman!" said *The Hollywood Reporter*.

"Five stars," said *The New York Post*. "Compelling," said *The New York Times*. All of it welcome news in ordinary circumstances, but these were not ordinary circumstances.

The following morning, with everyone purged of the tainted basil and pork, Norm's office was buzzing like the floor of the stock exchange. Everyone even remotely connected to the project was present and each held a different opinion of what the next move should be.

Norm: Write it off as an Orson Welles "War of the Worlds" one-off, a spoof, and return the series to the original cast for episode two.

Allen Flesh (network president): Don't look a gift horse in the mouth. It's a *hit*, and we'll save millions in cast salaries!

Other opinions: Go back to the original cast, but make the Second Team a spin-off; combine the two casts; make a documentary about what went down and have Monty Marshall narrate it. There was no wanting for suggestions. And, as if the zoo of suits didn't create enough of a maelstrom, the original cast showed up, Monty Marshall acting as spokesman. He declared that after due consideration (in truth, a brief meeting of their collective minds in Norm's lobby), the cast would be suing all parties involved in "the travesty" for defamation of character.

Monty's announcement silenced the room for a nanosecond, and in that briefest measure of time,

Norm turned to, of all people, me. "What do you think, Andy?" Again, the room fell silent.

"I quit," I said.

. . . .

It's been years since that fateful summer, but I remember it like it was yesterday. The press that had, at first, exalted *Unofficial Business* as a ground-breaking, revolutionary gesture, a flagship of social justice, learned of the true circumstances surrounding the broadcast and did an abrupt one-eighty. Norm and the network were declaimed as opportunists, frauds, and Hollywood elitists. Their table at Spagos was given to a new breed of execs. The show never aired again.

The original cast found work on other sitcoms, because in show business there is no such thing as notoriety, there is only fame. The second team continued to work as stand-ins—though inconceivable to those who see upward mobility as the only acceptable goal in life, they truly loved their station. They loved their work. They saw themselves as artists, and so do I.

Monty, now in his nineties, is still treading the boards, mostly on college campuses; his King Lear, though a little hoarse and a great deal less mobile, is still garnering praise in local papers.

Norm retired to his yacht and the simpler charms of Catalina. According to locals, he rarely comes ashore.

Henry stayed with it and got good. He was even nominated for an Oscar, but lost to a Korean actor in an action film. (It seems that every year the Oscars have an unspoken theme—a tacitly understood agreement that the awards should all go to some group that has been short-sold in the past; Henry's year, unfortunately for Henry, was "Hats off to Asia.")

And me? Well, I must have been listening closely when Norm gave me his Sermon on the Mount, because I now find myself the owner of twelve hundred acres of sheep ranch in the foothills of Montana. No more "Hi, honey, I'm home." I *am* home. And guess what? I don't own a television.

MILLER'S ISLAND

He had himself tested. But only for those illnesses that were undetectable by X-ray, by stethoscope, by MRI or EKG; only for ailments invisible on slides or swabs. He presented a litany of the elusive—migraine, insomnia, vertigo, and double-vision diseases that only existed by virtue of his say-so. He gladly surrendered carafes of urine, dozens of doggie-bags of stool, spit, hair, and fingernail clippings. He offered both knees to the little rubber hammer. He took deep breaths and held them at the doctor's request. He coughed on command. He stuck out his tongue. He pushed for more blood to be drawn and analyzed, for more "thinking outside of the box." But he already knew the problem. He wasn't sick. He was just sick and tired.

Truth be told, it was his hope that nothing untoward popped up on his chart. No dire or painful condition or, worse yet, grapefruit-sized, inoperable tumor, imminently fatal, that would just draw a crowd of so-called family and so-called friends, dutifully hanging over his bed and cooing their "I'm so sorrys" and their "Is there anything I can dos."

Even one of those rare conditions that quarantined the victim in a plastic bubble and required space-suited nurses would still garner unwanted visitors; the newsworthy aspect would bring God-knows-who to his hermetically sealed chambers. Wasn't that just what he was trying to avoid? People. That was what he was sick of. People, who, no matter what, always wanted something from him. Sick, too, of responsibility, of doing the right thing, saying the acceptable, eating at the designated three times a day, wearing shoes, and brushing his teeth.

It actually wasn't illness he was seeking after all; it was freedom. He had spent sixty-two years on the straight and narrow, stopping at stoplights, paying his taxes, waiting an hour after eating before going swimming, and all his obedience had earned him was another day to do more of the same. He wanted to make choices of his own, even foolish ones, and follow through on them undaunted by social mores. He wanted to floor it through school zones, leave public bathrooms without washing his hands, throw coffee grounds in the recycling bin, leap before he looked. But who gets away with that? Crazy people, that's who.

And it was that realization that fostered his plan. He would play crazy. Not in a danger-to-himself-or-others, schizo, paranoid, or homicidal way. Not in a lock-em-up, throw-away-the-key, hopeless-state-of-religious-delusion way. Not in a screaming-at-the-sky-in-a-rant-devoid-of-punctuation way. But in a way that allowed him the freedoms afforded only to children. He would have Alzheimer's.

He had his reasons, he felt. Good reasons. The world had simply become too much for him. For all of his life he had played the game. Never winning, but never really losing either. He had done his best to be adorable as a child (he knew the tricks, kept a mental ledger of what brought praise or smarmy smiles from his parents, his aunts, his uncles). He did his homework. He knew his multiplication tables, the states and their capitols, his tenses: past, present, perfect (future was never that clear to him). He had the same haircut as the popular guys. He went to college and majored in business because everyone said that was the sensible way to go. He asked Joanne—the short, mousy girl who worked in the bookstore—to the homecoming dance because he knew she was desperate enough to say yes. He'd made out with her under the bleachers, stopping short of anything serious because rules were rules. He'd married her because everyone said she was a "keeper." He held a job. Worked his way up to head accountant. Was employee of the month at the Magnifica Shower Curtain Company, April, 1981. He paid his taxes, mowed his lawn, and saw a dentist twice a year for cleaning.

Then, one day, it hit him. He realized that he was asking people, "How are you?" when he couldn't give two shits how they were. He realized that when he put his suit on in the morning he felt like an undertaker dressing a corpse for a funeral. He had thoughts of unplugging Joanne's infernal sleep apnea mask and watching her gasp her way into breathless oblivion. It dawned on him that he was neither Democrat nor Republican. He wasn't even Independent. He was nothing. And, at his age, he knew that the actuarial tables allowed him maybe another decade, give or take, of continued nothingness. In a rare moment of clarity and self-assertion he decided that was unacceptable.

(The epiphany had come to him while he was watching an old rerun of *The Match Game* on the Game Show Channel. Gene Rayburn had said something that made no sense whatsoever and everyone had laughed and applauded. Amazing, Herb thought. Then it came to him like the voice of God: "If Gene Rayburn can get away with being insane, why can't I?")

He would ease into it. He researched the big A at the Howard Taft Memorial Library, his local haunt of choice. (He couldn't look for anything on his home computer without nosy Joanne knowing what he was up to, and, besides, the library was his sanctum sanctorum, one of the few places he could go where he wasn't driven to near tantrum by the sound of people talking.) He plotted his course with a mariner's precision. He'd start with small gestures, little quirks that even his wife, numbed to his presence after thirty years of routine, would have to be dead not to notice.

He could sense Joanne staring at him when she broke the after-dinner silence. "Herb, are you aware that you're wearing two different socks?"

Herb reacted with a mild, calculated startle. "What are you talking about?"

"Your socks, honey. They don't match. Don't you see that?"

Herb took a longish gaze at his feet, removed his glasses, looked again, and replaced his glasses on his nose. "I don't see it," he said.

"Jesus, I hope this isn't the same problem you had with that double-vision business two years ago. *That* was a nightmare."

Herb half smiled at the recollection. "Joanne, if I had double vision, I'd be seeing four socks and I see two."

"A real nightmare," Joanne continued, not dropping it. "All those visits, all those eye drops, and $8,500 down the hopper even after the co-pay."

"So what are you saying?" Herb asked with seemingly genuine concern.

Joanne returned her attention to the hairstyle magazine she was reading and spoke more to the air in the room than to Herb, "I'm just saying that your socks are two different colors, that's all."

"Well, then I guess I must have another pair just like them, don't I," he half-chuckled, and pulled his pant legs up to reveal the issue in full splendor.

"A real nightmare," mumbled Joanne to her magazine.

. . . .

"Herb, I can't mail it like this," she said, thrusting the gas bill envelope in his face. "They won't accept it."

Herb regarded the offending envelope with mild curiosity. He had carefully placed the stamp dead-center on the envelope, covering the gas company's address. "I missed the corner by a little bit," he said. "Big deal. It's still the proper postage, isn't it?"

Joanne stared at the ceiling. "What am I gonna do with you?" she sighed. Then she turned, exasperated, and strode into the kitchen, picking at the stamp with her press-on nails.

. . . .

He still went to his office at the Magnifica Shower Curtain Company where he was the head accountant in the billing department. He had been there for twenty-six years, and his workplace patterns were well established: never late; twelve-minute bathroom break, 10:20-10:32. (Despite his alleged illnesses, many of them gastric in nature, Herb was as regular as Greenwich Mean Time, his voidings as regimented as a Catholic mass.) He ate his Arby's take-out lunch (noon to 1:00) at his little desk, which occupied all of his windowless accountant's cubicle (in a previous incarnation it had been a janitor's closet). His work station was more hidey-hole than office, insulating him from the intolerable annoyance of fellow workers dropping by to schmooze. Likewise, his work, which was unassailable, kept him virtually invisible to his superiors. He might as well have been an ice fisherman in an igloo. So it was out of the ordinary for Joanne to receive a midday phone call from Ray Slack, Herb's boss. She had never spoken to the man. Herb rarely mentioned him by name.

Ray introduced himself and, in a businesslike manner, asked her if she'd noticed any changes in Herb's behavior lately. He wouldn't go into specifics, but it had something to do with singing during a board meeting. Joanne thought that highly improbable but promised Ray (who seemed to be in a rush) that she would keep an eye out. Satisfied, Ray ended the call with an odd and somewhat ominous, "Good luck."

Joanne confronted her husband about the call the minute he got in the door. "Singing? You?" she asked. Herb dropped his briefcase at his feet and clutched both hands into fists. "Ray Slack is an asshole!!" he exclaimed. Then, suddenly calmer, he escorted his wife into the living room and indicated for her to sit. It was obvious he had something important to announce. With the tone of voice of a righteous barrister, he proceeded to tell her that Ray Slack was not only not to be trusted or believed, but that he was a communist infiltrator with a direct connection to Putin and was secretly developing a poison that could live on shower-curtain plastic and that these curtains would be installed in a men's gym frequented by senators and Supreme Court Justices. He further instructed her not to breathe a word of this to anyone. Joanne was dumbstruck. "Ray Slack!!?"

Herb looked at her quizzically. "Never heard of him," he said flatly.

Before he walked out of the room, Joanne would later swear he had called her "Mommy."

. . . .

And so it went, each day a further slip from normalcy. After an uncharacteristic announcement that he was "going shopping" (he never went shopping), Herb returned home with two bags containing four athletic supporters and an orange. He stuck yellow smiley faces on the heads of all the disciples in Joanne's framed *Last Supper* reproduction that hung in their den. He grew his fingernails to absurd lengths. One morning, upon waking in an empty bed, Joanne searched the premises for her husband and discovered him sleeping in his car wearing all four supporters. Ray Slack called again. This time Herb wasn't just singing, it was more like yodeling. A loud, atonal ululating, possibly in tongues. For this melodic transgression, Herb was asked to clean out his desk. Herb did his best to seem devastated. "What am I going to do, Mommy?" he wailed. Joanne's response was to be expected. "What am *I* going to do?" she asked God.

Because you can't phone God, she phoned her mother—her safety net of wisdom, whom she had always relied on. It was Belle who had held her hand and proffered bromides and encouragements during all of Herb's previous dalliances with illness. Belle used to be a nurse (pediatrics: colic, measles, mumps, skinned knees) but still had no more real medical knowledge than, say, a palm reader or an astrologer. Though always suspicious of fraud and malingering, Belle would reluctantly give Herb the benefit of the doubt, tapping into her superior experience to give tips on how to bring her son-in-law back to health. She instructed her daughter about cold compresses (not *too* cold!), how to properly boil water, and the unreliability of anal temperature taking. She stayed attentive on her end of the phone, while Joanne sobbed helplessly and relentlessly, and offered the maternal "I knows" at just the right moments. And it was Belle who, time and again, talked her daughter out of the obvious solution of divorce—not because she loved Herb, or even liked him (she didn't), but because he was making good money and would continue to do so for as long as people needed shower curtains.

Herb's misanthropy had begun its slow boil very early on, growing by increments to include virtually everyone he knew or met, some dogs, and most cats. (Let's be honest here, *all* cats.) But it was Belle who quickly became his venom's chief target. Belle was the bullseye toward which his animosity aimed. He hated her from the moment he met her. Hate at first sight, it was. He hated her bejeweled sunglasses, her salmon pantsuits, her over-round vowel sounds, the clipped and high-pitched giggles she always awarded herself after she said something she thought was clever, and, most of all, he hated the hunch he had that these off-putting traits, by virtue of simple genetics, were probably germinating at this very moment in his wife.

That his wife seemed to need her mother, and that mama filled a hole he could not fill for some reason, did not dampen his dislike for Belle. It increased it. He was not grateful in the least that Belle offered support or sage advice to her daughter regarding matters of homemaking (double-sided tape under the corners of rugs. You'll never slip again!!) or, God forbid, matters of the heart and soul (here's a website where you can check out your chakra balances!!). His only source of pleasure regarding Belle was that she had Type 1 diabetes, and that it had advanced enough to recently cost her a left leg from the knee down. With one skillful swipe of the surgeon's power saw, the possibility of travel had fallen off the table (as did her leg). This, he thought, meant there was no further possibility of Belle ever again smelling up their guest room on visits that seemed to last for light-years.

Of course, Belle's inability to hop on a plane (the thought of her "hopping" made him smile) meant that Joanne would spend countless hours on their phone, tying up their only line—they were a one-number household—but that actually was killing two birds with one stone. No Belle stinking up the joint, and when his wife was embroiled in a phone call she was as good as gone from the planet. This left Herb to his devices. Now unemployed, he could devote himself full-time to his ruse. He started writing lengthy letters to the Pope, which he left in places Joanne would have to find them—like the refrigerator, or carefully folded into the pages of the TV guide. He redid his sock drawer, making all of the pairs mismatched. He shaved one of his legs. He ate a whole stick of butter.

Already his behavior had begun to reap benefits. Joanne no longer asked him to perform even the simplest of household chores—he couldn't be trusted with the vacuum cleaner, a broom, a dish towel; even taking out the garbage presented too many opportunities for misdirected mischief.

So as not to seem too happy about the situation, Herb would volunteer for certain tasks like bringing in the mail. But even here, Herb would seize the moment, and he casually began referring to Mr. Blankenship, their wizened old postman of twenty-odd years, as "Your Highness." Then one day he upped the ante, adding Blankenship to the list of people he now called "Mommy."

Blankenship voiced his concern to Joanne, who immediately called her mother, who immediately insisted she call Adult Protective Services.

"But he's acting like a *child!!*" she protested.

"Then call *Child* Protective Services!!" her mother screamed. "Call *some*one!!"

And never having done so before, she hung up on her daughter.

Joanne called Child Protective Services, and, when the heavily accented East Indian girl asked how old her child was, she said, "Sixty-two." The following pause was long enough that Joanne thought the phone might have gone dead. Then the receptionist said something that Joanne, try as she might, could not understand. It sounded like someone trying to sneeze with a mouth full of salad. Joanne asked—nicely, she thought—if there was someone there who spoke English. The receptionist gave an untranslatable response and put her on hold for the next ten minutes. Seconds before she was going to hang up, she got a recording giving her 911 instructions and a list of phone numbers for snow removal, gas leaks, lost dogs, fire-hydrant replacement, and, finally, Adult Protective Services. She dialed the number, hoping for someone who had been born here.

"APS, what can I do you for?" said the man, clearly a man, clearly an American. He had the vacancy in his voice of a telemarketer who hated his job.

"I'm calling about my husband," she almost whispered.

"Is he beating you up?" he asked, mechanically. She had the feeling he had a checklist in front of him in his little cubicle.

"No, no. I mean, yes, but not 'beating up' beating up. More it's just really been hard." Good God, she thought, should she be telling this to a stranger?

"Is he hitting you or not? Yes or no? It makes a difference who I farm this to." Patience was obviously not this man's strong suit.

"No, no hitting. He's just not *himself*, I guess you'd say."

"Then who is he?"

"He's my husband. I told you that. He's..." She gathered her strength. "He called our mailman 'mommy.'"

"Does anyone else call him that? Neighbors? Is it a nickname?"

"No," she swallowed.

"I'm gonna put you through to Hajda. This is his kind of thing."

"Please tell me he speaks English," she pleaded.

"Pretty damned well, all things considered," was his gruff response and he transferred the call.

. . . .

"Hada," he said. The "J" was silent. She decided to just come right out with it.

"My husband is losing his mind." Once she started, it all came rushing out.

Hajda proved to be a good listener and, despite the hint of an accent now and then, a decent talker as well. Joanne ran down the list of the current inexplicables, slowing up a bit when he told her he was trying to write this all down. He then asked her for a brief family history, length of marriage, number of children, and spent the remainder of their twenty-minute chat getting the i's dotted and the t's crossed regarding their finances and insurance coverage. When he was satisfied, he said so.

"I'm satisfied," he said.

"So what do we... where do we go from here," she stammered.

"House call," he said. (It sounded a bit like "howz cow," but she got the drift.) "I could come by tomorrow depending on the weather." It was the heart of summer and this made little sense to Joanne.

"I'm sorry. The weather?" she wondered aloud.

"My wipers are shot. If it's raining, I'm not going anywhere. I'm not getting in an accident just because your husband doesn't know his mother from the mailman. I'm sure you understand."

She assured him that she understood and gave him their address. After hanging up, she immediately checked for the weather on her phone. 10% chance of showers.

It rained cats and dogs for the next three days. Joanne, now a nervous wreck from a tidal wave of "what-have-I-done's," did her best to busy herself in the house, doing all manner of chores to avoid any contact with her husband. She dusted, then re-dusted; she arranged her pantry's supply of canned soups by expiration date; she put a sweat sock on the end of a straightened coat hanger and poked out any and every speck of lint from around her dryer. She stayed invisible. Only once did she peek into Herb's bedroom (they now each had their own), finding him naked, watching the Game Show Channel and folding hundreds of paper airplanes from pages torn out of the Yellow Pages phone directory.

She knew better than to say anything. At breakfast, normally a completely silent affair, she had mentioned, as offhandedly as possible, that someone might be dropping by for "just a minute or so." Herb, true to form, exploded.

"Are you crazy, Joanne?!!!" he screamed. "Do you have any idea what kind of germs and pathogens you're talking about? I'm not well, you idiot!! I'm one microbe away from the ICU. Two microbes away from a body bag!!" And with the door slam that always ended such discussions, that was that. This left grave doubts in her mind as to whether Hajda would ever get a chance to meet her husband and assess his condition.

What she didn't know was that Herb, on the other hand, had reconciled himself to the necessity of having someone with proper credentials sign off on him if he was ever to become a full-fledged member of the Alzheimer's Club. So he watched the Game Show Channel with the sound off, one ear cocked for the sound of the doorbell.

. . . .

The next day the sun burst through with a vengeance; the TV lady said it was going to be a scorcher. At precisely 10 a.m. the doorbell rang. Joanne quickly undid her apron, wadded it into a ball, threw it in the broom closet, and, taking deep breaths, headed for the front door.

Hajda wasn't at all what she'd pictured. First of all, on the phone he had said he was forty-three years old (for some reason she had asked), and this fella looked about seventeen. Skin and bones. It was like a mahogany-colored head had been placed on top of clothes still on the hanger. She had also never seen hair quite like that—coal-black and so shiny that it made the matching buns he had twisted it into on either side of his head look like Christmas tree ornaments. His moustache could have been drawn with a pencil. And those eyes! Like bullet holes in marshmallows.

"Hello," he smiled, and handed her his card. "I'm Hajda, the one you called to complain to." She took the card and quickly scanned it: HAJDA RAPUNISASOTAMOVISTA, ASSISTANT

UNDER-DIRECTOR OF ADULT FACILITY PLACEMENT. His name, his hair, his child-like appearance, and his obvious discomfort in a suit and tie instantly flashed together in Joanne's mind and gave her a category to place him in: finalist in a spelling bee. With the comfort that pigeonholing someone always gave her, she smiled and said, "Please," and led him into their air-conditioned lair.

"Do your people drink coffee?" she asked, gesturing like Vanna White to their Mr. Coffee machine. Ignoring the slur, Hajda smiled and said that he'd already had his daily dose. He went on to say that he had an eleven o'clock on his schedule and that the sooner he met her husband the sooner he'd be out of their hair.

"I'll see what he's up to," she said, and led him to the living room to wait. When he lowered himself onto the couch, a large whoosh of hot air escaped from the confines of the clear plastic slipcovers. "Herb?" he heard her shout as she disappeared down the hall to the bedrooms. He took out his small, leather-bound pad and his pen. "Herb... short for Herbert? Or herb, like oregano? Possible childhood name association problem?" He slipped the pad and pen back into his jacket and looked around the room for any telltale signs or signals. There were none. It was the blandest, most ordinary room he had ever seen. All the furnishings (save the hulking BarcaLounger) were a muddy, dishwater brown and seemed somehow to be covered in moss. There were no pictures anywhere, no art, no photos. Burglars could use this place for aversion therapy, he thought to himself, and considered making a note about that but decided it was a waste of paper. He patiently crossed his legs and another whoosh came out of the slipcovers.

Joanne opened Herb's door to find him dressed—well, at least covered if not properly attired for visitors. He was clad in a tie-dyed T-shirt and turquoise sweatpants, the pants pulled up to mid-thigh as if to call greater attention to his non-matching knee-length hose. "Company?" he asked, almost chipper.

The meeting got off to a rocky start with Herb declining the offered handshake. "Oh no! I'm sure you wash your hands, pal, but God knows what's festering under your nails!" Hajda forged ahead and asked Herb if he had any idea why Joanne would have wanted him to come by. Herb seemed to take forever to understand the question and finally, lowering himself a notch further on his BarcaLounger, said, "Joanne who?" Hajda pulled his pad out again and would not stop his notetaking for the next half hour.

Herb had waited until the now-filled pad was safely back in Hajda's pocket before he began his planned speech. "You want to know what's going on, my little brown friend?" he bellowed. "I'll tell you, oh yes, I will tell you," Herb continued, his voice one of barely concealed rage. "I don't know what it's like in *your* country, but life in *this* country is HARD! REALLY HARD!! I work a full shift as a steamboat captain every day. I've got 3,300 employees under me clamoring for raises. From midnight to six I work in a plant where they package the little bags of peanuts for the airlines—at minimum wage with no bathroom breaks. I don't sleep. But when you work for the CIA like I do, sleep is a luxury. I've got four sons: Herb Jr., Herb III, Herb IV, and Herb V—the last goes and changes his name to Jessica because he's as gay as a sunset, as gay as a charm bracelet, as a wedding cake with two grooms, and wants his cock cut off. None of them have the same mother. I can count backward by sevens, and I have a bullet-proof shield around me that was a gift from aliens from Voltar in exchange for information about the electoral college. Hitler is alive and writes me letters. I can touch my toes with my tongue. I swear this is all true, just ask what's-her-name over there," he said, pointing at Joanne.

Herb suddenly stopped. And just as suddenly, left the room. As he stomped down the hallway he thought to himself, "Did I leave anything out?"

Because he didn't want to leave any stone, any pebble, unturned. He'd thrown it all on the table, maybe a little too much, a little too fanciful, too unhinged, he worried. But what the fuck, when the stakes are this high, you swing for the fences, bet the ranch. He wanted to ensure that there was no explanation for his behavior other than Alzheimer's. Alzheimer's, his ticket to a paradise of irresponsibility and political incorrectness, one-way, first-class, aisle seat.

. . . .

Joanne and Hajda sat silently for several minutes after Herb had left the room. Hajda broke the awkward silence. "Maybe I *will* have that coffee," he said. Joanne jumped up, welcoming his request like a prisoner on death row getting a reprieve.

"I can make new or nuke it. It's still pretty fresh," she said.

"Nuke it is fine," said Hajda rising from the couch with another whoosh of air. Joanne left for the kitchen and Hajda excused himself to fetch materials from his car. He let himself out and he let himself in, now with a small library of pamphlets and printouts under his arm. "I hope you like to read," he smiled.

They settled at the kitchen table and Hajda patiently showed her the information, some of it highly technical, filled with graphs and pie-charts, some of it user-friendly with titles like "So You're Living With a Mental Patient" and "What To Do When There's Nothing You Can Do."

Joanne was able to grasp the essential gist of things: Herb was not in his right mind. She needed to immediately switch her role from wife to full-time caretaker. Herb was capable of saying or doing anything. The house (which he should *never* leave unaccompanied) needed to be retrofitted as one would retrofit for a toddler—plastic covers on electrical outlets; nothing sharp, flammable, or of value on lower shelves (even though Herb was six-foot-one, you couldn't be too careful); all medicines child-proof capped and hidden—ideally in a locked box like a gun case. Most importantly, never take anything he says at face value, and *never* take it personally. Hajda put his hand lightly on Joanne's and, in his most comforting tone, said, "Remember, it's not Herb talking, it's the Alzheimer's."

Herb, who had tiptoed into the hallway and secreted himself behind a closet door to overhear as much as possible, heard the magic "A" word and couldn't help himself. He punched a fist into the air and, as softly as possible, said, "Yes!!"

. . . .

Life in the little bungalow on Miller Street was strained. (Herb, whose last name was Miller, had chosen the place because he thought the coincidence of nomenclature might give him a neighborhood authority, a leg up, a seniority of sorts. He quickly came to realize he had no interest in neighborhood matters or neighbors, period. Solipsistic? Yeah, so what, he thought. Neighbors, like family, are overrated. It's solitude that gets the short shrift.)

The house became quiet, eerily so. Though they both still lived there, slept there, ate there, no pretense was offered that they were still man and wife. Joanne had grown tired of Herb's introducing himself to her (as one would to a complete stranger) whenever their paths would cross. She had grown weary of fixing his special meals, served on his tray with only a spoon and butterknife as utensils. (No fork or steak knife was allowed. If the evening's menu included steak, chicken, or anything that required cutting, Joanne would meticulously predice it in the kitchen.) Often, she would return to his room to fetch his tray and find it sitting on the floor outside his door, like it was a hotel, with nothing eaten but the ice cream and glazed donut he insisted on having with every meal. In the interval between these repasts, Joanne would retire to the living room with the drapes drawn and reread the brochures and pamphlets Hajda had provided. (She had taken off the clear plastic slipcovers because of the noise they made. She didn't want anything to wake Herb should he be asleep—she never knew, he kept odd hours. Often, she would awaken in the middle of the night to adjust her apnea apparatus and find him silently hovering over her, only to leave as silently as he arrived after she asked if he needed something.)

The more she read, the worse it got. She compared all of Herb's quirks to the case histories in the guidebooks, and he ticked every box. Quirks, indeed. She was forced now to see his memory lapses and fantasies as very serious symptoms, absent-mindedness as dementia.

Herb wasn't coming back. He was well on his way down a meandering path that led inexorably to the loony bin; then (she could picture it) to his being strapped to a gurney like a gas-chamber bound murderer paying his debt to society, flailing and screaming; then, finally, mercifully sedated until the curtain came down.

Questions bounded and rebounded in her brain. Had there been earlier signs she had missed? Had there been a telltale tic in his step as he led her under the bleachers at that fateful homecoming dance? Then the big questions: "Did *I* do his to him?" followed by "How long does he have?" followed by "How much of *my* life will be left if I ever want to... My God," she thought. "Am I already really thinking like this? Thinking of finding another man some day? At my age? An older man, of course, it would *have* to be. And, with my luck, someone who would put me through this shit again!" And, when thoughts like these started to make the room spin, she would call her mother.

Belle's phone rang fifteen times before she picked up, but that was par. Belle hated the cell phone Joanne had bought her, refused to use it, insisting she could only hear clearly on the landline, which meant a trip to the kitchen on one leg. That could take a while.

"Who is this?" Belle said gruffly, just in case it was another of the goddamned robo calls that she'd been getting at all hours.

"Hey, Mom," Joanne said, trying not to sound too troubled.

"Hey, you," said her mother.

"I didn't wake you, did I?" asked Joanne.

"Joanne, it's 6:30! Why would I be in bed? I was just watching *Wheel of Fortune*."

"Oh, I'll let you get back to it. I really don't have anything to say," Joanne said, a little embarrassed at assuming her mother had turned in for the night while it was still day.

"Show's over," Belle said. "The fat guy got the car but not the vacation. Now, what's up? Is it Herb again? What did he do this time?"

"Well, it's always Herb. You know that." Joanne paused for a sigh. "I'm sorry if I'm bothering you. I guess I just needed to hear your voice."

"Well, here I am," Belle said, and drew in a breath to begin her motherly advice. "Honey, I think you're taking on too much. He should be in a home somewhere with other people who like to tell lies and run around naked. I've told you that before, and it's still what I think."

Joanne sighed again (she was doing a lot of sighing these days). "OK, Mom. I'll probably call you later."

"Call me anytime you want, honey. I'm not going dancing, that's for sure."

Joanne would call her again in an hour and have virtually the same conversation, except any mention of *Wheel of Fortune* was replaced by Belle's concerns for Alex Trebek (she was now watching *Jeopardy*). She couldn't believe that someone *that* handsome could get sick. Joanne took this observation as an oblique assessment of Herb's looks.

. . . .

Herb only left his room to use the toilet and to make his late-night prowls once he was convinced that Joanne was asleep. He had pretty much everything he needed in his room: a bed; pillows; a TV; a deck of cards (playing solitaire was a balm of sorts that soothed him during those rare moments of self-reflection when he wondered if what he was doing was actually a good idea); phone books to make his paper airplanes; a ukulele; paper; crayons; and, shelved on either side of his one window, a complete set of the *Encyclopedia Britannica*. (Herb had discovered that Joanne had secreted a baby-monitor camera between two of the leather-bound volumes and he deftly draped a necktie over the lens.) He had no responsibility other than wiping his ass.

He sat quietly on his bed in the glow of a muted TV game show and wondered to himself, "What do I miss?" A good question, he thought, because there were things that he *did* miss. Most of them were things that he imagined any man his age would miss. Namely, those strengths and abilities that one only has in youth; not just a body that was resilient and flexible, capable of movements that would now be ludicrous to even imagine (sixty-two-year-old men don't climb ropes up into tree huts, don't cannonball off the high board, don't take the stairs two at a time), but also the sense of wonder, the tingle of surprise upon seeing something for the very first time—like snow (at the age of two), or the awakenings of armpit hair (at the age of twelve), or seeing a naked woman stepping into the shower for the first time (Joanne had made him wait until he was twenty-eight before she was willing to share her toilette). He could go further, lengthen the list, but it would always be far shorter than the list of what he *didn't* miss. That was the list that kept him going, kept him steadfastly insisting on his faked condition.

He could write out his *didn't miss* list, but that would just be begging for writer's cramp. Had he done so, it would have started with The Magnifica Shower Curtain Company, or, as he called it, "the shithole." Sitting in a windowless cubicle eight hours a day, five days a week, fifty-two weeks a year (the last two weeks of August all the lemmings at the office took vacation—which meant that, regardless of where he went, or what he did, there was a chance of running into the *very* people from whom vacation should blessedly distance him). He hated the actual work, though he was surprisingly good at it. He had the instincts. For instance, when a buyer came in to order thirty-five curtains for a local motel, he researched the guy. If it turned out his mom-and-pop dump was part of a franchise, he'd offer a still-profitable discount and parlay the thirty-five into a thousand, nationwide. (Well, he'd done it just the once, winning his Employee of the Month award, but still.)

What he really detested about the job was the product itself: cheesy, Made in China, polystyrene garbage, with the world's ugliest patterns. Little belching tugboats, ugly ducklings, red beach umbrellas (that turned to a dirty pink at the first contact with water), and those goddamned, googly-eyed guppies and stenciled seahorses. Who came up with this shit? Retards? Nuns?

His thoughts returned to what he was missing. Joanne, what about Joanne? I can't say I miss her since she's still here… but would I miss her if she wasn't? OK, be honest. Do I still love her? Even *like* her? She's hung in there longer than I thought she would, so I've got to give her *some* credit. But that doesn't mean I *love* her, does it? Don't they say that you have to love yourself before you can… yadda yadda yadda… oh, come on, can you love someone just because they're patient? And, he had to admit, helpful.

Yes, Joanne was helpful. It was Joanne who brought him his meals, did his laundry, made sure he had toilet paper and toothpaste. Helpful, absolutely. And for the thirty-one years of their marriage, helpful above and beyond the call of duty. It was Joanne who ate the shit sandwiches life would throw at them. Not only nursing all his feigned illnesses but the big stuff, too. (When his parents both died in a fifteen-floor elevator plunge at the Holiday Inn in Salt Lake City—his father had made what would prove to be a fatal decision to attend a national U-Haul convention—it was Joanne who handled all the details. She shipped the bodies, arranged the funeral, cleared up their bank accounts, and sold their house. Herb, falsely claiming to have crippling grief, didn't have to lift a finger.) But that was then, this was now, and now she had become… what was the right word…? Boring? Sure, boring would do. "In fact," he said (he was now speaking aloud, nearly shouting), "the only thing about her that isn't boring is watching how every goddamned day she turns a little bit more into her goddamned mother! Face facts, you big schmuck, you haven't been in love in ten years!!"

This last remark had been said loud enough for Joanne to hear. Stung, she briefly considered confronting him but opted instead for the safe harbor of a call to her mother.

Joanne was startled when, after only two rings, the phone was answered. That was very un-Belle.

"Hello?" said a female voice, not her mother's.

"Who's this?" said Joanne, still startled.

"Oh, hi, Joanne. It's your sister," said Estelle.

(Estelle was her older sister—older by only a year, but quick to use that advantage to make her sister feel less aware, less informed, less in control.) "Jesus, Joanne, don't you recognize your own sister's voice?"

"I just wasn't expecting it to be... What are you...? Why...?" stammered Joanne.

"Take a deep breath, Joanne, it's nothing to get worked up about. Mom just asked me to keep an eye on the place and feed Ralphie while she's gone." (Ralphie was her mother's parakeet.)

"Gone?!!" said Joanne.

"I thought she'd be there by now," her sister mused.

"Estelle, would you please tell me what the hell is going on?!"

Estelle obliged. Apparently, their mother had gotten very concerned about Joanne and had decided her daughter needed the kind of moral support only a mother can supply. (Being a monoped, she couldn't offer much physical help around the house, but she could at least be an ear to listen, a shoulder to cry on.) She had made up her mind to pay a surprise visit. She didn't drive, so she had enlisted Jamal (an Uber driver who sometimes delivered her groceries) to make the three-and-a-half-hour trip for a flat rate of $400. She wasn't sure how her stump would do on what for her was a long trip, and they'd gotten a bit of a late start—leaving at 5:30 p.m., the heart of rush hour—so she had allowed for the possibility of doing the trip in two legs (the irony of which didn't escape her). If need be—after, say, an hour or two on the road—they could spend the night at a motel. She would pay for both rooms, of course—she had her "mad money" that had come from the sale of her late husband's bobblehead collection, and it had remained untouched for just such an emergency.

"Anyway," Estelle went on, "that's probably what happened, and mom should more than likely be there bright and early tomorrow morning." She then went into a seemingly endless story about how she couldn't find her mother's parakeet for the longest time—the little door on the cage had been left open. She had toyed with the idea of going to the pet store to find a replacement but knew that none of the birds would have the same markings as Ralphie, and that her mother would spot the difference instantly and throw a tantrum. Well, long story short, she finally found him in the pantry pecking away at an open box of Ritz crackers.

Joanne didn't know what to say. A surprise visit? God bless her, she meant well, but even when it's your own mother, your confidante, your wailing wall, a house guest is still a house guest. She was already overwhelmed and, connected as she was to her mother, keeping the relationship telephonic was a hell of a lot easier than entertaining a one-legged chatterbox while her husband spun into looney-land.

"Got it. I gotta go. Say hi to Ralphie for me." She hung up and headed for the linen closet to pull out the duvet for the couch.

The duvet wasn't there. Herb had obviously commandeered it for part of the "tent city" he now had in his bedroom. (He had draped bedding over the windows, plunging the room into darkness, and tied his blankets and sheets together to create what looked like an Arab's desert hideaway.) So no duvet. Her plan was to let mom sleep in her bed—it was just a couple of hops to the bathroom—it would be easier for her. Joanne, herself, would sleep on the couch. She'd be fine. She still had spare sheets and pillows and, if it got too chilly, she could cover up with bath towels. While she was contemplating her options, the doorbell rang. She went to the door and, before opening it, sang out, "Hi, Mom!"

She opened the door and was greeted not by her mother but by an older, looming man with grey-black circles under his eyes (think Abe Vigoda in *The Godfather*). Flustered, she drew in a quick breath.

"Oh!" she said.

"Hello," said the Abe Vigoda impersonator.

She had completely forgotten (or gotten her days wrong or something), but it all came back to her when she read the business card he offered. CARL COLETTO, AMALGAMATED INSURANCE GROUPS INC. He was there to verify Herb's disability claim. (As it turns out, The Magnifica Shower Curtain Company had employee coverage that wouldn't lapse for six months after retirement or, as in Herb's case, termination.) In fairness, they hadn't made a hard and fast appointment time—only saying that someone would be coming by for an assessment in the next ten days—but she was hardly prepared for anything other than her mother's arrival on this warm August evening. Certainly not a sit-down examination with her raving husband and Abe Vigoda.

"Come in," she smiled, and indicated he should sit on the couch. There was an awkward silence as they looked at each other.

"Did anyone ever tell you that you look like Abe Vigoda?" Joanne asked, her subconscious getting control of her brain and her mouth. She smiled like it was an ordinary thing to say.

"No," he stated flatly.

After another brief staring contest, Joanne said, "Let me see if I can find Herb."

Joanne took her time walking down the hallway to the little Baghdad where Herb was holed up. It wasn't like this was all new to her. She'd been through assessments before—hundreds of them it seemed. How many times had THE AMALGAMATED INSURANCE GROUPS, INC. people sent someone to check on Herb's disease du jour? (For a while she actually believed he *was* ill. Worried for him, for them, for their future, only to one day see the truth of the matter. He wanted time off. That was all. He was no sicker than the man in the moon.)

This realization had hit her like a runaway bus. It was one thing to hornswoggle The Magnifica Shower Curtain Company and the AMALGAMATED INSURANCE GROUPS, INC., but quite another to hornswoggle his own wife—taking advantage of her caring nature, her honest concern, her meals on trays. Yes, they had always sent reps to check up on Herb's claims, but it had always been young, crew-cut trainees who wouldn't know a smoker's cough from TB. This felt different. She not only felt that (for once) Herb was in truly dire straits, but the man they sent seemed more like an under*taker* than an underwriter. He looked like the grim reaper. She tried to remember if Abe Vigoda's character got killed in *The Godfather*.

Carl Coletto rose to greet Herb and, realizing there would be no handshake, no howdy-do, he sat back down and pulled some printed pages from his vest pocket. He looked them over for less than a minute. "OK, Herb," he began, "I've got your history here. You've already taken the max in sick leave on this agreement. I could say, and be perfectly within company policy, that we won't go another penny. But AMALGAMATED INSURANCE GROUPS, INC. has a heart. We don't throw people on the street in times of crisis. Why? Like I said, we have a heart. And, on top of that, it wouldn't look good from a PR point of view. People get their noses out of joint over stuff like that. On the other hand, we can't keep paying sick people's salaries forever. We'd be broke in six months. I'm sure you and Mrs. Miller understand." This last was said with a knowing nod to Joanne. "So, let's figure this thing out," he went on, taking a pen from his pocket and poising it over Herb's printout. "What seems to be the problem this time, Herb? Physical?" He looked hard at Herb, who was staring into space, drool collecting in the corner of his mouth. "Or mental?"

Herb said nothing. It was not as if he hadn't heard the question, it was as if he didn't know anyone was in the room other than himself and his "new friend," Joanne.

Joanne answered for him. "Mental," she said. Coletto wrote something on the printout as Joanne continued. "We had this very nice East Indian fellow come by and he said, in no uncertain terms, that Herb suffers from Alzheimer's. He said it was age-appropriate and that Herb had all the symptoms. I'm not going to go into all of them. You'd just think I was making it up. But 'mental,' yes. Definitely 'mental.'"

"And you're the only caregiver?" asked Carl.

"I am," she said, stoically.

"No one else in the house?" he asked.

And, as if on cue, the doorbell rang.

. . . .

It took some effort getting Belle's wheelchair up the half-step from the foyer to the living room, but between Joanne, Jamal, and Coletto, they managed it. Jamal lingered a bit, obviously waiting for a tip. Joanne gave him three $10.00 McDonald's gift certificates. (She had purchased several as Christmas gifts and had never used them.) Jamal jammed them in his pockets and with a grumbled, "Fuck me," trudged off to his car. Herb had not moved. Belle wheeled herself into the living room and, catching her first glimpse of her son-in-law, exclaimed, "My God!!" Herb's drool had finally let loose and was cascading down his tie-dyed tee.

For the next twenty minutes, Joanne, Coletto, and Belle discussed options. In Coletto's professional opinion the situation was beyond what could be handled by a single untrained caregiver, and having a handicapped eighty-one-year-old as a backup didn't alter that opinion. Belle was the first to agree and, after some outright sobbing, so did Joanne.

When the decision was reached that Herb should be in an assisted living facility, his eyes betrayed a small satisfaction that no one noticed. This had, of course, been his plan from day one: a room of his own, a bathroom of his own, his personal needs professionally met (he might even request a special diet—ice cream, donuts) and no one expecting anything of him. If he wanted to sleep for three days straight, he could. If he wanted to ignore any other lifeform on the planet, that was his right. Free as a newborn babe. He couldn't wait.

Golden Slumbers was the name of the joint. Years ago it had been a lumber yard (Golden's Lumbers) and to this day the various wings were still referred to as "2x4s," "plywood," "siding," and "hardware." Hardware was the wing that catered to the "memory-challenged." Herb's initial down payment had been covered by his insurance; the ongoing monthly fees would have to come from his social security and their modest savings. By Joanne's estimates, they could swing another six years until they were dead broke. (Six years, she had learned, was an optimistic prognosis for the disease, but he could very well live more, or less, than that. The scientists and doctors were split on the issue.)

Belle didn't go with them to Golden Slumbers. She had sworn that the Uber junket was the last time she would take a car trip of over ten minutes. So it was Joanne and Herb who made the twenty-seven-mile trip. (Joanne drove; Herb had insisted on sitting in the back seat.) Joanne had fruitlessly made attempts at conversation with a near-catatonic Herb. Or at least he wanted to appear catatonic—he was, in fact, very excited, and to mask his excitement he had undertaken the distraction of silently playing license-plate poker.

After a brief lunch stop at Dunkin' Donuts (ice cream and two glazed), they arrived under the porte-cochère of Golden Slumbers. A Mexican man (he seemed, and sounded, Mexican—he could have been from anywhere south of Kansas) greeted them, grabbed Herb's bags, and led them through a maze of hallways to Herb's new home.

Herb's new digs were more spacious than what he'd had on Miller Street. The double bed was motorized and articulated—it could, with the push of a button, become a recliner, a hammock, an easy chair, an astronaut's perch on his way to the moon—and it was perfectly level with the flat screen (mounted high on the wall, hospital-style). There was a small closet, more than enough space for the handful of things Joanne had packed for him. The hangers were fat, tubular, and plastic. (No wire hangers was a Golden Slumbers policy— the last thing they wanted was an "accident" that could lead to a malpractice suit.) The bathroom was beyond clean, as blindingly white as a blizzard. The tub was equipped with a jungle gym of chrome-plated steps, handles, grabbers, and nozzles that made getting a good soak a walk in the park even for the gymnastically challenged. But, to Herb's great delight, the shower curtain was plain white canvas.

Herb was instantly ten years old. He bounced on the bed, flushed the toilet, ran the hot and cold water, put the adjustable bed through its paces, switched on the TV—it was all he could do to refrain from dancing.

Once she'd delivered him to Hardware, Joanne's work was pretty much done. All that remained was the painful goodbye. Joanne teared up (as much from the disinfectant smells of the hallway as from the obvious difficulty and awkwardness a parting always presents). She had mixed emotions, two of which were abandonment (which she talked herself out of) and relief.

Yes, relief. Her life of late had not been an easy one. She had come to feel widowed without the space to grieve that an actually dead husband would provide. It was terrible to think of it that way, she told herself, but it was the truth. She needed this break. Badly. So, with both a heavy and lightened heart, she put her hands on Herb's shoulders, said, "You're going to like it here, Herbie," and pulled him closer. Touched, Herb momentarily broke character and kissed her lightly on the cheek. Then, back in character, he said, "I know, mommy. I'm a big boy now!!"

. . . .

Joanne didn't drive straight home. For over an hour she cruised the neighborhoods near theirs and looked at the houses. Who did they think they were kidding with their fire-engine-red front doors, their lattices and trellises, their bird baths and golden retrievers lounging on the front porch? Did they really think they'd pulled off the old Ozzie and Harriet? Or, more likely, were these one-story, three-bedroom, two-and-a-half bath boxes filled with all manner of degradation? All the little stuff like the flu and cat allergies, like morning sickness and runny noses. Or the big stuff: adultery, spousal abuse, cancer, or contemplated murder? She'd watched her share of crime TV. She knew what unthinkable horrors could be lurking on the other side of the chintz curtains, knew that the house next door might be the home of the guy who was "kinda quiet, always kept to himself" and then macheted the entire family of five and carried them out in garbage bags. You could almost count on it. She calculated that, on a sliding scale, she could be a lot worse off. So, still feeling like a victim, but less so (more like the victim of a schoolyard teasing than a full-on assault), she turned the final corner and headed for Miller Street. When she got home her mother had Rice-A-Roni waiting.

. . . .

Alone at last, Herb pirouetted in the middle of the room. He felt the joy of an economy-level hotel guest who has been inexplicably upgraded to the presidential suite, free of charge. Fortune was smiling on him with big white teeth. It was when he was drinking in his new surroundings and admiring his window view of the leafy, manicured grounds that the bubble burst. Not thirty feet away from his room he saw two Hazmat-suited attendants wheeling a gurney, and on that gurney, the unmistakable cargo of a body-bagged human. It hit him like the proverbial brick: people come here to die. Before this truth could fully sink in, he grabbed the blanket from his bed and draped it over the window. The room instantly felt like Miller Street all over again. Baghdad redux.

And soon, for both Herb and Joanne, life settled into a pattern.

Joanne's pattern: She was now off the couch and sleeping in Herb's old bedroom (after a thorough cleaning). Her mother still slept in Joanne's bed and had mastered the three hops it took to get to the john. Joanne and her mother shared the household chores—her mother limited to what she could do in her wheelchair or on one leg. (She had become surprisingly adept at single-leg activity. She could vacuum, for instance, using the vacuum cleaner's extendable nozzle as a kind of crutch.) Despite the close quarters, Belle and Joanne did not become contentious; if anything, they became more tightly knit, settling more often than not on exactly the same page without any disagreement. They played Scrabble. They watched Ellen.

Phoning Herb at Golden Slumbers was a nightmare. First of all, regardless of what time of day or night it was, the receptionist invariably spoke English as a second language. ("Is *everyone* from India?" Joanne wondered.) Secondly, Herb wouldn't answer his phone once they'd figured out how to patch it through. So she wrote letters. Not long ones, mostly "here's what happened today" stuff. She wrote him once a week, mailed the letter on Thursday so it would be there by Monday, hoping it might cheer him up and give him strength for the upcoming week. Herb never wrote back. Unbeknownst to Joanne, he never even opened the letters. Just shoved them into his sock drawer.

. . . .

Herb's pattern: Within hours of his arrival at Golden Slumbers, Herb got his first hint that this wasn't going to be the Valhalla he had hoped for. He awoke to find a "daily schedule" shoved under his door. Before reading any further than "Experience Sharing" (activities were listed alphabetically, starting with Art, then Bowling, ending with Zzzzzz, indicating a nap), he was interrupted by a knock at his door. Dr. Xohalli-Berman. At barely five feet tall and swimming in his lab coat, he seemed more mascot than doctor.

"Good morning, Mr... [He glanced at the paper in his hand] Miller! Did you sleep well?"

"I'm not done," said Herb.

"Not done *sleeping?* Now don't be silly. It's 7 a.m.!! The early bird gets the worm!!"

(It was the first of seventeen thousand bromides with which Xohalli-Berman would pepper his speech.) "Rise and shine!" "Carpe diem!" "Time waits for no man!" It was maddening.

But Herb bit the bullet. Though he found it almost physically painful to sit in group therapy sessions and loathed the windowless room where Mrs. Gondo, the art therapist, coaxed them through an assortment of paint-by-numbers (Herb was given *The Last Supper* and remembered the smiley faces he had put on Joanne's print), he balanced his discomfort with the knowledge that the "social" part of the day ended at two and he would have the rest of the afternoon and all of the evening to himself.

Still, it wasn't what he'd bargained for. He was tired of trade-offs. Wasn't that what everything was? One big trade-off? Think about it, he thought. You don't have a car (everybody else does), so you go to work (say, on the automotive assembly line), and you earn enough money to buy a car, but it's not the new car you've been working on, it's a used car, because they don't pay you enough to buy the new car you've been working on, and then you have to buy insurance on your used car, which you hope never to need, and pray that the guy who smashes *his* used car into you has insurance, and if he does, and it's *his* fault, then, once you've paid all the lawyers (which will be a huge chunk of it), you can collect enough money to buy fifteen of the cars you've been working on, but you can't drive any of them, because you've been crippled in the accident. Now you can't go back to work and have to sell the fifteen cars just to eat. Trade-offs.

The worst part (even worse than Xohalli-Berman's attempts at bonhomie) was the "buddy system." In the Golden Slumbers Hardware wing, socializing was deemed an anodyne to senility. To this end, everyone was assigned a "buddy"—you shared a table at meals, you held his or her hand during enforced walks around the grounds, you were encouraged to chat. Herb's buddy was Edgar, a toothless octogenarian who ate everything (even hot dogs) with a spoon. Thankfully, Edgar was as prone to lengthy silences as Herb, so it could have been worse. But, put it all together, as Herb would do lying sleepless in his adjustable bed, and it wasn't the slam dunk he had envisioned. Yes, he no longer had to deal with the vindictive Ray Slack. Yes, he didn't have to helplessly watch Joanne morph into her mother, and, no, he didn't even have to clip his own toenails, they did that for you. But, still... But, still...

. . . .

It was almost Belle's birthday, and she wanted a party. She was turning eighty-two. Her birthday, falling as it did on December 25th, had always played second fiddle to Santa Claus. Even the big ones, the red-letter birthdays—16, 21, 50, and 70—had been bleached out by the glare of Christmas lights. She was forced to accept that Christmas trumped birthdays (unless, of course, you're Jesus). That's just how it was. Now, with her children, Estelle and Joanne, themselves of a "certain age," and her only grandchild, Estelle's Maryanne, a million miles away in Oakland, she felt she could finally shift the focus off the yuletide and onto herself. Yes, she wanted a party, and (diabetes be damned) she wanted *cake!!*

A little sugar wouldn't kill her, she thought. The truth was that she hadn't been sticking too closely to her diet since moving in with Joanne. She blamed it originally on stress, the whole "Herb situation," but even after life at Miller Street had settled into a sort of rhythm, she found her sweet tooth undeniable. She understood fully that these cravings were what had cost her an appendage but figured that was a one-time event. Currently, she had no symptoms of anything untoward. (Yes, her numbers were sometimes a bit on the wild side, but that was probably her age, she reckoned.)

But the birth of Jesus still posed a problem. Estelle's husband, Alan, was a somewhat devout Lutheran and a Christmas fanatic. (He did their 4,000 outdoor lights; the animated, plastic Santa and sleigh on their roof; the eight-foot, star-topped tree.) No way was he going to allow Estelle to be anywhere but home on the 25th. Joanne felt a bit of a conflict as well. She had, for some time, planned on visiting Herb on Christmas. They had, after all, had some pretty good ones in the past—the year she got her washer and dryer, the year he got himself the BarcaLounger and she thought a visit might trigger memories of better days. He was probably beyond hope, but she wanted to try.

After much discussion, they arrived at a compromise. Belle would get her bash, but it would be on the 23rd. Joanne wouldn't even put the tree up until the 24th. All focus would be on the big birthday.

. . . .

Christmas at Golden Slumbers was a tricky business. Priding itself on being tolerant and egalitarian, the management had to consider the feelings of their Christian, Jewish, Muslim, Hindu, agnostic, and atheist residents. Decorating the halls and meeting places with representations of everyone's holiday symbology was more work than anyone in the already overworked janitorial staff wanted to undertake. (At the pre-holiday "help staff" meeting, Mrs. Gondo, the art therapist, had suggested she make a large poster to put over the main entrance—a red-suited Black man holding a menorah and a letter addressed to "Allah Claus." The mostly Middle Eastern board members nixed the idea.)

None of the patients exchanged gifts or had the wherewithal to do so—patients had no access to actual cash/money. Instead, they each had an "account" that their deliverers set up with the Golden

Slumbers facility—a fund that they, themselves, could not dip into. It was there for emergencies only (and for rolls of quarters for the laundry machines that were distributed weekly). This policy had been instituted after a wealthy, schizophrenic gentleman had flashed a wad of hundreds in front of a younger, depressive, female patient (a girl who had made a point of declaring herself, loudly and often, to be a famous biblical prostitute) and demanded she accompany him to the pool-supply shed for "favors." There and then, patients with ready cash were deemed a bad idea.

So, rather than do nothing and be seen as callous by the patient's families, Golden Slumbers celebrated the winter holiday season with a makeover of the patients' rooms. They spruced up the joint. On December 23rd, while the inmates were treated to a movie in the meal area (this year it was *Dumbo*), the staff swapped out the tired bedspreads, the stained sheets and pillowcases, the towels—virtually everything that wasn't bolted down. The plan was that the patients, their spirits already buoyed by the movie (no one on the staff had considered that *Dumbo* was, in fact, a pretty sad tale), would return to their rooms and find everything shiny and new. It wasn't the same as opening presents but, for most of the patients, it was a pleasant and unexpected surprise.

It was an unexpected surprise for Herb, but not a pleasant one. He was already in a surly and restless mood after sitting next to Edgar (eating popcorn with a spoon) for an hour and a half of what Herb called "Dumb"—no "o." He had, of late, been feeling more and more unsure as to the wisdom of his charade. He had wanted freedom. He had wanted, essentially, to be Tom Hanks and his soccer ball on an island. Instead, he was holding hands with Edgar, filling coloring books under the hypercritical eye of Mrs. Gondo, and being plied and manipulated into "sharing" with groups of people he would never give the time of day to in real life. He was ripe for a rethink. And when he saw his shiny new bedding (they had taken down the blanket he used to block his view of the corpse parade) and stepped into the bathroom, the shit hit the fan.

They had traded out his plain white shower curtain—with one of Magnifica's googly-eyed guppy-and-stenciled-seahorse monstrosities!!

"NO, NO, NO!!!!!" he screamed into his clutched fist. He tore the curtain down with such force it bent the rod in half. He was shaking. He was sweating. He caught sight of himself in the mirror. A madman! Was this what he'd become? He didn't want to see it. He grabbed the shiny new ceramic soap dish and smashed the mirror, the tiny slivers of glass tinkling on the floor tile like Christmas bells. "NO!"

He ran back to his bedroom, threw a few clothes in a pillowcase, and headed for the door.

He paused for a deep breath, then returned and dug Joanne's letters out from under his balled-up socks and shoved them into the pillowcase. Another deep breath and he was out the door.

. . . .

Belle's party started first thing in the morning. The girls brought her breakfast in bed—Honey Nut Cheerios (her favorite), OJ (from concentrate), and coffee. While she chewed and sipped, Joanne and Estelle began the decorating process. They hung crêpe paper streamers (no red, no green, nothing remotely Christmas—mostly yellow, Belle's favorite color). It was a flurry of activity, the girls resting only briefly to replenish their oxygen after orally inflating the dozens of balloons that now bounced around the rooms. The house looked like a Chuck E. Cheese.

It was decided that the big meal of the day, the "party meal," should be on the early side. At two days shy of eighty-two, Belle was not much of a night owl. After much discussion, they had eventually decided on ham—honey-baked ham, well done. The sides would all be Belle's favorites: microwaved peas and carrots, tater tots, and a Jell-O mold with fruit salad magically suspended within. And, of course, a cake: vanilla, with tidal waves of vanilla frosting. (It looked, Estelle laughed, like a suitcase someone had put in a plaster cast.) The number of candles was argued about. Eighty-two was out of the question—"We'd burn the house down!"—and one large ceremonial candle seemed insignificant. They settled on seven. It was Belle's "lucky" number.

Belle loved her dinner. While Joanne cleared the plates and carried them to the sink, Estelle brought out their mother's gifts. From Joanne: a yellow, chenille bathrobe. (When it was unfurled it looked big enough to cover a car.) From Estelle: a framed photo of Belle's only grandchild, Maryanne. The picture was a little blurry, probably taken on a cell phone and blown up, and showed her standing in front of an Oakland head shop, her hair spiky and dyed pink and purple. Maryanne's hands were thrust in front of her, her fingers pointing oddly, in what appeared to be a gang greeting. In the upper right corner it said, "To Grams!!" and in the lower left corner it said, "Peace out! Love, Malaysia Rain." (Estelle had neglected to tell her mother that Maryanne had changed her name, claiming that she could no longer "identify" with Maryanne Godalphski.) None of this mattered to Belle. She was having the time of her life.

"There's one *more!!*" Estelle giggled.

"What?!" said Belle. "You guys are gonna spoil me!"

Estelle handed her the gaily wrapped shoebox, which Belle tore open like a child. It was a single slipper. Belle didn't get the joke right away. "Is this from Herb?" she asked, unamused. "It's the kind of thing *he* would do."

"No, mama, we just thought it might be kind of funny," Joanne said softly and regretfully.

Belle looked back and forth at her daughters, and it hit her like remembering an old song. These were her *daughters!* The same sly little rascals who had pushed her to the limit so many years ago. Her daughters. But now, somehow, they weren't. They were all grown up—senior citizens like herself. It was an old gal's club now. A limited-fun and limited-games club. She had to forgive this black-humor gift, this seeming lapse in taste. They were just trying to give her a good laugh. So she laughed, boy did she laugh.

She was almost giddy, suspiciously so. Of course she was—she had been sneaking nibbles from a plate of fudge in the refrigerator since early morning and had polished off two massive wedges of her cake—giddy as a six-year-old. And, in a wink, giddy turned to dizzy. The room began to spin—the yellow, pink, and blue balloons and streamers flashing psychedelically like a special effect in a fun house. But it wasn't fun. Belle keeled over like a drunk in an alley. Estelle ran into the kitchen to get the backup packet of frozen peas and carrots to use as a cold compress. Joanne called 911.

. . . .

Herb's timing couldn't have been better. The Golden Slumbers staff party was in full swing and anyone who might otherwise be patrolling the hallways and exits was three drinks into a holiday stupor. He didn't see a soul as he walked right out the front door.

It was later than he thought; the streetlights were on. There was a seasonal nip in the air. Now what, he wondered to himself. About a half mile up the road he saw the low lights of a housing development. And, shouldering his pillowcase of worldly goods, he began to lumber toward the light. How he hated housing developments. Cookie-cutter blips scattered at uniform distances across acres of un-landscaped land. He was always reminded of hair-transplant plugs. Still, he moved toward them and was soon amidst the hair plugs. He looked around to get his bearings. He saw the meager Christmas décor: drooping, plastic lawn Santas, colored lights that flickered annoyingly like a migraine, Styrofoam candy canes duct-taped to mass-produced screen doors. And, through the front windows he saw the twinkling lights on the stunted Christmas trees, blocked from view on occasion by the shadow of an overweight homeowner—glass in hand, trying to make the best of it.

"*People*," he said, disparagingly. "They buy into the whole fucking thing."

Hoisting his sack to the other shoulder (Please, God. Don't let some kid see me and think I'm Santa Claus!), he walked on.

He walked for probably another two miles before he saw the fire.

Not the world ablaze as might have fit his state of mind, but a small campfire—a hobo's fire, complete with hobos, a dozen or so, all of them men. Or what used to be men. Now they were barely recognizable as humans. Any thought of haircut, shave, or bath long ago abandoned, any thought of fashion discarded. An odor that almost masked that of the trash-fire wafted from under threadbare rags worn over layer upon layer of more threadbare rags. And they were as silent as snowfall. They seemed oblivious of each other, staring into the flames, barely blinking. Trying to remember something? Herb wondered, or trying to forget? He was definitely sure it was one or the other, but then he wasn't so sure. Maybe it was neither one. Maybe these were people who had tried everything ordinary life had required of them—maybe even succeeded, become wealthy, popular—and, when all was said and done, they felt duped. That hollow feeling one has when one realizes he's bought a bill of goods. Maybe this silent staring at a trash fire, deep in what he assumed was thought, was a kind of graduate school. A silent seminar in how to live life as an intransitive verb: "Don't just *do* something, *stand there!*" Maybe they've solved the riddle of the Sphinx? And, of course, there was the real possibility that they were just drunks, junkies, and the hopelessly mentally ill.

Regardless of any of these possibilities, one thing was certain: They were very much alone—spaced around the trash fire at distances that prohibited conversation—not even flinching when the fire gave off a loud snap or crackle. Each had his own piece of earth, his own weather. His own island. His own *island!!* Herb thought, and almost jumped. Good Lord! They did it!! They're Tom Hanks!! No palm tree or soccer ball, but they *did* it! It may be a pile of shit and not sand, but they had *their own island!!* And then the thought slammed into him that it was true of *everyone*. The whole human race was an archipelago—just a chain of individual islands, one-person island nations—and all social interactions nothing more than a series of fragile trade agreements, of visas, of truce talks, and détentes.

"Well, well, well," he said to himself, "well, well, well."

At that very moment, one of the larger men (Central Casting, get me a Norse Viking) stood between Herb and the fire. He offered a three-toothed half-smile. "Ever want to get wet?" he asked.

"I'm sorry, what?" Herb replied.

"Get wet," said the Viking. "Get off the island."

Herb was dumbstruck, barely managing to say the word.

"Island?"

"What I said. Just don't go in over your head." And with that postscript he walked away as silently as he had arrived.

Herb had been forced to go to Sunday school as a lad. He had heard the stories about angels bringing messages, and he'd thought, even then, even at the age of eight, that it was all bullshit. But the man had said "Island!!" Are you kidding me? Was this guy reading his mail?

Then the word *mail* hit him—he pulled Joanne's letters from his pillowcase, ripping open the first one he could grab. Five twenty-dollar bills were nestled in the following note:

Dearest Herb,
In case you need something special. Because I think you *are* special.
All my love,
Joanne

Herb jumped to his feet, shoved one of the twenties into the wool-mittened hand of his Viking angel—"Buy yourself a soccer ball," he told him, and ran off.

It took forty minutes for the EMTs to arrive because the holiday season always meant high volume for 911 calls (an unusual number of overdoses, housefires, and alcohol-infused family slugfests). While they waited, Estelle continued to apply the frozen peas and carrots to her mother's brow, offered "There, there," and checked her color, her pulse, and her temperature every few minutes. Belle was still amongst the living.

Joanne, the calmer of the two sisters, used the time to pack an overnight suitcase for her mother: underwear, toothbrush, nightie, her new robe, and joke slipper. She checked that all the faucets, stove, oven, and space heaters were off, knowing that it could be a while before she was back home. There was nothing more they could do but wait, so they watched *The Bachelorette* until the doorbell rang.

The EMT crew was the picture of efficiency. Belle was slung on a gurney and slipped into the back of the ambulance in the time it took Joanne and Estelle to find their coats and purses.

Minutes later (the ambulance's red rotating beacon stealing the show from the neighborhood holiday lighting), the two vehicles (Joanne and Estelle were following in the Miller's Honda) careened across town, running red lights, and forcing late-night shoppers to jump back onto the sidewalk. "This is like a *movie!!*" Estelle squealed. Joanne, her eyes fixed on the ambulance's fleeing taillights, didn't respond.

. . . .

Herb wasn't sure where he was headed. He saw a faint glow of light on the horizon, and though he had no idea as to its source, it was either head there or head into the woods. He chose the light. An hour later he was glad that he did.

Grafton was a penny-sized town—a few stores bunched along a narrow main drag, a clock tower that let him know that it was 8:46 and (thanks to an inscription below the dial) that Grafton was "Where We Do Life." There was no one on the street.

Herb looked for an alleyway or covered door front where he might curl up for the night.

Then, from out of nowhere, he saw a solitary cab, inching its way down the street. He ran after it, waving his hands like a crazy man. The cab slowed to a halt.

In the next few minutes Herb would learn that things that could never, *ever* happen sometimes do. Herb reached the cab, breathless, and looked into the driver's side window—it was Hajda! For a second, Herb thought that he had actually, honestly, this time for real, lost his mind. This was impossible!! But Hajda recognized Herb instantly and said so, and, after Herb showed him that he had money, he said, "Hop in." Herb slid gratefully into the back seat.

Hajda agreed to drive him to Miller Street (he remembered exactly where it was). As Herb settled into the welcome warmth of the cab, Hajda began his soliloquy. He had been demoted to part-time by the Adult Protective Services (whom he suspected of being racially motivated, and he wasted no words in stating this suspicion) and, after short stints as a crossing guard and telemarketer, had settled on driving a cab. When he finished his rather lengthy bio, he asked Herb what he was doing wandering around Grafton.

Herb told him the truth. The whole truth.

. . . .

The emergency ward was a beehive—a steady stream of people complaining of everything from earaches to bullet holes. Belle, probably because of her age, was taken through the double doors within seconds of their arrival. Joanne and Estelle found seats in the waiting room and watched the fire drill of humanity in awe. Dozens of doctors and nurses, dashing in and out of swinging doors, trading clipboards and mumbling frantic instructions through their face masks. Joanne couldn't help but notice something: "My god," she whispered to herself, answering a question she had asked herself when Hajda had made his house call, "They *are* all from India!!"

Time crawled, and the only magazines were *Us* and something put out by AARP. It was nearly 10 p.m. when a young nurse approached them.

"She's out of woods," said the turban-headed girl (who looked to Joanne to be about twelve years old). The nurse then pointed to the check-in desk. "They give you room number." And she was gone.

"Thank God," said Joanne.

"Amen," said Estelle.

They entered Belle's room (Joanne felt weird

to come empty-handed but that was just who she was) and found their mother resting comfortably.

"Hi, girls, some party, huh?" said Belle, sheepishly.

The three shared a sigh of relief.

. . . .

After an hour or so of just sitting there with really nothing to say (Belle had fallen asleep), Joanne clasped her hand over her sister's.

"Estelle, sweetie, I've got this from here. I've been through a lot worse, believe me. Alan needs you for Christmas. You should go."

Of course Estelle refused to leave, even though she knew she wasn't needed and wanted desperately to go. So, "caving in" after a protocol of insincere arguing, Estelle kissed her mother's cheek, hugged her sister, and was out the door. Joanne sunk back in her molded-plastic chair, hoping to find a position that might let her sleep.

She fell asleep, and had a terrifying nightmare about her niece, Malaysia Rain (she could never get used to that name change, not in a million years). Malaysia had been kidnapped by a drug cartel in Mexico, had escaped, miraculously, and was hiding under a bed at Golden Slumbers, covered with spiders. Just when it seemed that all was lost, Abe Vigoda had come and rescued her. She woke with a start and realized that she was hungry.

. . . .

Herb, too, had fallen asleep, thanks to the drone of Hajda's diatribe. He was jolted awake when the cab slammed to a stop in front of his Miller Street home. He threw his handful of twenties at Hajda, told him to "keep the change," and dashed for the front door. What he saw was a note, a long one. It began: "Dear UPS, FEDEX, DHL, and Amazon, Please leave all packages next door at the Kugler's." It went on, for two legal-sized pages, to explain in great detail everything that had happened, as if any delivery man would give a shit. The last line revealed the name of the hospital.

Herb yelled for Hajda, who had just started pulling away, once again waving his arms like a crazy man. Once again, Hajda stopped. Herb piled in, and they were off to Our Lady of Elyria General.

. . . .

Assured that her mother would more than likely sleep through the night, Joanne headed down to the coffee shop. It was a smallish enterprise, tucked in a far corner, that someone (in the hope of lifting the spirits of concerned visitors) had made into a "themed" restaurant—paper palm trees, and little tiki-shaped salt and pepper shakers. It was called "The Island." Joanne had a booth all to herself.

Miller's Island

. . . .

Herb hustled to the check-in desk and got the room number. After what seemed an interminable wait for the elevator, he finally arrived at Belle's room. She was snoring away. No Joanne.

His day, so far, had been blessed with bad luck (seeing that fucking shower curtain almost put him in cardiac arrest) and a decent amount of good luck—he had escaped from Golden Slumbers, met a Viking who transformed his thinking, and caught the only cab in Grafton, but now it seemed his good fortune had run out. Back in the reception lobby and headed for the exit, he saw the neon sign that said, "The Island." You gotta be kidding me, he thought.

It was impossible for him not to see her. She was the only one in the place. And it was impossible for her not to see him. There was a moment of pregnant silence and then Herb gave her a smile she was sure she hadn't seen since that night under the bleachers at the homecoming.

"Hi, mommy," Herb said.

Joanne eased over in the booth to make room for him.

"Hi, daddy," said Joanne.

. . . .

"What did we ever do before plastic, eh, Herbert?" said Otis, the sweat-drenched bartender, as he held

Herb's Mastercard close to his face, then further away, then close again, trying to find the focal length for his myopia. "Herbert Miller," he read aloud.

"It's 'Herb'," said Herb. "I prefer 'Herb.'"

"Then Herb it is. Anything else I need to know?" Otis asked with a toothy smile.

Herb slid his empty glass toward Otis, indicating he needed another. Then, for reasons he could only later chalk up to some form of "good citizen fatigue," some sort of last-ditch-at-being-human deathbed confession, some urge to come clean, he said, almost in a whisper, "It's my birthday, sixty-five."

The Shangri Lounge was the quintessential neighborhood watering hole. It had stood at the corner of Sycamore and Broad for thirty years and Otis had been planted behind the bar from the day it opened. First-name basis was the law of the land here. An easy enough law to uphold since the bar, when filled to legal capacity, held only twenty-five people, counting Otis. Every patron was a "regular." These drinkers had all sought sanctuary at The Shangri Lounge for years. They knew more than each other's names—they knew each other's histories, the darker sides hidden behind a lush's grin. However, even though they were privy to potentially explosive information, there was a tacit understanding to never delve beneath the surface, beneath the prosaic, the hail-fellow-well-met recounting of daily events. "Get that roof finished?" "You ever talk to that guy about hip replacement?" "I see that rash cleared up." Nothing about what might have driven them to habitual drunkenness—what pitfalls, indignities, romantic traumas, IRS audits, and social disenfranchisements had turned them into barroom fixtures—rum-soaked human furniture as much a part of the décor as the plastic hurricane candles on the tables, the sawdust on the floor, content to slur aside the torment of their inner lives. It was a club. And Herb was not a member.

This did not mean that they treated his presence in their clubhouse as trespassing. There had been no cold shoulders or leering stares when he entered—just a nanosecond of quiet awareness that a new face was present (and not even *that* present—the regulars were all seated at two- and four-person tables, while Herb had selected a stool at the farthest end of the bar). Otis mechanically and somewhat ceremoniously threw down a coaster in front of Herb and, as if it were a signal, the drinkers instantly stopped their subtle gawking and resumed their boozy chatter as if Herb's stool were empty.

They must have kept one ear open for anything irregular, however, because when Herb said it was his birthday (and he had said it softly, he thought, almost internally), the room fell dead silent. Herb felt like he was the keynote speaker at a Rotary Club luncheon and had just clinked his glass with a butterknife to call for everyone's attention. They smelled a story.

"Sixty-five, huh! Well, you don't look it!" Otis lied. "I was gonna *card* you!"

"Right," Herb said, barely audible—the last thing he wanted was to start a conversation.

"Your birthday!" said Otis, putting a fresh Jack Daniel's in front of Herb. "I'll be damned. Then I guess this one's on the house."

Herb mustered a smile that said, "thank you," and took a long sip of his drink. Looking over the rim of the glass, he saw that he was still the center of everyone's attention—as if he were doing a magic trick; as if a dove would fly out of his mouth after he swallowed, his coaster reveal itself to be the missing queen of hearts. Please don't let these strangers sing happy birthday, he thought (because they looked like they might). Please *no*. But they didn't. They went back to the business of getting blotto.

Herb continued to sip, and Otis continued to hover.

"Celebrating all alone, huh?"

"Trying to," Herb said, with a bit of a leave-me-alone edge.

"Well, technically, you're not. You're celebrating with Jack Daniel's. If you want to add Johnny Walker and Jim Beam to the party, I could get you a table," said the bartender with practiced wit.

"I'm fine," said Herb.

Otis could see that it was a troubled man who sat before him and replaced his smile with a look of deep concern.

Miller's Island

"Listen, if there's anything you want to talk about. Like in those old songs, those old movies, set 'em up Joe, one for the road, you know, where the bartender lends an ear, puts a Band-Aid on your troubles, that kind of thing. Well, I'm here if you need that stuff."

Herb considered the man's words. He looked long and hard at him and could discern no malice, no devious soul-stealing curiosity, no threat of judgment. For reasons he would never understand he decided to open up.

"It's a long story," said Herb.

"We're open 'til two," said Otis.

. . . .

It may have been the Jack Daniel's. It may have been that Herb had indeed remembered those old songs and stories where the bartender becomes a lay therapist, a faceless priest taking whispered confessions through a tiny grill, or it may have been the exhaustion that comes with years of self-imposed emotional isolation. Whatever it was, the dam burst. Breaking only for a reflective sigh or an occasional slug of his cocktail, Herb told his life story. (Though Herb was already several sheets to the wind, he still maintained a semblance of an editor's reserve, and did not start his story from day one—he knew that there was nothing of interest about his youth or his parentage.) He decided to begin his story midstream: the feigned Alzheimer's debacle. In a slow, dispassionate, laundry-list manner (an accountant reading out the quarter's profits and losses), Herb spun his tale. When it came to the part where he spotted Joanne in the hospital diner, Otis, who hadn't said a word, stopped him.

"Herb. Gonna have to put a cork in it. It's two." Otis pointed to the Miller High Life clock to underscore his statement. It was actually five after.

Herb downed the last of his drink and wiped his chin.

"I called you a cab. You shouldn't be driving and, if you walked here, you shouldn't be walking," Otis said.

Herb nodded. It was true. He was seeing a couple of Otises at this point.

Then, as if there were only one cab driver in the world and the whole evening had been staged and choreographed, the front door opened and Hajda stepped in. "Taxi!" he said, scanning the room for his fare.

Hajda was now forty-six and no longer looked like a spelling bee finalist. His odd, double-bun hairdo was gone, cut as short as a banker's, and steel gray at the roots. He had been driving a cab full-time now for three years—his tenure with Adult Protective Services cut short after too many of his reports had been deemed unacceptable. Typos had been his nemesis. Not simple mistakes like "cunt" instead of "aunt," but more a form of typist's

Tourette's. He would inexplicably insert words like "cocksucker," "shitface," and "bumfucker" into his patient's reports. He didn't do it on purpose. He didn't speak this way. It was only when he typed. He had tried to pass it off as a translation problem—Hindi to English—even claiming that Gandhi had suffered the same difficulty. (Hadn't the famous Indian holy man once referred to Americans as "wiener-heads?" He was sure of it, but, try as he might, he couldn't produce any hard data.) Adult Services had to let him go.

By the time the cab pulled away from the Shangri Lounge, Herb was sprawled across the back seat, fast asleep. Hajda pulled to the curb in front of Herb's Miller Street home.

"Herb, we're here," he said softly. When Herb didn't budge, he said his name again, this time louder. Then again, and again, each time with more volume. Nothing. Hajda got out and opened the back-seat door and shook Herb's shoulder. "Wake up, Herb," he said. Herb was out cold. Hajda began poking him, first on the chest, then on the cheek, poking like someone urgently trying to enter a pin number into a stubborn ATM. Finally, after a knuckle-deep probe, Herb's eyes fluttered open. "What?" he complained.

Hajda had to literally breech birth him out of the cab and then perp walk him to the front door. He found Herb's keys in his pocket, opened the door, hoisted him over the threshold, and plopped him like a bag of wet sand onto his BarcaLounger. Herb instantly fell back asleep, snoring like an outboard motor in shallow water.

Hajda, who was a featherweight, unmuscular man, was still breathing hard from lugging Herb's two hundred fifteen pounds of helpless flesh. He needed a second. He sat on the couch opposite Herb and, for a longish moment, just looked at him, wondering aloud, "How does a man get to this point in his life?"

Because no one lives happily ever after. They just don't.

. . . .

Three years earlier, when Herb had caught Joanne's eye in the low fluorescent lighting of the hospital coffee shop, he was as puzzled as she was. This chance meeting was not part of a carefully plotted caper, he knew that much. Was it fate? Inevitability showing its inevitable face? Was there some almighty puppet master, sitting on a cloud somewhere, pulling the strings on his little marionettes, thrusting them into situations beyond their comprehension, just to tickle his tired old fancy? Or was there some form of magnetism that attracts two incomplete souls to the same time and place, the same level, like layers in a dessert parfait?

With no ready answer to any of these questions, Herb had negotiated the odd configuration of the little Formica tables and slid into the booth beside his wife. He had no words on the tip of his tongue, no words anywhere near his mouth. After the world's longest silence, he pointed to the coffee pot on their table and arched a questioning eyebrow.

"Sanka," answered Joanne.

. . . .

Opening gambits were awkward and halting, both parties looking for a lingua franca that would allow for any conversation. Even the sound of each other's voices seemed foreign in this strange moment of kismet. After several minutes of dead air, Herb smiled at her in a way that seemed vulnerable enough for her to open up, and soon they were bringing each other up to speed, recounting the events they each had recently endured, rattling them off like news anchors giving updates. They both listened to each other (they hadn't really done that in years). There was pathos. There was bathos. There was the undeniable realization that they were inextricably connected. Then and there they resolved to try and keep the marriage afloat. (This took the hard stuff, real coffee. Sanka couldn't handle an issue of this magnitude.) Herb offered his mea culpas. (Though she felt no guilt of her own, Joanne offered mea culpas as well, just to keep the playing field level.)

After an hour of this delicate banter, the mood lightened. Joanne could not get over Herb's new philosophical outlook (and that he'd gotten it from a "hobo" no less!). Hoping his new mindset would include forgiveness, she admitted to her feelings of "good riddance" during Herb's stay at Golden Slumbers. Herb was surprised, not pleasantly so, but hey, it's all on the table now, he thought. Time to move on.

For the three days that Belle remained hospitalized, Herb and Joanne were a team, a model couple—taking shifts at Belle's bedside, bringing each other snacks, fresh clothes, always saying "I love you" when they left each other's company, even if it was only to go to the bathroom.

It was all an act, of course, but both parties hoped that through repetition and muscle memory the act could become the reality. But, let's be honest: What they had endured could not be dismissed as a marital "spat." It was a sea change—a shift of the tectonic plates that ruptured the already fragile foundation of their union. It would take some major engineering to rectify the damage. The marriage had to be rebuilt, and — since neither one was any longer a youthful, vital specimen, brimming with sexual energy — the biggest challenge was finding something about their mate that they found even remotely attractive. Anything at all that might engender a spark. Not the easiest job in the world for either of them. Joanne had to somehow forget that the balding, fidgety man with the stomach like an enormous blister had spent most of their married life lying to her, and Herb had to see

Joanne in her frayed flannel nightie, all entwined in the luggage of her sleep-apnea apparatus, and picture Lolita. Herculean tasks.

The new housing arrangement didn't help matters. Belle, deemed out of the woods, had been discharged from the hospital and was now ensconced in the Miller's master bedroom. Joanne again took the couch. (She claimed she liked it, but it was more that it served her self-image as victim.) Herb had his old room back, fighting the urge to return it to the Baghdad tent that had been his womb just a few months earlier.

Belle needed constant attention. She was no longer able to pull off the three hops that would put her on the toilet—it was now a bedpan situation, which Joanne assumed as her personal chore.

"You shouldn't have to deal with my mother's doo-doo," she said.

"You're too kind," said Herb.

In fact, she *was* too kind. She waited on her mother hand and foot, day and night. Special meals, foot (singular) rubs, blood tests, thermostat adjustments, and constant chatter. (Herb's deep fear that his wife was turning into her mother was heightened by these endless conversations; he was having a harder and harder time distinguishing one voice from the other.) Had Herb wanted attention from Joanne it would have been a dealbreaker, but he was content to keep their contact at a minimum. He soon found himself spending his days, weeks, and months gaping slack-jawed at game shows again and knew if he didn't do something it would be "same song, second verse" in no time. He had to get out of the house. He had to get his job back.

. . . .

Months of ice cream, donuts, and watching daytime TV had taken its toll. His blue business suit was beyond snug—his shoulders felt like he'd been lassoed at a rodeo, his pants buttonable only after a deep, swimmer's breath. (And the pantlegs seemed too long—was he actually at the age when people start to shrink?) He tried his other blue suit, the one his wife called his "funeral suit." It was worse. He grudgingly muscled back into the first one. He had to tie his tie three times before he got it right. What had once been habit had devolved into clumsiness. Dressing for work, he discovered, was not as recallable a skill as riding a bicycle. Finally, as presentable as he could manage, he displayed himself to Joanne for her approval.

"You look nice," she said, automatically.

"Don't patronize me, Joanne. I look like a burrito."

"Well, how about your funeral suit?"

"Worse. I had to take the jacket off just to tie my fucking shoes!"

"Then wear your loafers!!" boomed Belle's off-stage voice. (She'd been eavesdropping from her bedroom hideaway.)

"Belle, please, stay out of this," he yelled back. "My loafers are *brown* and my suit is *blue!!* Think about things before you throw in your two cents, for Christ's sake!"

"No one is going to be looking at your shoes, honey," said Joanne soothingly. "They're all just going to be happy to see you again. Now, go get 'em, Herbie. You can do this!"

She tried to give her husband a hug but, given the restrictions of his suitcoat, he couldn't reciprocate.

"Here goes nothing," Herb muttered, picking up his briefcase.

His briefcase. His holy grail. His only possession that he thought of as exclusively *his*. Joanne learned early on not to touch it. (Belle, he suspected, may have tried to probe its locked innards at one time, but he couldn't prove it.) Not that it contained anything shocking, disreputable, illegal, or immoral—no contraband, secret love letters, salacious documents, or porno playing cards. It was just a *thing* he had for his briefcase. Today, however, it was virtually empty: his birth certificate; a handful of printouts of government regulations regarding fair hiring practices (in case he ran into unexpected bias); his embossed, official certificate proclaiming him Employee of the Month (just to jog their memory); and a ballpoint pen.

Off to work he went, oddly nervous, considering it was something he had done almost automatically for twenty-six years. For twenty-six years he had taken the three steps up to the massive wooden door with the peeling gold-leaf MAGNIFICA on it, opened it, heard the old-timey jingle of the rusting sleighbell that announced a visitor, and mounted the stairs to his cubicle without even a glance over his shoulder.

He had begun his career as a low-level assistant accountant and worked his way up the corporate ladder—his raises, more often than not, were in title only, not in salary. (Ray Stark would cry poor when pressed for a bump, citing rising overhead and inflation, citing taxes, citing whatever it took to placate employees and offering the abstract notion of "job security" as if it were something edible.) As of his termination, Herb held the title of Head Accountant of the Billing Department—but his paycheck had grown only by a meager five percent since his first day on the job. Today, he would ask for his job back and consider himself fortunate to have the same salary.

He took the three steps and noticed that the door was no longer the wooden behemoth of his memory; it was burnished aluminum and emblazoned with a large black M. He had to be buzzed in. Well, *that's* new, he thought.

Once inside, he fought the instinct to head for the stairs as he had done for twenty-six years. Instead, he entered the waiting room—a room he had never entered before or even noticed. It was small, with a dun-colored shag rug, pale drab olive walls with blades of light from the venetian blinds that slashed through dozens of framed samples of Magnifica's absurd and ludicrous shower curtain patterns. (Without this "art" it could have been a police station; with it, it was an Uffizi of the john.) He took a seat on one of the cracked lime-green vinyl chairs, placed his briefcase on his lap like a TV tray. He had barely begun to leaf through the current Magnifica Shower Curtain catalog chained to his chair when employees started to stream in.

He recognized no one. Not that the employees he remembered were all that memorable. They had all been middle-aged white men in blue suits, some with glasses, some without, most of them smelling of cigarettes. He had never been a very keen observer of the passing parade, but he was sure all of these people who now presented themselves were recent hires. First, there were women as well as men—that was new. Second, the men all seemed to be barely into their twenties. And, lastly, the *outfits!* Not a suit and tie to be seen. All of them, even the women, seemed to be more appropriately attired for washing the car than doing business. Jeans, sweatshirts, short-sleeved pullovers, sneakers, T-shirts with the names of heavy metal bands scrolled across them like wearable billboards. "And I was worried about wearing *brown shoes?*" he thought. And, while we're at it, the *hairstyles!*

He could understand how pride could have led the African American guy to grow that mushroom cloud of hair, but the other do's were inexcusable—shoulder-length mops, ridiculous braids, and none of it looking like it had ever seen soap. "How can you sell shower curtains if you've never even taken a shower?" he said to himself. For a second he was unsure that he'd come to the right office and approached the young receptionist to ask.

"Of course it's Magnifica, silly," said the ponytailed teenager behind the desk, her voice as innocent and fairy-like as her face. "Mr. Slack is coming down to get you *any* minute," she smiled.

Herb thanked her and returned to his chair. Okay, things change, he thought, go with the flow. "We're all islands," he repeated to himself, searching for reassurance. But he wasn't ready for the next island to present itself. The man approaching him was *not* Ray Slack. He was much younger and snappier. He almost clicked his heels when he stuck out his hand.

"Herb Miller? Jason Slack. I think you knew my father."

Ten minutes later, Herb was up to speed. Stunned, perplexed, but up to speed. Jason held nothing back in his explanations, embarrassing as they might be. His father was in prison. While Herb had been languishing at Golden Slumbers, Ray Slack and his brother (who Ray had hired to replace Herb) had been caught with their hands in the cookie jar—to the tune of three and a half million cookies. Ray had been double dipping for years, fudging the books, offshore accounts, Ponzi schemes, you name it. His brother had laundered the proceeds. The trial had been swift and the sentence severe. The Stark brothers would have eight to twelve years to regret their ambition.

In reviewing the history of the company's financial records, it was noted that Herb's books were singularly spotless—everything hunky dory right down to the penny. Herb's previous office shenanigans (his unprovoked singing, his frequent lapses into catatonia) were dismissed as products of a midlife crisis and forgiven. It was, after all, Jason, the new-ager, who had loosened the hiring practices to allow for the parade Herb had witnessed filing to the elevators. Jason would bend over backwards to be able to write NO in the box that said "ageist" in his progressive moral checklist. He was thrilled to take Herb back. Herb was even offered one of the coveted corner offices. To put the cherry on the sundae, Jason ordered up five hundred business cards for Herb while Herb sat there silently drinking his coffee.

Silently, yes, but internally realizing, and lamenting, that his play-acting in the office—his atonal rendition of "Don't Blame Me" during the board meeting and his attempts at Swedish yodeling in the hallway—had not fooled anyone, certainly not Ray Stark. Ray had seen through it and pounced on it as an opportunity to can his ass and replace him with his scamming brother. Boy, you think you know the people you love, and you think you *really* know the people you hate, but he never thought Ray would stoop so low. He toyed with the idea of visiting Ray in prison just to laugh in his face. He was steamed. It took a few sips of the coffee to counter the bile in his stomach and put him back on the sunny side of the street.

Bygones be bygones, he thought. He had his job back. Game on.

Herb's good news was received rather casually at home. No bells and whistles, no popping champagne corks. In fact, Herb got no more attention and praise than a neighbor showing off his new lawn mower. Not that the girls were jealous or resentful of his good fortune; they were just too tightly knit to allow new, outside information into their shrinking world. They had almost become one person—one three-legged, disease-obsessed talking machine. It seemed to Herb that they *never* stopped talking, never took a breath. They had even gone so far as to create a verbal shorthand so they could say more in less time.

"Have you..." said Belle.

"They're in the..." said Joanne.

"Well, I need the..." said Belle.

"But those aren't..." said Joanne.

"Then where's my...?" said Belle.

"Pillowcase," said Joanne.

Herb found it maddening.

And when they weren't talking, they were eating—picnic-sized spreads at the foot of Belle's bed. Belle's diabetic diet was supposed to exclude certain foods, but, from what Herb could see when he passed by the room, there wasn't much that was off the table. Baskets of rolls, mountains of mashed potatoes, pizzas, pastas, gallons of Pepsi-Cola, and (quickly hidden when Herb peeked in) boxes of assorted candies and chocolates. When Herb confronted Joanne about Belle's eating vis-à-vis her disease, she confessed that the sweets and carbs were for *her*, not for her mother. Stress, she claimed, was the culprit. Well, she had him there. Herb could not deny that stress abounded in their little house, so he dropped the subject. Over the next three months, Joanne gained eighty pounds.

Herb, on the other hand, lost weight. Not intentionally, but he was glad he could fit in his suits again. His weight loss was the result of pushing himself at the office—he often worked through lunch and skipped dinner in favor of sleep. It wasn't that he had to prove himself at the office—Jason was easily impressed—it was a way of hiding. Long hours and the occasional Saturday and Sunday at Magnifica meant fewer hours at the yammering hen party at home. Keeping his attentions horse-blindered on his ledgers of accounts receivable kept him from acknowledging the presence of his coworkers, whom he came to regard as a sideshow, a casting call for some bizarre Fellini film which he would never watch, even with subtitles. His tireless work ethic served the purpose of isolation even better than his fraudulent Alzheimer's ever had. As a joke on himself, he bought a soccer ball and placed it on the chair opposite his desk. Herb Island.

. . . .

And for many months, then a year, then two, then two-and-a-half, this was the stuff and substance of the Millers' life. Neither rut nor groove, simply pattern. Simply ritual. Herb continued to work, Joanne continued to eat, and Belle continued to age. Working, eating, aging—a fairly accurate, if not very romantic, description of human life. Carpe diem? No. One didn't seize the day, one simply tried to get through it.

. . . .

And then a red-letter day that would change everything.

The man who had been shown to Herb's office was unimposing, well dressed, and soft-spoken. His name was Bjorn Borgberg, and he was the CEO of Nordia Cruise Lines—a fleet of five luxury cruise ships based in Oslo, Norway. Their business, while still profitable, needed a little goosing. To this end, he had decided the boats needed a total facelift. All of the cabins and suites—over three thousand in total—would be refurbished. This meant new shower curtains, of course. But Borgberg didn't want any of the cutesy, garish patterns that he saw in the Magnifica catalog. Instead, he wanted a custom job that incorporated his new logo: an octopus in a top hat holding a cocktail in each of its tentacles. Magnifica had never done custom work, relying on their stock images to satisfy the lack of taste of most of their clients. But Herb wasn't going to lose this windfall. He told Borgberg that it could be done. It might be a little more pricey, but yes, it could be done. He would have a figure for him tomorrow. He bid Borgberg a fond adieu, then got on the phone, found a designer who could work with the eight-armed, alcoholic logo, and started crunching numbers.

After working well past quitting time, Herb looked at the bottom line on his spreadsheet and realized that this would be the biggest sale in Magnifica's history. He also realized that Borgberg could be shaken out of his pipe dream once he saw the costs, think he was being gouged, and take his business elsewhere. Herb had no idea what would happen. He was not by nature a businessman, not in the wheeler-dealer sense. He was an accountant and had chosen accountancy because it was a one-man operation—perfectly suited to his feelings of distance from his fellow man. Yes, he'd assumed a new, non-hostile tolerance of people after the "island" epiphany, but that's all it was—a tolerance.

He was worried that he hadn't shown more warmth to Mr. Borgberg. (Not that Norwegians are all that familiar with warmth, he thought; it's supposed to be fucking freezing there.) Would his personality (or what Joanne often reminded him was his lack of one) blow the deal?

Screw it, he thought, I'm sixty-four years old, almost sixty-five. I'm not going to change who I am for some reindeer wrangler—not going to overhaul my character over a boatload of shower curtains.

He slept like a baby that night.

. . . .

Bright and early the next morning, Herb was in their little kitchen scarfing down his breakfast when Joanne poked her head in. She was still wearing her apnea mask, the long hose dangling like some prehistoric trunked animal.

"Mwratopin. Waopieng," she mumbled.

"Take that damned thing off if you're going to talk," Herb said. "I can't understand a word you're saying." Joanne removed the mask.

"I *said* you're up early."

"I've got a big day," Herb answered curtly.

Joanne's eyes went to the donut Herb was shoving into his mouth.

"I hope that's not one of *mine*," she barked.

"Like you need it," Herb replied, wiping his mouth on his coat sleeve. Joanne gave a humph, replaced the mask, and headed back to her makeshift bed on the couch. Once she was out of his sight, Herb took the last donut from the package, put it in his briefcase, and headed for the door.

. . . .

Herb had set the meeting for half an hour before the other employees were due to arrive. He didn't want what he saw as the unprofessionalism of the new hires to squirrel the deal.

Borgberg was punctual and, after a few awkward pleasantries, asked to see the offer. He read it quickly and, without a word, grabbed his fountain pen from his suit jacket and signed on the dotted line. Done deal. He couldn't be more pleased—letting it slip that the Magnifica offer was substantially less expensive than he had expected. (Hearing this, Herb felt like *he* had been taken. That old Ray Slack and his thieving brother would have cleaned this guy's clock. Thank God they're in prison, he thought, and not here to berate him for his lack of business acumen.)

Borgberg was happy. Beyond happy. So happy that he wanted to sweeten his end of the deal.

"You like to cruise the *islands?*" Bjorn Borgberg asked.

Herb was confused. He wondered if there was anything in his life that didn't in some way involve the "i" word. "What?" he said.

"A cruise. For you and Mrs. Miller. It's the least I can offer for your kindness," said Borgberg.

He proceeded to detail his offer: round-trip, first-class airfare to Miami; a suite on their finest ship; six days at sea with stops in St. Thomas, St. Croix, and St. Barts—all expenses paid.

"Leave your wallet at home," he chuckled Nordically.

Herb was speechless, then found his tongue.

"Deal," he said, grinning for the first time in years.

All that remained was setting up a time for the Miller cruise. Herb remembered that his birthday was coming up and could think of no better way to celebrate reaching sixty-five than to be gazing at a palm-tree-clustered isle from the upper deck of an ocean liner.

Borgberg made a thirty-second phone call, and it was all set.

For the rest of the day, Herb was split between elation at his good fortune and conjuring lies he could tell Joanne so he could take the trip solo. He couldn't think of a good one.

. . . .

"Hi, honey, I'm home!" he chirped as he came through the door. (He had never said such a thing in his life.) Joanne, already in her flannel nightie, came quickly out of her mother's bedroom, an alarmed look on her face.

"Good Lord, Herb, what's wrong?" she said breathlessly.

"Wrong? Nothing's *wrong*. I've got some great news, that's all."

"That doesn't sound like you," she said warily. "Do we need to talk?"

"We sure do," he said proudly.

Leaving nothing out, he described his day and his good fortune to Joanne who listened intently. At first, she thought he was lying, since that would have been the norm in years past. Slowly she came around to seeing that it was the truth—they had been offered a free dream vacation. (Lacking a reasonable lie, Herb had decided not only to bite the bullet and include Joanne, but to do his best to be happy about it. Maybe a change of scene was all they needed, he'd reasoned, a chance to be young again, to start over.)

As Joanne absorbed the information, a patina of victimhood slid over her face.

"I can't go anywhere, Herb. You *know* that. Sometimes I think you say things just to be mean."

She clouded up, tears in the making.

"No, sweetheart, I'm serious. Really. *This* time I'm serious," he said. "Look, there's got to be a way we can do this. It's the chance of a lifetime!" She thought she sensed a whiff of sincerity in his words—enough so that she was willing to at least talk about it.

For the next hour and a half they talked. Herb, who was an accountant down to the marrow, not a salesman, did his best to pitch his sale. "Opportunities like this never come around for ordinary people like us—we're not getting any younger—we haven't been anywhere in years—it's the perfect time of year to head South—it won't cost us one red cent!" His pitch had the ring of being rehearsed because it had been. All afternoon he had crafted it after deciding to include Joanne in his windfall. She couldn't deny any of it. The trip would be spectacular. That wasn't the problem.

Herb saw clearly what the problem was. Somehow, he had to get her to sever the umbilical cord with her mother ("sever" was too strong a word, and would never happen), or more like "tie it off" for six days.

"Not even a whole *week*!" he pleaded. His pleading led him nowhere, so he brought sympathy, he brought understanding, he brought empathy and humanity and, when he sensed she was leaning his way, he brought practical ideas.

"Estelle can take care of your mother," he said.

"Not like *I* can," said Joanne.

"Of course not, sweetheart, there's no one like you. But she can do whatever's needed for six days."

"Mom's afraid of burglars," Joanne countered.

"We'll put in a surveillance system, get her a little pistol. She can hide it under her pillow."

"Estelle sleeps hard. She won't hear if mom needs her."

"We'll get a baby monitor, turn it up to ten," said Herb.

"Mom's diet," Joanne went on.

"Written down so even Estelle can't screw it up."

"Her meds."

"Labeled and pre-measured before we go."

"Herb, I'm afraid."

"Of course you are. That's part of the *fun* of it!"

"I guess I should be excited," Joanne said, faintly smiling.

"Yes, you *should!*" said Herb, squeezing her hand. It was the first time they'd touched in months.

"Okay," said Joanne.

. . . .

For the first time in his life, Herb was walking on air. (His walk, even as a child, even as an adolescent, a young adult, had always been a weighty shuffle, heavy, plodding, like someone wearing snowshoes, trudging through a drifted field.) His high spirits were engendered not by thoughts of tropical weather and on-the-house dining, but more by the fact that he had pulled it off without lying. All of his previous coups—the Alzheimer's ruse, his other "illnesses," even his marriage proposal (he had promised Joanne a happy life, knowing in his soul that he probably couldn't deliver) had been lie-driven enterprises. Now he fairly bounced around the office, even chatting with the Crayola box of new employees in the hallways, wearing his newfound morality like a bespoke suit. And, speaking of clothing, he purchased his first bathing suit. He had never owned one and wasn't sure as to what was proper. He tried on five of them at the department store, couldn't decide which one made him look thinnest, and purchased them all. He would model them for Joanne. Let her decide. Yes, their relationship had warmed to that point.

Why wouldn't it? Joanne had jumped on the bandwagon, too. She dropped eleven pounds in the first week (near-starvation dieting and morning workouts with a TV fitness guru that left her drenched in sweat). She dyed her hair an almost Lucille Ball red and had it styled in a perky flip. She mail-ordered a new nightie, sundresses, and a bathing suit for herself—a modest, skirted, one-piece number (she was still over two hundred pounds). She pored over the brochures that Herb had been sent, checking off the activities she thought they could manage, reading the menus.

But, for all these efforts, Joanne still couldn't shake her concern for her mother's well-being. She insisted that Herb follow through with all of his promises of increased home security—which he did.

Her sister, Estelle, had agreed to babysit and actually said she was eager to spend the time with their mother.

"She's eighty-four, Joanne," she had said. "You never know when it's the last time you're going to see someone."

That was the wrong thing to say to Joanne, who now spent every second that she wasn't preparing for the trip nestled as close to her mother as possible, even sleeping with her on several occasions. Her suitcase might be packed, but Joanne and her mother were still essentially three legs, one mind, and one heart.

. . . .

Estelle arrived the night before their departure and was immediately assailed with instructions, checklists, and schedules regarding Belle's safekeeping. All of the information had been printed out, in duplicate, and the more urgent requirements underlined in red Magic Marker. Joanne had left no stone unturned; contingency plans for any emergency were clearly laid out. She'd done all she could, she thought, as she curled into bed with her mother.

The departure date arrived at long last. Herb was up first (well, not technically; Joanne had never really fallen asleep—a nervous wreck). A quick cup of instant coffee, a couple of donuts, and Hajda was at their door, his taxi idling in the driveway. Hajda hefted their luggage (one suitcase was particularly heavy as it contained Joanne's sleep apnea apparatus) and loaded them up. Herb had to physically pull Joanne away from his mother-in-law.

"Mama will you be...?" said Joanne.

"I'm gonna..." said Belle.

"I'm..." said Joanne.

"It's..." said Belle.

"Okay, good..." said Joanne.

"Yeah, good..." said Belle.

Jesus, thought Herb, they can't even add the *bye* to "Good*bye*..."

Estelle—the only one who seemed to be enjoying the moment—took picture after picture on her iPhone and kept up a steady stream of "Don't worrys" and "Bon voyages." Hajda mentioned several times that it looked like rain and he was worried about his wipers. Herb was screaming about being late. It was a madhouse.

Eventually, after a brief argument about seating arrangements (Herb, with his long legs, wanted to sit in front, but Joanne claimed to need him by her side), they were underway. They both turned to look out the back window at Estelle waving madly, as if they were astronauts off to Mars.

· · · ·

The charm of flying first class was diminished to a great extent by the family seated across the aisle—an oversized Arab woman, her hajib revealing nothing but a pair of angry revolutionary's eyes, and her twin babies, who seemed to be having a crying contest. Who could be louder? Who could go longer?

Miller's Island

The Millers retreated to their headphones. Though they did little to muffle the little screamers, they prohibited conversation, which would have been just Joanne voicing her concerns about her mother anyway. Instead, she devoured the in-flight, duty-free catalog while Herb ogled the stewardess (never missing the moment when she had to bend over to reach a window-seated passenger). They each had a Bloody Mary. They both opted for the chicken. Their meals arrived just as they hit turbulence. After an hour of bouncing around the sky, their fingers cramped from white-knuckling, the jumbo jet set down on the tarmac in Miami.

The limo was long, white, and spotless. Borgberg had pulled out all the stops. Once settled, the Millers found a chilled bottle of sparkling water, two cut-glass flutes, a bowl of peanuts, a small box of chocolate-covered cherries, and two T-shirts (both large) emblazoned with the ridiculous, tippling, top-hatted octopus logo. There was also a tote bag, similarly emblazoned, filled with lotions and unguents, sun blocks, and more snacks.

Herb explored the bag of goodies while Joanne dug her iPhone from her carry-all and frantically dialed her sister.

"How is she?" asked Joanne, not even bothering with the traditional "Hello."

"Oh, hi, Joanne. She's fine," said Estelle.

"Everything's good?" Joanne asked, eager to hear more.

"No. Everything's *shit*. Don't you watch the news?"

"What are you saying? Is something wrong?!!" Joanne became increasingly concerned.

"Oh, lighten up, Joanne. Mom is fine and dandy. I'm talking about the outside world," said Estelle.

"Well, we're *in* the outside world, Estelle, and it's definitely *not* shit! We're in a *Cadillac!!*"

"So were the Kennedys," quipped Estelle.

"I can't talk to you when you're like this," Joanne said wearily.

"I had a glass of wine, okay? Shoot me," said Estelle.

"You're *drinking!!*" said Joanne, horrified.

"I'm *kidding*. Jesus, just relax and enjoy your little trip, will you? Our mother is *fine!*"

"Alright. I'll call you again in a little bit," said Joanne, and ended the call.

"Everything hunky dory?" asked Herb, opening the box of chocolate-covered cherries.

"I guess so," Joanne said with a sigh. "It just feels weird, that's all."

Herb offered her a chocolate-covered cherry. "Here," he said, "let's try and enjoy this if we can." He hoped his soothing voice and the sugar rush would calm her nerves. By the time she was done chewing, she was on the phone again with Estelle, the second of five calls she would make before they reached the dock.

Miller's Island

. . . .

The blush came off the rose when they entered their "suite." It was a matchbox: just a double bed with tiny, flat pillows, crammed into an alcove with what looked like barely enough room for Joanne's apnea gear on her side of the bed. (Herb's side opened directly into the miniscule bathroom.) No chairs, no romantic loveseat, and no TV. (Herb decided this was not a cost-cutting gesture—they probably couldn't get a signal at sea.) It was awful. Alright, Herb thought, it wasn't a galley with sweat-soaked, chained Nubians struggling in unison with massive oars, but a *suite?* Come on. If this is a suite, then what in the hell was it like in the single units below decks? In steerage?

He inspected the bathroom—a one-person-at-a-time situation, that was certain. He made note of the tired towels, the unwrapped soaps, and his trained eye went to the shower curtain. It looked like someone had used it to wash their cat. Jesus. No wonder Borgberg had initiated the makeover. If there was anything at all "suite" about their quarters, it was the smudged and scratched sliding glass door that opened to a three-by-three-foot porch overlooking the sea. My God, he thought, six days like this? I was better off at Golden Slumbers!

There were no shelves or closets, so, with the exception of the one containing Joanne's sleep apnea apparatus, the suitcases were left unzipped on the floor—like an odd buffet of clothes and toiletries. The sleep apnea apparatus took some doing. The compressor, after a few forceful nudges, finally fit on Herb's side of the bed. (It just meant that the bathroom door had to remain open.) The breathing module, regulator, and monitor device were coaxed into Joanne's side of the bed. This meant that the electrical cord, as well as a long section of breathing tube, would span the bed, side to side, pinning Herb in a position where he could not move his arms without fear of unplugging it and sending Joanne to a gasping end. Six days, he thought. Six days.

Joanne called her sister again, and again was reassured that all was going swimmingly. Satisfied with the report, Joanne announced that she was exhausted and needed a nap. She asked Herb to blind his eyes while she slipped into the new nightie she had purchased for the trip (there was no privacy to be had, even in the bathroom, thanks to the apnea junk blocking the door), and he complied. When he was given the "all clear" and looked, he saw that her new nightie was yellow with big blue polka dots. It was also comically baggy. Seen in conjunction with her new barn-red hair, Herb couldn't shake the vision of a clown.

"Sleep tight," he said. (He fought saying something like, "Sweet dreams, Bozo.") "I'm gonna go look around this barge."

Despite the letdown of their accommodations, his step was still a little lighter than usual. He was determined not to let the thumbprint-sized suite sour his trip. Sour his suite, he smiled to himself. He liked that one. That was a good one.

He had changed clothes for his deck-side promenade—now sporting off-white Bermuda shorts that were precisely the same color as his hairless legs, giving him a waist-down appearance of wearing pantaloons. Topside, he wore a pink and green, floral Hawaiian shirt. He couldn't bring himself to wear the giveaway octopus T-shirt, although when he took his first gander at his fellow passengers milling about on the deck he saw that he alone had made that decision. Everyone else *was* wearing their octopus. This sameness of attire was underscored by a sameness of age (old), of mannerisms (halting waves, coughing, constant adjustment of sunglasses), of hairdos (gray perms), and conversations (little to none). More than passengers, they seemed like a cult. "If the Hindus are right, and there is a caste system," Herb wondered aloud as he slalomed through the loiterers, "then 'tourist' has to be just a hair north of 'untouchable.'"

Oh, where was his hairy, philosophizing hobo friend to help him find the wisdom needed to invest these people with individuality—to make them a part of the human archipelago? Let it go, Herb thought, let it go. He had a boat to explore.

He set off at a decent pace. The deck was wooden, like a weathered boardwalk, dappled here and there by ancient women, baking to burnt umber in ill-advised two-piece swimsuits. Now and then, he'd spot an actual family, the mother anxiously sheep-dogging her children away from the climbable railing that separated them from the roiling waters below. There were a few sulking teenagers, hating the fact that their vacations were being spent with their parents instead of sneaking cigarettes with their pals back in Buttcrack, Iowa. There were a few little shops selling every imaginable lotion and souvenir ashtrays (once again, octopus-themed). There were countless rental stations for lounges and umbrellas, and Herb wondered if his carte blanche covered such amenities. He toyed with the idea of stopping at a little tiki bar and getting one of those cutesy cocktails with the umbrella and saw that it would mean standing in line. He hated standing in lines. He continued on, taking some steps to a lower deck and discovered it was virtually devoid of humanity. His kind of place. He found a chaise lounge and lowered himself onto it as a spectacular sunset appeared before him. This is more like it, he thought. Christ, I feel like I'm in a postcard!

Within minutes, he was fast asleep.

Miller's Island

. . . .

The foghorn woke him. My God, he thought, it's dark! He checked his watch and saw that, sure enough, he had been asleep for nearly two and a half hours. It was now nearly 10 p.m.—long after he had told Joanne he would take her to dinner. (They had chosen a restaurant from the brochure—a semi-dressy joint called "The Squid"—and had made reservations for 8 p.m.) He jumped to his feet and started running (well, doing something as close to running as he could manage; he was, after all, a sixty-four year old accountant). Losing his way on occasion in the maze of stairwells and decks, he finally found the hallway that led to their suite. He stood, breathing hard, and was silently rehearsing the excuses he would offer when he saw the tray of half-eaten food sitting on the floor outside their door. Joanne had dined. He was going to face a shitstorm.

He took another deep breath, steeling himself for a tongue lashing, and slowly opened the door. "Joanne?" he said, cautiously. No response. "Joanne?" he said a little louder. Then, in full voice, "JOANNE?" She wasn't there. Not unless she was hiding—an impossibility in their phone-booth quarters. He went back into the hallway, looking both ways, calling her name. No Joanne. Just a disembodied male voice from another suite who shouted, "Pipe down!!" Now he was starting to panic. He went back in the room for another look and saw her phone on her pillow. She *never* went anywhere without it. Something was *very, very* wrong! He picked up the phone and saw the text:

MRS. MILLER

I REGRET TO INFORM YOU OF THE PASSING OF YOUR
MOTHER AND SISTER. I AM VERY SORRY FOR YOUR LOSS.
PLEASE CONTACT ME AT YOUR EARLIEST CONVENIENCE. FOR FURTHER DETAILS.
DETECTIVE SGT. RAMON D'ESTE, ELYRIA POLICE DEPARTMENT

(216) 578-8651

Herb let out a wordless, primal scream. And that's when he noticed that the sliding glass door to their tiny porch was open. He ran out there, screaming her name at the ocean. Powerless to do anything else, he hung his head in despair. When he opened his eyes, he saw the shred of yellow flannel with blue polka dots flapping on the railing.

. . . .

After two days of fruitlessly searching the ship and radar-probing the waters where the ship had been at the time of the "accident," Borgberg sent his private yacht to bring a very shaken Herb back to shore. Joanne had jumped. Herb just had to accept that. Never, in his wildest imagination, had he considered that suicide could be part of Joanne's DNA. Maybe the idea of life without her mother had just been too unthinkable—swimming with the fishes a less terrifying option. Now he had to face a similar dilemma: life without Joanne. He'd deal with that later. First, he had to find out what the hell happened to Estelle and Belle.

Everything had been going well. Estelle had followed Joanne's instructions to the letter. The meals, the meds, the massages, all of it. On the to-do list was a daily change of bedding. This maneuver required Belle to perform an awkward pirouette on one leg while Estelle fitted the bottom sheet.

Belle had earlier complained of a slight lightheadedness, so, when she attempted to stand, the room began to spin. To steady herself, she grabbed for the knob on the headboard and came up emptyhanded. "Estelle!!" she shrieked, as she headed for the floor. Estelle, panicked, quickly grabbed an armload of pillows and threw them down on the floor in front of Belle, hoping to cushion her fall. A fatal mistake. The little .22-caliber pistol (Herb, as promised, had given it to her to protect against burglars) was dislodged from its hiding place in her pillows, hit the hardwood floor, and fired. Estelle took the single bullet in the middle of her forehead.

Belle, instantly in a state of shock from the sound of the gun and the sight of blood dripping from her daughter, was still somehow able to crawl to her phone and dial 911. When the paramedics arrived, Belle was virtually incoherent and already feeling severe chest pains, a throbbing down her left arm. Before she lapsed into complete unconsciousness, however, she was able to babble out the whole story to the policeman, who had been summoned after the medics had discovered the bullet hole. She went into full cardiac arrest on the gurney and was gone by the time they got to Our Lady of Elyria General.

All three ladies: gone.

. . . .

It's been said that we love our friends more after they're gone. It was certainly true for Herb as he tried to absorb the idea of life without Joanne. He was a wreck. Back home again, he did his best to find a spot in the house that didn't feel ghostly—didn't remind him of all the good things about Joanne. Any negative feelings he had previously harbored toward her had disappeared with her physical presence. He rebuilt his little tent city, climbed inside, and, assuming the fetal position, proceeded to mourn his heart out. This is how Jason Slack found him when he made his wellness check.

"Herb, I brought you a sandwich," he said, tentatively poking the bag into the flap of the tent.

That simple act of kindness pulled Herb out of his doldrums just enough to discuss a memorial.

Jason had a softness, a sweetness, that caused Herb to question his parentage. He couldn't be Ray Slack's son. He was probably adopted. Ray was a prick, and this guy was a saint. A hint as to the source of Jason's gentility came when Jason told him that flowers for the service would not be a problem.

"My partner is a florist," he said, proudly.

"Of course," said Herb.

It was decided there would be a memorial that honored all three women at one time. Jason would take care of all the arrangements. Did Herb have a list of people who might like to pay their respects?

He did not. He personally had no family, save the ones in the urns. Estelle's husband had passed away a year ago from pancreatic cancer. That left Estelle's daughter, the recently renamed Malaysia Rain, as the only family member, and she was a couch-surfing beatnik in Oakland. Forget her.

. . . .

The Millers were not churchgoers (at her brother-in-law's urging, Joanne had given the Lutherans a crack and had found them less than uplifting). Herb was on the cusp of agnostic/atheist. So, finding a facility for the memorial was not an easy task. Jason was undaunted, however, and after much looking around was able to secure the back patio of a local pizzeria for the event. Given the solemnity of the occasion, the restaurant would not accept any payment—just Jason's assurance that the affair would not start until the lunch bunch had cleared out and would end before the dinner crowd swarmed in. 2-4 p.m. was the agreed-upon window.

As for décor, the restaurant had insisted they leave up the large Italian flag and the green and red balloons that echoed its colors—inappropriate, to say the least, for a funeral, and garish enough to make almost invisible the two dozen roses sent by Borgburg and the dainty arrangements created by Jason's partner. At full capacity, the patio sat only about ten people, but it was more than enough for Herb's limited guest list. The chairs were arranged to face the bandstand (a polka band played there on Thursday nights) and Jason had set up a cheap pasteboard podium and microphone for anyone who wanted to speak.

On the day, Herb rose from maybe an hour's sleep—his cascading tears and bubbling snot more like an allergy attack than grieving—and forced himself into what Joanne had always referred to as his now aptly named "funeral suit."

Jason, ever dutiful—now acting almost like a son—fetched Herb for the ceremony and gently walked him to a seat toward the rear of the assembled guests. There weren't many:

Mr. Blankenship—mailman
The Baumgardners—next door neighbors
Allison Krepp—book club member
Jason

Jason began the ceremony with a few generic platitudes—he had never met any of the women and was hard-pressed to embellish his remarks. He indicated to all that it was an "open mic." The first to rise was Ed Blankenship, their mailman.

Ed commented on Belle's pleasant voice (he had heard her through the closed door but had never actually set eyes on her) and Joanne's sweet smile. He also praised Joanne for always remembering him with a fat envelope at Christmas time, adding how she adjusted his tip each year, which showed an awareness of the world of economics. Every time he referred to Joanne by name, it was as Mrs. Joanne Miller, 2461 Miller Street, Elyria, Ohio, 44035. He ended his remarks by saying that he was sure that Mr. Herb Miller, 2461 Miller Street, Elyria, Ohio, 44035 would miss her.

Next up were the Baumgardners. They were older, and frightened by the microphone, but managed to say that they appreciated looking out their window at the well-kept front lawn of the Millers and especially liked her new drapes.

Allison Krepp then took the mic. She had known Joanne a few years back when they were both in a book club. They had since drifted apart, but she still had some memories of how Joanne could "read between the lines," "tell you the whole plot and not ruin the ending," and, most impressive to Allison, "actually *could* judge a book by its cover!"

The podium sat unattended for a few minutes and there was a general sense that the event had drawn to a close. Amidst the rustle of departure, the finding of hats and purses, no one noticed when the slight Filipino man entered the room and ascended the stage. "Testing," he said tentatively into the microphone, and the mourners sat back down. Herb, who had been sobbing continuously, stopped for a moment in wonder. Why was the cab driver here?

Hajda began his prepared speech. Harkening back to his days with Adult Protective Services, he fondly remembered Joanne and her great concern for Herb during his Alzheimer's phase. How giving she was. How selfless. He was eloquent. There was even the injection of a humorous anecdote to soften the moment. A great speech, except for one problem: He had typed it. His "typing Tourettes" revealed itself three minutes into his testimonial, when he dropped the f-bomb five times in a six-word sentence. The mourners were speechless. It was when he called the restaurant a "dago shithole" that the owner ripped the microphone from his hand and ordered everybody out.

Jason grabbed the three jade-green plastic urns in one arm and Herb in the other and drove him back to Miller Street.

· · · ·

Alone now, Herb was cried out, hollow. He looked in the pantry for anything alcoholic, thinking, This is the time when anyone in their right mind would get drunk. Cooking sherry. That was it. So, though he'd never done anything like this before, he set off, on foot, for the Shangri Lounge. He walked the two miles with swarms of thoughts: thoughts of loss, thoughts of possibility, thoughts of past and future, moments wasted, chances taken, mistakes made. The man who thought he could fool them all now felt the fool. He tried to mold these thoughts into a semblance of sense and direction. He was unable. He tried to mold them into a prayer. None came to him. By then, he was through the door of the tavern.

· · · ·

And now here he was, sleeping like a slobbering baby in his BarcaLounger. Hajda watched Herb's chest rise and fall with each snore. He felt terrible about his blurting out at the memorial. It was a disease. He'd meant well, and it had gone south in a heartbeat. He wanted to make it up to Herb somehow but couldn't think of anything. I'll just stay here with him for a while, he thought, make sure he's okay. After a moment, he rose from the couch, knelt in front of Herb, and gently removed Herb's shoes, setting them neatly by his chair. There, he thought, I've actually performed a real adult protective service.

And the drunken birthday boy dreamt of Bora Bora.

. . . .

Hajda had become almost like a son after the memorial disaster (perhaps in atonement for the locker-room language of his oration). It was he, alone, who helped Herb with the difficult task of deciding which relics of Belle and Joanne's lives to keep, what to donate, what just needed cleaning, and what to trash. Joanne's clothes found a home with the homeless. (Belle's were bagged and tossed without ceremony.) The hardest part for Herb was realizing that virtually everything in the Miller Street house had Joanne's fingerprints on it, her smell, the enduring reminders of her peculiar tastes. She had chosen the drapes, the couch, the towels, the bedding, the plates, the silverware, everything. It was her voice on their answering machine.

Miller's Island

Hajda never stopped working. He pushed and pulled his way through Herb's bouts of nostalgia and melancholy and, thanks to his efforts, every Tuesday when the garbage trucks came by, there were five or six more hefty bags waiting at the curb for pickup. Soon the place was as generic and impersonal as a home "staged" for a real-estate showing. It felt cavernous, anonymous, and, as much as Hajda had insisted it promised a "new beginning," Herb was unmotivated. He would sit for hours in his BarcaLounger (the one thing he had picked out himself) listening to his chat shows on his transistor radio and counting on Hajda to bring him a pizza.

Hajda watched this downward spiral with a heavy heart and decided it was time to put on his "Adult Protective Services" hat.

"What are you thinking?" Hajda asked as Herb bit into his pizza.

"I'm thinking I should have jumped in after her," Herb said.

"Well, I, for one, am glad you didn't. You have a lot of life ahead of you, my friend."

"Bullshit!" blurted Herb. "I have *old age* ahead of me. That's it! Feebleness, aches and pains, dry rot—and now nobody to complain to."

They sat silently while Herb chewed. Hajda considered his next move.

"Have you thought about going back to work?" he ventured tentatively.

"You're kidding, right? God, Hajda, you don't get it, do you! I'm *done!* It's curtains for me," he said (amazing himself that he had resorted to such a tired old saw to express his feelings of doom. I've become an old fart, he thought).

Hajda smiled, knowingly. "There! Do you see what you just did? You heard me say the word 'work' and you immediately went to the word 'curtains'! Your subconscious still relates to your job, Herb! You know what they say... You can take the shower curtain out of the country, but you can't take the..."

Herb popped his eyes and mouth open in mock, theatrical astonishment. "My God!! You're right! And I'm eating pizza because it's warm, wet, and 'V' shaped!! I must *subconsciously* need a woman! Probably an Italian!"

Hajda was visibly hurt. "I'm just trying to help, Herb."

Herb could see he'd gone too far and placed his hand on Hajda's shoulder like a father consoling his son after a Little League loss. "You *have* helped, Hajda. A great deal. I couldn't have gotten this place sorted out without you." With his hand still on Hajda's shoulder, he gently guided him toward the door. "I truly appreciate your concern."

"Will you at least think about it?" asked Hajda, as he stepped into the night.

"Of course," said Herb, and he closed the door.

. . . .

But he didn't think about it. His brain was going a mile a minute in a different direction.

He was in full soul-search mode—laying his life on the table like a ledger at an audit. He looked at everything he had ever been and done and conceded that he had made mistakes. Many of them. And, to his credit, he thought, he had (perhaps bumblingly, desperately, at times maybe even dishonestly) rectified most of the errors and forged ahead. It was not a brutal self-assessment—he was kind enough to himself to allow that certain missteps were normal growing pains, that others were the luck-of-the-draw results of bravery and risk-taking. The biggest regret that he had was the bogus Alzheimer's fiasco. He had wanted a situation where he could be left alone, completely and utterly, and had foolishly chosen "disease" as the meal ticket. He should have known that disease is a magnet. People flock to disease: wives, doctors, specialists, social workers, even strangers with morbid curiosities. Worse than simply acting concerned and probing for information, the healthy seem to enjoy a certain empowerment from the fact that they are *not* sick. They're all over you. So you end up in a place like Golden Slumbers. There had to be a better way.

. . . .

Returning to his hobo-guru's sage advice about being an island, Herb realized that he didn't just want to *be* an island, he wanted to live on one. In his fantasies, he had always pictured the classic Robinson Crusoe scenario: a small, lush atoll, surrounded by emerald-green waters, teeming with tuna, and shaded from the golden sun by a grove of swaying palms. Forcing himself to see the less fanciful side of the coin, he had to concede that, in the eyes of a more straitlaced, more materialistic man, his tropical paradise would be seen as merely a piece of deserted real estate, just a pile of sand in the water. And that's when it hit him. It needn't be defined by limited acreage, climate, or being surrounded on all sides by water. An island can take other forms. What was Howard Hughes's high-rise Vegas hideaway? What was Buckingham Palace for the queen? The Vatican for the Pope? Oh, sure, they made a few token excursions into the fray, but, for the most part, they lived insular lives. He decided that the Miller Street house would be his island. His brown and dying front and back yards: his roaring surf. His maple tree: his palm.

He went a bit over the edge, clearing everything from the living room save his BarcaLounger. The living room would be his beach. (He even went so far as to randomly scatter plates and saucers on the floor to replicate seashells. He dumped boxes of sugar and salt on the floor to give his bare feet the feel of sand.) He even named the island: Millerania.

As with most men of his age, he had become a creature of comfort. He continued to sleep in his little tented bedroom, but his days were spent, sunup to sundown, basking in his BarcaLounger. His only contact with the outside world was supplied by the endless stream of radio call-in talk shows, to which he was now addicted. (He had called it quits with TV—even his beloved game shows—they were just not the same anymore. Witty, attractive, personable celebrities who had been the lifeblood of such shows as *Match Game* and *Tattletales* were gone. Now the contestants were "civilians." (*Judge Judy*, featuring the commonest of the common, bib-overall and undershirt-clad plaintiffs who swear they can't pay the $50.00 fine but have $300.00 manicures on nails as long as knitting needles. Or *Family Feud*—generations of morons willing to call out each other's shortcomings for a shot at a new Nissan: "My mother's snoring keeps the whole family awake!" "The survey will say 'mostly anal.'" Were they kidding? Wasn't that just what you turned on TV to avoid?)

Odd, then, that the talk-show callers would hold his attention so raptly. You couldn't get less "celebrity" than this underbelly of society—the maimed, bankrupt, jilted, morally bereft, and clueless dregs of humanity, who had lost even the sense of shame that keeps normal people's mouths shut.

An endless supply of people willing, in fact *eager*, to broadcast their failures and confusions, their infidelities, their inabilities to cope.

Herb's initial reaction to hearing these tales of woe had been a somewhat smug notion that, by comparison, he was in fat city. None of these losers sounded like they were lounging in a recliner at an indoor beach. He was the king of Millerania, and, as long as his problems remained less than those of the callers-in, he would remain so. The disembodied voices of the callers were his court jester, a source of amusement, of diversion. But after a few days, he started to recognize the names and voices of recurrent callers: Susan B., Alfred Z., the guy who just called himself Bozo, and felt something just shy of kinship. He wasn't sure what it was. He tried to understand the feeling in terms of his "we're all islands" philosophy, and he had to admit that these islands that suffered very severe weather (monsoons, tidal waves, and hurricanes) were a source of some odd concern. Alone on Millerania, he was insular. But he wasn't insulated. He felt for them.

He felt for Susan B. She was a regular caller to *The Ross Portman Show*. Every day, sometime between 2 and 3 p.m., Susan would take over the airwaves with sobbing descriptions of her sordid, soap-opera life. It was as if she was keeping a spoken-word diary. Poor Susan B. She had been married five times, her first husband fried by lightning on a golf course, the next three each carted off to prison for a variety of felonies, and number five a no-show on their honeymoon (he had disappeared with her maid of honor right after the ceremony and was never to be seen again). She had four preschool age children who shared her drafty, unheated mobile home. The two youngest were plagued by allergies to virtually every known substance. Her current complaint: She had received a letter from the Publisher's Clearance House Sweepstakes stating that she had won the million-dollar first prize, and then never heard another word from them. Her question for Ross: "Can they *do* that?"

Ross softly explained to her that "They do it all the time." Then, like an uncle (like a pastor, really, he was more a confessor than a radio host), he inquired of her children's health.

"Hanging in there," said Susan B.

"Well, that's something," said Ross. "I'll talk to you tomorrow."

He felt for Alfred Z. When he first heard Alfred's voice on his little transistor radio, he was certain that the man could have no problems. His voice was beautiful—rich, creamy, like hot fudge. Women would swoon, Herb thought. Herb pictured Alfred as young, well built, handsome, with blindingly white teeth and a full head of sandy hair. He was right. On top of that, Alfred was rich—born into a department-store fortune. So what was the problem? For all his other perfections, Alfred lacked the one thing that separated him from the lower primates: opposable thumbs. He didn't have them. It was a birth defect. (His uncle had the same condition.) Where thumbs should've been, Alfred had two boneless, fleshy flaps—like elongated earlobes with a useless nail on the tip. He could do nothing. Hold a spoon? A fork? He had to be fed. Drive a car? He couldn't hold the steering wheel. (Hitchhiking was obviously not an option.) Tie his shoes? Handle cash? Brush his teeth? He was paralyzed. He could dial the push-button phone to call Ross, but his mother had to hold the receiver to his ear. His complaint today? People's cruelty. So-called friends who would tell him to "Get a hold of yourself," or worse, "Get a grip!"

Ross listened. He was a very good listener (paid to listen, after all). He would hold his comments until he could say something that would lighten the caller's burden—something more matter-of-fact, but still respectful, that might help the caller through the day.

"When they say something like that, give them a 'thumbs down.' You only need gravity to do that," Ross said, warmly.

. . . .

Alfred was the last caller of the day, so Herb decided to go to bed. He slept at odd hours these days—being alone, he had no schedule to follow.

He had no to-do list. He slept like the proverbial log. And the dreams! Such dreams!! These were not pedestrian "we were in this big house," "my father had a horse's head" dreams—they were production numbers: epic technicolor travelogues invariably set in balmy tropical landscapes.

He spent as much time asleep as he did awake, so reality could go either way. He could easily assume that the brick-and-mortar reality of his actual situation was the dream and the dream the reality. One morning he awoke (or did he?) and, upon opening his eyes, he saw blue sky where the ceiling should've been. He craned his neck to look around and noticed that the walls were now tropical shrubbery. He heard waves crashing in the living room. He went into the kitchen and discovered it was no longer a kitchen—it was a tiki bar nestled under a palm, azure waters lapping at the bamboo barstools. The air smelled of saltwater. He heard gulls. His gaze led him to the window where he saw the passing cars and vans transformed into a breathtaking display of leaping and frolicking dolphins, the lumbering busses now mammoth whales, bursting from the water to spew their geysers of exhale. He saw his beloved briefcase and felt no connection—now merely a piece of driftwood. (There was a part of him, a sliver of sanity, that knew this was all fantasy, as make-believe as any child's bogeyman under the bed, but he stifled it. If sanity were to retake the reins, then this whole tropical paradise would revert to the colorless, suburban, one-size-fits-all tract home on Miller Street. Who in their right mind wouldn't take their own private island over a prefab in a subdivision? More, accurately, who in their *wrong* mind. Sanity be damned!!)

He tore down one of the blue floral drapes in the living room, wrapped it around his pasty, naked body like a sarong, settled into his BarcaLounger, and turned on his radio. (He now saw his radio as a ship-to-shore instrument that had fortuitously washed to shore after a shipwreck.) It was his only lifeline to the real world.

The first caller was Bozo. Bozo fancied himself a poet. His problem (and the reason he called Russ—sometimes as often as three times a day) was a nagging inability to come up with the right word. He was synonym-challenged. "Ross, what's another word for 'meat?'" he asked. Ross offered him: beef, pork, mutton, veal, venison, steak, hamburger, and brisket. "No," he said to each offering, "not the word I'm looking for." Ross offered him tenderloin, filet, T-bone, flank, giblet, sausage, sweetbreads, weenies. "Nope," said Bozo, who shifted to another verbal dilemma. "Can you give me another word for 'afternoon?'" he asked.

"Late afternoon or early?" Russ asked patiently.

"I'm not sure. It depends on the word for 'meat'," said Bozo.

That was the verbal ping-pong Herb was absorbing when his doorbell rang.

In his deranged state, Herb thought it was a ship's siren, a signal of distress from some wayward sailor, adrift for days and ripe for rescue. Eager to play the hero, he went to his front door (the "dock" in his current imaginations) and opened it. It was a woman!! He was completely unprepared for such a sight, and it threw him deeper into his delirium. "A mermaid!!" Herb exclaimed. "A beautiful mermaid has swum to shore to share her carnal delights with the lovelorn castaway!! Oh, my lady of dark and sultry eyes and amazing pink and purple spiked hair, welcome!!"

It was Herb's long-lost niece, Malaysia Rain, and she had a suitcase.

She stepped inside and took a quick look at the plate and saucer-strewn living room.

"Uncle Herb?!!" she said, startled.

Herb opened his arms in a gesture that offered an embrace and his sarong fell to the floor.

"WHAT THE FUCK?!!" Malaysia screamed.

Her scream was warranted. He made quite a sight—three-months' worth of unshaven beard and uncut hair sitting on top of roll after roll of unwashed flesh. And dead center, the little pink nose peeking out from a thatch of greying pubic hair.

"WHAT THE FUCKING FUCK?!!!" Malaysia screamed again, dropping her suitcase and, as if knowing intuitively where to go, running to the safety of the master bedroom. (She would later see the irony of seeking sanctuary in the very room where her mother had taken a bullet between the eyes.) She quickly locked the door. Herb followed her, tried the door, then knocked gently. "Are you alright?" he asked stupidly. Her only response was more wailing and sobbing.

He sat all night outside her door, not making a sound, just waiting and listening until, finally, her sobbing subsided. He wasn't sure if mermaids slept. What did they eat? Did they need to be in water? Should he run a tub? He wasn't sure of anything right now.

When morning came, he heard rustling in the room, then the mermaid's voice as it rose and shattered into frantic curses, desperate pleas, and subsided back into deep, guttural sobbing. Herb had no idea what to do. Here he was, the king of Millerania, and he was helpless. He held the power of good and evil, right and wrong, the permitted and the taboo, and he couldn't even deal with a crying mermaid. *Some king!* he thought. He wracked his brain for any solution to the hysterical mermaid problem. Who would know what to do? As he tied his sarong back around his bulbous girth and made his way to the BarcaLounger, the answer came to him. Ross Portman would know!!

He had been a loyal and dedicated listener, never missing a word of Ross Portman's radio wisdom. But the idea of being a "caller" was terrifying.

Miller's Island

It was not just the fear of blowing his cover (there *was* a tiny bit of that). Mostly he feared the judgements of other listeners who would call after he'd hung up and voice their two cents about something they couldn't possibly understand. He'd heard that scenario played out many times. There were a lot of stupid islands out there. But his emergency was the definition of emergency. He had no choice. He had to call.

Somehow, he remembered that his old flip phone was still in the vest pocket of his "funeral" suit. Like a madman on a scavenger hunt, he rummaged in the boxes that held his clothes and found his phone. Miracle upon miracle, it still held a charge. He made the call.

"You're on the air with Ross Portman. What's up?" crooned the seasoned voice through his standard opening. Herb took the deepest breath of his life.

"Hello, my name is Herb M." Herb paused a moment to decide how much to reveal and decided to reveal all of it. "I am the king of the island nation of Millerania and there is a beautiful mermaid locked in my dead wife's bedroom. She ran in there when she saw me naked. I think I might be her uncle."

Before Herb had even gotten to the word "uncle," the studio engineer (who had been trained to do so in emergencies) traced the call to Herb's address and notified the police and the mental health authorities. The engineer then made circular motions with his finger to let Ross know he should keep Herb on the line and Ross nodded in understanding.

"The mermaid *ran* into the bedroom?" Ross asked, like it was a normal question. "I didn't think mermaids had legs." Herb took the bait. My god, he thought, I'm on with Ross Portman!

"I know," said Herb. "And I didn't know that mermaids had pink and purple hair! There's so much we can learn from nature!"

They bantered like this for several minutes before Herb heard the loud banging on his front door. "I have to go now. Thanks for listening, Ross," he said, and hung up.

. . . .

It took months of legal wrangling and botched bureaucracy, but Malaysia (who changed her name back to Maryanne and her hair back to brown) was given title to the Miller Street house. She transformed it back into a home and lived there alone— though she had ventured out for two dinners with Hajda, whom she found curious and a bit exotic.

. . . .

Herb's old room at Golden Slumbers was taken, but his new one was identical. They all were. Herb was given a smorgasbord of drugs in hopes of lessening his delusions. He held the pills under his tongue and deposited them into the toilet after the nurse had left. He didn't see his fantasies as delusions. He saw them as adventures—a flailing out against a life sentence that would have otherwise made him just another old accountant who loses his sight, his hearing, his color, who marks his mornings by new aches and pains, who stares at a TV and watches his country morph into a youth-filled, thankless mayhem, and quietly dies of something unchic.

He still had his transistor radio and listened to Ross every night as he went to sleep. Tonight's caller had a different message. He asked Ross if he would be permitted a success story in lieu of the usual tale of woe. Ross was delighted to give him the airtime.

His name was Walter H., and he was the CEO of a chain of sporting goods stores: a multimillionaire. But years ago, he had been down and out, homeless and penniless. Sitting around a hobo's campfire one night, a complete stranger whom he had befriended suddenly thrust a twenty-dollar bill into his hand and told him to "Go buy a soccer ball." He did. And the rest was history. He'd always wanted to find the man and thank him but never could.

Herb held his little radio to his ear and listened to Walter H.'s tale of unexpected windfall. A small smile crept across his face. For a moment, he toyed with calling in and identifying himself as the good Samaritan with the twenty. No, he thought, some things are better left as myth, as fairy tale, as the inexplicable whim of an unpredictable God. He closed his eyes and slipped into the deepest of sleeps.

    HERBERT L. MILLER
    JUNE 3, 1946—NOVEMBER 23, 2019

CONCESSION

He was losing the election. Well, not him, personally. The guy he voted for.

Truth be told, he wasn't that crazy about either of the guys who were running, didn't really have a dog in the fight, was just exercising what he'd been taught was his civic duty—and, though, long ago, experience had shown him that his vote didn't *really* count, regardless of how constantly the candidates said it did, a part of him wanted to be a good citizen. Whatever that was.

No matter who wins, he thought, they'll end up being the same guy in four years, eight if they don't fuck up too bad. Either one would eventually become an old, bromide spewing, mouthpiece for lobbyists, big-money campaign contributors, this or that union; stoking fear that so-and-so now has nuclear capability, that the sky is falling, and, probably, espousing whatever *cause celebre* their much-younger wife had currently adopted: hearing ear dogs for the deaf, for instance. So, big deal.

So, why then, if he really didn't give a shit, was he now watching the returns on his flat-screen as

Concession

diligently as he was? Because it was an event. It was like sports. He loved watching sports. And also because there was nothing else on. Every network had the same thing playing. Heavily made-up, Armani-clad news-anchors, all of them prancing around digital screens showing states, counties, red and blue swaths of countryside, and numbers that seemed to change as slowly and inaccurately as weather forecasts. Every network the same, save one: an obscure cable channel that offered infomercials for dog blankets, acne medications, garage-door openers, and Russian nesting dolls. Unwatchable. So he stuck with the returns.

Though the talking heads and prognosticators all seemed to be interchangeable, the predictions and body counts differed from one network to another. One would have his candidate in a neck and neck, while the other had him losing in a landslide. He decided to stick with the landslide channel, hoping it would be the first to air the concession speech. He loved the concession speeches. There was something about watching a person admit defeat on a grand scale that made the losses in his own life seem diminished, more manageable. And, certainly, more private.

The TV folks must have shared his appetite for the loser's mea culpa, he thought. They kept switching their feed to his streamer-draped, balloon-filled ballroom; the empty, waiting podium; the long-faced supporters milling about aimlessly, now wearing their buttons, badges, and banners like a scarlet letter. Roving cub reporters would corner dejected would-be partygoers and ask them the stupidest questions: "Did you see this coming?" "Are you sad?" "Will you be moving to Europe?" Most of them would just shrug their shoulders and lumber off past the bandstand where the musicians sat quietly, wishing they could smoke.

Why haven't these people taken off their buttons, badges, and sashes and, with hanging heads, gone back to their homes and called it a night? For the same reason that they stand ten-deep around car accidents, watching as the Fire Department plies the jaws of life to extract some miserable son of a bitch with a steering wheel through his sternum. The reason they watch the locker-room interview with the *losing* team. Because it puts you in your place. It makes you count your blessings that it's not you who has engendered mass disappointment. Not you who is going to have to somehow explain to millions of people that their five- and ten-dollar campaign donations (five- and ten-dollars? Are you kidding? Some gave thousands, millions even) weren't just pouring money down a rathole. And I'll bet neither of them spend all of it on the campaign, he reckoned. I'll bet they both salt away a chunk in case they don't win. Maybe even *know* they won't win and start stashing it on day one. Maybe the whole thing is rigged from the get-go. Maybe. And, if the guy I voted for was that crooked

Concession

to begin with, why did I vote for him? Because I thought the other guy was a bigger asshole? Maybe that was it. The other guy certainly *was* an asshole, no question, but a bigger one? Jesus, he thought, that was my choice? The smaller of two assholes?

Maybe, he thought, it wasn't a matter of asshole diameter. Maybe it was just that he felt he had a little more in common with William Borden, the guy he'd voted for, than Kendall Murphy, the guy he didn't. Well, first, there was the name thing. He was Billy Mott. Billy—short for William—and though he'd been a Billy for all of his seventy-one years, he was technically a William. So there was that. Borden was also seventy-one, so throw that into the mix. As far as platform went, he had no real idea what either of them had in mind for the country. The speeches were all pretty much the same: bromides, bumper-sticker slogans, undeliverable promises, and pathetic attempts to seem like "regular folks." They'd both visited assembly lines and looked like the guy in The Village People in their hard hats; they'd both had a hamburger at some greasy-spoon diner in some agricultural crossroads; they'd both tried to master a few words of Spanish.

So what was the difference? What was the deciding factor that made him vote for Borden? The question nagged him as he watched the two candidates in their election night headquarters. Then he saw it. He saw why he had voted for Borden. Borden seemed more exhausted. He seemed too tired to ever do anything if he was elected. He'd let things stay the same.

Billy liked that. He was perfectly content with the way things were with his country. (Murphy used the word "change" a little too often for Billy's taste.) Change? What are you talking about? Change *what?* Billy Mott liked the *status quo*. As far as he was concerned, the *status* should be even more *quo*. In Billy's opinion, it was an "if it ain't broke" situation, and it wasn't broke. He had no complaints. He'd had a reasonably good life—not one filled with limousines and tuxedos, but who would want *that*?

His country had treated him fairly. He went to public schools, elementary and high. If his grades were such that college was out of the question, well, that was *his* fault, not his country's. He had volunteered for the Army, and was told that, at five feet two, he was too short. (He was a late-bloomer, not reaching his full five feet five until he was in his mid-twenties.) He opted for trade school (or, as he liked to call it, "Technical" school—it sounded smarter, sounded like it might involve math or a science of some sort). So he wasn't book-smart, so what? So he didn't know who T.S. Eliot was. (He once saw a book of T.S. Eliot's on his son's desk and wondered what the hell his full name was—he decided it was Tom Sam Eliot.)

He discovered he had a way with motors. The spark plugs, carburetors, pistons and cylinders all made sense to him. He did his "thesis" in lawn-

Concession

mower repair and got his certificate. He never met a mower he couldn't fix. Piece of cake. He could do it in five minutes and do it blindfolded. (His skill was such that he had to charge by the job—if he charged by the hour he'd be broke in a day.) And because people could always be counted on to run over stones or sprinkler heads, to leave their mowers out in a driving rain, to let them rust away, untended, during snow season, he had a job.

By the age of twenty-five (and finally his full five feet five), he decided to pursue the American dream with vigor. He opened his own shop. *Vrooom!* was the name of his company, so named for the mouth sound he always made when he proudly started up his customer's repaired mowers. He made a decent living, paid his taxes, and managed to save enough to buy a double-wide with a garage and a small lawn. (Needless to say, his lawn was mown to perfection.) He knew he'd never become a rich man, but he'd always have food on the table. Work, dinner, TV, bed. His life had assumed an almost military regularity. Then he met Charlotte.

Oh, my dear Charlotte, he thought, as he looked at the matching recliner next to his, the one with the embroidered "Mama Bear" pillow. How he missed Charlotte. It had been two years now since the cancer had invaded her pancreas and then spread like wildfire, touching places that he felt were his alone to touch. He didn't want to think about her like that. Certainly didn't want to think about those last days, his Charlotte tented in steamy hospital plastic, tubes running in and out, filling her with poison, flushing her of life. No, he didn't want to go there.

Instead he remembered the good times. He remembered all those nights she had spent watching the election returns with him. Like himself, she felt a certain disconnect from the proceedings. Didn't root for either of the men running. Her idea of a president was someone like Jefferson, Washington, Lincoln. Someone whose picture was on money. (He remembered the day when Kennedy had been shot. The lady next door had run into their yard screaming, "They killed our PRESIDENT!!!" Charlotte had absorbed that information and then stated flatly, "Well, then maybe it's time we didn't have one.") Yeah, she was one of a kind.

Billy could count on non sequiturs like that. She would let him listen to the news folk, their predictions and analyses, and then, during the commercials, offer some observation about a candidate's haircut or the lack of eye contact between the candidate and his wife. She had a great bullshit-detector, could cut to the chase in an instant. And she had loved him. He never questioned that. She would bring him his beers, his Cheetos. All that was changed now. *Change*. How could Murphy want change when all it ever brought was grief?

There. He had his reasons, and he'd cast his vote. Now all that was left was to watch the returns

Concession

and see how little his vote mattered. He lowered his recliner another notch and waited for the concession speech.

Three beers and half a bag of Cheetos and still no concession speech. However, the numbers in the bottom third of the TV screen were now jumping around, flicking forward as quickly as the gallon/price readout on a gas pump. Now, even the channel that had Borden headed out to pasture in a landslide showed the gap narrowing. It was almost midnight. Three hours later than his normal bedtime. And, here in Texas, I'm two hours ahead of them, he mused, no wonder Borden looks so exhausted. And the numbers kept changing.

He had turned the sound down a while ago, but seeing what seemed like a renewed excitement amongst the newscasters, he turned it back up. Thinking, maybe it *is* going to be a horse race, maybe I can get interested enough that I'll stop thinking about Charlotte, knowing that he would *always* be thinking of Charlotte. She had been his whole world, had given him a son who *was* college material, who had a degree in something Billy didn't understand, *bio*-something, who couldn't wait to move to New York, who called on his father's birthday, Christmas, who was far from a chip off the old block, and had to be cajoled many times by his mother into at least being civil with his father. Charlotte had a way with him. She had a way with everyone. They broke the mold with Charlotte. God, how he missed her.

He returned his gaze to the screen. Something was afoot. He tried to put Charlotte out of his mind, to concentrate on what the talking heads were saying. "Down to the wire," one said. "Anyone's ball game," said another. Billy tried to follow the flickering numbers, the lower-third super of info. Apparently, Guam was still uncounted, as was North Dakota. A freak, early-November blizzard had hit the state, making any form of travel out of the question. Walk-in voters had turned tail from the polls, fearing frostbite, unwilling to exchange fingers or toes for a voice in Washington. Mail-in ballots would have to be delivered by sled. North Dakota never seemed like a real place to Billy, so he couldn't understand how it could be such a big deal.

. . . .

2:30 in the morning. He hadn't been up this late since he and Charlotte had attended the New Year's party at the country club. He wasn't a member, nowhere near wealthy enough to ever be. He had merely serviced their golf course mowers and this invite was just their way of fishing for a discount on next year's repairs. He had known that, but they went anyway. Hey, free drinks? Are you kidding?

2:30, and now the talking heads had outlived their makeup—their faces etched with powder-encrusted lines, their hairdos gone flat as a failed soufflé. Human after all, he smiled to himself.

Concession

They no longer were even trying to be unbiased. Their ecumenical, one-size-fits-all, "voice of everyman" posture had been eroded by too many hours of filling dead air. Some were now unabashedly for Borden. Others shamelessly pro-Murphy. Each extolling the virtues of their man and belittling the opposition. If this broadcast went another hour it could get ugly. Come on, North Dakota! Come on Guam! Let's wrap this thing up!

Something was happening. From seemingly out of nowhere, Borden was garnering votes. Out of what had seemed like a cakewalk for Murphy, a tortoise-and-hare situation had arisen. It was a dead heat. Popular and electoral college votes in a virtual tie.

He was headed into the kitchen for another beer when his phone rang. "Who the hell?" he wondered aloud, picking up the receiver.

"Dad?" It was Billy Jr. "Are you awake?"

"I answered the phone, Billy, so yes, I'm awake."

"Oh, Jesus, Dad," Billy Jr. blurted. "I'm scared shitless."

The three beers instantly lost their effect; Billy was cold sober, concerned.

"Why? Is there someone outside trying to break in? Are there shadows in the yard? Someone trying your doorknob? Did you call 911?" Billy Sr. asked, trying to keep his rising panic from his voice.

"No, it's bigger than that."

"Is it one of your kids? Sue Ann or Willy? Is it your wife?"

"Judy... She has a *name*, Dad."

"Don't act like that. I *know* her name. Is it *her*? Is it Judy? What is it?"

"What *is* it?!! Jesus!! Are you *watching!!!?*"

"The returns? Yes, I'm watching. I'm waiting for the concession speech," Billy said, relieved that his son's house was not on fire. He opened his beer and took a long pull.

"I hope you mean *Borden's* concession speech!!" Billy Jr. all but yelled. "He *can't* win, Dad. He just *can't!!* He's against everything we're for!!"

"Who's *we*?" said Billy Sr.

Billy Jr. blew out a long, exasperated breath.

"Who's *WE*, Dad? *WE* are anyone who has a brain! Don't you watch the news? Don't you read the papers? Murphy's trying to save the planet and Borden just wants to sit on his ass. He wants to send us back to 1950!"

"I had a good time in 1950," Billy Sr. stated, nostalgically.

"Oh my God, I can't believe we're having this conversation!" said Billy Jr.

"Can I just say something?" Billy Sr. asked, slowing his speech to a fatherly pace.

"Please don't say something stupid," said Billy Jr.

"I'm going to say what I have to say, and when I'm done, you can decide for yourself if it's stupid or

Concession

not. I don't really care." He took another long pull on his beer, his speech fermenting as he swallowed.

"I'm guessing you're on a cell phone. Well, I'm on a landline. That right there should tell you something. I'm also guessing that you're standing in your stainless-steel and granite kitchen next to that meadow-sized island with the built-in wine cooler fridge, and that the other fridge is wall-sized and has nothing in it but kale, kohlrabi, wheat germ, bean sprouts and yogurt, and that for all the cupboards you have, there is nothing with gluten. I'm going to keep guessing. I'm guessing that there's a cutesy little bulletin board with schedules for yoga classes pinned to it. And I'm guessing there are five different garbage cans, one for metal, one for glass, one for white paper, one for colored paper, one for cardboard. I'm guessing that the pajamas you're wearing are made from recycled hemp, and that your slippers are ergonomically designed and made by hand in a commune in Vermont. How'm I doing? Let's go outside. I'd bet the ranch that your car is electric. And so is Joan's. I'm sorry: *Judy's*. Now, let's look around the yard. Your pool: solar heated? I'll bet it is. And, last but not least, your lawn. I'll bet you've never mowed it yourself. Did I get any of this right?"

"Dad, are you drunk?" Billy Jr. asked, in lieu of an answer to the lawn mowing question.

"No. I'm not drunk. I'm just in a mood. I've been thinking about your mother," Billy Sr. said, climbing back down from his tirade. Mention of his mother usually put Billy Jr. in a position where he didn't know what to say. Not tonight.

"*Mom* would have voted for *Murphy!!!*" Billy Jr. blurted.

"You don't *know* that," said Billy Sr. "You don't even know for sure who *I* voted for. This is America. Votes are secret!"

And then Billy Jr screamed, "*SHIT!!!!*" and hung up.

The reason Billy Jr. screamed was right there on the TV. North Dakota had somehow managed to count enough votes to indicate a decisive trend in Borden's favor, and Guam had thrown the final log on the fire. Borden had won!

The younger news anchors looked shaken, as if they'd been blindsided, mugged in an alley. The older ones looked tired and occasionally a little smug. They announced the final tally and went on to say that Murphy would be addressing his flock shortly. Borden's acceptance speech would wait until Murphy was done. (Billy was certain that Borden would use that time for a nap.)

So here it was, finally, the long-awaited concession speech. It called for one last beer. Billy opened it and settled into his recliner.

Murphy looked like he'd been shipwrecked. His top-of-the-line suit now hanging on him like a tropical moss. His smile, still illuminated by his too-white teeth, now seemed applied, ironed on,

Concession

a rictus of false bravery. He thanked everyone he could think of, praised them for their support, their diligence, their wisdom in seeing the future for what it could be. He hugged his red-eyed wife (whose hair had miraculously not moved since the morning news shows), and suffered his antsy, preschool age children to his side like a savior manqué. By the end of his remarks, there seemed to be a slightly tearful tinge to his voice. He never mentioned Borden by name. He ended his speech with a prayer. An odd prayer, in that it never mentioned God or even America, just "our planet" and "the collective souls of our heaving masses." Amen.

Billy watched the whole thing. As concession speeches went, he would have to give it a seven. No, a six.

And, as he watched Murphy and his family make their way off stage, his attention was drawn to his supporters on the stage behind him. They looked like a glee club, sharing an anger and disappointment that they had nothing to sing. They were every size, shape, and color imaginable, with the notable exception that none of them had gray hair. All of them were *young*. All of them. Billy Jr.'s people.

Billy turned off the TV and lumbered up to bed, knowing that in four years—a period of time that can fly past a man of his age in a nanosecond—Murphy, or someone even younger, would be President of the United States.

THE ENCORE

I had no intention of becoming a musician. I had every intention of becoming an orthodontist. Why an orthodontist? It certainly wasn't because I was thrilled with the thought of spending my functioning years up to the elbow in somebody's ramshackle mouth, bending wire around what looked like a box full of used hotel soaps, straightening incisors that stuck out like a taxicab going down Fifth Avenue with both rear doors open. Nor was it the knowledge that restructuring the bites of hundreds of preteen "Bucky Beavers" could indeed make me a wealthy man.

No, my decision to be an orthodontist wasn't based on any thinking of any sort. I never weighed the pros and cons. I accepted it as fate. Put more simply: My father was a wealthy orthodontist and he was willing to pay whatever it cost to make me one, too. In other words, a free ride. Being, as a teen, almost catatonically lazy, this exemption from responsibility appealed to me. I didn't even have to think about my future; I knew what it would be. In a dozen years or so, I would be given a document that read: Marcus Phillips, DDS. And that would be that. I would become an orthodontist. Game. Set. Match.

Then I bought a guitar.

It was the last thing in the world that I thought I'd do. Music was not a part of our household when I was growing up. My father listened to nothing but wall-to-wall news. My mother would, on rare occasions, softly croon to herself while she was puttering around our ranch-style kitchen—I assume it was a medley of 30's and 40's pop tunes—but her lack of anything resembling pitch made her efforts more akin to an asthma attack or Gregorian chant than anything recognizable. We didn't own a stereo. Unlike most teenagers, I would not blast the radio when I drove. I never even learned to whistle. Music was for other people.

So, why then, three years into my pre-med studies at Tufts did I buy a guitar? The cheap and easy answer to that question would be just to say it was peer pressure. That would be accurate to a point; it was the sixties and everyone and his brother seemed to have a moustache, long hair, and a guitar. But now, with the benefit of hindsight, I think that it was more than just wanting to fit in. It was biological. It was the mating urge. One didn't need a sociology degree to see how the sex-on-campus scene played out. Guys who could play the guitar got girls. And there was a subset of truisms under that fact: Guys who played *folk* music got the mousy, nerdier, usually overweight, "world peace" girls; guys who played rock and roll got the prettier ones. If you were in a band and the band was halfway decent, you got the halfway-hot ones. If you were in a band and it was *good*, then you got the hottest of the hot. I, of course, wanted to be on the top of that pyramid, but currently found myself as far under it as a mummified Pharaoh. I wanted the hottest of the hot. That's why I bought a guitar.

It's also why Kirk and Perry, my equally unpopular roommates, decided to follow my lead and bought their own guitars. Needless to say, the fact that we *owned* the instruments meant nothing. We were not instantly part of the in-crowd, or swarmed by adoring coeds. We had to learn to *play* the damned things. So, as our studies of gum structure, overbites, and mandibular displacement (all three of us were pre-med, orthodontia majors) fell further and further off the table, we practiced. We practiced and practiced, grew our hair and moustaches, and practiced and practiced.

We had purchased the guitars in September, and by the following April, I could manage the three chords needed for "Louie Louie" (and the five or six chords needed for most of the Rolling Stones catalog). No fancy licks, no flourishes, but competent. Kirk, on the other hand, found the guitar confounding. In his odd, mathematical and pot-enhanced logic, he reasoned that the electric bass, having two less strings than the guitar, would be one-third more learnable. He also liked the fact that the bass played only one note at a time. He traded his guitar for a Fender electric bass and soon caught up to me on the competency chart. Perry was the most musical of the three of us (thanks to his parents' insistence on childhood piano lessons), but he, too, found the guitar a daunting challenge. So Perry traded his guitar for an electric piano.

By the end of May, we had settled into our respective roles: Guitar, bass and piano. We no longer saw ourselves as orthodontia wannabes, we were rock 'n' rollers. We had become hirsute and skinny, ingesting more alcohol and pot than solid food, and carried ourselves with the tentative swagger that we associated with the uber-hip. We thought of ourselves as blood brothers in a noble cause, world-beaters despite the fact that our music had never been performed outside the confines of our shitty apartment. Night after night, we'd blast our brains on weed and play the same ten songs, over and over, into the wee small. But, even on those rare occasions when we managed a mistake-free performance of our little repertoire, we came to the same conclusion: It didn't feel like music. The three of us were not enough. We were incomplete. If we were going to change the world, then we would need a drummer and a singer.

Now, in a perfect world, I would simply go to the school bulletin board and see Post-its from a terrific drummer and a great singer who need work.

As it happened, the world was partially a perfect one: there were Post-its from both a drummer and a female singer needing work, but there was no way to know if they were any good. Just names and phone numbers. (Also, the phrase "need work" could be a stumbling block. We had no work, and probably wouldn't have any work until we had a drummer and a singer—a Catch-22 situation.)

We spent an entire evening just looking at the Post-its, smoking dope, and trying to decide what to do. Perry was worried that adding anyone to the band would upset the dynamic of our threesome. He was doubly concerned that the singer was female. He countered with the suggestion that we get an electronic drum machine and learn to sing for ourselves—forgetting, it seemed, the disastrous attempts at singing that we had already endured. Kirk and I were adamantly opposed to this idea. In the end, majority ruled. Two to one. We held sway. I volunteered to call the singer, Kirk would call the drummer. Perry would pout.

Kirk arranged to meet our would-be drummer at the lunch counter of the Greyhound Bus terminal—a scenario that suggested that this was a last-ditch effort on the part of the would-be Ringo. If the meeting went south, he'd probably hop a bus to greener pastures, become a telemarketer, marry his high school sweetheart, and have five kids. But the meeting went north. Kirk liked the guy. His name was Nathan Kaufman. He looked like Ben Stein in the *Ferris Bueller* movie, only a little shorter. For the last four months, he had been working with a bar band that was the permanent fixture at The Last Call, a local, somewhat sleazy watering hole. That sinecure came to a crashing halt two weeks later when the owner decided that the current uptick in vandalism (graffiti on every available surface, peek holes punched between the men's and women's bathrooms, a blanket of broken bottles in the parking lot) was created by the band's fanbase. "You guys draw a rough crowd" were the last words the owner said before demanding that they remove their equipment. Nathan's drums were still in the bar's basement.

Getting this information from Nathan necessitated patience, he was not a terribly talkative man. When he did speak, it was softly. Odd that a drummer, whose job was one of the noisiest one could have, would be so quiet. But, as I said, Kirk liked him.

Kirk had a VW van, a high school graduation present from his well-to-do parents, and volunteered to take Nathan to The Last Call and fetch his drums. Kirk also paid for Nathan's BLT and Sprite, no doubt giving him the false impression that there was money somewhere and that he might be getting a salary in the near future. I wasn't home when they arrived and unloaded Nathan's traps into our already-crowded apartment. I was chasing down Phoebe Nipper, the singer.

Phoebe, or "Feebs" as she preferred, was little, almost tiny, but so well-proportioned that, when seen in the selfie photographs that covered every inch of her apartment walls, she appeared full-sized and curvaceous. She was pretty. The camera liked her. So did I. I hate to use the word "bubbly" but that was what she was. She made us instant coffee, sat me on a beanbag chair, and immediately launched into her story.

She had been a theater major at Tufts and had dropped out when she got what she thought was a shoo-in audition for an Off-Broadway musical. The part was perfect for her—could have been written for her. She didn't get the part. She was stunned. It was the first time she had lost anything. Prior to this setback, she had won a baker's dozen of titles: Miss This, Miss That, gold medal in the "Tomorrow's Stars" competition sponsored by Alcoa Aluminum (her father was an exec at Alcoa), the list went on and on. She didn't even make understudy. But Feebs was not one to give in to failure. She subscribed to the philosophy of so many Broadway tunes that urged you to "pick yourself up, dust yourself off, and start all over again." The lyrics of those showstoppers were her Bible. She openly admitted that her forte was the Broadway song, the heart-wrenching "Climb Ev'ry Mountain" tear-jerker. She had never sung with a band, never sung rock and roll except in the shower. She was currently supporting herself as a driver for Meals on Wheels. She said she liked my moustache.

The Encore

Oh boy. The last thing we were looking for was a miniature Ethel Merman or Bernadette Peters. If she hadn't been so damned cute, I would have thanked her for her time and hit the road. Instead, I took my guitar from the case and asked her to sing for me. I tried to think of a song that might be somewhere in her ballpark and suggested the Beatle's "Yesterday." To my surprise, she not only knew it well, she sang it beautifully—an enormous voice coming out of that little frame. I'd seen and heard enough to make up my mind. We had our singer.

The first rehearsal felt like anything but. It was awkward to say the least—like how it must feel to be trapped between floors in an elevator with strangers, forced to put on a good face, to be nice to people you don't know. Perry wasn't being nice. He was being pissy, acting put-upon because Nathan's drum set took up some of the space where he usually set up his piano. He was holding on to his notion that the dynamic of the three of us was being destroyed, and may have even said something to that effect. Kirk was yammering away, almost assaulting Nathan with questions, hoping to bring Nathan out of his nonverbal shell. Nathan responded by quietly assembling and re-assembling his hi-hat. I ordered pizza.

I assumed it was the pizza guy when the doorbell rang. It was Feebs.

She was all dressed up—not like she was headed for the prom or anything, but pretty fancy. She had on a little flowered dress and platform shoes that made her almost five foot five. Her hair was piled on her head and held in place by one of those black plastic combs that flamenco dancers wear. She had on a shitload of makeup. I'm making this sound too negative. The fact was, she looked great. So good, in fact, that it took me a minute to notice that she had a bundle of sheet music in her hand.

Sheet music? Was she kidding? What did she think we were? Real musicians? Perry had maybe been forced to read music during his piano lesson days, but Kirk and I (and, I assumed, Nathan) were clueless when it came to deciphering what looked like pigeon tracks in the snow. Our inspiration didn't come from those scribbles, it came from dope. Dope and beer and trial and error.

Poor Feebs. She must have felt like the proverbial fish out of water. I could see her drinking in the sight before her—the hippie squalor, the cramped quarters, the oversized bong on the coffee table. I fully expected her to run. Nathan saved the day.

"Phoebe Nipper?" he said.

"Yes?" said Feebs, confused.

"It's Nathan. Nathan Kaufman. Remember me? I was the drummer in that Alcoa Aluminum orchestra," said Nathan.

"Oh, my God," Feebs squealed. "That was in…"

The Encore

"October 17th, 1968. You sang 'Send in the Clowns.'" said Nathan, like he was reading back the minutes of a meeting.

"Wow, you're right. Good memory," she said.

"You *won* that night!" said Nathan, smiling broadly at the memory.

"Yeah, I did," said Feebs.

And Nathan, who had seemed so tight-lipped, opened up, chatting amiably about her triumphant evening—an evening that sounded like living hell: amateur accordion players, six-year-old tap dancers, a four-hundred-pound guy who did impressions. Nathan's enthusism was enough to thaw Feeb's angst. Soon, we were all chatting it up.

Once we'd memorized each other's names and exhausted the small talk, the subject turned to music. She named a few tunes we had never heard of, we named a few that she didn't know. Stalemate? No. As anyone who has ever been in a jam session knows, when all else fails, you play the blues.

We tuned up, hit the bong (Feebs abstaining), and launched into "Stormy Monday." Feebs began to sing in a halting, gentle, almost Billie Holiday way, and then, out of nowhere, came this belting Bessie Smith growl. It was unbelievable. This little thing making that big sound.

Two hours later, we were blowing the walls out of the apartment with a throbbing version of "Satisfaction"—Feebs giving it her all, even strutting around the cramped living room like Mick Jagger.

Nathan was soaking wet, Kirk and I both complained of burnt fingers. We needed a break. While we sat there, finishing the last of the beer, Perry picked up her sheet music and looked through the selections with a knowing eye. Apparently, he knew what the scratches meant. He held up one of the sheets.

"'Bye Bye Blackbird,' you know this one?" he asked of Feebs.

"Pretty much," she said demurely.

What ensued was a version of the old standard that could have brought a stone to tears. Feebs was the real deal. More importantly, it was obvious to all of us that we were now a band.

A band, whether it's a duo or an orchestra, is made up of individuals. Each individual contributes what he or she can, and the end result, hopefully, is a sum greater than its parts. For the most part, the five of us were able to keep our personal peccadillos in check—no one fighting for solos or startime, no one assuming a leadership role. Even Perry stopped being pissy. We kept it as democratic as possible. We started talking about names for the band.

Perry wanted to call us "Ménage à cinq." Kirk hated the name. He thought the whole French thing was pretentious and I tended to agree with him.

"Sank?" I said, pronouncing it correctly.

"It means five," Perry said with a pedantic sigh.

"Then why not just say 'five?'" said Kirk.

"Ménage à 'five,' that's a terrible name," said Perry.

"I agree," I said.

"Does 'The Orthodontics' do anything for anybody?" Kirk asked. No one even bothered to respond.

"I got it," said Nathan, unexpectedly. "Feebs, Dweebs, and a Hebe!"

There was a moment of stunned silence before we realized he wasn't serious. Then we all laughed.

And so it went, well into the night, the four men stoned as geese, throwing out one bad name after another. We loaded up the bong for one last go-round and again offered it to Feebs who declined.

"No thanks," she said. "Sorry to be the odd man out."

"Odd *woman* out," Perry corrected her. His words hung in the air for a second.

"That's it!" I almost shouted. "*Odd Woman Out*." That's our name!"

Maybe it was the hour, maybe it was how hammered we were, but we all agreed. Odd Woman Out. It had a ring to it. We were now a band with a name.

One thing the members of OWO (because, of course, you need an acronym) shared was a healthy work ethic. For the next three months, rehearsal seemed virtually nonstop. We were actually getting good. Our repertoire was essentially the hits of the day, a decent cache of material if the goal is to be a bar band. We, of course, wanted to be more than that. Copy bands were a dime a dozen. Sure the

Beatles started out that way but… No, we needed our own material. Nathan had tried to write a few tunes (well, "tunes" would be inaccurate. Being a drummer, his "songs" were atonal—rhythms rather than melodies—and being preternaturally nonverbal, he was at a loss for lyrics.) Kirk, Perry, and I tried our hand, but had equally bad luck. Our efforts were stilted, trite, and decidedly amateur. Dope didn't help. Booze didn't help. At the end of each laughably unproductive "writing session" we all were faced with the undeniable truth that we were pretenders—that the best our little combo could ever hope for would be to roughly mimic other truly creative people. Lennon and McCartney we were not.

Then, because sometimes the unthinkable happens, Feebs dropped acid.

You heard me right. Little Miss "no thank you" when it came to smoking dope, little Miss "maybe half a beer" when it came to alcohol, went the full monty. LSD!! One day she didn't show up for rehearsal, wasn't answering her phone, and, concerned about her, we decided to make a wellness check. The door to her apartment was open, and when we went in, we saw her sitting on the floor, surrounded by reams of paper—she had been writing songs. Tons of them. She told us, very matter-of-factly, that a little door had opened on the top of her head and the music had just poured in. She made it sound like the most natural thing in the world.

The Encore

With the exception of being barefoot (she never went barefoot because of her height), she seemed perfectly normal, perfectly sane. Had she not told us that she had taken the drug, no one would have guessed. She proudly showed us the lyrics and sang a few of the melodies. They were great.

We were blown away. She still had a few more to sing for us when she suddenly announced that she was very, very tired and disappeared into her bedroom. We carefully collated and sorted the various papers, knowing that it was our goldmine and, genuinely concerned for her well-being, waited until she woke from her nap. Seven hours later, she emerged from her room. She was the old Feebs.

We had the old Feebs. We had the new songs.

Since Feebs did not play an instrument herself, it took a bit of trial and error, and a lot of patience on her part, to convey the melodies and chord structures to the band. She would sing her songs over and over and we would improvise behind her until she said that we had it right. We never worked harder.

Oddly enough, given the psychedelic source, the songs were solid. The lyrics were not blown-mind ramblings—no references to unicorns, vibrations, or third eyes—just good music, in a variety of tempos and genres. After discarding a few ballads that we all (including Feebs) deemed a little too precious, too Broadway, we still had enough material for two, hour-long sets. We were ready to grab the world by the balls and swing it. Now we needed a gig.

Kirk, Perry, and I were still technically enrolled at Tufts, even though we rarely went to class and were fully prepared to flunk out. We didn't care. We were OWO, not DDS. Despite our absence on campus, we still had a few friends who were students in good standing. One such friend was Warren Berkman. Warren was a business major who would come around now and then and listen to the band rehearsing. He became a fan. He was also part of the Winterfest planning committee. Winterfest was a semester-ending gala at Tufts that culminated with a concert by a big-name band. This year it was to be The Young Rascals, who were still milking the dregs of a one-hit wonder career. Warren had the idea that OWO should be the opening act and set to work to make that a reality. He proved tenacious, a real carnivore when it came to business, and was able to coax the others on the Winterfest committee to at least come hear a rehearsal. They did, liked what they heard, and the deal was done. We would be the opening act for The Young Rascals at Winterfest. We were ecstatic.

. . . .

The Winterfest committee had done their best to transform the Tufts gymnasium into a wonderland: crêpe paper streamers, Styrofoam snowmen, balloons, a disco ball hung precariously from the rafters. We piled all of our equipment into Perry's VW van, headed for the venue, and, upon arrival, were given a printed rundown. The Young Rascals would load in first, setting the stage for their convenience. (We would have to set up our equipment in a way that didn't infringe.) Next, it was a sound check for The Rascals. We sat in awe as they blasted through a couple of numbers. They were road-hardened, slick, and, above all, loud. The gym literally shook from the sheer volume they generated. (I was certain that the disco ball would come crashing down, shards of glass flying like shrapnel.) If that decibel level was what it took to win over a crowd, then we were dead in the water. Our pathetic little amplifiers were half the size of theirs.

Now it was our turn. We carefully snuggled our gear between the Rascal's monumental amps and did a bit of the old "test, test," tapping the microphones. We hadn't even attempted to play anything when the Rascal's roadie hollered out, "Five minutes, you guys. We gotta do our lights." We frantically plunged into our opening song, which sounded like a weak sister of what it did in the apartment, and, seconds later, the roadie grabbed Feeb's mic and began shouting instructions to the lighting man. So much for our sound check. We would make our debut flying blind.

Showtime, and we were at every disadvantage, save one. That one advantage was the fact that the audience wasn't completely drunk yet. They were actually attentive, polite, and when the emcee told them that OWO was a band made up of their classmates, enthusiastic in their response. Buoyed by their welcoming applause, we launched into our opening number. Feebs strutted and belted like a seasoned veteran. The audience was quickly and demonstrably on our side—cheering us on at every turn, jockeying for positions closer to the stage. Magical. The thirty-five minutes allocated for the opening act flew by. We finished our last song, pumped our fists at the sky and screamed "Thank you!!" and "Tufts rocks!!!" and started for the wings. The audience would have none of it. They wanted more. It got very loud. The Rascals' manager stepped on stage and grabbed me, screaming into my ear. "One more. That's it!!" Over his shoulder, I could see The Young Rascals' personnel, they looked none too pleased with the turn of events. But, back out we went. Feebs had written a kick-ass tune that we still had in our pocket: "Dancin' on Mars." We turned our amps up to the max and let it fly. When Nathan's cymbals finally stopped sizzling, the audience rose to its feet, cheering its collective head off. We felt like the Beatles at Shea Stadium. We were still bowing and thanking when the Rascal roadies shoved us aside to set the stage for their boys.

The Encore

I never saw The Young Rascals show. None of OWO did. We were too busy toasting our accomplishment. Warren Berkman had purchased a bottle of cheap champagne on the off chance that we would do well. It was gone in five minutes. A case of beer miraculously appeared and was quickly consumed. The boys and I lit up heavy-duty doobies. Our little dressing room must have looked like a Hells Angels birthday party when Max Diehl, the Rascal's manager, stuck his head in the door. We feared the worst, but he was all smiles.

After a flurry of glad-handing and praise-throwing, he let us know that he and Warren had reached a deal whereby we would tour with The Young Rascals as their permanent opening act. What?! (Was Warren now our manager? Did we even *want* a manager?) It was all happening so quickly. No one had any time (and thanks to all of the stimulants, any ability) to think. The deal was done. We were going on the road.

OWO had done the impossible. We had, in the space of one night, gone from being a nonentity to a touring band. From zero to sixty in one second. We would be spared the endless sets at spurious bars, would never have to endure the stench of a vomit-filled fraternity party, never have to drive hundreds of miles to play at some out-of-the-way State Teachers College or high-school prom. We never would suffer any growing pains. Feeb's song said it all. We *were* "Dancin' on Mars."

The next three months seemed like three days. So many losses and gains crammed into such a short period of time. On the loss side: Kirk, Perry, and I all dropped out of Tufts. This led to a loss in terms of my relationship with my father—he refused to even take my calls. With Perry and Kirk it was much the same story. All three of us, however, were convinced that when the band made its first million, got its first gold record, these wounds would be instantly healed. So we put any feelings of being orphaned in our back pockets.

There was also a loss of innocence, of playfulness. Our schedule didn't allow for much goofing off. Our pipe dreams of what it would be like to be rock stars were quickly replaced with the reality that music was an industry. As the touring began, life divided itself into two distinct activities: performing and traveling. Trenton, Philadelphia, Wilmington. D.C., Memphis, Dayton, Columbus, Indianapolis.

Kirk and I did our best to make a party out of it. After each concert, we would search out the "hotties" that would linger in the alleyways outside our stage door. (Hadn't that been the dangling carrot since day one? The reason we bought the guitars in the first place?) We now had the opportunity afforded by fame, however meager that fame might be. We had it down to a science. Step one: decide who was at least eighteen. Step two: who was the prettiest. Step three: coerce them back to the hotel. Step four: a little cocaine, a little pot, a few shots of Jack Daniel's, and then whatever you could get away with. Step five (if I wasn't passed out by this point): the chivalrous calling of a cab for Debbi, Kiki, Ramona, Dee Dee, Cookie, for Whoosis with the tattoo on her boobs. Step six: crash, and hope to be rested enough to get through Baltimore, Charlotte, Atlanta, Mobile.

I don't know if I was physically stronger than Kirk or just morally weaker, but soon it was just me sowing my wild oats. It became a bit of an issue with the band, and a bigger issue with Warren. Hindsight tells me that my bandmates were concerned for my well-being. Warren was more blunt in his accusations, complaining that my musicianship was faltering; calling me a skirt-chasing drunk, a junkie, a PR disaster. The truth was that I had not improved as a musician since the early days at the apartment. The rest of the band had grown in their skills, in their professionalism, and musicality. I was hanging on by a thread.

My most vocal defender was Feebs. Was it because I was the one that had found her, because I was the one that had coaxed the astounding rendition of "Yesterday" out of her and hired her on the spot? Did she feel she owed me one? Hard to say. But it was only her who would take the time to have heart-to-hearts; only her who would tell me that I needed to eat something when I slipped under a hundred and fifty pounds, only she who would volunteer to sit next to me on the airplane and let me fall asleep with my head on her shoulder. Yes, Feebs was my life-insurance policy with the band. She was, after all, what made the band unique. They would never get rid of her, and she would stay loyal to me. So, on to Nashville, St. Louis, Evanston, Dubuque, Kansas City.

Chicago was my Waterloo. We arrived at the hotel the night before the concert, and so did a blizzard of Biblical proportions. By morning, the city was at a standstill. Fourteen floors below me I could hear the snowplows clearing the roads, so I knew that the concert would still go on. I also knew that, having no desire to wander around freezing my balls off, I wouldn't be leaving my room prior to the sound check. Fine by me. I had all that I needed to occupy me until showtime: a gram and a half of cocaine, a little over an ounce of decent pot, and the little hotel refrigerator filled with a variety of alcoholic beverages. I hung the Do Not Disturb sign outside my door and began my spiral into the abyss.

I must have passed out, because the pounding on my door seemed to be coming from far, far away. I looked at my clock: It was only 2:30, too early for the sound check. (And I *had* hung the Do Not Disturb sign, hadn't I?) I tried to clear the cobwebs and figure out what was going on and came up empty. I made it to the door, opened it, and there stood Warren and the whole band. They were all smiles, smiles that instantly turned into open-mouthed gasps as they drank in the sight before them. The room was trashed and so was I.

What ensued was a band meeting unlike any we'd ever had. I sat, near-fetal, on my bed, fighting a monstrous hangover while the others fidgeted, hoping that whatever was going to happen would be short and sweet. Warren was the only one who spoke.

"I'm sorry, Marcus. I really am," he said.

Those six words set the tone. I knew Warren had his doubts about me as a team player, but why would he bring the whole band with him to confront me? Because they hadn't come by to confront me. They had come by to share *good* news. They had come by to tell me that we had secured a record deal. We were going to make our first album. That's why the initial smiles. But now, faced with the trainwreck in front of them, other steps had to be taken. I was told that I was no longer a member of OWO, that I was a liability they could no longer afford, that tonight's concert would be given without me.

"Without me?!!" I managed. "How can you do the music without me!!"

"Easily," said Warren, an icy edge to his voice that I had never heard before.

Warren delivered this judgement and I could see from the averted eyes of Perry, Kirk, and Nathan that there was unanimity. Only my dear sweet Feebs offered anything conciliatory.

"We'll get you some help," she said, her saucer eyes glistening. That's when I realized that I was, and always had been, in love with her.

. . . .

Feebs did send me a couple of letters while I was in rehab. Chatty, newsy letters—the album had done well, making the Top 100; she had written more songs without the help of LSD; Perry had quit and gone back to college (and the new piano player was *great!!*); they were headlining now, no more opening for The Young Rascals. Hope you're feeling better. All the best, Feebs. Those letters arrived during my first week at Fresh Start Farms, then nothing.

. . . .

The time I spent with a guitar in my hands is like a giant comma in a sentence that begins, "I went off to college [giant comma] and I got my degree as an orthodontist." Because that was what I did after rehab. After much soul-searching—beating myself up for being essentially an imposter in the world of music, then forgiving myself for simply being nothing more than an aimless, vulnerable, and cartoonishly horny adolescent—I went back to Tufts. The admissions people were understanding enough to let me return. After what felt like

The Encore

a century of schooling, I finally got my degrees and began a career inside the mouths of people who had post-apocalyptic teeth. From there, my bio was predictable, down the straight and narrow. I made a lot of money, married my nurse after an unremarkable three-year courtship, and fathered a son. And then, although barely into my forties, I had my first stroke.

In baseball, it's three strikes and you're out. In life, it's three *strokes* and you're out. At least usually. In my case, I wasn't completely out after the third stroke, but I certainly wasn't at bat any longer. I was hospitalized in a long-term facility. I was told by my doctors that I would, with hard work, probably be able to regain the ability to walk, to talk, to feed and wipe myself. Of course that's what they said. (I was a doctor myself, and knew how easily false hope could be distributed.) But walk and talk? Well, let's just say that I can sometimes get soup to my mouth without spilling, use the TV remote, and, every now and then, put together a sentence that, if you know what you're listening for, might sound like English. Anything else? Forget about it. For the past twenty-some years I've been stuck in this room.

My wife, Claire, took a powder after the second stroke. Remarried, she lives somewhere in upstate New Hampshire. We haven't had any contact in at least fifteen years, but my son, Noah, lives nearby. He visits as often as his schedule allows. He'll bring food and spread it out at the foot of my bed like a picnic. Every now and then, he'll take me out of the home for activities that can be accomplished in a wheelchair—a push around the park, a brunch at a sidewalk café, a drive to look at the fall color painting the leaves.

Noah has learned how to decipher my speech and loves to get me talking about the OWO days. At twenty-four, he's too young to see the tragedy of it; he sees only the romance. And, to be honest, there's a part of me that likes having my son see me as a rock 'n' roller and not just an old man in a bed.

Noah came by today, all excited. He had learned that OWO would be performing in Hartford—a short drive from my quarters. Like many of the bands of the seventies and eighties—the Doobie Brothers; Crosby, Stills, Nash & what's-his-name; Flo & Eddie—OWO had reformed for a last go-round, hoping to cash in on the nostalgia that old hippies embraced. "Jesus," I mumbled. "They have to be in their late sixties, seventies maybe!" I was seventy-one. I couldn't imagine it.

Noah had purchased tickets. He called ahead to make sure that the venue was wheelchair-accessible. It was. He refused to take "no" for an answer.

The venue was more theater than concert hall, maybe five-hundred seats, and only half of them were filled. Our seats were in the last row, the easiest for me to maneuver. My stomach and heart kept trading places, my thrice-stroked brain under

The Encore

siege with questions. Was this really happening? Would it be the people I had known, or would it be just another group using the name OWO to their advantage? Would I remember the songs? If the lights came on in the theater, would they see *me?* If they did, would they recognize me? Would I recognize *them?*

The lights dimmed dramatically and a disembodied baritone barked through the public address system: "Ladies and gentlemen, Odd Woman Out!!!" And out they walked. Not with the bouncy step of days gone by, but at least unassisted.

Nathan was first out. Bearded, completely bald, and even shorter than I had remembered. He looked like he should be running a deli or a failing bookstore. Next was Kirk. Kirk had kept his long hair, now bone-white, and seemed to struggle a bit getting the instrument strap over his shoulder. He looked old. Would Perry have come back for the reunion tour? No. The piano player was a kid, and you could see from the concern he had for Nathan and Kirk (Were they plugged in? Were they comfortable?) that he was hired as much as a babysitter as a musician. Feebs always entered last. My heart felt like kettledrums. The spotlight swung to the wings and she walked out, her hands in the air, acknowledging the applause.

Feebs, dear sweet Feebs. Time had taken its toll, and she was fighting it like a trooper. Gone were the platform shoes—the risk of falling way too great—gone was the postage-stamp miniskirt, a caftan in its place. Her hair was still the reddish-brown I remembered, but unnaturally so, probably bottled. She had gained a few pounds and, if it were possible, had grown even shorter. If I had crossed paths with her on the street, I wouldn't have recognized her. It wasn't until she smiled that anything about this little old lady resonated. Feeb's smile. Unforgettable.

The applause died down and she took the microphone in her hand.

"Before we begin," she said, "I'd like to do a shout-out to someone who is here tonight. Someone who made all of this possible many, many, years ago. His son sent me a note saying he would be here tonight. So... Marcus Phillips... if you *did* show up...? [And then that little laugh of hers that breaks your heart]... stand up and take a bow!!"

Of course I couldn't. Noah started to stand for me and I urged him not to. It was all too much. The tears were racing down my face.

"A 'no-show,' I guess," said Feebs. "Well, if any of you know him, tell him we miss him."

And, without further ado, the show began. Feebs could still sing. Not with the ferocity and adventure that had once defined her, but well enough. The band was adequate, the audience supplying the energy the players lacked. They finished their set and were called back for an encore. "Dancin' on Mars" ended the evening.

The Last Two Months of Ed Furst

Noah asked me if I wanted to go backstage for a quick hello. I did not. I just wanted to go home, get in bed, and have a dream where I could still walk and talk and play the guitar.

THE LAST TWO MONTHS OF ED FURST

Ed Furst worked in a health-food store. Of course he did. Health was everything to Ed. His body wasn't just a temple, it was a whole diocese. It would be safe to say that staying alive was Ed's lifework. So of course he worked in a health-food store. Being within arm's reach of anything and everything his current fixation might deem necessary for his well-being was paramount. He had encyclopedic knowledge of the homeopathic wares that stocked the shelves: the herbs, the pills, the unguents, supplements, vitamins, minerals, oils, balms, creams, and salves, and he was always quick to act the shaman in imparting his wisdom to his customers. He was also quick to help himself to the inventory, constantly swallowing or chewing some tincture, philter, or decoction that he was convinced was the panacea du jour. And to supplement his supplements, he ingested a steady stream of carob brownies, beet pulp, bales of kale, and dozens of gluten-free cookies.

Given this intake, one would think he'd be big as a barn, but he was not. He was reed-thin, barely cast a shadow, and, for someone so intent on being healthy, had the pallor of a cave-dweller under house arrest. His stringy, shoulder-length hair would often go unwashed for weeks (though he had discovered a non-acidic, low-sulfate shampoo made from elderberries and palm fronds, he was still afraid it would dry out his scalp), and its long tendrils clung to his neck as if coated in Stickum. His fingers looked like asparagus stalks. All of these characteristics, which a normal person might find alarming, he regarded as positive signs that he was "ridding himself of toxins." If something as prosaic as sniffles or an itch presented itself, he knew just what ground-up Chinese mushrooms or fizzy elixir would make it all go away. He was forty-nine years old and planned on seeing one hundred. So he was more than a little concerned when he woke up with an inexplicable pain in the hollow under his ribcage.

To the extent that he was inclined to trust the holistic approach, he was doubly inclined to mistrust Western medicine's needles and knives. He felt that their oath to "first, do no harm" was the height of hypocrisy. Doing harm was their stock in trade. He'd seen it way too often: unwarranted surgeries, invasive probings, lethal medicines masquerading as harmless pink candies. Doctors weren't to be trusted, neither were dentists—he'd pull his own teeth if it ever came to that. Chiropractors, to their credit, never crept inside body cavities, but were still on the "do not trust" list.

So he ravaged his home larder for anything "natural" to ease this newfound gastric discomfort. The almond-bark tea and the yam root did nothing to alleviate the pain. The celery-water-piñón-nut cream likewise. He lay back down on his waterbed and tried a combination of breathings: half-Lamaze, half-pranayama—a yogic routine that usually calmed him. He was still uncomfortable. He toyed with the idea of calling in sick, but there were two problems. First, he was the only employee, so who would he call? Second, one doesn't call in sick to a health-food store. It's oxymoronic.

The store had been a fixture in New Milford, Connecticut, for over two decades. Ed and his UConn roommate, Eddie Burke, had founded it. Both men were premed students; both were struggling with the curriculum; both had doubts about the efficacy of Western medicine; and both were drawn inexorably to the wisdom of the East. They began their enterprise by selling various herbs and vitamins out of their dorm room—there was an endless stream of disillusioned hippies, searching for alternative lifestyles—and soon found it was a full-time job. They rented a storefront, and MOLLOY & MALONE was born. (There had been a moment when they had considered calling it ED & EDDIE'S, but felt it sounded too cutesy, too much like an ice cream store. MOLLOY & MALONE was concocted from the titles of two Samuel Beckett books, which they both found ponderous enough to lend the store an occult mystique.) Business was instantly brisk, enough so that they hired an attractive, young redhead to run the checkout counter. Her name was Marriott James. (Named after the location of her conception.) The store did well enough that they were soon able to buy the building.

Ed, Eddie, and Marriott were a well-oiled team. Eddie managed the financial end of things, Ed the inventory and the informational expertise. Marriott was the eye-candy behind the counter that lured in many a young male customer. Ed had been so ensconced in uncovering the mysteries of the holistic world that he never noticed the blooming romance between Eddie and Marriott. So he was surprised, to say the least, when they arrived at the shop one morning and announced that they had gotten married. Married?!! This called for glasses of carbonated birch-water and carrot cake! The newlyweds would be taking a week off for a honeymoon, they said, and Ed assured them he could hold the fort.

It was the honeymoon that brought tragedy to MOLLOY & MALONE. Eddie had been on the top step of the hotel escalator, his camera aimed at his new bride as she pirouetted in her yellow sundress three floors below. Putting her in focus must have altered his sense of distance, because his next step connected with nothing but air and sent him bouncing like a basketball all the way to the hotel lobby's granite floor. His neck had been broken. He was gone.

Marriott was heartbroken, inconsolable. She lost all interest in the store, retreating to the sanctuary of the couple's tiny cottage to mourn. Now MOLLOY & MALONE was Ed's alone. (Marriott did retain her late husband's half-interest, however, and Ed was dutiful in splitting the proceeds—visiting every month to give her a check for her share.)

So the store was his, and if it was going to stay open he'd have to forget about whatever was causing the pain in his stomach. He went to work.

The pain did not subside. Over the next few weeks it increased exponentially and was accompanied by dysphagia, a difficulty in swallowing. He wrote this difficulty off to the dryness of some of the pills and herbs he was ingesting. He tried slavering them in yak butter before taking them, but still the condition persisted. He was also passing a lot more gas than usual. He hoped that problem would stay in abeyance today when he visited Marriott to give her the monthly check.

Marriott answered the door in her signature muumuu and Birkenstocks. (Some things never change.) But where age might have given her laugh lines, she had wrinkles etched by despair—tiny crevices in her still porcelain skin that betrayed a lonely existence. A shame, really, because she was still pretty, like women who somehow maintain a girl's face well into adulthood. As always, when she opened the door, she had a cup of steaming tea in one hand and a Kleenex in the other.

"Hey," she said, long-faced.

"Hey," Ed responded, handing her the envelope containing the check.

They settled into two old wicker chairs in Marriott's warm and tiny sunporch. Marriott had offered tea, Ed had politely refused.

"You usually want tea, Ed. Is everything okay?" she asked, her eyes narrowing in concern.

"Oh, I'm fine." Ed pointed to his mouth. "I'm just chewing something I don't want to dilute. That's all."

"Seriously? You don't chew *gum*. There's *sugar* in gum!"

Ed laughed, but barely. "Gum? Oh God, no!! It's balsam-bark and chicle. It's supposed to be an antacid."

"Is your stomach still bothering you? It was bothering you the last couple of times you were here. Maybe you should..."

"Nothing major," said Ed, waving it off. And then, as if on cue, his sphincter opened. It sounded like a medium-sized audience applauding. A stinging cloud of methane filled the sun porch.

"Jesus," said Marriott.

After a flurry of red-faced apologies from Ed, the decision was made to retire to a larger room.

"I'm worried about you, Ed. You've told me a thousand times that you know your body better than anyone and that's probably true. But maybe..."

"I'm not going to a doctor, Marriott. I was created by Nature and I'll be healed by Nature. It's not even open to discussion."

"The doctor was created by Nature, too," said Marriott.

"Oh, please. Not gonna happen. I'm not about to have some jerk who thought thalidomide was a good idea poke me and probe me when, as far as I can see, I'm just a little low on zinc.»

"Have you taken zinc?"

"I probably haven't taken enough."

"A *doctor* could tell you..."

"Marriott! I don't want to hear that *word!*"

"Listen to me, Ed. I know that you believe that every baby should be born at home in a bathtub, and that colds can be cured by wheat germ, and that it's just the additives they put in our food that keeps us from being a hundred and twenty-five years old. But I've got news for you. There weren't enough herbs in the world to help Eddie when he was laying on that granite hotel floor. If he had let them put him in a collar and lay him on a board and take him to the hospital he might still be here. But no, not my Mr. Natural. And now he's gone. I'm just saying that sometimes you need a *real* doctor!! I don't want to lose you, too!!"

Eddie rose to his feet to leave and another fetid gust escaped his pants. He sat back down, his head in his hands, his pride and defenses gone with the wind.

"I wouldn't know who to go to," he said submissively.

"Go see Walter," said Marriott.

Walter was Marriott's brother and a GP. For Eddie and Ed, his practice of Western medicine had been the source of countless arguments and shout-fights at family gatherings. Eddie and Ed were often reduced to calling Walter a "moron" over pie at Thanksgiving dinner. But Walter was never swayed from his belief in Western medicine. He stuck to his guns and built a reasonable practice as a general practitioner. He never chose to specialize, content with a steady income from flus, mumps, and sprained ankles. His patients loved him. He had a soothing, avuncular presence that put them at ease even during times of crisis. Oddly enough, it was this non-alarmist, even-keeled temperament that had led Ed to admit on one less-confrontational occasion that "if I ever break my arm or something where I *do* need a doctor, I'd probably go to Walter." He had this thought again as Marriott repeated, "Go see Walter," this time more of an order.

Ed was in too much discomfort to fight. He knew that Marriott cared about him and wouldn't let this drop. So, as he made his way to the door, accompanied by what sounded like randomly popping corn, he promised that, if he was still hurting after the two-week regimen he had devised for himself (everything south of rhino-tusk), he would give Walter a call.

Two weeks later he felt like he had eaten a bag of nails. He was doubled over in pain and had to have Marriott drive him to Walter's office.

Walter's nurse, a slight man named Dieter, ushered him into a consulting room, instructed him to strip to his socks and shorts and put on the paper gown. Ed did so, and Dieter left him to wait for Walter. Ed looked around the little room: cabinets filled with what he considered poisons and other instruments of torture: lancets, scalpels, space-age looking machines, posters of the human body sectioned off like cuts of meat. He was terrified. He was in pain. And he was cold. Why do they keep it so cold, he wondered—to prepare you for death?

After what seemed an eternity, Walter came into the room. He greeted Ed with the same warmth with which he greeted all of his patients. For Walter, ever the professional, any intellectual differences he and Ed might have held, vis-à-vis medicine, were ancient history.

"Marriott said you're having some tummy trouble," he said kindly.

"She insisted I see you."

"And she can be a pain in the ass if you're on her bad side, right?"

"Yeah, a pain in the ass," Ed agreed.

"And any other pains. Ed? Besides the pain in the ass and the one in your tummy?"

"No."

"Well, let's see what's going on there," said Walter, and he began to poke a bit around Ed's stomach area. Ed reacted to one poke like it was a dagger.

"Ooh, that's not good," said Walter, concerned. "Tell me, have you been experiencing unusual flatulence? Difficulty swallowing? Heartburn?"

"Yeah, all of it."

"For how long?"

"Last few months."

"A few *months*, huh? Why'd you wait so long to come in?"

"I thought I could get a handle on it. I still do. I think it might be low zinc."

"Well, I guess there's always that possibility," Walter said condescendingly. "We're going to find out. I'm going to have Dieter get your urine and some blood, and I'm gonna have you do an upper GI test."

"Oh, Christ." Ed shivered, a small fart escaping his gown.

"It's no big deal. You just drink this stuff that tastes like a milkshake. It'll tell us what we need to know. Do you need anything for the pain?"

"No. I don't believe in that shit."

"Of course you don't. I remember," said Walter.

He called for Dieter, who appeared magically, and Walter shook Ed's hand. "Hang in there. We'll figure this thing out." And he was gone.

Ed surrendered his fluids reluctantly but dutifully. He pocketed the milkshake Dieter provided and, still fighting the bag of nails in his stomach, left to open the store.

He waited until the shop was empty to drink his milkshake, knowing that he could never explain his consuming a Western-med beverage to a customer.

. . . .

Okay, I'm going to stop you right there, Mr. Third Person. It's *my* story, after all, I should be the one to tell it. You've done a reasonable job setting the table—I'll give you that—although there were a number of things you either omitted or gave short shrift. Your description of the store, for instance, was colorless and lacked detail. Two decades of blood, sweat, and tears went into making it the jewel it is today—there are over five-thousand different remedies and supplements on those shelves. A little respect, please. You also failed to mention that I, too, had a thing for Marriott, and when she went off with Eddie it spelled the end of my romantic interest in anyone. If there had been a "one for me," then it was her, and when it couldn't be her, well... I guess the store became my woman. What else? Your description of the pain. Since it wasn't yours, there was no way you could know how to describe it, but to say it was a "stomachache" would be like saying that decapitation is a "pain in the neck." I don't think I could put it in words either, so you're forgiven your uninspired "bag of nails" metaphor. What else? What else? Oh, my hair isn't "stringy"—I like to think of it as shiny. And you didn't mention that Walter's "warmth" is an affectation, as far as I'm concerned. Finally, you make it sound like all of the holistic medicines I took were a form of pissing into the wind. Not true. Ninety-nine percent of the medications and supplements I took did exactly what they were supposed to do. There's more, but it's kind of pointless to dwell on anything prior to that milkshake—the milkshake that shook the world off its axis. So go get yourself a cup of coffee, Mr. Third Person, I got this now. Here we go, Ed Furst, head-first.

. . . .

For forty-nine years, I had managed to avoid any contact with doctors. Even with all the bumps and bruises that fill the gap between cradle cap and acne, never a need to "see someone." (My parents were functionally Christian Scientists, though it had nothing to do with religion, merely economics—doctors were simply too expensive.) As an adult, I watched my diet diligently, did my sit-ups, looked both ways before crossing busy streets, and never took my well-being for granted. It should be noted that the fucking upper GI milkshake was the first milkshake I ever had in my life—an irony that I now find as difficult to swallow as that shake itself.

Because the results of that upper GI exam caused the concern that would put me through living hell. I flunked the test. Something was growing in my stomach. Walter immediately ordered an MRI. (If you are a capital "M" masochist and really want to put yourself through a torture like no other, I suggest you have an MRI. If you can't afford the thousand bucks then you can replicate the feeling by crawling headfirst into a tiny heating duct in an aging home and having someone bang on the pipes with a sledgehammer for twenty minutes.) The MRI validated Walter's suspicions and he called in a specialist: a cancer doctor—because that's what the MRI revealed, cancer. Walter and Dr. Weiss, the specialist, sat me down to break the news—news which I greeted with complete denial.

"Well," I said, "that's bullshit. There's got to be something wrong with your machines."

"I'm afraid not," said Walter and Weiss in one voice.

"You don't *know* that!" I barked.

"Unfortunately, we do," said Walter. "We saw the tumor on the screen."

It was their smug self-assurance that got to me as much as their diagnosis. I made the jump from denial to anger.

"You believe everything you see on your little fucking screen? TVs can lie!! Christ, that's what they *do!* Mr. Ed couldn't *talk!! Star Trek* wasn't filmed in *space,* it was filmed in *Burbank!!*

"That lump could have been a shadow of one of my ribs. One of your fucking nurses could have had a finger on the lens. It could have been the congealed remains of that fucking milkshake, the remnants of yesterday's lunch. It could be a thousand things that *aren't* cancer! You don't *know!!*"

"It was the size of a lemon," said Weiss, calmly.

"A lime," countered Walter.

And that's when I felt my eyes rolling back into my head. The room began to spin, all gravity and horizon up for grabs. I closed my eyes and it was worse. I opened them and saw what looked like an iPhone movie of a Japanese earthquake, furniture flying like runaway kites, Weiss and Walter reduced to anatomical parts. And the sound! It was like gravel being unloaded on a steel floor. The last thing I remember was the two young nurses, their powder-blue paper gowns rustling and cracking as they lunged for me. Their hands were giant, their fingernails like talons of some prehistoric creature. I blacked out.

They said it was a fairly common anxiety attack and that I was only out for a couple of minutes, but it felt much longer. When I had barely come to, they offered me water and a pill. (Had I been in possession of my full faculties, I would, of course, have refused the pill—having never taken one in my life.) Slowly, I returned to normal. And then a little *better* than normal. Jesus! What *was* that pill? Valium, they told me.

I'd heard about Valium and, like all Western medicine, considered it taboo. But, I have to say, I could see why people carried a bottle of it in their pocket—how that might offer the sense of security cowboys felt having a six-gun on their hip. In fact, I would have to say that if it wasn't for the soothing effects of the Valium, I would never have been able to sit there and listen to what Walter and Weiss rolled out as a treatment program: exploratory surgery, chemo, radiation, more MRIs, more bloodwork, even last-ditch experimentals—hypothermia, gene therapy, unpronounceable drugs with potentially devastating side effects: Dichloroacetate, Quercetin, Yervoy.

As they rattled off their list of deadlies, I nodded my head obediently, trying to act as if I understood everything they were saying, trying to give the impression that I would be a willing and grateful patient. I agreed with them that time was of the essence, that we should get right on this. They had me fill out a ream of permission slips, insurance forms, and the addresses of my next of kin. It was decided that I should report to the hospital at 7 the following morning. Again, I nodded in agreement. When they were satisfied that I was on board, they asked me:

"Is there anything else you want to know?"

"How long do I have?" I asked with a resigned sigh.

"Untreated? Two months," said Walter.

"And treated?"

"That's up to God," smiled Weiss. There was an awkward silence that ensued. Walter broke the silence.

"In the meantime, is there anything we can do for you?"

"Valium," I said.

. . . .

Once I had escaped their grasp, I went straight to the store, pulled every relevant book off the shelf, and searched for a holistic answer to my problem. There was mention of Salvestrol Platinum, vitamin B-17, and apricot powder, but nothing was deemed surefire. There were testimonials from patients who had gone to Mexico for Laetrile, but Laetrile was iffy and still a Western solution. By the end of the day, I had no answers. Well, that's not completely true. I knew that I had been given two months. A fact that begged a bigger question: How would I spend them? I went home, said, "Fuck it," took two Valiums, crawled into my waterbed, and slept like the proverbial baby. I also had the most extraordinary dream of my life.

As is often the case in my dreams, I didn't look like myself. For starters, I had short, dry hair. I was also forty pounds heavier and it was all muscle. I poked my stomach and found I was pain-free. The room, which I did not recognize, was filled with people, balloons, streamers—a party of some sort. Everyone was the picture of health, the men swathed in the glow that comes with worldly success, the women each more beautiful than the next. And, for once, I was not the anomaly. I was one of them. But the most astounding thing was that we were all drinking alcohol, eating pizza, dipping potato chips into pools of onion dip, smoking cigarettes, and passing joints. Every hedonist pleasure that I had denied myself for nearly half a century was in full flower. Then, as can only happen in a dream, I saw the skinny, underweight, cancer-stricken Ed Furst appear in the midst of the revelers. The A-listers greeted him with astonished, silent stares—a pariah in their midst. A circle formed around him, giving him space. Then, as if on command, he pulled up his shirt and, to the horror of the partygoers, revealed a bloody, gaping hole where his stomach should've been. You could see right through him. He groaned loudly and began to stagger. A pretty young girl (could it have been Marriott?) caught him as he started to fall and her boyfriend shoved a slice of pizza in his mouth; another man gave him a glass of scotch. "Good for what ails ya!" the man exclaimed. And it was. Within seconds of ingesting the pizza and scotch, the hole healed over seamlessly; the sickly

The Last Two Months of Ed Furst

Ed Furst magically returned to health. He began to dance. He twirled and swung, sashayed and stomped and, catching my eye, opened his arms and ran at me like an old army buddy recognizing his foxhole mate in a bar after twenty years. He embraced me. And when he did so, he melted into me, absorbed like a second skin, like good news, like the welcome heat of a fireplace on a cold day. We two became one. Cheers and applause filled the room. I would have stayed in that dream forever if the phone hadn't rung.

It was Walter.

"Yeah?" I said.

"Ed? It's Walter. Where the hell are you? It's seven-thirty. You were supposed to be here at quarter to seven. I've got a whole team standing by." I didn't know what to say, so I said nothing.

"Ed?" Walter again. "Are you there?" I gathered my strength.

"I'm here."

"Well? What's the story?" Walter said impatiently.

"Change of plans," I said.

"What are you talking about?"

I took a long, deep breath, recalling the ecstasy of my dream.

"Walter, do you remember when you told me I only had two months? Well, I've been thinking about that. It doesn't scare me. When you think about it, *everyone* reaches a point where they only have two months. A thirty-six-year-old that won't see thirty-seven. A ninety-eight-year-old that won't see ninety-eight and a half. A seven-year-old who's had his last birthday cake. Babies that don't make it full-term. Everyone. Because no one lives forever. No one. We *all* have our last two months. The sad part is that most people aren't given notice, aren't given the chance to change their tactics like a football team given the two-minute warning—aren't told to really enjoy and appreciate a beautiful sunset because it's the last one they're going to see. Jesus, stock traders know that they better have their portfolios together before the closing bell, boxers know when it's round ten. We should *all* get the news you gave me. And, if that were the case, if we all had a head's up that the other bookend was so near at hand, how many do you think would opt to spend that time suffering the horrors of chemotherapy, of radical surgeries, of drawing that last breath through a plastic tube shoved down their throat? Not me. No thank you."

"You've lost your mind," said Walter.

"No, I've *found* it," I crowed. Walter was silent for a moment, then emitted a long and defeated sigh.

"So you're just going to do *nothing?*" he managed.

"*Nothing?* Oh, no, just the contrary. I'm going to do everything!! I'm going to live like there's no tomorrow, because there isn't." And I think I laughed. That's when Walter hung up.

It's Mr. Third Person again. Ed's handed me the reins while he takes a little nap.

Ed rose and dressed on that fateful morning and, instead of going straight to the store, went out for breakfast. He walked to the tiny diner two blocks from MOLLOY & MALONE. In the past, the smell of heavy grease and bacon had made him almost nauseous when he was forced to walk past it—today the aroma was a siren's song. He took a stool at the counter, grabbed the menu, and read it as if it were a poem. He ordered the works. Eggs, sausage, biscuits with mounds of butter, a bagel with cream cheese and lox, a sticky, sugar-encrusted pastry, and real coffee with cream and four sugars. He got six donuts "to go," which were gone before he reached the store. For the first time in memory, he didn't take his morning vitamins.

There was still a vestige of common sense to Ed, which worried that his overindulgence might push his lemon-sized lump to a grapefruit, might further increase his stomach pain to unbearable. It did not. If anything, he simply felt full, his pain no worse, perhaps even a bit less. His farts were less frequent. He stopped thinking about it. Instead he thought about lunch. He had never had a hamburger, a grilled cheese, French fries; and today he would have them all. What's more, he would find them at a bar and grill so he could wash them down with beer. Yes! Alcohol! He was a man on a mission: fill the last two months with everything he'd ever denied himself. Go out with a roar.

Ed spent a high-energy morning at the store. He was even more loquacious and effusive than usual with the patrons (offering free samples, two-for-ones, deep discounts. When asked about certain remedies and supplements, he would short-sell their impact, suggesting fresh air and sunshine as a more viable alternative). When the shop was empty he found busywork, alphabetizing the vitamins on their shelves, sweeping, dusting, sharpening pencils. Every second now seemed precious.

On his way back from lunch (he had held back nothing, had ordered everything, topping it off with pie à la mode) Ed stopped into a chic hair salon and made an appointment to get a cut and blow-dry. At the corner newsstand, he picked up a copy of *People* magazine to research what was current, what was hip, not wanting to miss out on any pleasure that might be out there for the taking. Afternoon traffic at the store was light, so he popped another Valium and read the *People*, dog-earing several pages. He saw the biceps on the action-movie stars and knew he'd have to join a gym. He saw the sun-drenched complexions of the *Bachelor* finalists, and knew he'd have to find a tanning salon. He read the confessions of an alcoholic rock and roller—the no-holds-barred lifestyle he had led before finding AA—and felt jealous of his *pre*-sober antics. After locking up for the night, Ed walked back to his cramped studio apartment, stopping off to pick up a large pizza (he wracked his brain to remember what was on the one in his dream: Was it pepperoni? Onion? Artichokes? He decided to go with the works). He bought a bottle of Jack Daniel's.

Ed ate the whole pizza and made a decent dent in the Jack Daniel's. He sank into his beanbag chair and took another Valium. (He then counted the Valiums that remained in his little bottle: 39—he'd have to be judicious in his use, he thought.) The combination of food, booze, and drugs caused his thoughts to cloud in a postprandial fog and then, with a start, they sharpened. He needed to make a list. A "to do" list.

Get haircut.

Join gym.

Get tan.

These items were already on his mind so they were easy. Then he dug deeper, and the list became not so much "to do" as "what I never did and should have."

Eat a hotdog at a ballpark.

Skinny-dip.

Smoke pot.

Buy a suit.

Grow a moustache.

And then, as the Valium and Jack Daniel's grabbed the reins, the list exploded into a litany of activities, many of them impossible, absurd, and illegal.

Go on African safari.
Run naked down the street.
Get my back waxed.
Shoplift.
Shoot pool with a Hells Angel in a bar.
Run for governor.
Fight a bull in Spain.
Mani-pedi.
Tap dance.
Hooker?
Burn my old clothes.
Tattoos!!
Do a lap at the Indy 500.
Rustle cattle.
Naked food fight with Beyoncé.
Tea with the Queen.
Go without underwear.
Open a liquor store.
Yell "Fire!" in a movie house.
Yell "Movie!!" in a fire house.

The Valium finally hit full force and his lids grew heavy as he tried to formulate a last addition to the list.

Tell Marriott how much I... But he couldn't put the thought into words.

. . . .

For the next three and a half weeks, Ed spent every moment trying to make his life-changing dream a curative reality. Three and a half weeks of the new regimen now under his belt (quite literally under his belt, he had gained fifteen pounds). Well, it wasn't really a "regimen," was it, since there was nothing off-limits—he wined and dined like a politico; spent hundreds of dollars on clothes, tanning salon visits, a watch that gave him the time of day anywhere in the world. He leased a fire-engine red Mustang convertible.

Was it mind over matter? He couldn't say. But somehow this living like a profligate Arab prince had an analgesic effect. He was virtually pain-free.

. . . .

It's me again. Back from my nap, and not a moment too soon, I should say. Mr. Third Person is, once again, guilty of omitting certain things and glossing over others. I don't know where he got that "profligate Arab prince" bullshit. I was just living my life the way I saw others live theirs. I didn't dive into anything and everything edible or potable like a starved dog. I tasted first, sipped, held myself to just three meals a day and went light on the condiments, the salt. Though I'd been told that I might have only two months to enjoy myself, I didn't jump in the deep end. I'm not an idiot. He makes it sound like I had to be rolled out of restaurants, bum-rushed out of bars. Not true.

He also makes it sound like Walter gave up on me. Again, not true. Walter called me as relentlessly as a telemarketer. Each conversation would devolve into the same stalemate—Walter retreating to his data, his Harvard-medical-school hunches, his doomsday prognoses, and I to my unwillingness to become a guinea pig for the butchers of Western medicine. He begged me to come in. I refused. He told me that my actions were suicidal. Tried to play the shrink with statements like: "Life is worth living." And I would counter with "*living* is precisely what I'm doing!" So it went, day after day. Soon the calls ebbed to a trickle, and then none at all.

It was now the end of the month. I had to deliver Marriott's check. Even though the ritual harkened back to my previous life, I was looking forward to it. I had gotten my hair cut and styled, put on needed weight (and a little muscle, courtesy of the gym), tanned myself the color of an old penny, and would be decked out in stylish attire. All but a small part of me assumed that she would see my metamorphosis as nothing less than extraordinary. That small part was concerned that she had been fond of the old Ed Furst, warts and all, and would find the new one an unlikeable stranger. So the small part took a Valium. I was down to five left.

I pulled the Mustang, top down, into her driveway and hit the horn twice. I wanted to make the full impression. Marriott, tea and Kleenex in hand, opened the door a crack, took one look, and

The Last Two Months of Ed Furst

slammed the door. She didn't recognize me. I saw her face appear in a window and I waved the check in my hand, smiling broadly. She slowly closed the curtain as I walked to the front door and knocked. She opened it warily.

"It's Ed!" I said cheerfully.

"My God! Ed! What happened to you?" she exclaimed.

"Good stuff, Marriott, all good stuff." I handed her the check, which she quickly scanned.

"What is this? *Seventeen* dollars?"

"I know. It's a lot less than usual. The store took a little hit this past month. I haven't been able to be there as much as I normally am."

"Ed, what have you done to yourself?" she said, returning her stunned gaze to my artificially bronzed face.

"Well," I said with a chuckle, "I've cured myself of cancer for starters! Can I come in?"

We sat in her little sunroom, sipping tea. (I have to confess that, given the tension, I would have preferred my Jack Daniel's, but when in Rome...) I wouldn't even call it a conversation. Half of the time was dominated by Marriott's crying—seeing me no doubt exhumed memories of her long-lost Eddie—and the other half by argument. She wasn't buying my claim that I was out of the cancer woods. She acknowledged that I *looked* better but took the position that looks can be deceiving. Looks were the exterior—my problem was interior. I told her how the pain had dissipated, and she said that could be a bad sign as well as a good one. I asked her how she could think such a thing, and she said that the cancer could have spread to my brain, killing off the receptors for pain. I said, "That's preposterous," and she again burst into tears, the floodgates fully opening in gut-wrenching sobs.

"You don't get it, do you," she cried. "I can't lose you *too!* I hope to God you're right about all this, I really do. I hope you're all better. But I'm not going to get any peace of mind until I hear it from Walter!!!"

"I don't need to see Walter," I said calmly. "I'm fine."

"Well, if you're *fine*, then let Walter *see* that!" She was almost screaming now. "Walter would be happy for you, Ed. Walter is *family!!*"

"He's a doctor."

"But he's my *brother* first! He's *very* concerned about me. He knows I couldn't handle another loss. Jesus, Ed, all I'm asking is that you go see him, let him see the miraculous recovery you're claiming. If you're all better, then you have nothing to worry about. If not, well... Can you just do this for *me?* Please? I love you, Ed."

The true test of a man's conviction is whether he can stand his ground while a sobbing, beautiful woman is saying "I love you." I couldn't. It wasn't just a collapse of character, I actually *did* think that I was clean and clear and that Walter would

The Last Two Months of Ed Furst

see that immediately. I would be in and out of his office in ten minutes.

. . . .

For starters, Walter was running late. So I had to sit there in the cramped quarters of the waiting room, with nothing to amuse myself besides *Today's Health* and *AARP* pamphlets. When he finally bustled into the office, he walked right past me. *He didn't recognize me!!* I literally had become a new man. In fact, "new man" was the exact term he used when, two minutes later, he ushered me, like a visiting dignitary, into the examining room. He couldn't get over it. He had me remove my shirt and started poking around my abdomen, searching for the lemon/lime. Nothing. No lump. He pushed his forefinger deeply into my stomach. "Does this hurt?" he asked. It didn't. He called in Dieter to take some blood, sharing his amazement with the young nurse. "Get some urine, too, Dieter, but I have a feeling it's going to be pointless. I think this guy is good to go. Astounding!"

While I was surrendering my fluids, Walter asked me if I had discovered some herbal wonder drug or mega-vitamin program, assuming that would have been the road I would have taken, and I proceeded to tell him the whole story: the burgers, the Jack Daniel's, all of it. He was dumbstruck. As I started to put my shirt back on, Walter said,

"Wait a minute. I'm going to ask a huge favor of you. Not just for me but... well, for medical history, as it were. I'd like to do one last MRI to make sure that this miracle is documented."

"An MRI?" I said. "Not gonna happen. The last one was the worst twenty minutes of my life."

"We'll do a short one then. Ten minutes tops."

"Why?"

"Honestly? Because your story of how you cured yourself would be earth-shaking in the scientific community, and *I* want to be the one who writes the paper on it for the *Journal of American Medicine*. That's why. Call me selfish, but this is a once-in-a-lifetime opportunity for me."

"Great. And what would *I* get out of that?" I said.

"Are you trying to work a *deal* with me? Jesus, Ed, I don't know. Maybe... Well... How about I give you my services, free of charge, for the rest of your life?"

"Not what I had in mind," I said.

"What, then?" Walter asked, his face a frown of confusion.

"Valium," I said. "An open-ended prescription."

. . . .

Mr. Third Person, back again. I'm going to grab the baton and run the anchor leg of this relay. First of all, the MRI showed a stomach that was perfect. No lemon, no lime, not even a kumquat, not even a raisin. His tummy was pink as pork. Walter couldn't believe his eyes.

. . . .

Ed got his prescription, thank God, because he needed it to deal with all that was about to transpire.

Walter got right to work on his paper for *The Lancet*, the official periodical of the American Medical Association—like most writings that appeared in the journal, it would be a highly technical piece, filled with charts and bar graphs, lengthy paragraphs of arcane patois that only doctors or Latin scholars could decode. He took a leave of absence from his practice to devote himself full-time to the project.

Meanwhile, Dieter, whose prying eyes and ears had been privy to Ed's diagnosis, testing, and miraculous recovery, used this motherlode of eavesdropper's info to write his own story: a much more pedestrian description of Ed's saga. It was entitled "Health-nut Glutton Beats the Big 'C'" and subtitled "Local man turns pigpen diet into miracle cure." He sold it to the local paper, *The Hartford Courant*. Three days later, Dieter's story covered four columns on page two, sharing the page with an ongoing story about the mayor's much-ballyhooed divorce.

The story caught fire. It seemed that everyone had a vested interest in the tale. There were, of course, the cancer-afflicted, who pounced on Ed's radical approach as a possible alternative to their own failing treatments and demanded to know more. There were the junk-food addicts who could now hail their diets as not only reasonable, but nothing short of a preventive vaccine. There were the by-the-book, Western medicine advocates who claimed that something smelled fishy. There were call-in radio hosts who opened up their phone lines to anyone and everyone who had an opinion, no matter how pithy. There were bookies willing to take bets as to whether Ed would make it the full two months.

Ed hadn't seen the paper. So he was confused, to say the least, when the crowd started forming outside MOLLOY & MALONE. Friends and long-time customers alike—people he had advised and escorted down the path of holistic remedy—were screaming that they wanted their money back. They were very vocal. *"Fraud!!»* they screamed. *"Charlatan!!"* Ed locked the door, snuck out the back, and literally ran home. He collapsed breathless in his beanbag chair, poured himself a huge Jack Daniel's, and popped three Valiums. He called Marriott.

"People are trying to kill me!" he slurred.

"No, they're *not!*" said Marriott. "They're just... well, have you seen the paper?"

"I don't read the paper.»

"Well, there's a whole story on you. Walter's asshole nurse wrote it. Walter's furious."

The Last Two Months of Ed Furst

"Walter wrote a story about me?" said Ed, his thinking now muddled by medication and alcohol.

"No, you're not listening to me. His *nurse* wrote it. Walter fired him the minute he found out."

"And the story's about *me*?" Ed mumbled.

"Yes. He didn't use your last name, just called you 'Patient Ed' and said you ran a health-food store. Christ, this is a small town. He might as well have given them a photograph of you. It's all about your bad habits, Ed, and your 'miracle' recovery. People are calling into radio shows trying to take credit for the turnaround: Morton's Deli, The Liquor Barn, U-Go Rental Cars, The Tan-atorium where you got all brown."

"I'm all *brown*?" he said. "When did *that* happen?" He could barely form the words.

"Ed, you sound terrible. I'm worried about you. Why don't you take a nap and call me when you're coherent."

"*Brown?*" was the last thing he said before hanging up. He slept on and off for the next two days.

By the end of the week (this would be week seven of the two-month life expectancy Walter and Weiss had given him) things were pretty much back to normal. (The mayor's divorce, now somehow linked to the Mafia and human trafficking, was once again the top story.) Ed went back to work and did his best to soothe the store's irate constituency, offering bromides like "one man's meat..." and "what's sauce for the goose..." in an attempt to reinstate his belief in the efficacy of the goods he was selling. The customers seemed placated. Business slowly picked up.

He was, for a time, treated a bit like a celebrity when he patronized the deli and the liquor store, the Tan-atorium, but even that waned quickly. It seemed his fifteen minutes of fame had mercifully elapsed.

Walter, on the other hand, was on the shit list with the hospital's ethics people—Dieter's story had broken virtually every law regarding doctor/patient confidentiality. It took a team of lawyers (generally reserved for his malpractice suits) to get him off the hot seat. It cost him a ton of money—enough to buy a fucking yacht, he would later say. But he was reinstated in full and went back to writing his *Lancet* article.

Marriott invited Ed to a candlelit dinner. She agreed to try a sip or two of the Jack Daniel's. Once again, she said "I love you." Ed said the same thing back to her and one thing led to another.

When he awoke the following morning, he poked his head out from under the floral-scented duvet and saw his clothes, heaped in a frantic pile on the floor. Then he saw her clothes, folded demurely on the little wooden bedroom chair. As quietly as possible, he turned his head to look at Marriott. She was sleeping peacefully. An angel. He could see the little, now-dry, snail trails of tears on her cheeks. (Marriott was a crier, whether it was pain or pleasure.) He inched himself to a semi-sitting position and looked out the window. As his eyes adjusted to the morning light, he could see that there were new buds on the trees. Spring was in the air. All was right with the world.

For about an hour.

Because it was that same Friday morning that *The New York Times* ran *their* story—less lurid and judgmental than Dieter's, it was nonetheless more powerful than the *Hartford Courant's* coverage by virtue of its being a national publication. The upshot this time was not a pedestrian buzz but a flurry of calls and texts from medical professionals who were outraged that a publication as influential as *The Times* would even suggest that Ed's recovery was anything but a hoax. Big Pharma's nose was particularly out of joint, sensing a loss of billions of dollars if any part of the tale was true. Noted cancer physicians around the world were incensed that their theories and methods could be challenged by what they saw as a fairytale. By mid-morning, the cable news shows were all over it.

It was the incessant ringing of Marriott's phone that finally roused the lovebirds.

"Who *is* this?" Marriott said, annoyed.

"It's Walter," Walter said. "Turn on CNN." And he hung up.

Marriott and Ed did as they were told and watched in stunned silence as a steady stream of "experts" manned the airwaves, debunking Ed's claims. The *Times* author, desperate to save his reputation, appeared on one of the shows, stating that he had relied on "unnamed sources" and that "further investigation" might be called for. But the cat was out of the bag.

Now *Ed's* phone began to ring, and ring, and ring. Marriott acted as secretary, fielding the calls—"No, he's not here" and "I don't know where he is" her stock answers. Ed took sanctuary in his Valium. He was somewhere north of la-la-land when he realized that Marriott had been on the last call for some time. He raised a quizzical eyebrow and she motioned for him to come to the phone. "Who is it?" Ed mouthed. Marriott covered the mouthpiece with her hand.

"NBC," she whispered. *The Good Morgan Show*.

(*The Good Morgan Show* was NBC's flagship morning show, hosted by Tommy Morgan and co-hosted by one-time Broadway actress LeeLee Inglehaur. Tommy did the hard news and the legitimate interviews, LeeLee was there to add color and the occasional non sequitur that would leave Morgan rolling his eyes before saying, "We'll be right back.» It was a hit show. So Ed was surprised and a bit starstruck when Marriott told him it was actually Tommy Morgan, the man himself, on the line.)

Ed took the phone. "Hello?" he said, and that was the last thing he said for the next ten minutes. He just listened. How could he not? Tommy Mor-

The Last Two Months of Ed Furst

gan's voice was legendary—a soothing baritone that had informed, convinced, and reassured millions of listeners for over three decades. He could, with a turn of phrase, make the catastrophic seem prosaic, the earth-shattering merely everyday. His was the voice of God. Ed broke his silence at the end of the call: "Thank you so much, Tommy. I'll see you then." He ended the call and grabbed Marriott in a hug.

"I'm going to be on TV!!" he said, beaming like a child who's been promised a new toy.

Morgan was a diehard Catholic who believed in miracles. He had, years ago, taken his own mother to Lourdes in an attempt to alleviate her discomfort with an arthritic hip. It was unsuccessful, but his belief in miracles was undaunted. He thought Ed's recovery worthy of the term. It *was* a miracle, case closed. He also felt it was almost a violation of the first amendment that Ed's story was not being told by Ed himself. Ed's story needed to be told by Ed. *The Good Morgan Show* would offer him the opportunity.

The Good Morgan Show didn't air on Saturday or Sunday, so Monday was set as the day of the interview. Ed and Marriott both shut their phones off to avoid further harassment and concentrated on their trip to the Big Apple. (They did little things, like Marriott fixing pocket-sized plastic bags of dried fruit and trail mix for the two-hour train ride, and Ed getting a last blast of fake sun at the

Tan-atorium). Their excitement, now multiplied by their newly discovered romantic connection, was all-encompassing. Between bouncing on the bed and packing and repacking their bags, the time seemed to fly.

Sunday afternoon. The train departed right on time and, with the exception of an obese couple who slept rather noisily, they had the car to themselves. It was the perfect opportunity for Ed to rehearse what he would say on TV. Marriott coached him and quizzed him, helping him remember the anecdotes that would not only sell his story but endear him to the listeners. By the time the train pulled into Grand Central Station, Ed had his patter down pat.

Their hotel (arranged and comped by NBC) was just a few blocks from the *Morgan* studios. Ed and Marriott were greeted in the lobby by one of the show's production assistants and given the schedule for Monday morning: The show aired from 6 a.m. until 9 a.m. Ed would need to be there by 4:30 for hair and makeup. (I'm as tan as a beachcomber, Ed thought, I don't need makeup. But he wasn't going to argue.) He asked the girl behind the desk for a 3:30 wake-up call. So much for their big night on the town in New York. He'd need to go to bed almost immediately. There was only time for a quick room-service cheeseburger and fries, and some Valium for dessert. It took five to knock him out.

The big day. Ed was still fighting the cobwebs of his narco-sleep when they arrived at the studio. He was shown his dressing room, where Marriott remained as Ed was hustled into makeup. LeeLee was in the other chair, undergoing what looked like a complete makeover. They were working on her lips so she couldn't say hello. Tommy, already coifed and pancaked, stuck his head in the door.

"Hey! Is that my miracle man?" he chirped. "Welcome!!" Ed turned to respond but Tommy was gone.

Ed was dressed, powdered, and camera-ready by 5:45. Now the big wait. They were shown to the "green room," a tiny cubicle with a TV monitor flanked by two couches. He and Marriott took one of the couches, the other already occupied by the show's other guests: A Honduran man who had fallen out of an airplane and survived, and a one-hundred-and-two-year-old silent film actress who was hawking a memoir. There was no conversation, only a feeling of shared angst as they stared at the blank screen, waiting for it to spring to life. Though it was somewhat chilly in the "green room," Ed could feel that he was starting to sweat.

The screen lit up like a flashbulb going off. "Good Morgan, America!!!" boomed the well-known voice of Billy Pirillo, Tommy's announcer since the beginning of time. "And Good Mooooorgan Tommy!" The show's logo dissolved to reveal Tommy beaming behind his desk. As Tommy effortlessly bounced through the headlines of the day, Ed could feel his sweat increasing, his breath quickening. He grabbed Marriott's hand.

"You're soaking wet!" she said.

"Just a little nervous. I'll get over it," he said, trying to convince himself as well as Marriott.

He grabbed a bottled water and drank it in one gulp.

Ed would be Tommy's first guest, so the production assistant came to escort him to the wings.

"Break a leg, Eddie," Marriott said.

"*Eddie?*" the word rang in Ed's head. I'm not *Eddie!* I'm Ed!! She called me *Eddie!* He's *dead!* Is Marriott crazy? Am *I* crazy? Where the hell am I? *Who* the hell am I?!!

And thoughts such as these ran amok as he waited to be introduced. Thoughts that had no basis in reality. Unhinged thoughts. He had no idea who he was, what he was doing. Oh, God!! Not again, he thought, remembering the devastating anxiety attack he had had in Walter's office. Not here! Not now!!!

"My next guest was told he had two months to live," said Tommy.

"That's one-sixth of a year," chirped LeeLee. Tommy rolled his eyes.

"Yes, LeeLee. That's what it is. Anyway, please welcome..."

Ed heard his name, the fight-or-flight instincts quickly taking over, and flight was winning. But, though the order to run held the upper hand, he fought it like a trooper. He took as deep a breath as possible and walked onstage. He shook Tommy's hand, he took the offered seat next to Tommy's desk. He tried to be present, to smile. He really did. But the stage was spinning like a Devil's runaway merry-go-round, the studio lights jabbing him like blazing, pulsing suns, LeeLee's toothsome rictus hovered above him, looking like an exhumed cadaver, turning to dust before his eyes, Tommy's bow tie twirled like a knife blade, a lethal propeller, and Ed's heart, now double in size, now triple, throbbed and pounded like someone locked in a closet. His pulse hammered, up became down, right became left, horizon up for grabs, gravity abandoned him. Unthinkable thoughts swarmed him. The surreality and fear became too much to bear. He *had* to get out of there!! He burst from his chair, leaping to his feet.

CRACK!!!!!! The top of his head slammed into the boom microphone that had been hovering above him. The sound, doubly loud because the weapon was a microphone, was horrific.

And, just like that, Ed's two months were up.

. . . .

What I'm about to tell you may or may not be so. But, as his friend (I am his Mr. Third Person, after all) I certainly hope it's true.

Ed did not pass away the second the microphone cracked his skull. He lived for another thirty seconds. That's eight times longer than a man falling off a ten-story building, and, supposedly, when one falls off a ten-story building, one's whole life flashes before one. Ed had more than enough time to see his life—the fits and starts, the ups and downs, the heydays and doldrums, the sweeping overall view—and I think he was content. I think he saw that his life was indeed a full one. He did not see a life cut short, but rather a series of lives, each fully realized. He had been a boy, complete with baseballs and bicycles. He had been a medical student who had seen the folly of his ways. He had been an energetic advocate of healing through roots and berries, and had changed the diets and outlooks of hundreds of followers. He had, with his miraculous recovery, become the poster boy for untold numbers of hopeless cancer sufferers. He had raised questions in the medical community that would be years in the answering. His tale would surpass urban myth and become legend. He had, in the end, always been true to himself, even when that self seemed the complete opposite of the one that had preceded it. He had marched to his own drummer, regardless of the tune. He also saw that his departure came on the cusp of his decline—that he had been mercifully spared the aches, pains, and confusions that attend the elderly. In short, he had died happy, feeling in many ways like the hero of his own story. Hey, he got the girl in the end, didn't he?

As for his last act on *The Good Morgan Show*? Well, some people just aren't cut out for show business.

WARREN PACE

It was his second divorce in as many years—Kitty, then Kelly, neither a good match for Warren, but dead ringers for each other. Both were on the buxom side and pencil-thin below; both were blue-eyed dishwater blonds; both were undereducated waitresses from Pennsylvania (Kitty from Harrisburg, Kelly from Philadelphia), and both were irrepressible and unquenchable alcoholics. Neither would be at the top of a responsible young man's list of possible life partners, but Warren's self-esteem had never been anything to write home about and, consequently, he set the bar fairly low in terms of finding a mate. In truth, it had really only been their willingness to match him drink for drink that had attracted him. And it was the volatility that accompanies an alcohol-based relationship that had put the kibosh on both marriages. Warren, when drunk (which was all of the time), tended to retreat to a quiet self-examining stupor; the wives tended toward aggression, name-calling, and dish-throwing. The marriage to Kitty somehow survived four tumultuous years before critical mass was attained: a kitchen fire, deliberately set. (Warren had casually observed that the lasagna was burnt. Kitty responded: "Burnt? You want burnt? I'll give you burnt!") Warren's reluctant decision to drop the arson charges did little to mitigate her assault on his finances in the ensuing divorce settlement. She cleaned his clock.

Six weeks later, he met Kelly, the classic rebound. That marriage lasted less than a year. The tipping point came on the heels of a torrent of inebriated invective which ripened into a 911 call, a restraining order, and Warren being left on the street. And now he was seated in the all-too-familiar overstuffed leather chair in her lawyer's claustrophobic office, staring down the boiling Kelly and her no-nonsense, bloodthirsty attorney.

Warren's senses had been all but destroyed by drink. His eyesight (no doubt as a result of countless hours of a drunkard's double vision) was the first to go. He now needed glasses just to find his glasses. His hearing, too, was conveniently slipping away, as much a case of selective listening as alcohol-related nerve damage. Taste and touch had been reduced to the finger-numbing chill of the ice-filled glass and the tangy fire of its contents. That left smell. And, as he intentionally fumbled with the ballpoint pen in an attempt to forestall the signing of the divorce agreement, he thought he smelled something.

He couldn't put his finger on it—or his nose, as was the case. It wasn't the absurdly tropical scent of the lawyer's aftershave, nor was it the decades-long buildup of Lemon Pledge on his meadow-sized desk. Kelly was known to douse herself in "Tabu" to mask her personal climate of ashtray and bar-room breath, but that wasn't it. Was there a cat box? Had he stepped in something? Then it hit him. It was the smell of despair. He reeked of it. His thinning hair, his droopy, unkempt moustache, his ratty Walmart clothes—all steeped in hopelessness. At least he'd identified it. Robotically, he signed the papers that would leave him virtually destitute and, without another word, slunk out of the office, his despair in tow.

On his way home, he was pulled almost magnetically to the liquor store. If losing half of your worldly goods wasn't a good reason for a cocktail or two, then he couldn't think of what was. (Regardless of the outcome of the day's negotiations, come evening, he would have had a glass in his hand, either celebrating or grieving.) Tonight it would be grieving, so he bought three bottles—just in case the malaise carried over into the next day, and the day after that. He pulled the aging VW Bug (Kelly had been awarded the Buick) into the old-fashioned, prewar driveway—two narrow strips of cracked concrete divided by a once-grassy patch and sat in the car for a moment, gathering strength. He got out, locked the car (as if anyone would steal the twenty-year-old rust bucket) and made his way to the side of the house and down the crumbling steps to his basement apartment.

Holding the bag of bottles like a swaddled infant, he fumbled with his keys and eventually made it inside. Instantly the odor of despair was enhanced by the stronger aroma of bachelorhood—cigarettes, dirty socks, festering scraps of pizza and burnt coffee. He set his precious cargo on the tiny Formica counter and searched the overhead cabinet for a clean glass. None there. He'd have to wash one. Or not. Fuck it. He opened the fridge to see if his ice had been made yet (he had used the few remaining cubes from the last batch for this morning's Bloody Mary). No ice. Again, fuck it. He pulled one of the new bottles of Johnny Walker from the bag and actually smiled at it, as if appreciating the artistry of the label—a somewhat stupid smile that radiated "here we go again." He filled the cleanest glass he could find with a generous helping, found the TV remote under a cushion, and plopped on the threadbare couch to begin his evening.

Ironically, the program was *Jeopardy!* He missed what the question was, but the answer was "what is paradise?" (He figured it was the name of some small town somewhere, but knew it certainly wasn't where he was sitting.) He was right. It *was* a small town. The bulbous, beehived housewife got the answer right and walked away with $15,400.00. He turned the TV off, refilled his glass, and could sense that he was headed for another bout of self-assessment. It was his pattern: numb yourself, and then beat yourself up. Usually, the fourth or fifth cocktail would put an end to the self-flagellation, but sometimes (and tonight felt like it would be one of them) he would be afforded a moment or two of clarity. It was only in these brief flashes that he could see himself as having any future whatsoever—as having honest, all-too-human needs and desires, as redeemable. It was also, during these respites of sanity, that he was able to place blame where it was deserved. Tonight, he and his buddy Johnny Walker would take a cold hard look at who he's been, who he is, and where he's headed.

First, he had to let his parents off the hook. Yes, they were shitty parents, delinquent even. Self-absorbed, status-conscious, and contentious. As a child, his home was nothing more than an arena for their Friday night fights. As angry and hateful as the relationship was, they both seemed to revel in it. Though they both seemed to take great glee in diminishing the other, there was never any desire expressed by either party to call it quits. Had they split up, he doubted that either one would have wanted custody of little Warren. Were they drinkers? He couldn't say. They certainly acted like sloppy, aggressive drunks, and yet he couldn't recall seeing either of them drinking—maybe they did and he just never saw it (or didn't want to see it). No, they were just shitty parents. But then, aren't *all* parents remiss in some way or another? It's an impossible task, bringing another person into the world and setting them straight. No, he couldn't blame his parents.

The fiasco of his failed marriages was all his own doing. Oh, he could say that he was trying to find in them the love that his parents had refused him, but that was too easy, and too much like some Dr. Phil psychobabble. At one point during the prizefight that passed for their marriage, Kelly had suggested therapy. Warren went once. He found it unbearable—Kelly sitting there smugly while he stewed in the Naugahyde hotseat. The whole idea was preposterous, invasive, unrewarding, and ridiculously expensive.

No, he couldn't blame his parents. Even if he did, he couldn't confront them. Both had died years ago, whisked away on a cloud of carbon monoxide on one of the rare occasions when they shared a conjugal bed. For all the threats they had thrown at each other over the years, it was a faulty furnace that had proved their undoing.

Could he blame Kitty or Kelly, his doppelganger wives? Not honestly. They were pawns in a game that he wasn't even aware he was playing.

Kitty, a high school dropout, was all of twenty-two when they married. Smooth skinned, pretty, and an athletic lover, she was hardly the sharpest knife in the drawer. Dumb as a bag of hair, Warren once mused. At first, she tried to compensate for her disability at intelligent conversation with what she deemed to be the perfect execution of a housewife's duties. Meals were cooked, shirts ironed, rugs vacuumed. But she could sense Warren's increasing boredom. In an attempt at actual companionship, she started drinking with him. She soon could put him under the table. So, for the first two years, their life was bifurcated into two distinct activities: drinking to oblivion, and bed. Year three saw her ceasing all attempts at homemaking, constant fighting, and a romantic hiatus that was subsidized by week-long disappearances and infidelities by both parties. Year four was when she set the kitchen on fire. (In the divorce settlement, she got the house and enough cash to renovate the damage.)

He never saw Kitty again, though he thought he had when he saw Kelly. She could have been a clone. The same face, the same figure. The only difference was that she was smiling, laughing even, as she served him his beer and hamburger at the smoky little bar in Philadelphia. (Of course she was smiling and laughing, she was already half in the bag, sneaking drinks in the kitchen.) He saw it as a second chance. A chance to do Kitty over again and get it right this time. After a week-long bender in Buck's County, they tied the knot with a justice of the peace and that was that.

Six months later, after a tornado of screaming and shoving, he was forced to pack his suitcase.

He had to admit that he never really saw either of the women as a real person, more as a prop—a piece of the puzzle that he needed to make him whole. He never loved either of them. What he loved was drinking.

Yes, he loved drinking. This was the inevitable realization he came to when he did his soul-searching. The big question. *Why* did he love drinking? And, plunging deeper still, *how* could he love drinking when it had led him to the abyss where he now found himself? In high school, he might have a few beers with the guys after the football game, a few more at unchaperoned parties, but nothing untoward or excessive. There were pals of his that drank quite a bit; several had wrecked the family car, been suspended from school, but not Warren. Despite the massive dysfunction that ran rampant in the Pace home, Warren was a typical, cookie-cutter teenager: decent grades, a handful of friends, a few racy jokes he could share in the locker room. However, when his hormones kicked in, unlike his buddies who bounced around from one girlfriend to another, searching for the one that would be the "easiest," Warren's erotic fantasies centered on one girl, and one girl only: Mary Lou Higgins. He had had a crush on her since the fifth grade.

Mary Lou didn't look like either Kitty or Kelly. She was tall, legs forever, a cascade of brown hair that showed flecks of gold in the sunlight, and eyes big as those of a baby deer. She was smart as a whip, always the first to answer in class and always with the right answer. She played field hockey, soccer, and basketball. She was in the choir, editor of the yearbook. She was the complete package and Warren fell like a piano off a ten-story building. He had feelings he'd never experienced before—an actual tightening in his chest at the sight of her, an inability to focus when she wasn't in view. His homework suffered, his eating, his sleeping. He paid previously unthinkable attention to his clothes and his hair. He actually found himself writing "Mr. and Mrs. Warren Pace" and "Mary Lou Pace" on scraps of paper, crumbling them up embarrassedly and chewing them to a pulp. Jesus, he thought, this is what *girls* do!

One day, at lunch, he could contain himself no longer. The screaming urges of teen love manhandled any sense of decorum. He took a deep breath, smoothed his shirtfront, stepped right up, and introduced himself.

"I'm Warren Pace,» he said, as directly as a trial witness under oath.

Mary Lou laughed—a genuine, uncontainable laugh.

"Oh, I'm sorry!" she said, covering her mouth with her hand. "That was *so* rude! It's just that I thought you said, 'I'm *War and Peace*.'"

(Needless to say, Warren had been hearing this since he could remember. The phonetic similarity was obvious and shopworn. The not-too-obscure reference to Tolstoy's masterpiece had been intentional, his father's drunken idea of a joke. His father's sophomoric sense of humor often wandered to what he considered funny names: Ben Dover, Connie Lingus, Frank Furter—nothing funny. To alleviate what might be a lifetime of ridicule, his father had given him "Bud" as a middle name, certain that it would stick and the joke would go away. "Bud" never stuck. He would forever be Warren Pace.)

Warren wasn't offended by Mary Lou's gaffe. In fact, he was charmed. There was something about the way Mary Lou had stated it—a childlike glee in making the connection, as if she were the first to ever hear the similarity—as if she'd discovered the profile of the Virgin Mary in a potato chip. She pulled her hand from her mouth and extended it toward Warren.

"I really *am* sorry. I'm Mary Lou Higgins," she smiled.

"It's nothing," Warren managed, shaking her delicate hand. "I get it all the time."

"I'll bet you do!" said Mary Lou.

"Yep," said Warren.

An awkward silence ensued that Mary Lou felt obliged to break.

"Have you ever read it? *War and Peace*?" she asked, genuinely curious.

"No," said Warren.

"I have," said Mary Lou. "Well, I *had* to... for advanced placement English. I'm college prep. Well, not *college* exactly, junior college. My dad says it's a lot cheaper and a good idea until I really know what I want to do."

This was far more of a conversation than Warren had anticipated and he found himself tonguetied. "Smart," was all he could muster.

"I'm going to Harrisburg Central JC. I've already gotten early acceptance," she said, placing her lips seductively around her straw and drawing in some chocolate milk. Seeing her lips gently tighten around the straw was too much for Warren—a metaphoric image that would stay forever lodged between the ventricles of his heart, forever tattooed on his brain.

"That's where *I'm* going, too!!" he lied, without really planning to. He had no idea where those words came from. He had simply panicked at the thought of never seeing her again and blurted the first thing that came to his mind—anything that might connect him to Mary Lou.

"Really?!" Mary Lou exclaimed. "That is *so* cool! Have you seen the campus?"

Now he was caught. What did I just do? He had to think fast. Of course he'd never seen the campus—had never even heard of it before. Think. Well, it's a junior college, the odds are that the campus is nothing to write home about. If there even *is* one. He decided to go with that hunch.

"Not much of a campus," he half-mumbled, hoping he was right. He was.

"I know," said Mary Lou. "I mean, I've only seen pictures. I was thinking of going there next weekend for a better look."

"Next weekend?" Warren echoed weakly.

"Yeah. Hey! Why don't we drive down there together? I could pick you up. My dad bought me a car for graduation. It's a red Camaro. It'll be fun. What do you say?"

"Next weekend?" Warren said, with a smile that reached both ears.

"It's a convertible, wear a hat," she grinned.

Warren wracked his brain for what he might have done in a former life that would warrant a blessing such as this. Lou Gehrig isn't the luckiest man on earth, he thought to himself, "*I* am!!"

. . . .

But it was never to be. Two days later, on an unseasonably cold April evening, Warren, who, regardless of the weather, always slept with his window wide open, dreamt of his future with Mary Lou, while his parents, hermetically sealed in the chilly bedroom they only shared when they were drunk, filled their lungs with carbon monoxide and ceased to be.

With the passing of his parents, Warren's world shifted on its axis. He instantly became a high-school dropout, ass-deep in funeral directors, lawyers, insurance adjustors, and police investigators. He never saw Mary Lou again.

. . . .

He poured himself another tumbler of whiskey and, glass in one hand, bottle in the other, made his way to his unmade bed to resume his life's inventory.

The next twelve years were what made him what he was and what he wasn't. He found work as a typewriter repairman. It was a skill that became less and less in demand as computers made their inexorable inroads—the need for his services diminishing in invisible increments as did most other aspects of his life. What few friends he had, after a period of dutiful contact where they referred to him as "poor Warren," left for higher, less traumatic ground. It was just like the song says; nobody knows you when you're down and out.

The house became hollow. Most of his meals were taken at a local bar and grill, more out of ritual than hunger. Whatever he was hungry for, it couldn't be satisfied by a hamburger or fries. It was here that he met his new best friend: Johnny Walker. Johnny listened. Johnny soothed him. Johnny numbed him. Johnny deftly led him away from thoughts of what could be, what ought to be, and from thoughts of Mary Lou. All Johnny asked for in return was his diligence in keeping the friendship alive.

And he kept it alive. Alive, and increasing, through the lean and problematic years of unemployment. Through the two failed marriages.

And, tonight, as he had done on countless other occasions, Johnny Walker gently tucked him into bed and closed his eyes.

Usually, after consuming nearly the whole quart of Johnny Walker, Warren would pass out—a state more akin to unconsciousness than sleep. Therefore, he would rarely dream. Tonight would be an exception. He had a short, surreal episode where he found himself in a gymnasium filled with rabbits—talking rabbits—speaking in a language that sounded like backwards English. As suddenly as that dream appeared, it vanished, as if it were the cartoon before the feature film. Now he found himself sitting on the rickety porch of a lakeside cabin, a place completely foreign to him. An open door behind him revealed the interior of the cabin—a windowless cubicle no larger than a phone booth. Curious, he entered the little room, the door slamming behind him, plunging him into complete darkness. He groped around overhead and found a string, pulled it, and was instantly awash in an amber light. He saw a table with a bottle on it. The bottle was throbbing, as if it had a pulse. It was, essentially, Alice's "Eat me" cookie. He grabbed it, brought it to his lips, and, as he did so, one wall of the tiny compartment turned to glass, revealing a beautiful female in a field-hockey uniform. "Don't!!" said the Mary Lou lookalike. He ignored the warning, took a long swig, and watched in horror as she exploded in a cloud of scarlet dust. Seeing this, he threw the bottle away and ran from the cabin. He ran and he ran and he ran. When he finally woke up, he was soaking wet and shaking.

He stumbled his way to the bathroom and saw himself in the mirror. The man he saw didn't have the gray and haggard look of the professional drunk, the expected crossed-eyes; in fact, he seemed, surprisingly clear-eyed, capable. He stared at himself for a second and the dream replayed itself in detail. It was too real and too profound. He couldn't shake it, seeing it now not as a fantasy, but as an instruction—marching orders. Warren and the man in the mirror came to an agreement: two resolutions—he would quit drinking, and he would find Mary Lou Higgins.

The more he considered his plan, the more sense it made. That the bottle was killing him was beyond question, nor was there any question that Mary Lou Higgins was the only person he had ever truly loved. Kitty and Kelly were pale substitutes, stopgap maneuvers, warm bodies to drink with. Merely handy, and ultimately, not even that.

That he could have these thoughts surprised him. Somehow the dream had swept his brain, left him clearheaded. All of his prior foolishness was suddenly glaringly apparent. To continue in such a fashion was now unthinkable. It was time for a change. A big change. It would require rescuing the remnants of self-determination from the wreckage of his life. It would require flexing mental muscles that he'd never used before. He had always seen life as an acceptance of the misfortune heaped on him and never as something that could be molded, controlled, or directed. He would have to make plans and, for Warren, making plans had never been a more elaborate process than making sure he didn't run out of alcohol.

Oh, alcohol! He could feel the tendrils of craving already. This was going to be hard. To say goodbye to Johnny Walker would feel like a form of suicide. No, not suicide, murder. He would have to kill the man that Johnny knew. Let that drunken fool wither and die. Mary Lou wouldn't want that man anyway. She'd want the new Warren. And he had to deliver him.

He took a long shower, slowly adjusting the valves so the water got colder and colder. He wanted to be at his sharpest for the odyssey that awaited him. He lathered his face to shave, pausing for a moment to consider his moustache. For years it had been as much a part of his face as the bloodshot nose that protruded above it. Mary Lou had never seen him with a moustache. It had to go.

As long as he could keep Mary Lou in his sights, he could keep the bottle at bay, he reasoned. Yes, his sobriety would be fueled by thoughts of

Mary Lou. These were, however, thoughts that couldn't really be called memories, because his reminiscences were of events that never happened. He conjured tête-à-têtes, trysts, walks in the park, late-night passionate phone calls, furtive fumblings in the back seat of her red convertible, all of it made from whole cloth. All make believe. His mind did not know how to handle his heart.

The February morning air was colder than his shower. He sat behind the wheel of his aging VW, his breath fogging the windshield with lacelike mandalas of ice. Belted into the passenger seat were the two unopened bottles of Johnny Walker. He would attempt to return them for cash—more a statement of newfound resolve than a need for money, though the need for money was always there.

After several asthmatic attempts, the VW coughed to life, and he was off to start his quest.

Sal's Liquors took the bottles back, reimbursing him for all but the taxes. "Can't fuck with Uncle Sam," Sal had said. Fortunately, there was little other conversation, and no explanations demanded. Had there been any questions, Warren wasn't sure how he would have answered them. It was all too new.

Forty dollars to the good, Warren found himself on the street, unsure of his next move. Half a block away he spotted a phone booth, inscribed head to toe with graffiti, its glass door shattered and unhinged. He assumed the phone would be gone—ripped out by junkies in need of its treasure trove of dimes and quarters—but he held the hope that there still might be a directory hanging from its rusted chain. There was.

The directory was brittle from age and cold, smelled of urine, and had had many pages removed. Names starting with "H" were still there, however, and he thumbed his way to "Higgins." There were quite a few: Aaron through Zeke, but no Mary Lou. Did he really expect it would be this easy? Had she left Harrisburg? Did he know for a fact that she was still a "Higgins"? Had she married? Was she now Mrs. Mary Lou Jones? And then the stultifying thought: Was she still alive? He had to find out.

Warren hated computers. It was a hatred founded in economics. When he turned sixteen, his tight-fisted parents put an end to his weekly allowance—paltry as it was. So, to keep his little ship afloat, every day after school (and on most Saturdays, as well) he would repair typewriters at Bledsoe's Office Supply. He could fix the Remingtons, the Olivettis, the Smith Coronas, the Royals, and, eventually, the daunting IBM Selectric. He had a preternatural gift. No amount of wear and tear or mishandling was beyond his healing touch. His skill was instinctive and remarkable. He soon became the go-to guy, handling a steady stream of desperate machines. He had begun a savings account that was growing steadily. He had plans to one day open his own typewriter repair shop. It was as close to making plans as he had ever come. Then the stream of work grew shallow; soon barely a trickle. Mr. Bledsoe had to let him go. All thanks to computers.

Of course, he had the brains to add the computer to his list of patients, but he refused to own one. God, how he hated computers. And now he knew he'd have to use one. If, yesterday, someone had told him he'd be going to the library, he'd have asked what they were smoking. Likewise, if they had told him that he'd be sober. But both facts were, unimaginably, true.

It was still early, barely eleven, so the library was uncrowded. Once inside, Warren stood for a moment, blowing on his hands to warm them, and tried to look inconspicuous as he took in his surroundings: a waning bun-haired dowager behind the front desk, a handful of people reading, another handful prowling the stacks, and the expected cluster of homeless, sprawled on the benches, fast asleep.

Warren's eye settled on a hirsute, unkempt teenager, his nose buried in his laptop. He sauntered toward the boy, and peered over his shoulder at the image on his screen: topless women, pouting at the camera. The boy sensed Warren's presence and slammed the computer shut.

"It's okay," said Warren, like an understanding parent.

"Fuck off!" said the boy, rising from his chair, the computer shoved under his arm. Warren stopped him with an open hand, like a cop directing traffic.

"Wait a minute, pal. I said *it's okay*, I *get* it."

"What do you want?" asked the boy, still backing away.

"A favor," said Warren. The boy squinted suspiciously.

"Well, not a *favor*, really," Warren continued. "I'm willing to pay you." The boy continued to eye him warily as Warren pulled the two twenties from his pocket.

The kid was a whiz. In less than twenty minutes the young porno-cruiser had Mary Lou's info. No recent photo or current address, however. Simply the fact that she had indeed attended Harrisburg Central JC and graduated with honors. That would have been twelve years ago. The kid searched through social media and came up empty. Maybe she hated computers as much as he did, thought Warren, that would be one more thing they had in common. The kid searched deeper, to no avail. Then Warren spotted something.

"What's that?" he asked.

"Reunion," said the kid, opening it for more information.

Here was the information: Mary Lou's Harrisburg Central class was holding their annual reunion, a dinner with the hackneyed title *Winterfest*.

The time and place were posted: the Ramada Inn on Chester Street, 8:00 p.m. on Saturday, the 18th of February. Three days away.

Warren thanked the boy, paid him, and made his way to his VW, grateful that his mind was clear—he had some thinking to do. Was this reunion the breadcrumb that would lead him to his beloved? Odds were against it. (God, he wanted a drink.) The thought that she would be there, radiant, open-armed, waiting for him was too ridiculous to even entertain. But maybe someone there would have kept in touch with her—would know where she was now—would direct him to his destiny. (Excited now, he *really* wanted a drink.) He looked at the car seat where the two bottles of Johnny Walker had sat and wanted them back. What was he doing?

He rubbed his face and felt the rough stubble where his moustache had been. He had shaved it for a reason. A good reason. "No booze," he told himself.

The next three days were an eternity. His brain was a war zone—one side pushing him toward Mary Lou, the other pulling him to the liquor store and relief from his tremors and mounting anxiety. Sleep helped, but sleep was hard to come by. He had forgotten how to fall asleep, relying on the soporific of drink to be his sandman. He tried to read the newspaper, tried to watch TV, tried to tidy his squalid quarters, anything to fill the time. How had he filled it before? He hadn't. Johnny Walker had filled his time for him. God, he wanted a drink. Twice, he drove to Chester Street, reconnoitering the Ramada Inn. Timing the drive, pre-selecting where he might park. On the second trip he saw the signage: WELCOME HARRISBURG CENTRAL ALUMNI!! His heart leapt at the sight.

Friday night finally arrived and, with it, the forecast of a blizzard—the TV news promised eight to twelve inches of snow. Warren worried that Mary Lou might stay home, that the event might even be cancelled, that his rust-bucket VW would be helpless against the drifts and icy roads. Thinking, "Better safe than sorry," he decided to leave at once, before the blizzard hit. He could spend the night in his VW in the Ramada parking lot. Why not? He wasn't sleeping anyway. And maybe seeing himself as bold and capable, like a frontiersman facing the elements to rescue the damsel in distress, would take his mind off the comforts that were just a bottle away. He showered, shaved, dressed, found the thermos that had always served him as a flask in too-public gatherings, and filled it with hot coffee. The frozen wind was howling when he pulled out of the driveway.

The blizzard never came. Neither did sleep. He spent the night unsnug in his bug, the only flurries were thoughts: thoughts of self-effacement, of futility, of grave disappointment with his life. And thoughts of drink. Many thoughts of drink. He felt mentally ill. Didn't they say that alcoholism is a disease? If he had diabetes, he'd be given insulin. If he had cancer, he'd be given morphine. He had alcoholism, he should be given alcohol, damn it. He fought these thoughts with images of Mary Lou, but the habit was marrow deep, its fingers wrapped around every part of his being. Fighting these thoughts certainly wasn't made any easier by the fact that he could see a flashing neon sign that said *McNally's Bar and Grill* at the far end of the parking lot. It would take him less than a minute to get there.

Oh, Mary Lou, he thought, oh, Mary Lou. He took another pull on his thermos of coffee. "The things we do for love," he said aloud to himself, the words turning to vapor and clouding the windshield. And so he spent his day, slouched behind the wheel, waiting for nightfall.

He wiped the windshield clear with his coat sleeve and saw a car arrive; then another, then several more. He checked his watch: 7:45. Game on.

Warren tried his best to get a good look at the arriving partygoers, but his breathing had sped up with excitement and the windows kept fogging over. He weighed his options and decided to join the queue, albeit from an eavesdropper's perspective. He took a position in an alcove near the hotel's entranceway and tried to catalogue the faces as they entered, but it seemed now like everyone had arrived at the same time—a chattering gaggle of people, hugging each other and hurrying to get out of the cold. Was Mary Lou one of them? Had she walked right past him without his seeing her?

He checked his reflection in the window. Did he look crazy? No, he decided. Could he pass for one of the invitees? Sure. He blew a breath into his cupped hands to check his breath and went into the hotel.

The hotel's function room was on the small side, dimly lit by candles on the tables, and bustling with people hanging their coats and chattering loudly. The congestion was such that Warren's progress was halted at the check-in table. A female voice reached out to him.

"Name?" said the woman behind the table.

"What?" said Warren, his eyes still darting around the room in search of Mary Lou.

"Your name, please,» said the woman, waving a guest list in her hand impatiently.

"Oh... uh, Warren Pace."

And, of course, she laughed. "War and Peace?" she said, and laughed a little more as she scanned the list of invitees.

"Pace," said Warren, impatiently, "P-A-C-E." He was in no mood for this encounter.

"I'm sorry," the lady said, "It sounded like you said..." Warren cut her off.

"I know... I know... Look, lady, I'm just trying to..."

"I don't see you here," she said, scanning a second page. Warren felt himself redden with both embarrassment and anger. He hadn't planned on this.

"Oh... I know why. That's because I'm... I'm... I'm... Mary Lou Higgins's husband," he blurted out, desperately. Again, the woman laughed, like this was an impossibility.

"Mary Lou's *husband!!?*" she said, incredulously. But before she could consult her papers again, Warren had slipped into the throng of graduates.

The guests began to settle, each finding their assigned table and, once seated, turning their attention to the podium on the small riser. Warren slid just behind the door to the coat closet, hoping to stay inconspicuous. From here, all he could see were the backs of heads. He looked for Mary Lou's distinctive locks and came up empty. Oh, Mary Lou, where the fuck are you?

A bald-headed man rose, walked to the little stage, and took his place behind the podium.

"Hi, gang! I'm Rob Merchant," said the man. "Now, I know a lot of you are thinking 'No, that can't be Rob Merchant, Rob had a lot of hair.'"

There was a smattering of polite laughter.

"Well, what can I say? Hair today... gone, well, you know the rest." Again, a tepid laugh.

Rob continued. "Now I know we've got a lot of people who want to get up here and share their stories, and I'll bet Keri and Marie are gonna want to sing for you, but first things first. As is our tradition, we'll start this party with a benediction. Reverend, if you'll be so kind?"

Warren was trapped. He couldn't see Mary Lou anywhere and he couldn't walk out during a prayer. (Well, he *could*. He was going to hell anyway.) But, no, he didn't want the attention. So he watched as a very large woman in a voluminous black pantsuit rose from her seat and mounted the stage, the plywood structure groaning under her ponderous weight. Her hair was cropped short as a man's, her face as plain as a nun's. Rob Merchant gave her a perfunctory hug and turned to his audience.

"Let's give it up for our very own Reverend Mary Lou Higgins!!!"

Warren felt the blood rush from his head, his knees turning to water.

No! he thought, no, it can't be!! No, No, No!! But when he looked a little harder at the eyes, the subtle sparkle of her stubbled hairdo, he saw that this blimp with the buzzcut was indeed his Mary Lou. He had found Mary Lou. But she had found God.

"Jesus Christ!" he said, uncontrollably, and loudly enough for people to turn and see the source of the blasphemy.

"Shush!" said a woman in the back row. But Warren was beyond shushing.

"Jesus Fucking Christ!!!" he screamed.

Over the years there had been many instances when Warren, a little too far into his cups, had been asked to leave a drinking establishment. He had always done so without incident. He'd never been physically tossed out. So tonight was a first. He was literally bum-rushed out of the Ramada Inn by a quintet of very angry male graduates. Literally grabbed by his collar and the seat of his pants and tossed out the door. Adding insult to injury, he was cold sober.

The reality of the situation was so bizarre that he was hard-pressed to even formulate a thought. He just picked himself up, brushed the snow from his knees and his elbows, and wandered through the snow (the blizzard had finally arrived). He plunged himself behind the wheel of his freezing VW. As he sat there shivering, his head cleared. He knew what to do.

There were very few patrons in *McNally's Bar and Grill*. Warren stomped the snow from his shoes and made his way to the bar. Within seconds he had downed his Johnny Walker double and had ordered a second. New drink in hand, he selected a table near the space heater and sat. Thanks to Johnny Walker, warm blood was returning to his extremities.

Out of nowhere a waitress appeared. Warren couldn't believe his eyes. Was it Kitty? Was it Kelly? It could have been either. Was there a factory somewhere where they manufactured these look-alike, dead ringer girls?

"What's your name?" asked Warren.

"Katie," she smiled.

"Of course it is," said Warren.

She handed him a menu.

"Is there anything I can do for you?" she asked, coquettishly.

"Oh, I'm sure there is," said Warren Pace, handing her his empty glass.

Hard Cider Press is a back-of-the-barn operation run by the editors and publisher of *County Highway*. The Press was founded in 1887 when our original editors sought to meet demand for a local Almanac. The first printing of the Almanac is said to have been bound together with glue made from the hooves of the Editor-in-Chief's favorite horse, Thaddeus, following his exposure outdoors during a thunder-storm.